ALL OR NOTHING

LO EVERETT

FOREWORD

To the readers that feel a little broken and the books that put them back together piece by jagged piece. It's okay to not be whole.

AUTHOR'S NOTE

Cruz and Delilah's story is filled with heartwarming, swoony moments, because, above all else, I want reading my books to be fun. However, we all know that not everything is sunshine in rainbows in the literary world, or in the real one.

I would be remiss if I didn't call attention to the parts of the story that are less warm and fuzzy before you begin reading. It's important to know that, both Delilah and Cruz have been through their own trauma, which is shared on these pages.

Please know that I truly care about you and your mental health, and your priority should always be to take care of yourself. If you're feeling a little beat down after the more emotional chapters, know that there's a well-placed dopamine dump coming soon. But it's also okay if you need to set the book down and come back to it. Cruz and Delilah will be here waiting when you're ready.

Trigger Warnings: This book deals with the topics of sibling death, end-of-life care, and cheating by a past partner. There is also mention of recreational drug usage (not by the MC's).

Note: The justice system isn't perfect and often works more slowly than many of us would like. For the purpose of this storyline, I've sped up that process and taken a few liberties with the criminal and legal proceedings because, after all, this is a work of fiction.

Happy reading!

PROLOGUE

TOOL SHED

TWO YEARS EARLIER

I blow a wisp of blonde hair, that's fallen free from the disaster masquerading as a messy bun on top of my head, out of my face, while the dough I'm molding into scones sticks to my fingers. Over the speakers my phone chimes, interrupting the classic rock I have pumping through the coffee shop and bakery I own, aptly named *Buns & Roses*.

"Hey Siri, read my text messages," I call out as I continue to work.

"You have a text from *Fiancé*." The robotic voice starts. "Hey Dee. Can't make it to brunch this morning. I think I have food poisoning. So gross. I'll call you later."

Abandoning the dough, I use my elbow to flip the sink on and wash my hands so I can call Brad to see what's going on. His phone rings three times before going to voicemail. I know he's not sleeping since the text just came through, but I suppose he could be in the bathroom.

DELILAH:

Are you okay? Can I bring you anything?
I'm sorry you're not feeling well.
Don't worry about brunch.

BRAD:

I'll be okay. Better stay away..
I don't want you to get it if it's something else.

DELILAH:

You'll call if you need something?

BRAD:

Of course. I don't want you to miss dress shopping with the girls this week-end. I know how excited you are.

DELILAH:

Love you. Hope you feel better.

BRAD:

Same, baby.

I pace the floor of the kitchen, nibbling on my thumb before I pick my phone back up and dial my long-time employee Mikey.

"Hey Lilah, what's up?" he asks when the call connects.

"Hey Mikey, I hate to ask, but Brad's sick and I want to go check on him. Are you interested in coming in early?"

"Sure. I can be there in thirty minutes."

"Thanks Mikey. I owe you."

"Don't even worry about it Lilah, I know you'd do the same for me. See you soon."

When the call disconnects I finish up with the scones so that all Mikey has to do is take them out of the oven.

"Hey Lilah, I'm here," Mikey calls out as he pushes through the back door of the shop.

I drape my apron over the hook as he clocks in. "Thanks so much Mikey. I'm going to grab some supplies from the pharmacy and go check on him. Call me if you need anything." I gather up my things, making a mental list of things to make Brad feel better.

I balance the bag of supplies I picked up at the pharmacy on my hip while I unlock the door using the key Brad gave me. It's crazy to think that in just a few weeks, we will both be living here. I smile, thinking about all the things to come for us. Moving slowly, I shut the door behind me carefully in case he's sleeping it off. Sliding my shoes off, I set the shopping bag on the floor and make my way through the kitchen to the master bedroom.

I'm halfway down the hallway when I hear giggling coming from the bedroom. My steps falter. *Maybe he's watching TV.* My hand lands on the knob and I freeze in place when I hear a familiar voice from the bedroom.

"You're already hard for me again, babe." Grating laughter rings out as I try to comprehend what I'm hearing.

My stomach bottoms out. *No fucking way this is happening.* My body keeps moving forward on its own, even though I am not consciously moving my feet. I can't get enough air in. The door swings open and my whole-body shudders with disgust and anger at the scene in front of me.

"Shit, Dee. It's not what it looks like," Brad says with a panicked look on his face.

I swallow down the rising bile. "Oh good, so that's not my college best friend in your lap, riding your dick like it's her favorite pony."

Bridget buries her face in Brad's neck as he pulls the sheet up around her protectively. Like modesty and *her* embarrassment is the biggest issue we are facing right now.

"Oh, for fuck's sake, I have seen you both naked before. Although never at the same time, so that's new. If you have anything to be ashamed of, it's not the actual nudity but the fact that you are fucking each other behind my back. We"—I glare at my *ex* fiance—"are supposed to be getting married, and you . . ." I shift my gaze to Bridget, the fucking traitor. "*You are supposed to be flying in this weekend to help me pick out a dress.*" My voice catches as the reality of what's happening hits me: my fiancé is cheating on me with one of my bridesmaids—my best friend. My whole world feels like it's crashing down around me in the most horrific fashion.

"I—I'm sorry. I decided to come early. I changed my flight." Like that explains anything.

A laugh rips out of my chest at the absurdity of her statement. I sound deranged even to me. "Did you come early? Cause I never get to come at all unless I do it myself . . . Fuck!" I yell, stomping my foot before I turn on my heels so fast that it leaves me dizzy. There's no way in hell I can stand here one more second. I leave the same way I came in, shoving my feet back into my shoes without bothering to untie them.

The sound of Brad padding after me, bare feet smacking against the wood floors, has me straightening up. It takes every ounce of strength I have to hold back the tears that are threatening to fall. I just want to get out of here and get home where I can fall apart in private.

I take an unsteady breath as I turn around. Brad stands there, holding a pillow over his crotch.

"Dee, stay. We can talk about this," he says, looking anywhere but my eyes.

"Stay? Brad, you're my *fiancé* and you're screwing someone who is supposed to be my *best friend*. There's nothing to say, no reason you can give me that will make any of this okay."

"I love her, Dee."

I rear back, his words hit me like a blow to the face. That's not what I thought he was going to say. Maybe "*it was a mistake,*" or "*it didn't mean anything,*" or how about "*you're the love of my love, please forgive me.*"

"Well, congratulations." I pull the ring from my finger and slap it down on the counter, the sting of the contact barely registering. It's more Bridget's style anyway, the large square stone and blinding platinum metal. "Marry her then because I'm sure as hell not marrying you."

"Dee, don't do this." His voice shakes now like he might actually have some remorse over ripping my heart out.

"Stop calling me that. I hate it." I look down, not able to look at him like this. He doesn't deserve to act like this hurts him. "How long have you two been together?" I bite each word out, needing to know while equally dreading the answer.

"This time. Three months." He has the decency to at least sound ashamed.

"This time?" My voice hits an octave I didn't know was possible. "What does that even mean?"

"We . . . um . . . hooked up in college for a while during your study abroad. I—fuck. I never meant for this to happen. It was supposed to be me and you, but . . ."

I feel the sting of tears trickle down my face. "That's enough. I can't, Brad." I wipe my hand across my cheek and turn to the door, dropping my key on the counter next to my ring as I leave.

It wasn't always this way. Things used to be so good, but this isn't the man I fell in love with. He hasn't been for quite some time and he's treated me like a doormat for far too long. And I let him get away with it because I'd invested so much time into our relationship.

My dad's right, I'm too nice for my own good. Brad's lackluster proposal and near constant inattentiveness these last few months should have been enough to end it.

God, I feel so naive!

When I hit the stairs, I take off running, sucking in deep breaths of air as soon as I hit the sidewalk. I run as hard as I can, pumping my legs like I'm running a 200-meter sprint and not the twelve blocks back to my apartment. By the time I get there, my lungs and legs burn almost as much as my eyes.

I throw myself on the couch and scream into the cushion until my throat is raw and tears stain the fabric. Punching the pillows, I let the anger and hurt flow out of me. But it's not enough—the screaming, the tears, the hitting, the physical exertion of running—nothing dulls the rage that feels like it's tearing me limb from limb.

PROLOGUE

THE AFTERMATH

TWO YEARS EARLIER

In a stadium full of tens of thousands of people the only thing I see is the one, teal seat that's glaringly vacant.

For the first time since I got her tickets, my best friend is a no-show. It was the first thing I noticed when I stepped onto the field after warm-ups. The metal seat gleaming in the sun has continued to taunt me each inning when my eyes inevitably find it—drawn to it like a magnet. It's been almost ten months of having her in the stands cheering me on. Delilah rarely misses and if she's going to, she always lets me know.

Each time my eyes find her empty seat the panic coursing through my body escalates another notch. I couldn't even tell you what the stats or highlights of the game were. Each inning I went out there, counting down the seconds until I could get out of there. I haven't been that unfocused since last year, after I lost my brother, Jarrett, in a tragic accident.

My knee bounces, making the bench shake while Coach Wilson gives his postgame speech in the locker room. I nod along as he reviews the critical moments in the game, but it's all background noise. As soon as he's done talking to us, I grab my phone, frantically checking for a message or call from her. Anything to let me know she's okay.

There's nothing.

The pit in my stomach grows deeper until it feels bottomless. I shoot off a text and take the world's fastest shower, hoping that when I'm done, there will be a message from her.

Nothing.

Her phone just rings and rings when I try calling her as I walk through the player's lot. I'm practically running by the time I disconnect.

It's a miracle I don't get pulled over as I race towards her apartment. The entire way, my heart is beating wildly at the visions that flash through my head like a sickening slideshow. It's one I have seen before, but this time it's Delilah in a hospital bed, with a breathing tube—eyes closed in a permanent sleep. My palms are damp as I grip the steering wheel tightly, hanging on like it's the only thing that's keeping me from losing it completely. One more block.

I pull into the first spot I see and run toward her building. Taking the stairs two at a time, instead of waiting for the elevator, I skid to a stop at her door.

My fist comes down on her door harder than I intend with the anxiety coursing through me. "Delilah, are you there?" My voice shakes as I continue knocking. "*Delilah!*" I bark again, seriously considering kicking the door in.

It seems like hours before the knob turns and the door swings open. My eyes roam over her, checking to make sure she's okay. Her eyes are red-rimmed and swollen. I cross the threshold without a word and wrap her in my arms. As soon as I have her in my arms, my muscles uncoil for the first time since I spotted her empty seat.

She clings to me, her whole body shaking as a sob escapes her. The door clicks shut behind me and I squat, scooping her small body into my arms.

"Talk to me, Delilah. You're scaring me," I beg as I move us through the apartment, keeping her cradled against my chest. We sink to the couch together and my hand comes up to brush her blonde hair back, but it's stuck to her tear-streaked face. After smoothing it out of the way, I tilt her chin up. She sniffles and tries to bury her face back in my shoulder, like whatever is happening makes it too hard to face me. "Is someone hurt? One of your dads?" She shakes her head, still struggling to control her breathing. "Is Brad okay?" I ask just grasping at straws for what could have her this wrecked.

The maniacal laugh that comes out of her mouth alarms me. "Yes—no. Brad's fine. Better than fine," she chokes out the words, her chest heaving as she wipes the sleeve of her sweater under her nose. "I found Bridget in his lap—naked—this morning when he bailed on our brunch. Since when is fucking the groom part of bridesmaid responsibilities?" She looks up at the ceiling before looking back at me. "He told me he was sick and I went to check on him, like the fool I am."

Rage is bubbling just under the surface, but I lock that shit down. She doesn't need my emotions adding fuel to the fire. My hands come to the side of her face, cradling it and forcing her to see the sincerity in my eyes. "Jesus Delilah. I'm so fucking sorry."

"I'm so stupid. It wasn't even the first time. How did I not see it?"

I grit my teeth and place a gentle hand on her chin coaxing her to look up at me. "No. You're not gonna do that. This isn't your fault." By some miracle, I keep my voice mellow even though there's a battle raging inside me. I'm so fucking angry that she's blaming herself—that she's hurting, but as much as I try to shut it down there's a piece of me that's glad she's free of him. I rub circles on her back as she shakes in my arms, tearing my heart out. I want to kill him for hurting her like this—for not seeing what he's had all along. "He's a tool. No, a whole *shed* full of tools. Hands down the dumbest man on the planet to let someone as amazing as you slip through his fingers." My voice softens. "He's the problem, not you. What can I do?"

"Stay. I don't want to be alone."

"Anything Delilah." I kick my shoes off and shift under her, so my legs are extended in front of me, keeping her curled up in my lap. Her breathing slows as I rub her back until she passes out in my arms.

We stay like that until I'm certain she is asleep. Pushing off the couch with her in my arms, I carry her to her room and tuck her in before crawling in next to her. I don't want her to wake up alone in the middle of the night.

I slowly creep through Delilah's apartment to find coffee. She's still sleeping, and I don't want to wake her if I can avoid it. Mikey was already scheduled to open today, so she has the morning off.

When I find the grounds, I brew a carafe for the two of us. I have to get to practice this morning, but I'm not leaving here until the last possible minute. She was understandably devastated last night, and I need to see that she's okay this morning. I'll drag her along to practice if I need to.

I shake my head, trying to dislodge the memories still haunting me from last night. I thought she was physically hurt. The whole time I was trying to get to her, images of her in a hospital bed haunted me.

The drip of the coffee pulls me out of the dark memories.

I hear Delilah blowing her nose in the other room before she shuffles out. Her eyes are still puffy, but less red this morning. Golden wisps of hair fall free from her adorably messy bun sitting crooked on her head. It's not lost on me that even like this she's the most beautiful woman I've ever seen.

"You started coffee. That's usually my job." Her lips curl into a small smile that doesn't quite reach her eyes, but it's a start. "You need to get to the stadium soon."

"I do, but I wanted to make sure you were good. As good as you can be, I mean." She stops in front of me, dropping her hand on my arm.

"I'm so much better than I would have been if you hadn't shown up. Thank you for being here when I needed you, and for staying."

"Why didn't you call last night?" I lean against the counter and search her eyes, making sure she's really okay.

"You had a game. I didn't want to distract you." She shrugs like she's not more important than the game.

I couldn't have skipped the game, but I would have figured something out. "The thought of you here alone last night crying . . . it guts me."

"I didn't mean to worry you last night. When you got here. I could see that you were . . . upset." She bites on her plump lip, leaving two perfect little dents in it as she looks up at me through her lashes. Her voice is gentle, as if she doesn't want to say what she's really thinking.

I can imagine how I looked when she opened the door. She knows me well enough by now to guess that I went down a dark path. Delilah had a front row seat to my grief. We met right after my brother passed and my team in St. Louis traded me. She's been my saving grace as I figure out how to get through each day without him.

I push my hands through my hair. "I was fucking terrified when you didn't show up to the game and I couldn't get ahold of you. But none of this is your fault—not what he did, and not my reaction."

"I know, but I should've let you know I wouldn't be there. I wasn't thinking."

"Don't give it another thought. You'll come to the game tonight though, right? I don't want you sitting here alone."

"I'll be there. I won't pretend I'm not hurt and angry, and there will be moments where I just can't deal because I'm fucking gutted. But I refuse to sit around and cry over either of them. They've taken enough from me already."

"There she is. That's my strong girl." I pull her into a hug before we drink our coffee, sitting side by side and come up with a plan for what's next. She's got a long to-do list because of Brad's callus actions and if I know him, he's not going to lift a finger to help.

She talks and I make a list of the things that are urgent. Every once in a while she pops a caramel in her mouth, making a tiny mountain of wrappers next to her on the table. I make a mental note to restock her stash. The list grows as we work with things like: nixing the dress shopping this weekend, letting her extended family know the engagement is off, canceling wedding contracts, and talking to her landlord to make sure she can stay in her apartment.

She clutches my hand like it's her lifeline when she calls her dads to tell them the wedding is off. The tears streaming down her face as she reopened all the fresh wounds made me want to hunt Brad down and break every bone in his body.

No surprise, but her dads were both just concerned about how she was doing after finding Brad with Bridget, and the toll it would take on her to cancel all the wedding plans on her own. Her Pops sniffled along with her. While Dad was fuming just like me, threatening to tear Brad limb from limb for hurting his little girl.

They graciously offered, or rather demanded, to fly out and take care of her, but Delilah refused to let them do that. They eventually let it rest after the promise of daily Facetimes and reassurance that she wasn't alone.

"Thank you for your help with that. I would have broken down trying to get through that on my own." She nods to the piece of paper which is now stuck to her fridge. Making a plan seems to have helped her deal with a little of the pain she was feeling. Like breaking it down into tasks made it more manageable.

CHAPTER 1

THE BRIDGET BOMB

PRESENT

"Attendance is mandatory, and management is asking that everyone brings a plus one. It doesn't have to be a date. Bring your mom for all I care," Coach bellows at us as we all hurry towards the door. "Don't forget the dress code is black tie. Now, get out of here and go enjoy the rest of your day."

I cringe when I see the time on my watch—I'm supposed to meet Delilah for lunch. It's something we started doing weekly after her breakup with Brad. We've kept it up for the last two years. I needed to know she was okay, and it was a way to get her out of her apartment or *Buns & Roses,* so she couldn't hide herself away or bury herself in work while she worked through her pain.

Stepping into the crisp, fall air my feet carry me to my truck at a rapid pace. The old truck shutters when I slam the door shut. I turn over the engine, bringing it rumbling to life. While I let it warm up my fingers move across the screen, typing out a short message letting her know I'm running behind.

My head goes back to the night we met, when Brad was almost an hour late for their date. I don't ever want to be the guy that makes her question whether she's worth showing up for her. Turning left into the parking lot I find the first open spot, leap from the truck and hustle into the restaurant to find her already waiting for me at a table by the window of the Vietnamese bakery.

Delilah stands when I approach the table, and I don't think twice about pulling her into me. My chin rests on the top of her head, keeping her there a beat longer than necessary. As expected, the scent of brown sugar and coffee consumes me. It's so fucking intoxicating. Nothing smells more like home to me than she does. "Sorry I'm late. Coach was on a rant after practice. Have you ordered yet?"

"No, I haven't. You were two minutes late. It's hardly a big deal." She glances down at her watch, which is stacked with the bracelet I got for her birthday the first year we met. The watch is a recent addition. It's gold, like the bracelet, and inscribed with the letters BFF. It's cheesy as hell which makes it even better.

I gave it to her the morning of her birthday, at the park where we sometimes volunteer to walk rescue dogs. Afterwards she scolded me for spending so much on a watch only to have something so ridiculous etched into it. But I would have spent a hundred times more to hear a genuine laugh after all the shit she's been through.

My fingers skate across the delicate chain on her wrist. "Maybe not to you, but I hate the thought of you waiting on me."

Her brows furrow, eyes following the movement as my finger toys with her bracelet. She places her hand on top of mine. "Aside from my dads you're the most steadfast presence in my life. You wouldn't be late without reason. I'm the luckiest girl alive to have a friend like you in my life."

Friend. Right. Why does that sting a little more every time I hear her describe me that way? Maybe because my feelings for her have grown far beyond the boundaries of friendship. Lately, it's hard to push that aside and act like I don't need more. Every cell in my body is begging me to indulge in the feelings I've developed for Delilah.

I think I've known since we first met that there was more to it—to *us*—but I wrote it off as physical attraction. Delilah's gorgeous inside and out, with those stunning blue eyes that seem to see into every nook and cranny of my soul. She was the friend I needed when everything was clouded by grief, helping me overcome it day by day. She chipped away at the darkness that had caged me in. Then Brad broke her heart and—like she helped me—I did my best to be there for her.

All I know is that she understands me better than anyone ever has, except maybe Jarrett. But our timing has always been fucked. I'm still not sure that I'll ever be healed enough to love her the way she deserves. There are too many unanswered questions about what caused my brother's fatal injuries that still send me spiraling with anxiety more often than I would like.

But I don't tell her any of that. Because as much as I want her, that's not what she needs. She's on a self-proclaimed dating timeout after being in a relationship for most of her adult life and having her trust shattered. So we stay firmly in the friend zone, meeting weekly for lunch, while I wait, hoping one day she'll be ready.

"The Grilled Pork Banh Mi looks amazing, but so does the rice bowl. Such a big decision." She taps her lower lip with an exaggerated pout, looking irresistible. The girl is baiting me, and I don't even care. I'd order the whole damn menu under the pretense of being a growing boy just so she could graze off little bites of each—just the way she likes to. "What are you going to get?" she finally asks, dropping her menu to look at me.

"You get the rice bowl and I'll get the Grilled Pork and Spicy Tofu. You can try some of mine. But I get a bite of the rice bowl. And spring rolls . . . we need spring rolls."

Her face lights up like the scoreboard after a grand slam. "I love this plan. You know the way to my heart." *If only it were that simple.*

We place our orders and talk about her dads upcoming trip to visit. When they call her name, I go to grab the food. Turning back toward the table with the tray in my hands I find her with a wide-eyed look on her suddenly ashen face. My shoes squeak against the tile floor as I grind to a halt searching for whatever's caused the rapid change in her demeanor. Over her head I see the reason for her distress. Fucking Brad. He's walking up to the door hand in hand with Bridget.

Shaking off my shock at seeing him, I cross the small space and slide back into my seat, setting the tray down and turning Delilah's chin toward me. "Say the word and we'll leave."

Her head whips side to side, but she looks panic-stricken. Shockingly, Brad holds the door for Bridget. When she steps around him Delilah whimpers, her fingers lock around my wrist. "They're still together." After everything that happened she cut off contact with both of them, not bothering to keep tabs on what happened to her ex or her best friend. I was in awe of how fucking brave she was for making her mental health a priority. "And she's pregnant Cruz, they're having a baby." My heart ached for her, knowing Delilah was hurt and angry as she mourned the loss of a future she had planned for years. Her eyes gleam with unshed tears that I know are fueled by agonizing memories, not longing.

I would do anything to make her feel better, but the chance to flee without being seen is gone. My hand goes to her cheek, caressing it softly as I turn her head toward me. "Delilah, look at me," I whisper softly, touching my forehead to hers. "You are the strongest woman I know. They hurt you, but don't give them that power right now. Focus on me. Deep breaths—I've got you."

She nods and swallows roughly before steeling her features. I scoot my chair further into her space and wrap my arm around her shoulder, caressing her arm. I bury my nose against her hairline. "Put your hand on my knee and smile at me."

She takes a half-second to react, but she does so flawlessly. Once her eyes are on me, she lights up like I am her entire world. No one else would know that her heart is breaking all over again. With all my focus on Delilah, I lay kisses along her neck. She shivers underneath me, and I'd like to think it has everything to do with me and nothing to do with the anxiety over the footsteps approaching our table. "Focus on me, Hermosa," I utter against her neck.

"Mmm . . ." Delilah responds dreamily, but she jolts when a throat clears next to us.

"Delilah? Cruz?" I look up to see Brad looking down his nose at us.

"Hey, man, how's it going?" I have to force my voice to sound disinterested while I continue drawing lazy circles on Delilah's arm. But inside, it's taking every ounce of restraint not to lay him out for how he hurt her. Next to me, my girl just rests her head on my shoulder and sighs like she's bored with the whole interaction.

Bridget drops her hand to rest on the top of her stomach, and she dramatically rubs her belly. Delilah's eyes drop to where she's making exaggerated circles over the bump.

"Wow, looks like congratulations are in order," Delilah says sweetly and I swear I hear her tack on an almost silent *"better you than me."*

That's my spunky girl.

"Thanks Dee. Are you two . . . um, together?" Brad waves his hand between us, his forehead crinkling as he stammers over the question.

My fingers breeze down her arm, making her shiver under my touch. "Not sure that's any of your business. You lost the right to know what happens in Delilah's life the second you stuck your dick in someone else."

Brad's eyebrows shoot up to his thinning hairline—thank you karma—and Bridget scoffs next to him. *Because* I'm *the offensive one here.*

She links her finger through mine, beaming at me. "It's okay, Cruz. I am happier than I've ever been." My stomach flips and I drop a kiss on her head—wishing she meant those words the way I took them.

"Mhmmm. So fucking lucky," I mumble against her hair.

Bridget tugs Brad's hand. "Let's order, I'm starving."

"Yeah. Okay," he says, but stays rooted to the spot in front of us. His gaze drops to our linked hands.

"Babe." Bridget stomps her foot at him—still holding his hand, arms stretched between them. She yanks on his arm dragging him to the counter looking more than a little pissed at his lack of attentiveness toward her.

Thank fuck, they order their food to-go and are out of there in a matter of minutes. When his car doors slam shut and he pulls out of the lot, Delilah takes a full breath for the first time since they walked in.

I twist away from the window toward her, taking her face in my hands. "Are you okay?"

She covers my hands with hers. "Thanks to you. I freaked out for a second but I'm fine."

"Are you sure?" I search her eyes for any sign she's covering her pain. "It's okay to not be."

"I'm sure. So sure. I was shocked to see that they're having a baby, but I meant what I said." Her eyes soften and strokes my hands gently. "I'm happier than I have ever been, and you are a huge part of that. Things between Brad and I never would have worked. We both changed a lot during the last few years of our relationship. He became more obsessed about making partner and I buried myself in work to avoid the ever expand-ing crack in our relationship. I was so caught up in the life we planned together that I didn't see that it wasn't what either of us *needed* and that *he* wasn't the person I wanted it with anymore."

"There's my girl. I am so proud of how damn strong you are." I brush my lips across her forehead.

"Let's not waste anymore of our lunch talking about them. You said Coach was on a rant and that's why you were 'running late.'" She throws air quotes around that last bit.

"Yeah, about that, I actually have a favor to ask you. The front office is up our ass about this gala that's coming up. It's for a great cause, so I'm happy to go, but they're pushing all of us to bring a date this year." I push my fingers through my curls. "I hate to ask because it's kind of stuffy and mostly just rubbing elbows to get donations from a bunch of rich old dudes."

"Ask what, Cruz?" A sly smile tilts the corner of her lips up as she raises her fork to her mouth.

"Would you come with me?"

"With an invitation like that, who could say no?" She drops her fork into her bowl, laughter ringing out at my expense.

My hand freezes with my sandwich midair and I channel my inner golden retriever, giving her my best puppy dog eyes. "Are you mocking me right now? In my time of need. Right after I helped you?"

"Stop with the eyes. Just because God gave you those big brown weapons of mass destruction doesn't mean they'll work on me. I know you too well."

"Is that a yes?" Leaning in close, I pull out all the stops. Letting my accent come out to play and giving her a crooked grin I know makes my dimples extra deep.

"Of course, it's a yes you goon. Now put those dimples away, they did their job. Plus, it'll give Poppy an excuse to take me shopping." She spears a piece of pork that's covered in sticky rice and lifts her fork between us. "Try this. It's so freaking delicious. It might be the best meat I have ever had in my mouth. Mmm."

That's only because you haven't had mine—I stop myself. *Shit*, I am so fucked.

I raise my eyebrow at her, but Delilah just shrugs, and moves the fork closer. I wrap my mouth around the fork. She wasn't lying, it's incredible. But what I love most is how her pupils flare when I hum in satisfaction.

When I'm finished chewing, I pull out my wallet and slide my card across the table. She clears her throat as her eyes drop to the card, breaking that connection. "What's this?"

"My credit card."

"Thanks, Captain Obvious. I can see that, but why do *I* need it?" Her eyes roll dramatically, and I can't help but think if she were mine, I would kiss that sassy look right off her face.

"For the dress. I asked you to a black-tie gala. Since you would rather shop with Poppy than me, I'm giving you my card. Get shoes, a purse, and whatever else you need for the night."

Like a game of hot potato she pushes it back across the table. "I can buy my own dress."

"I know you can. I said I *wanted* to buy it for you. I'll pretend not to be hurt that you didn't refute my claim that you'd rather shop with Poppy." Both our hands still on the card, I slide it over the threshold back towards her half of the table.

She levels me with a glare that tells me she's about done with my nonsense. "Are you going to skip your away games to shop with me? I think not. I'm not taking your card. End of conversation."

I drop it for now, but there's no way this is over.

CHAPTER 2

DRESS SHOPPING

PRESENT

"What about this one?" Poppy holds a short, strappy, pink number up against her chest and bats her eyelashes at me. It's the first store on our "Lilah gets her groove back"—that's what she's calling it—shopping extravaganza and so far it's a bust.

My stunning, redheaded friend and I bonded over a love of dirty jokes when she walked into *Buns & Roses* to find me with bloodshot eyes one morning after the break-up. She was the first person to make me laugh after everything. And she kept coming back, claiming it was because my latte art looked less phallic than the other neighborhood coffeeshop. But really she just wanted to make sure I was okay. Now she's my partner in crime—the devil to Cruz's angel on my shoulder.

"I'm not sure what I am looking for, but I know it's not that." I flip through the choices on the rack. All of them scream prom or plaything, not black-tie gala.

"Hey, that's a start. Maybe if we rule things out, we can figure out what *the one* looks like." Poppy hangs the Pepto pink abomination back on the rack.

"Can you please stop calling it that? It's not a wedding dress."

"No, you're right . . . it might be more important. It's a drive-my-hot-as-hell-best-friend-crazy dress."

I feel the blush crawling up my neck and settling in my cheeks. Damn, why is it so hot in here all of a sudden? "That's not what this is. He needed a favor and I'm helping him out." I play it off with an eye roll. But if I'm being honest, Cruz, liking the way I look, is more appealing than I want to admit.

"Whatever you say, babe. Maybe I'm wrong, but that man wants you, and I think you might want him a little bit, too."

"Can we just focus on the dress? I'm not sure I'm ready for a relation-ship yet. I spent most of my adult life getting lost in one. I'm just starting to find myself again."

Her eyes soften from across the rack. "And I'm so happy for you, but we both know that sexy-as-sin best friend was there helping as you found your way through the shit storm that Douche Canoe Brad put you through."

"Nothing pink," I say, conceding to her plans but not addressing the bigger issue. She's right. Cruz has been my rock since I ran out of Brad's apartment that day. My fingers wrap around the velvet hanger and hold a silver dress against my body. "Not metallic either."

Poppy claps her hands excitedly. "Let's find you a killer dress that makes you feel good."

Several stores later, I'm beginning to think that finding a dress is hope-less and I'll have to shop in Poppy's closet. But, just as we were about to throw in the towel, we decided to make one last stop and find ourselves impressed upon entering the store. Partially because they have champagne, but also because they have a much better selection of dresses.

"I feel good about this." Poppy tips back her flute as we start combing through the racks.

"About the dresses? Or the champagne?" I lift a deep purple dress off the rack and hold it up for inspection. With a thumbs up it gets draped over my arm.

"Both."

The woman that greeted us with flutes of bubbly rejoins us, taking the dresses draped over our arms and starts a fitting room. Holding up an emerald green dress with a deep V-neck Poppy lifts one red eyebrow in silent question.

"That could work. The color would be better on you, but I like the cut."

We continue to pile dresses into each other's arms as quickly as the employees can run them back to the fitting room. By the time we finish our second glass of champagne, I have a stack of dresses taller than me to try on and the floaty feeling of a little buzz.

Dress after dress goes on and comes off. With each one that ends up back on the rack, I feel my confidence deflate.

My hair is a disaster and I'm exhausted when I tug the last dress over my hips. I let the green fabric drop around my feet and call Poppy in to zip me up. She slips through the door and dramatically touches the back of her hand to her forehead, fluttering her eyelids in a fake swoon.

"Just zip me, you freak."

She tugs the zipper into place looking at me in the mirror from around my shoulder. "The belly button deep neckline on this one is giving those sexy vibes we were looking for."

"It certainly does, but I kind of wish it was red. I'm also a little concerned about a wardrobe malfunction. These girls have a mind of their own." I adjust myself in the mirror and turn to the side. There's an obscene amount of cleavage on display.

A soft knock at the door has Poppy twisting around to pull it open. My jaw drops. The sales lady is standing there holding the most stunning dress I have seen all day. "I overheard you talking and wanted to bring this one over for you to try on. I think it might be what you're looking for." She turns it around so we can see the back and Poppy makes grabby hands at her.

It's crimson red with a high neck and an indecently low back. A thin crystal chain hangs in the middle, connecting the two straps midway down the back.

Poppy tugs the zipper down my spine and thrusts the red dress at me. "This is it. I can tell. Now strip!" Her feet don't move as she stands there and waits for me to change. I guess I'm not getting privacy for this.

The material is cool and silky against my skin—this dress fits like it was made for me, which is a miracle on its own considering I'm barely five-three. I turn to the side, running my hands down the front of the dress and my eyes go wide when I see the back. It's stunning and sexy as hell.

"This is perfect. Champagne to celebrate." Poppy hands me her flute for a sip. "You look super fuckable. Those baseball players are going to be begging to take you home. I hope the rich old donors have their cardiologists on speed dial because they're going straight into cardiac arrest when they see you."

"It's definitely a stunner, but I haven't looked at the price tag. Can you check it? I'm too nervous."

Poppy frowns but fishes the tag out before quickly tucking it back in.

"It's not good, is it?" I ask biting on my thumbnail.

"It's a little spendy."

I twist my body around and pluck that tag out craning my neck to read it. *A little?* "This is more than *Buns & Roses* makes in a day."

"Just think about it. Let's see if they will put it on hold until the end of the day. Get changed and I'll talk to Janey, woman to woman," Poppy says as the dressing room door clicks shut.

We spend another hour shopping, but nothing even comes close to the red dress. Feeling defeated, I suggest we drown our sorrows in tacos.

We are halfway through a pile of nachos while we wait on our tacos when Poppy slaps the table.

"I have a strappy black dress that would be perfect for you. It's not the red one, but it'll make you feel sexy. It's got a high slit and barely-there straps across the open back."

I smile. She's trying so hard and it's sweet. "Thanks Poppy. I'm sure it will be perfect." My hand slips into my purse, grabbing two caramels and holding my hand out to my friend so she can grab one.

"You can always go back for the red one if mine doesn't work." She lays her hand on top of mine.

I shouldn't be this bummed over a dress, but it made me feel more confident than I have in a while. It's been so long since I have really done anything outside of *Buns & Roses* for me. This isn't just about a silly dress— this felt like an opportunity to flaunt my femininity and feel really freaking good about it.

CHAPTER 3

GALA NIGHT

PRESENT

Chewing slowly on a bite of tart apple, I savor the peace between our morning rush and the crowd that comes in for lunch. I have my AirPods in with Ed Sheeran crooning to keep me focused as I work on payroll. I'm trying to get everything done before this afternoon.

Mikey is going to close up so I can sneak out and get my glam on. After the red dress slipped through my fingers, I splurged on having my hair and make-up done for the gala.

Poppy was right. I deserve to feel sexy, especially since I'll be surrounded by hunky baseball players and what, I'm sure, will be droves of model-like dates. As I double check the time entry, the front door chimes.

"Hey, Lilah girl, there's delivery for you," Mikey croons when his head peeks around the doorway.

"You can sign for it," I say, not bothering to take my eyes off the payroll program on the screen.

"Nuh uh. This one's all you."

I blow out a breath, trying not to be annoyed. When I step through the doorway to the front of the coffee shop he's leaning against the counter with the biggest Cheshire cat grin stretched across his face. He wiggles his eyebrows as he tips his head toward the big white box sitting on the counter.

It's wrapped up with a sleek black bow and there's a card tucked into it. I give him a puzzled look just as the courier clears her throat.

"Oh, right. Sorry," I stammer, coming around to sign the tablet she holds out. "Have a good day." I continue to stare at the box as the delivery man leaves.

"Are you going to open it or just look at the dang thing?" Mikey excitedly gestures toward the box.

I slip my finger under the seal on the envelope and pull the small card out. The front simply says: *"I'm sorry."*

"What the hell?"

Delilah, You know the saying, "It's better to ask forgiveness than permission"? This is like that. I hope you aren't too mad at me or my accomplice. Enjoy your pampering. Can't wait to see you tonight, Cruz.

"Who's it from?" Mikey's rocking back on his heels, looking downright gleeful—like it's a gift for him.

"Cruz, but if I had to guess, he had help from Poppy. What did those two do?" My fingers work the bow loose and lift the top of the box, revealing a layer of tissue paper. Silky red fabric comes into view and my hand shoots to my mouth covering my gasp.

Tucked in next to the dress is a pair of nude heels with crystal detailing on the wrap-around straps that match the one on the back of the dress.

There's also the most gorgeous, nude YSL clutch I've ever seen tucked in the box. Sticking out of it is a case of mints and another note.

Lilah- To keep your breath fresh around all those sexy men tonight. You may not be ready for a relationship, but that doesn't mean they shouldn't want to kiss your minty lips. Have fun and be nice to Cruz. He just wanted you to feel your best tonight. Love ya, Poppy.

"That dress is everything. You are going to look fine as fuck." Mikey peeks over my shoulder at the note.

"I really am. I can't believe they put their heads together to do this." I'm not even mad that they ignored my wishes. It's too damn sweet.

I run my hands down the smooth red fabric, watching how the bottom flutters around my red toenails. As my phone vibrates from the dresser, I take one more look at myself in the mirror, turning to see the back. Heat creeps up my neck and I fan my face to keep it from ruining my makeup. I had to get creative with my undergarments—namely, not wearing any. The back of this dress made that impossible.

I snag my phone, slipping it into the clutch and I apply a fresh coat of, what Poppy called, "fuck me" red on my lips. There's a knock at the door as I cap the lipstick. When I pull the door open, air whooshes out of my lungs at the sight.

Cruz is leaning with his forearm against the doorframe, his dark curls tumbling over his forehead where it is swept to the side. He's dressed in crisp black on black and it looks impeccable, from the way the tailored fit hugs his broad shoulders to how the satin finish looks against his caramel skin tone.

A devilish smirk plays at his lips as his gaze roams over me slowly. "Fuck, Hermosa. You look more stunning than I could have ever imagined," he says, straightening the matching, black tie that hangs down his broad chest.

I extend my hand in the air and give him a twirl.

"Holy shit. Delilah—you . . . the back," he stammers, running his hand along his jaw. "Poppy warned me, but she didn't do you justice. Her words were, 'you'll have the hottest date at the gala.' But she was wrong. You're the hottest date in the *history* of dates. You pulled out all the stops."

Heat prickles at my cheeks with the way he's looking at me like he's never seen anything quite like me in this dress. *This* is why I wanted the dress—I feel invincible and so sexy. But my date, he's my equal in that department. Cruz always looks good, but right now I'm questioning everything I've ever said about being just friends. This man is every woman's fantasy and I have to keep my hands to myself because he's my best friend.

Honestly, I am not sure how I'm going to manage because I think he could impregnate me with a wink. "I'm not the only one that pulled out all the stops." I step into him, giving the shiny lapels of his suit a gentle tug before smoothing down the tie. He just fixed it, but I can't resist the urge to touch him. "You look sharp in this suit. If you're not careful, you'll end up with a trail of women following you home like a sexy pied piper."

He gives me a gravelly laugh and holds his hand out. "The only woman I'm interested in spending time with tonight is you. You look breathtaking, Hermosa. Ready to go stun the world with our amazingly good looks?" His accent comes out to play, giving him an unfair advantage—one he definitely doesn't need because he's already the most charming man I've ever met. Top his sweet words with a voice that sounds like it's dripping in butter? How's a girl supposed to keep her cool?

I do my best not to let my fluster show and place my palm in his hoping he doesn't notice the slight tremble. He tucks me under his arm as we walk toward the elevator. "I've never felt more beautiful and confident and I have you to thank for that. The dress was more than enough, but the shoes and the clutch—you're too good to me. I'm grateful to have someone who looks out for me even when I'm being stubborn. It seems you know me better than I know myself."

He pauses, turning to face me. His hand cups my cheek and I lean into it, letting my eyes close. "Delilah, there's nothing I wouldn't do for you—big or small." His lips skim across my forehead gently before he tugs on my hand, leading me into the waiting elevator.

"You got us a limo." My voice is high-pitched and girly at the prospect of arriving at the gala in a limo. Sometimes I forget Cruz is famous and gets to do these kinds of things all the time. He's so down to earth, and, to me, he's just the guy who chatted with me one of the many times Brad was running late. Or the new friend that came by the coffee shop with a warm smile and jokes, the one who did everything he could to be there for me while I got my life back together.

"We didn't get all glammed up for nothing. You and I are going to walk that red carpet like we own it. But I'll just be background noise. All eyes are going to be on you." His warm hand drops to the small of my back, making me shiver at the roughness of his big hand against my skin. Opening the door to the limo, he ushers me in before sliding in next to me.

CHAPTER 4

GALA NIGHT

PRESENT

Delilah slides into the limo, smoothing her dress as her eyes dart around the interior. I take advantage of the fact that she's distracted and take her in. When that door opened, it took everything in me not to march her backwards into her apartment and keep her there all night, where only I would get to see her like this.

Poppy told me to prepare myself, but she left out a few things. Essential information like the way the slinky, red silk drapes across all of her curves, gliding over her hips and highlighting the best parts of her—the swell of her breasts and the delicate shape of her waist. I bite my lip just thinking about the way she twirled, revealing the open back and the way it grazed the swell of her ass.

There's no fucking way she's wearing underwear with that dress. I adjust myself, cursing the fact that all of the effort I had put in upstairs, to avoid getting hard over my best friend, had been pointless. Meanwhile Delilah leans forward, grabbing the bottle of champagne, and then I slide in next to her, plucking it from her slender fingers.

"Are you going to let me at least pretend to be a gentleman and offer you some?" I tease, grabbing two flutes as the driver pulls away from the curb.

Delilah takes them, holding them out while I pour. "What should we toast?"

"To beautiful friends, and a beautiful friendship, with many more years of making memories together."

The sheen in her eyes and the blush that blossoms across her cheeks makes me want to keep talking—tell her all the things I feel so she never stops looking at me like that. "Are you trying to ruin my makeup with that toast? It was perfect."

"Not yet. That comes later, when I get you all sweaty and mess up that hair."

Her eyes turn into saucers like the Maria doll my mom keeps on a shelf at home, and her mouth drops open and closes wordlessly. I replay the words in my head as her chest heaves with choppy inhales.

"Dancing Delilah, I meant dancing," I say with a nervous laugh, although the dirty thoughts of other ways to get sweaty with her are really fucking appealing. I mentally scold myself knowing she's not ready to pursue a relationship with anyone and, as her friend, I'm supposed to have her best interests at heart.

She ghosts a hand up over her throat holding it there and fuck if I don't imagine replacing it with my own. "Dancing, of course. How else would you make a mess of me?"

"Is that a rhetorical question, Hermosa? Or was Brad such a miserable excuse for a fiancé that I need to explain to you all the ways a man can mess up a woman's hair while getting sweaty together?"

Her throat works under her delicate fingers and I lift my champagne to my lips before I take this any further and ruin our night. I glance out the window to give her the space she needs, and I swear I hear her mumble a string of nonsense about her, *"best friend," "sex on a stick,"* and *"Buzz Lightgirth."*

When the driver pulls up to the curb, camera bulbs flash brightly as photographers snap pictures of my teammates and their dates exiting their cars. Next to me, Delilah's got her plump, ruby red lip trapped between her teeth.

"Ready?" I extend my hand to her as the driver comes around to open the door. "You look flawless. You're going to blow them all away."

She nods before tilting her chin up and placing her hand in mine. When the door opens, I help her from the car and guide her along the carpet with my hand nestled against the skin right above the delicious curve of her ass.

Walking hand in hand, we stop to pose for a few photos by the team photographer. Delilah snuggles right into my side, beaming up at me as the camera shutter clicks. I can't wait to see them, print one off, and display it where I can see it every day as a permanent reminder that I was lucky enough to have her like this, even if just for tonight.

The ballroom is already packed with guests dressed in their very best. Everyone is mingling as the band plays softly, accompanied by the tinkling of laughter and the hum of small talk. A server with a tray of champagne pauses as we pass, and I grab a flute for each of us.

"There's Linc. Let's go say hi and maybe grab some of those fancy looking appetizers on our way." Delilah points to a table with an array of small plates.

"I like the way you think. Finger food for the win. Make sure you eat now because once you see my dance moves, you're not going to be able to tear yourself away from the dance floor."

We grab our fancy plates, filled with boujee food and join Lincoln, my former teammate, at the bar. "Damn Cruz. How did you convince Lilah to come with you? Look at her, she's like a twenty out of ten and you're a solid four on a good day."

Delilah's shoulders shake with laughter. "I knew you were my favorite Bandit for a reason, Linc. But give him a little credit, with that suit, he's at least a six tonight."

"He's not even on the team anymore! But I can't be mad about the abuse—he's right, I'm out punting my coverage with you as my date."

"Damn straight you are. It's a good thing your personality makes up for your tragic looks. Oh, shrimp." Linc plucks a shrimp off my plate, dragging it through cocktail sauce before he bites into it with a smirk.

"Where is your stunning wife?" Delilah asks.

"I'm flying solo tonight. Maxi didn't want to make the trip with Lulu. She's had strep and is just starting to feel better," he says of his wife and daughter. "But you'll save a dance for me tonight, right, beautiful?" Linc smirks over his drink like he's not trying to push my buttons.

"That depends," Delilah teases. He was the first teammate I introduced her to after we met and the two hit it off from that first night, teaming up to give me a hard time any chance that they got.

"Oh yeah? On what?"

"Do you have moves?"

"Moves that rival Usher's," Lincoln says, spinning on the balls of his feet without warning.

"I'll be the judge of that." She pats his chest. "But you're going to have some stiff competition. Cruz has made some pretty big promises about what his dancing will do to me, haven't you, big guy?" she says, winking over her shoulder at me.

I almost choke on my champagne. This fucking girl. People underestimate her. They see her as the sweet baker, but underneath that sugary exterior, she's bold and brazen. She holds her own bantering with the guys.

"But first I need to find the ladies room. The limo champagne went right through me. Excuse me boys." I watch Delilah walk away in that godforsaken dress, trying, and failing, not to stare as her ass sways side to sides.

Lincoln whistles, letting me know I was not discreet, but I wasn't really trying to be. It's better that everyone sees me watching and knows just how fucking off-limits she is.

"How's Lulu? Feeling better?" I ask knowing he can't help himself when it comes to his family. It's guaranteed to get the attention off me.

"Much better and adorable as ever. I make the prettiest fucking babies. Look at this picture." I can hear the love in his voice for his daughter as he pulls out his phone. She might have been unexpected, but she's owned her dad's heart from the moment he found out about her.

"Hate to break it to you Linc, but I think she gets that from your wife."

Lulu is on the screen of his phone toddling around the yard with one of the small rustic cabins and the mountains in the background. She's chasing bubbles with outstretched fingers and has, what looks like, squashed strawberries coating her face. He's right, she's adorable.

"Enough with stalling tactics, tell me what's going on with Lilah. Have you two figured your shit out yet?"

"Not sure what you mean," I tell him, gripping the back of my neck.

"We're going to play dumb today? That's not your style."

"Still just friends. She's been all sorts of skittish about dating since Brad. She's only gone on a handful of dates and no one ever makes it past the second date."

"Are you just going to sit around, waiting on her forever? Don't you think it's time to make a move or move on?"

"You know I value your advice about a lot of things, but you accidentally married your wife and then got her pregnant all in the span of three months. I think you might be a little out of your depth."

"I'm going to try not to be offended. Maxi and I may have had an unconventional start, and sure, Lulu sped up our future, but we worked through our shit *together*. And it wasn't an easy journey. I've watched you and Lilah circle each other for years. As a matter of fact, I remember you threatening me after the first time I met her. If you think you're fooling anyone by saying you're just friends, you've lost it."

"Not holding back, I see." Not that I would expect him to, Lincoln's always been an ace at getting people to open up.

"It's not in my nature," he says with a laugh. "That's why I was such an awesome captain."

"Fine. Dust your captain's hat off and give me your best advice. What would you suggest I do?" It's not like I have much to lose at this point.

"That depends on you. Can you let her go? If you did, would you be able to move on?"

It doesn't take me long to respond. "She may not give me an option. But no, I don't think I could just move on."

"I don't think you really need to hear this from me, but you need to go after her. Tell her how you feel. You'll probably need to ease her into the idea of the two of you being more than friends. You already said she's skittish. The fact that you are her best friend is going to work against you as much as it'll work for you."

"I'm listening."

"She knows you. Knows that you have her best interest at heart. You've always been there for her, but that also means that she depends on you, and changing that dynamic is going to be a lot for her to process. You already treat her like your girlfriend in a lot of ways, but if it were me, I'd ramp up the heat. Get her thinking about what it *could* be like. Turn the dial little by little so neither of you gets burned."

"I think I can do that. Fuck, what if it doesn't work?"

"It'll work. Have you seen you? You've got those rugged good looks, big brown eyes, and bronzed skin. If all else fails, just flex and whisper to her in Spanish."

"Is that how you got Maxi to fall in love with you?"

"No man, I used a wink, my impeccable ability to give her multiple orgasms, and a whole fuck-ton of groveling. I recommend you try to avoid the need for groveling. That was the most miserable month of my life."

"I remember, but it worked out pretty well for you. It was all worth it."

"Yeah—it really was," he says as Delilah weaves through the crowd to us. "Don't forget to give her the orgasms though, those work wonders."

When she stops in front of us I pat Lincoln on the shoulder in a silent *thank you* before holding out my arm for Delilah. "Let's go, Hermosa. It's time to dance." I set my champagne down and lead her toward the dance floor. "Good luck getting her away from me once we get started!" I holler over my shoulder at my former captain.

"Someone's in a hurry."

"To have a beautiful woman in my arms on the dance floor? Absolutely." I tug Delilah against my chest as the band starts a slow song. It's the instrumental version of "Better Together" by Jack Johnson.

"You tell all the ladies that, don't you?" Her hands smooth up my chest before linking behind my neck.

"What ladies? I haven't dated since I moved to Colorado."

"Don't act like there aren't still ladies just because you aren't dating. Why don't you date? I mean, I know why you didn't date when we first met, but you're in a better place now."

"Thanks to you." It's true. Without her I'm not sure where I would've ended up. "Just waiting on the right woman," I tell her, searching her eyes to see any hint of where this is coming from.

"What qualities does the right lady for Cruz Tellez need to have?" Her fingers toy with the hair at the base of my skull. It's distracting as hell.

"Someone with a kind heart, but some sass. She can't be too sweet—I need someone to challenge me; a partner-in-crime that I can talk to about everything and nothing when I'm on the road. Smart and hardworking, but not too serious. Whoever I end up with needs to be able to let loose and have fun. She needs to be strong too, because this life doesn't come without its trials, but vulnerable enough to speak up when she needs more from me." I don't break eye contact while I speak—hoping she sees the emotions behind my words.

Her throat bobs as she swallows, but doesn't say anything. Instead, she steps into my space and rests her head on my chest.

We dance together like that for another slow song before Lincoln cuts in just as the band kicks up the tempo. Delilah laughs as he spins her in circles and dips her.

I remember the way Brad used to drag her to events like this—parade her around like she was a trophy on his arm but somehow still failed to see what was right in front of him. He was the luckiest fucking guy on the planet, but he never deserved her. The jackass even managed to make his proposal about himself, it took every ounce of willpower I had not to tell Delilah to walk away from him right then and there. Seeing her like this now, radiant and filled with joy, I regret biting my tongue. Maybe I could have saved her some heartache, but at the time I was too afraid to lose her to speak up.

When the song fades out, he slings his arm around her shoulder, and they walk back toward where I'm leaning against the bar watching.

"Honorable Judge Lilah, what's the verdict?"

"Mhmm . . . Hard to say. I only got a slow dance with Cruz. I'll need him to take me for another spin around the floor to reach a final decision."

She extends her hand to me, and I take it, following her back out onto the floor just as the band starts to play an instrumental version of "My Love" by Justin Timberlake. My hand falls to her hip and I pull her into me, lifting her hand with my free one and placing it on my shoulder. I gently stroke my fingers down her arm, watching the goosebumps explode across her smooth skin. She may not be ready to admit her feelings for me, but there's no denying she's affected by me.

When my hand snakes around her waist, coming to rest on her lower back, I have to focus on not getting a very public erection with the way my hands slip below the fabric of her dress as she sways. The rhythm of her hips causes my pinky to brush against the swell of her ass, making her breath catch and my dick twitch behind the zipper of my pants.

The song is far shorter than I would like, and as it comes to an end I bring my lips to the shell of her ear. "Hermosa, you are the most spectacular woman in this room. No one else compares to you—not even close. Being beside you makes these events worth all the hassle."

We spin around the dance floor for the rest of the night until I catch Delilah slipping her heels off under the table while she alternates taking sips between a glass of ice water and champagne.

"Let's get you home," I tell her, holding out my hand and leading her to the waiting limo.

Once inside she mumbles a soft, *"Thank you"* and brushes her lips across my jaw before falling asleep against my shoulder.

CHAPTER 5

PREVIOUS ENGAGEMENTS

FLASHBACK - TWO YEARS EARLIER

Looking around the restaurant, I search for Delilah in the crowded space. There are a lot of fucking people here. Based on the venue and attire, they're mostly Brad's co-workers, or clients. The thought makes my jaw clench. Tonight should be about Delilah, not Brad impressing his bosses.

I run my fingers through my still-damp hair, suddenly aware of exactly how much I stick out—never mind the fact that I make more than everyone in this room. My jaw is covered in a week's worth of stubble from the hitting streak I've been on lately. The team declared I couldn't shave because I'd jinx myself. I also opted to skip the blazer and cufflinks for a white button-up with rolled sleeves.

There isn't a single person in this room whose opinion I care about other than Delilah. But the kid who grew up wearing misprinted shirts from his parents' shop can't help but feel out of place surrounded by all the carbon copies of Brad—men with short, gelled hair in varying shades of blond and brown, starched shirts with suit jackets, and polished black shoes. All complete with pocket squares and tumblers of gin.

As I make my way around to the other side of the bar, I see a flash of blonde. I'm barely able to brace myself before her tiny body comes barreling into me, wrapping her arms around my waist. I return her hug, my shoulder relaxing as the smell of cinnamon and coffee surrounds me.

"Surprise," I whisper against the shell of her ear.

"What did you do? You finished playing less than three hours ago halfway across the country." Delilah looks up at me as she lets her arm fall to her side. I bury the disappointment I feel at the loss of her touch, something I'm getting good at—avoiding the feelings I'm developing for her. I'm going to need to get even better at it if my hunch about tonight is correct.

"Did you really think I would miss your birthday? What kind of best friend would I be if I did that?" My threat last year—after we met—to stop by the coffee shop daily and be her self-proclaimed best friend might have started as a joke, but fate has a funny way of giving you exactly what you need, in the way you least expect it. Delilah is that for me. She's the bright spot in some of the darkest days. "Don't worry about how I got here. That's not important.

"You made it?" Brad says as he approaches pulling Delilah against his side. "Dee didn't think you would. But we're glad you could be here. It's going to be a special night."

Delilah looks up at Brad smiling. She's thinking the same thing that I am. Well, maybe not the exact same thing.

This tool bag is about to propose to a girl he's nowhere near good enough for, and I'm trying really hard to be happy for her. But no matter how I spin it, nothing gets rid of the sinking feeling in my gut every time I think about Delilah saying *"yes"* to spending the rest of her life with Brad.

"Now that Cruz is here, what do you say we make a quick toast?" Brad weaves his fingers through hers and pulls her away from me before she even has the chance to respond.

She looks over her shoulder and smiles mouthing *"sorry"* as she trails behind him to the center of the room.

Brad picks up a fork and clanks it against his glass a few times to get everyone's attention. "Thank you all for coming tonight to help celebrate Dee's birthday." I roll my eyes at the nickname knowing she prefers Delilah or Lilah. Every time he introduces her to someone new as "Dee," she politely corrects it.

I haven't decided if Brad's too dumb or too inconsiderate to pick up on it. Maybe both. Definitely both.

"As many of you know, we've been together since college. In that time, we've spent countless hours planning out a life together. This one's been there for me through undergrad, law school, and making partner." Brad pauses, giving the room a self-important smile. "Now it's time for that next step and I couldn't think of a more perfect woman to live out my dreams with."

Brad drops to his knee and pulls a small blue box out of his pocket. Delilah's hands come to her mouth and tears fill her eyes. I roll my lips together, trying to muster some happiness, but I can get past the apprehension that this isn't what's best for her.

Delilah deserves so much better than a proposal filled with a list of her fiancé's accomplishments. The one thing he got right is that she's perfect. She deserves to be more than just his arm candy. Maybe I could be happy if she was with someone who values her thoughtfulness, tenacity, and passion. I look down at the gift bag still hanging from my finger and I think about the gift inside. All the thought and time I put into making sure it's right and her fiancé can't even do that for her on the night they get engaged.

"Dee, will you do me the honor of becoming my wife and building the life we have spent the last eight years dreaming up?"

No, I love you. No, I can't live without you. Jesus. What the fuck?

I grab a glass of champagne off the passing waiter's tray and down it, not bothering to wait for the toast that I know is coming. Across the room Delilah nods rapidly while Brad slides the chunky ring on her finger.

After all the cheers die down, I bide my time until I can pull her aside to wish her well before I duck out. Watching her agree to marry Brad was harder than I expected. Delilah and I aren't meant to be. I'm not the guy for her. She has whole life planned out and I can't give her the things she needs. I can barely give myself the things I need most days.

My guilt over leaving early is eased by the knowledge that we have plans to celebrate her birthday tomorrow with a trip to Saving Paws animal shelter. If she asks, I can blame my exit on jet lag but I'm feeling more emotionally drained than physically.

"Hey man, thanks again for coming. I know it means a lot to Dee," Brad says, clapping me on the back like we're buds. I plaster a smile on my face, tolerating Brad because he's important to her.

"Congratulations, Brad," I say, returning the pat on the back more roughly than I probably need to.

"There you are. My two favorite humans." Delilah comes between us and rests her head on Brad's chest.

"Congratulations, Delilah." Do I emphasize her full name to poke at Brad? Maybe. "You deserve all the happiness in the world."

She wipes a tear from the corner of her eye and wraps her arms around my waist. "Thank you for being here. You made this night even more special."

"Nothing could have kept me from being here for your birthday. I'll let you get back to your guests. I'm feeling a little worn out from the flight and I need all my energy for our dog walking adventure tomorrow."

Brad frowns over her shoulder but doesn't say anything. What's he got against dogs?

"I can't wait. I'm going to snuggle the puppies so hard. They might not let me come back. Seriously, that's how much cuddling I plan to do. I'm going to spoil the shit of those doggos."

"Bye, Delilah. Happy birthday."

The grief starts to press down on me like weighted plates sitting on my chest during the drive home as tonight forces me to think of all the things brother will never get to experience, and all of the things that I'll never get to experience *with* him. I'll never see Jarrett propose to the love of his life or stand next to him as she walks down the aisle. I'll never get to hold his children in the hospital and tease him that they got their good looks from their uncle.

The aching desire to call him and tell him about Delilah closes in on me. I want to ask him what I should do. It's a nagging thought I've had countless times since meeting her. He was the person I would go to when I needed to talk things out. But that was taken away from both of us and I'm still so mad at him, at the world.

When I get home, I settle into the couch and open up the folder of pictures on my phone of Jarrett and me. Every day without him feels like a battle against a deep dark sea of despair that tries to suck me under, but these significant life milestones make the black waves crash harder against my heart and leave me fighting for breath.

Flipping through the photos, I get lost in my memories—all the time we spent together at the ballpark, or in the garage building my Bronco together as teens. Remembering the way he was always playing pranks on me, or how his smile was the brightest in any room. He could make anyone laugh. Everyone loved being around him. He and Delilah would have been thick as thieves. God, the two of them would have been so much fun together, so full of life and joy.

I would give anything to have him back so I could introduce the two of them. I dig the heels of my hands into my eyes, feeling my emotions threaten to overwhelm me.

Closing out the folder, I stop the downward spiral before I can fall back down into that pit of despair. With a harsh exhale, I set the phone face down on the coffee table and walk to my master bathroom to shower and get ready for bed.

CHAPTER 6

HBD BESTIE

FLASHBACK- TWO YEARS EARLIER

The next morning I absentmindedly spin my engagement ring around my finger as I wait for Cruz to pick me up from *Buns & Roses*. Covering a yawn with the back of my hand, I consider adding another shot of espresso to my coffee. Brad and I stayed out later than I would've liked to celebrate our engagement with his friends and co-workers.

By the time we got back to his place, it was after midnight and I was here at four-thirty this morning to bake so that I could go walk dogs with Cruz for my birthday. Even though I'm tired, I know the puppies will re-energize me.

Cruz has volunteered at Saving Paws with the team before and set this up because he knows I love dogs. Since owning a coffee shop isn't exactly conducive to taking care of a fur ball, volunteering is as close as I can get to having one of my own, so I've been looking forward to this for weeks.

An engine rumbles outside as Cruz's forest-green Bronco pulls up to the curb, stopping in front of the store. He comes around the front with a big smile and a familiar gift bag in his hand. Brad was so busy parading me around last night after the proposal to show off the ring he picked out that I never got to open my present.

Cruz stops in front of me, extending his arm, letting the gift bag dangle between us. With a goofy smile that makes his dimples stand out, he asks, "Are you ready to walk some dogs?"

He looks so worry-free and happy at this moment. It's a better present than anything he could buy me. I didn't know Cruz before he lost his brother, but I like to think that this is him in his natural state. All dimples and lightheartedness.

"You have no idea. This might be the best birthday ever," I say enthusiastically, my eyes glued to his instead of the gift bag.

"Sit, we've got time." Cruz nods toward the table I just stood from. "Relax for a minute and open your gift."

I slide back into the seat and pass Cruz's usual order across the table to him. "One iced coffee."

"And one birthday gift for the birthday girl. I'm sorry I bolted so early last night." His lips pull down in a frown as he hands the bag across the table.

"Cruz, you chartered a flight home so you could be there for me. There's absolutely nothing to apologize for. You showing up at all was the best surprise ever."

He raises an eyebrow and glances down at my left hand, which is currently twirling the ribbon attached to the gift bag, his eyes snagging on the diamond there.

"That wasn't really a surprise. I mean—it was a little, but I suspected he was going to do it last night. We've been talking about it for years. Since making partner, he's been dropping hints." I lift my coffee to my mouth to stop my rambling. Talking about this shouldn't make my stomach flip with nerves, but my relationship isn't something that Cruz and I talk about often. And the way he's studying me makes my head swim with uncertainty.

"And you *are* happy? Right?" Cruz's eyebrows pull together as he continues looking at me like he can see something that I don't.

"Of course, we've been together forever. He loves me and he is going to make a wonderful husband." I clear my throat, wanting to change the subject. I gesture to the gift bag, hoping to break the tension. "Should we open this thing?"

Cruz's forehead smooths out, and he nods. I pull the paper out of the top of the bag, setting it to the side. When I reach inside, my fingers brush against the lush velvet. My eyes find Cruz watching me. His grin is so wide that his eyes crinkle at the corner. "Go on."

"What did you do?" Even the box looks expensive. "Cruz, you chartered a plane, and this looks like it's from Smithfield's. They only do custom jewelry and I've seen some of the price tags on their designs." I'm not sure I want to open it. Whatever's in here is going to be gorgeous and I'll want to keep it, but I can't accept a gift this expensive.

"Delilah, just open it before you freak out." Cruz sighs, laying his hand on top of mine. "Please?" The softness in his eyes when he asks makes my resolve melt away.

"Fine." I crack the top open just enough to see part of a gold chain. When our eyes meet across the table, I open it the rest of the way. When I look back down and see the bracelet, my hand flies up to cover my mouth.

The delicate gold chain is adorned with three of the smallest charms I have ever seen. A tiny coffee bean, a paw print, and a baseball—each separated with an equally dainty diamond.

"Cruz. This is the most beautiful bracelet I have ever seen. It's everything. And way too much. But I'm not giving it back." A snort slips free as I clutch the box to my chest. I shouldn't keep this, but this is the most "me" piece of jewelry I've ever owned. It's understated and personal.

He stands and comes around the table, pulling me up from the chair and into his chest where I rest my head. "I wouldn't take it back if you tried.

Thank you for being my friend. You were the first person after Jarrett died to make me feel like I could survive without him. I hope this year is even more wonderful than your last. You, *Mi Sol*, deserve all the happiness in the world."

I feel a hot tear glide down my cheek and bring my hand up to wipe it away before he can see. "Will you help me put it on?"

"Of course, and then it's puppy time!" he says, lifting the bracelet to my wrist. His forehead scrunches as his large fingers fumble with the tiny clasp. I press my lips together. It'd be rude to laugh at him, but he looks so serious as he works.

Once he has it secured, I slide the box back into the bag and follow him outside. Cruz opens the car door for me before rounding the front of the bronco to join me. When he cranks the key, the engine rumbles to life and his radio comes on playing "Weak" by AJR. His hand shoots out, turning the knob. He stares at the silent radio, a frown pulling at his lips.

He doesn't say anything as he pulls into traffic. It's rare for us not to fill up the blank space with chatter. He's got the same, withdrawn look in his eyes that I saw before he left the party last night. Witnessing his grief enough over the last few months, I know that he's thinking of Jarrett right now. He's trapped in a memory of his life before, and my heart breaks for him.

"You looked a little lost. Want to talk about it?"

He glances over at me for a second before he looks forward, keeping his focus on the road as his hands tighten on the steering wheel. His breath comes out in one long shaky exhale. "I'm not sure how to explain this without coming off like an asshole."

"Just tell me. We have always been open with each other and I stick around."

"It's because of my mom's esquites recipe, you can't get enough. That's what keeps you around." His grip loosens, and he gives me a quick smile, trying to skirt the topic.

"I can't deny the appeal of a decades-old recipe from your mom's family. But after this present?" I shake my wrist in front of me, admiring the bracelet again.

Cruz just shakes his head at my antics before glancing my way. On exhale he explains, "The big milestones in life remind me—more than a normal day—that Jarrett isn't here. That he missed out on so many things." Pointing at the radio, he adds, "Hearing his favorite band is a little overwhelming for me, right now."

I lower my hand to Cruz's knee, palm up, and he threads his fingers through mine, squeezing.

"I spent a lot of time last night looking at pictures of him and I together. Just to make sure I hadn't forgotten all those little details about him. Like the way his stupid hair would always flop to one side." That makes Cruz laugh, but his eyes are still misty. "Then this morning I was listening to AJR when I was lifting. I wanted to remember all the times he used to drag me to their shows. I'd pretend it wasn't my thing, but secretly I loved it because it made him so happy."

"Those are both really beautiful ways to remember him, Cruz. I'm proud of you for channeling those feelings into reminiscing instead of into something destructive. I can't imagine that's easy."

He shrugs his shoulders. "It's easier now that I'm here in Denver and that I'm on a team that supports me, and I have you. I meant what I said earlier, Mi Sol. You helped me find the light in all the darkness that cloaked me early on."

When I look up at him the light is back in his eyes. "It's okay to be sad and to miss him. It's even okay to call me when you are having a hard time. I'll come over and we'll dance to AJR together. You can teach me all his best dance moves and I'll do them right alongside you. If that doesn't work, we'll haul ass to the shelter and pet puppies." He squeezes my hand and lets his head fall back against the seat.

"I can't bring Jarrett back, but I'll do everything I can to help you celebrate him, or distract you. Whatever you need. And if that's still not enough, then you'll let me know and we will figure it out together."

Cruz nods and turns into the parking lot, finding a spot in the back where he can park this beast away from everyone else. He grabs the hat off the dash and pulls it down tight over his head before he rounds the truck and opens my door.

♥

"Follow me to the back. We have leashes and goodie bags for you," the volunteer covering the front desk of Saving Paws instructs Cruz and me.

"Goodie bags? Why do I think those aren't filled with birthday treats for us?" Cruz whispers under his breath. The volunteer leads us through the building and stops in front of a kennel holding two of the fluffiest, tawny colored puppers I have ever seen. Their tails wag excitedly, smacking off the side of the chain link kennel, causing them to rattle as Cruz bends to their eye level.

"Don't you two look happy to see us! You want to go for a walk with Delilah and I today?" he croons, holding his hand in front of the cage for a smell.

"Emmett and Rose are thrilled to have the two of you here to walk them."

Stooping down next to Cruz, I place my palm against the cage for a sloppy kiss from the smaller of the two dogs. "Are they siblings? They're both so dang adorable."

"They are. We got them as puppies and their siblings have all found homes, but these two were bonded. Finding homes for a pair is more difficult. They have been with us for six months," the volunteer explains stepping into the cage and leashing both pups. "Enjoy your walk today, guys," she says, handing Cruz and I the leashes and a few goodie bags, which are indeed poop bags.

The dogs lead us through the city stopping to sniff every fire hydrant along the way. Cruz tells me about a prank Lincoln played on one of the rookies during their last road trip while we wait at the corner to cross. The smile that tilts up his lips is blinding. It's a welcome change from the grief stricken look he wore this morning in the car. He nods over toward the park and we follow the trail into the greenspace.

"This is seriously the best birthday ever. Thank you so much for everything—being there last night, the bracelet, and now this. I'm thankful everyday to be your friend." We're seated on a bench, giving ear scratches to Emmett and Rose before we have to start the walk back to the shelter.

"*Best friend*," Cruz amends, giving me a chasting look. "Your trap worked. One well-placed coffee scent and you earned yourself a bestie for life. You didn't even need to lock me in the dungeon," he says, pulling me to his side and placing a sweet kiss on the crown of my head.

"You know you're not the only one with something to be grateful for. After Jarrett . . . I didn't know how much I needed someone until I met you. I was drifting in my grief, letting it pull me through life without much thought or care about the future. You helped me find my way out of the fog. You know I promised him I would try to live my life fully when he was gone, and it's been tough. I'm not there yet, but I get a little closer every day."

My hand comes to Cruz's cheek, turning his face, so he looks at me instead of Rose. "Cruz, you know I will always be here. On the good days and the days that the grief drags you back down."

He nods, but his eyes shift to the side and his lips flatten into a line. "Delilah, you are about to start your own life with Brad. I know things are going to—"

"No. I'm fully capable of prioritizing my marriage and still being a good friend to you. Nothing will change that." My words are firm. Brad knows that my friendship with Cruz is non-negotiable. He may not fully understand it, but he knows not to push it. "We need to get these two back so that you can get to practice," I tell him to end the conversation before he can argue with me.

CHAPTER 7

I MUST BE DREAMING

PRESENT

His fingers trail gently over my collarbone, mapping out the curve of it as he smiles down at me, making his dimples pop. Cruz steps further into my space, crowding me against the wall with his big body. He's so close I can feel the heat coming off his bare chest. And when his lips graze my temple I can't stop the shiver that races down my spine.

"I've thought about doing this since that first night at Sabor. Did you know how badly I wanted you back then? Seeing you with Brad killed me. He was never enough for you, but I promise you, I'm more than enough." The dangerous grin he gives me should be a warning, but I don't heed it.

He hooks his finger under my chin and tilts my face up so I can't look away—his hips pin me in place. He's clad in only basketball shorts and the thin fabric is doing nothing to hide his rock hard cock as he presses into me—searching my eyes, waiting for my answer.

"I didn't know. I thought maybe that first night, and again when you came into *Buns & Roses,* but you never—" The words die on my tongue as he lowers his mouth to my neck and pushes the strap of my pajamas off my shoulder.

"I tried to push it away, ignore it, when you were with him and then when you were healing. I've waited so long to make you mine. Tell me you want to be mine, Delilah."

His hand comes up to massage my breast, teasing my nipple into a peak as he grinds into me.

After all this time, he wants me.

I've wanted him for years, but I've been so scared. He's my best friend, and can't lose him. But all the reasons this is a terrible idea fly out the window the minute his tongue licks up the side of my neck, branding me as his.

This might be the worst decision of my life, but I want him too.

"Yes, Cruz. Make me yours," I say, reaching down to the hem of my tank top and pulling it over my head.

"Fuck, Mi Cielo. You are so beautiful." Cruz drops to his knees in front of me. His eyes are full of dirty promises as his large hands ghost over my hips. He toys with the waistband of my shorts, waiting for permission.

The moment I nod, he pushes my shorts down, letting them fall around my ankles. Strong hands grip my ass, tilting my pelvis towards him. His tongue darts out, flattening against my center. He hums in satisfaction as he licks me from my entrance to my clit, making me feral to hear the sound again. He circles the hard nub before sucking it into his mouth.

"Oh god," I choke out at the way he devours me.

"You taste so sweet, Hermosa, I knew you would. Even better than I imagined. Forget your sticky buns, this pussy is my new favorite dessert. I can't wait to see what you look like falling apart with my name on your lips."

My knees shake under the pressure of the orgasm that's building in my spine. I'm not sure how much more I can take. He pushes two fingers into me, pulsing them in and out as he continues to work me over with his tongue.

"Cruz. I ca—fuck." I comb his thick curls back with my hands so I can see his face between my legs as I tremble and I tighten around him.

"God damn, Delilah. You're squeezing my fingers so tight. I can't wait to get inside you." His tongue presses flat against my clit, bringing me higher until I can't take it anymore and shatter.

He continues working his fingers in and out of me, making me shudder with little zings of pleasure in the aftermath of my orgasm. I'm a panting mess when he finally pulls them out. "Are you ready for my cock?" He licks the evidence of my release off his lips with a wicked smile on his face.

I nod eagerly, unable to find my voice.

Rising in front of me, his hands fall to my hips and he spins me around, walking us over to the couch. He covers my back with his front and I can feel him everywhere. The beat of his heart hammering in his chest, the hard length of him pressing against my ass through his shorts, the press of his fingers biting into pelvis.

"Hold on to the back of the couch and spread your legs for me."

I reach forward, bending at the waist, and brace my hands against the couch—craving more of that commanding tone. He steps back and I miss the heat of his body, but he doesn't make me wait long. Cruz steps up against me, covering my body with his, nothing between us this time. Gently, he brushes my hair to the side, placing a kiss at the nape of my neck. "Tell me you want this, Delilah," he whispers in my ear.

"Please, Cruz." He rubs his length along my slit, coating himself with my arousal. Even though he just gave me an earth shattering orgasm, I already need more.

"Please, what?" he asks, his voice sounding strained with the restraint of holding back.

"Don't make me say it," I whimper, afraid that if I say it out loud, it will all be too real. I'm about to fuck my best friend and I know it will change everything.

"I need to hear it. I'm not giving you my cock until I hear the words," he says, rubbing himself up and down me painfully slowly, making the ache inside me deepen.

"I want you to fuck me." My breath whooshes out of me as he thrusts forward, entering me in one smooth stroke.

"Mi Cielo, you feel like heaven," he praises, as he draws back his hips.

I shoot up, grasping the sheet in front of me. I'm drenched, covered in sweat, and panting when I wake up. The dream has my blood pounding behind my eardrums. I can still feel the flutter of my orgasm between my legs. I bring my hands to my head, pushing them through my sweat damp hair. It felt so real. God, I could almost feel his breath against my thighs as he knelt at my feet.

"Ugh." Rolling to my side, I pull my pillow to my face and let out a frustrated yell—the image of him looking up at me etched into my memory. My feet thrash, kicking the covers off. It's too damn hot in here.

Now that I'm awake without Cruz beside me, I feel more alone than ever. Even after I left Brad, it never felt this empty.

I flip to my side, punching my pillow, only to turn back to the other side. No matter what position I'm in, or how hard I try, the dream sticks with me.

My palms cover my eyes like it will keep what I'm about to do from being a reality. I blindly root around in my nightstand drawer and pull out Buzz Lightgirth, my white and purple vibrator. I click the button seven times, skipping over the pulsing and wave settings. Going straight to the steady buzz that always punches my ticket. My hand slips between my legs, seeking relief from how horny that dream left me.

Trying to fill the emptiness with pleasure even if it's not what I need. At the very least, maybe it will help rid me of leftover lust before I see him later today when Poppy and I go to the game.

"Your hair is down today. I thought that was only for holidays and hot dates. Any reason, or just feeling frisky?" Poppy asks as we hustle through the gameday crowd trying to make it to the stadium for first pitch.

I squeeze closer to her as we make our way across a particularly busy crosswalk. "I'd really like to put an end to my dry spell. My elbow is getting sore from all the self-love." A self-deprecating laugh breaks free. I wish I was joking, but I think years of being mostly alone has caused an acute case of tennis elbow.

"Okay, wow. I love that you are comfortable sharing that with me. Let's make sure we fix that with an ergonomically correct vibrator. Maybe try switching up your position? Do you have anyone in mind to end the dry spell?" she asks as we pause at another crosswalk. "You do. Don't you?" Her voice gets higher than it was a minute ago.

I bite my bottom lip nervously. "I had a dream last night that I can't get out of my head, but I need to."

"Did you have a sex dream about Cruz?"

My neck heats as blush spreads across my face. "God, it was hot. I woke up sweating and out of breath. It had me so amped up that I needed to come a second time."

"Is now a good time to tell you I told Hendrix we would meet him after the game? I need to get the keycard for his apartment so I can water his plants while he's gone." Poppy wrinkles her nose as she explains why she needs to meet up with Cruz's new teammate and friend. He is a recent trade from the Los Angeles Diablos and the two guys grew close during spring training.

My eyes go wide. I had forgotten that Cruz invited me over for movie night. I've been so out of sorts over this dream that the text messages from the night before completely slipped my mind. At the time, the plan sounded fun. But after that dream, I'm not sure I can face him.

"Ugh . . . no. New plan. Hang with me here, I'm just spitballing." A half-assed plan formulates in my head to get out of spending one-on-one time with Cruz tonight. "I'll duck into the bathroom while you grab the key.

You make up a story about needing a girls' night and get rid of them." I can already feel sweat forming on my upper lip. Deceiving people isn't my strong suit. My dad always used to tease me because my tells were so obvious when I was trying to hide something.

"No way that works without Cruz getting suspicious," she tells me softly.

"Please, Poppy," I plead as we reach the front of the security line. Poppy hands me my family pass as she walks through the metal detector ahead of me.

"Lilah, of course I'll do it, but he's going to know you're avoiding him. Maybe you should just tell him."

Panic freezes me in place. "No . . . I can't. Absolutely not. He doesn't see me like that." Poppy rolls her eyes at me, but it doesn't stop me. "Besides, even if he saw me like that, I would never risk our friendship. Poppy, you saw me when Brad cheated. We had just met, but Cruz was there every step of the way. He let me cry on his shoulder . . . so many times."

"Hey, Delilah. Look at me. You won't lose him. You mean just as much to him as he does to you. You were his rock after his brother died," she reminds me.

"So, I can hide in the bathroom?"

"If that's what you need, we will hide you in the bathroom."

I grab her hands and give them a squeeze. "Thank you, Poppy."

"That must have been some dream," she jokes as we walk through the concourse.

"You know that joke, 'what's the difference between a golf ball and the g-spot'?"

"I can't believe you remember that joke, it was one of the first ones I told you after we met." Poppy laughs. "My one hope for all womankind is that we condition men to spend as much time looking for the g-spot as they do for a golf ball."

"It always stuck with me. Brad was a golfer, but couldn't find my g-spot with the help of a caddy."

She nods knowingly. "Good riddance."

"Dream Cruz had absolutely no problem finding the right buttons to push," I tell her quietly as we approach our section.

Down on the field, Cruz is warming up with Dom, one of the Bandits outfielders. When we find our row, I set my beer down in the cup holder and bring my thumb and pointer finger to my mouth, letting out a high pitched whistle that makes Poppy cover her ears.

Cruz smiles but continues warming up, throwing the ball to Dom a few more times before they huddle up. Dom tilts his head to where Poppy and I are sitting, and Cruz shakes his head, looking irritated at the rookie. Dom throws his hands up in defeat and heads back toward the dugout.

Scanning the stands to find me, Cruz grins and jogs over to the wall. He crooks his finger at me, and I respond with an eye roll. Even with me leaning over the railing, he's still a solid four feet below me. Pushing my anxiety about the dream aside, I plaster on a smile, hoping it hides how awkward I feel. The last thing I want is for Cruz to pick up on the fact that something is wrong. He's relentless when it comes to getting me to spill my guts. If he catches wind of the fact that I'm feeling anything but our ordinary friendly vibes, he'll drag the whole embarrassing story out of me before I even realize what's happened.

"Hey there, Slugger." My hair is down, which is a rare treat. I gather it up and pull it to the side, so it hangs in a curtain on the side of my head. "Are you and the rookie having a disagreement tonight?"

"He's just being Dom, but I set him straight." Cruz grins up at me. "Are you still coming over after the game tonight? I thought we could stay in and watch a movie?"

When he gives me that hopeful look, his full lips turning up and making his tempting dimples pop against bronze skin, I stand no chance. I nod, my whole elaborate plan of avoiding him going out the window.

"Good. Wait for me after the game."

The way he's looking at me causes a flashback to the image of him crowding me against the wall. The words, *"Mine, Delilah"* reverberate through me, and I feel a heat crawl up my chest, coloring my cheeks pink. His throwing hand disappears into the back pocket of his pants and he fishes something out. It's a caramel, my stress candy. With a smirk, he tosses it to me in the stands.

"Okay." All my resolve to run away crumbling at my feet as I clap my hands around the treat.

"Oh, and Delilah, you look incredible tonight. I like your hair down like that. See you after the game, Hermosa."

I bite my lower lip. I have always loved when he speaks Spanish to me and not just because it makes his accent stand out more. It makes me feel special. The only other time I've heard him speak it is when he's talking to his parents. But after the dream, those words hit differently. Landing somewhere a little further south than they usually do.

"Hey Cruz, good luck tonight!" I shout as he heads back toward the dugout. His steps falter and he looks over his shoulder, throwing me a playful wink. Oh, shit. Welp, there goes any hopes of me making it through the game with dry panties.

CHAPTER 8

MOVIE NIGHT

PRESENT

Delilah might think she's hiding her panic, but her expressive face gives her away. It also doesn't hurt that I know her better than anyone.

I hope she packed chapstick because she's gonna need it the way she was nibbling her lip raw earlier. She seems freaked out and I wish she would just tell me what's got her so worked up so I could fix it. Maybe she's feeling the way things have shifted between us since the gala? I know I have. But if I'm being honest it's been that way for me for much longer.

When Hendrix and I stepped out of the locker room, she was an adorable twitchy mess, babbling about movie night to Poppy who was clearly engrossed in Hen. Somehow, the two of them ended up getting invited to join us.

Now, we are all back at my place, bellies full of pizza and watching *Avengers*. Delilah's relaxed enough that she is no longer sitting stiffly on the couch next to me, but tucked into the crook of my arm, relaxing with a margarita.

Her eyes keep fluttering shut before they fly back open, but it's a losing battle. Looks like everyone will crash here instead of making the walk back to their respective apartments. And, based on the way Poppy and Hen are tangled up, he's not letting her out of his sight tonight.

When the credits on the movie start rolling, Deliliah is sleeping hard enough that every once in a while she sighs or hums softly like she's dreaming. Across from us, Hendrix and Poppy are stretched out. Her leg is thrown over his hip and they're asleep facing each other, looking like a full-blown couple instead of new friends.

I slide my arm under Delilah's legs and shift her to my lap. Standing from the couch, I adjust her in my arms so she's tight against my chest, and make my way through the dark apartment to my bedroom.

When I lay Delilah down on my bed, she stirs, but her eyes stay closed. I pull the blanket up and soak in the sight of her in my bed. I should just walk away, but I can't stop myself from dropping a kiss on her forehead. She looks so fucking beautiful like this.

When I go to leave, her delicate fingers wrap around my wrist.

"Where are you going?" Her voice is rough and her eyes are barely open. She's tugging at my heartstrings, and she doesn't even know it.

"To the couch."

She shakes her head and her hair tumbles into her face. "Stay." She scoots over and pats the bed next to her. She's more pliant this way than she was earlier, when she had herself all tied up in knots.

Fuck, this was not in my plans tonight. I'm not sure if I'm strong enough to sleep next to her without telling her everything I'm feeling.

"Please?" she asks, her hand making circles on the sheet.

This girl owns my heart. I can't say no to her—not now, not ever. There was never a chance I would walk away and end up on the couch once she asked me to stay. When Lincoln said to turn up the heat I don't think he meant *this* quickly. But I guess there's no time like the present. I reach down and grab the hem of my shirt, pulling it over my head and dropping it at my feet.

Her eyes are definitely open now. There's just enough light from the moon to see her pupils dilate as her gaze roams over my chest. When her tongue darts out to wet her lips, I take that as a clear enough sign that she is okay with where this is going and push my luck a little further. My thumbs hook in the band of my sweats, sliding them off my hips before letting them pool at my feet. I swear a whimper falls from her lips, but I can't focus on anything other than the skin she's revealing as she scoots her jeans down her body.

She keeps her eyes on me as she reaches behind her body in a practiced move and un-clasps her bra. I almost swallow my tongue when her hand disappears up the front of her shirt to move the strap down one arm and then the other. She drops both her jeans and bra off the bed into our growing pile. It's just a few articles of clothing, but it's so monumental that it feels like a mountain right in the middle of my bedroom.

I swallow roughly. It's going to be a long fucking night lying next to her, like this, in just her shirt and panties. There's no way I'm pushing things further than I already have, because I don't think either of us could handle it. Lowering myself to the bed, I sidle up next to her, lay my hand on the curve of her waist, and brush a soft kiss at her temple.

Delilah exhales curling into me and turning into the little spoon. I internally groan, willing myself not to get hard at the way she is pressed against me. I wrap my arm around her, holding her close to me.

"Buenas noches, Mi Cielo." Her breathing evens out as she falls back to sleep, but I can't even manage to shut my eyes. I want to soak this in and remember the way she looks at this moment, so soft and relaxed.

It looks exactly like I imagined it would, so perfect that it seems unreal. Her skin is warm and smooth. Her creamy complexion is a contrast to my bronzed skin. Eventually my body gives into her warmth surrounding me and the gentle tempo of her heartbeat against my chest lulling me to sleep.

I crack my eyes open cautiously and question whether my current state is a dream or maybe I died, and this is my own personal slice of heaven. The warmth of Delilah in my arms when the early morning sunlight streams through the window is easily the best way to wake up.

She shifts slightly in my arms, causing her ass to rub against me. Of course I'm fucking hard. Her top has ridden up so that her stomach is exposed and she's pressed up against me in all the right places. I bring my knuckles to my mouth, biting down and fighting the urge to groan or rock into her. Both equally stupid and far too tempting this early in the day.

She squirms in my arms again and I prop my head up on my palm, completely in awe of her. Dark lashes brush her cheekbones as she breathes softly next to me, her lips, slightly parted. I should probably put some space between us, but I am so sick of fighting this. It's time she knows all the ways she affects me. The hard as hell erection pressed between her ass cheeks should be a pretty clear indication of that.

A sharp intake of breath breaks me out of my thoughts. Delilah's eyes flutter open and she freezes, but only for a second before she goes slack against me.

Fuck it. There's a neon sign in my pants telling her how I feel. I may as well just go for it.

My lips brush against her temple. "Good morning, how did you sleep?" Goosebumps blossom across the skin of her stomach where I trace small circles on her skin with my finger.

Her throat bobs, and a sly smile tilts up her lips before she answers, "I was very comfortable. Must be these expensive sheets."

Expensive sheets. Is she messing with me?

"The sheets," I repeat as Delilah's lips tilt up further, spreading into a full-blown smile. "You're such a brat. Do you know what happens to brats?" Keeping one arm wrapped tight around her, my other hand descends on her ribs, zeroing in on the spot I know will drive her nuts.

"Don't you dare," she says, but she can't keep herself from dissolving into a fit of giggles when my fingers move along her ribs. "Cruz. Please."

She thrashes against me, and I know she can feel how hard I am, but apparently we're both just going to ignore that for now.

"What's wrong, does that tickle?"

"You know it does, you ass." She growls between the laughter overtaking her body.

"I'll ask again, why did you sleep so well?" My attack on her slows so she can speak.

"1200 thr—thread count Egyptian cotton," she squeaks out between gasps.

I shift above her so I'm straddling her hips, locking her in with my knees so both hands are free. She stills as her eyes travel over my chest and down my stomach. The way she's looking at me only makes my dick stand taller. Not bothering to hide what I'm doing I adjust myself in my briefs. When her stormy blues travel back up my body to lock with mine they're wide with shock. My heart feels like it might hammer straight through my ribs when her palms come to rest on my thighs, and she traps her bottom lip between her teeth. She's just as affected by me as I am by her.

Fuck, yes.

"Last chance. Why did you sleep so well?"

She looks away, but only for a beat before she brings her gaze back to me. Her breathing picks up and her nipples pucker under the fabric of the thin shirt, which is bunched dangerously high. I lean forward, trailing my hands up her sides slowly, like I am going to tickle her. Instead, I pull her shirt down so she's not at risk of showing me anything she's not ready for.

"You—I've never felt safer than I do in your arms. I could be sleeping in a burlap sack, and I would be just as comfortable as long as you were holding me." Her voice is so low that it's barely audible over my thumping heart.

"I will always be your safe space, Mi Sol." I roll off her and pull her with me. When we land side by side, I run my nose up the length of hers. "I have never seen you look more beautiful than you do right now. Even more so than that first night when you had on that stunning purple dress.

Her cheeks flush the prettiest shade of pink when she nods slowly. I run my hand up her arm, causing her to shiver under my touch. "But seeing you like this . . . You don't need the dress, or the hair and makeup. You laughing in my bed is the most breathtaking sight I have ever seen."

She drops her head to my shoulder and inhales a shaky breath. I'm not sure if I'm sparing her the need to respond, or if I'm too nervous that she might push me away when I say, "Let's go get you some coffee."

CHAPTER 9

BRAD THE DOUCHE CANOE

FLASHBACK - THREE YEARS EARLIER

He's late . . . again.

My eyes drop to where my phone rests on the smooth, black bar top of the trendy Venezuelan restaurant, Sabor, that Brad picked for our date tonight. It's been forty-five minutes since we were supposed to meet. Brad's assistant called right after I sat down at one of the tall, industrial style barstools to let me know he was stuck in a meeting with an important client. It took all of my restraint to not snap that there was *always* a client who needed his attention. But it's not her fault my boyfriend can't fulfill his commitments to me or shoot him a text himself.

I strum my polished fingernails against the cool cement, debating my next move. I need food, and the smoky aroma of meats cooked in chili peppers and garlic is only making me grow hangrier by the second. Knowing Brad, there's no telling how much longer it will be. When he's focused on work, hours can slip by without him noticing, regardless of the fact that I have to be up at 4 a.m. to open the coffee shop.

Whether I order takeout here, or head home and scrounge for food, it looks like I'm on my own tonight. My fingers fly across my screen, tapping out a text letting him know I'm ordering. Tilting my head back, I swallow the rest of my wine down and nod to the bartender, asking for a menu.

The soft fabric of my dress slips through my fingers as I toy with the hem. I could be home in my favorite leggings, the ones that have just the right amount of stretch, watching mindless TV on Bravo, instead of being stood up in a bar by my long-time boyfriend.

The dress I picked out for our date is a deep purple that makes my blue eyes stand out, and hugs every curve in the very best way. Normally it would have me feeling on top of the world, but right now it's just a reminder of the bone-deep irritation that's growing like a weed with each passing minute. My molars grind together as I think about the extra time and care I took curling my hair and shaving my freaking legs!

After waking up well before the rest of Denver, and working on my feet all day, putting on something other than an oversized t-shirt—sans bra— seemed like the equivalent of running a marathon. It's too bad I'll be the only one appreciating my efforts tonight. Once the merger goes through next month, Brad's promised things will settle down. But lately, there's always something pulling us in opposite directions.

"Do you mind if I take this seat?" someone asks as I look over the menu that the bartender just handed me.

"It's all yours," I say without looking up from where I'm debating between the arepas or pasticho. Both sound phenomenal, which is to be expected considering this restaurant is the trendiest place to eat right now.

"Thank you," he says in a rich voice that I can't ignore a second time. There is something warm and inviting in its deep tenor. I also can't help but notice a faint accent, the southern kind, that makes women everywhere break out in goosebumps.

My curiosity wins out and I glance at the man next to me. The first thing I notice is his chocolate-colored, intensely dark eyes—framed by lashes that are unfairly thick. *Why does God always grant men the courtesy of insanely beautiful lashes?* A dusting of dark stubble covers his square jaw and when he catches me looking, he smiles, revealing the most adorable dimples I have ever seen on a man.

It's the only thing adorable about him. Even seated, he towers over my five foot three frame. His broad shoulders stretch the seams of his crisp white shirt, which plays off the sliver of warm bronze skin showing where he has the top three buttons undone.

"Have you eaten here before? The asado negro is excellent," he says, still smiling warmly at me, but there's something sad in his eyes. "It's almost as good as my abuela's recipe, but don't tell my dad I said that. I'd be ousted from the family."

"I haven't. Thanks for the recommendation. Any thoughts on desserts?"

"Don't bother, they aren't very good." He leans in closer, ensuring that the bartender and other patrons can't overhear. "Their baker quit, and they haven't replaced her."

"How often do you eat here?" I eye him curiously.

"Too often. I just moved to Denver and live close by. It's convenient, but it also reminds me of home. So I end up ordering takeout more than I should."

Catching the bartender's eye, I get his attention and ask for the asado negro, and opt to skip the dessert. When he walks away, I turn back toward my new friend.

"This is my first time here. My apartment is right down the street and I own a coffee shop nearby, but I usually prefer someplace a little less . . ." Pausing to consider my words, I don't want to offend him since he's clearly a regular, but I am honest to a fault. "I'm meeting my boyfriend, but he's running late. Normally, this place really isn't my vibe. It seems kind of pretentious."

He barks out a husky laugh. It seems to catch him off guard, and I watch the pain in his eyes dull a little. "It's become pretty pretentious, ever since it went viral thanks to a few food blogger reviews. But the food is fantastic. That's part of the reason I started ordering my food to-go. I'm afraid if I stay too long, they'll convert me." He looks pointedly around the restaurant, pushing a clump of dark curls off his forehead.

Men in suits or button-down shirts fill the tables. It's like the Stepford wives, but with cufflinks and tumblers of gin. "Oh, my god . . . they're all clones." I can't stop the giggle that breaks free. "I don't know you, but please don't turn into one of them. We don't need more Chad in Finance clones."

The wicked smile that spreads across his face gives those dark eyes a dangerous glint, and I forget all about calling his dimples adorable earlier. "Not a chance, Hermosa."

My neck prickles with heat in a way I haven't felt in a while from his flirtation. I forget for a minute that I'm supposed to be here with my boyfriend and bask in the glow of being desired. The two of them could not be more different—Brad with his buttoned-up attitude, blond hair, and his lean build from years of road biking, while the man sitting next to me is the epitome of tall, dark, and dangerously handsome.

"Hey Dee, sorry I'm late," the familiar voice startles me as he strolls up beside me, dropping a hasty kiss on my cheek. For a moment, guilt consumes me. I was allowing this stranger to flirt with me and worse, I was enjoying it. But the guilt fades when I see Brad is absorbed in his phone as he leans against the bar. "Did you order?"

"I just got the asado negro *to go*. My new friend recommended them to me."

He holds out his hand to Brad. "Cruz."

Cruz. I let the name echo through my head. Something about it just sounds right to me, like it fits.

"Hey, thanks for keeping my girl company until I could get here." Brad gives his hand a pump, straightening as he sizes him up.

"My pleasure," Cruz returns, but his tone is clipped, and the look on his face tells me he's not impressed.

The bartender brings Cruz his to-go container, and he stands to leave. Before he walks away, he looks over his shoulder. "What's the name of your coffee shop? I've been drinking coffee from the corner store. It's terrible." He makes a face like he just tasted something bitter, causing the tan skin around his nose to wrinkle.

"*Buns & Roses*."

"Maybe I'll see you there, Dee, is it?"

I shake my head. Brad is the only person who has ever called me that. And he only gets away with it because I thought it was endearing when we started seeing each other in college. "It's Delilah. Enjoy your dinner. Don't let the clones get you on the way out." Warm laughter rumbles from deep within him, before he disappears through the bar, giving the host a fist bump as he steps out onto the dark sidewalk.

"Do you mind if we eat here? One of the partners from the firm planned to stop by for a drink." Brad's fingers fly across his phone, completely engrossed in his email.

As a recovering people pleaser, my first instinct is to default to what will make everyone else happy, but I am working hard to put myself first more. "It's already eight and opening a coffee shop comes early." I infuse as much conviction into my voice as I can muster.

My dad is always telling me I'm too nice for my own good. It's times like this where I'm likely to believe him, even though my Pops always retorts that my compassion is my best quality. It's next to impossible not to be empathetic when you are raised by two people that had to fight so hard to have a family. I won the dad lottery, with a little help from science. Our house was always filled with overwhelming gratitude that we had each other, even when things weren't always easy. I'm learning to balance that without being a doormat.

"We need to find you some help at the coffee shop, so you aren't there so early every morning. I need you by my side at some of these dinners."

His whiny tone grates on my nerves and I steal my backbone, channeling my dad's *take-no-prisoners* attitude.

"I'm not ready for that yet. Financially, the shop is still too new to take that risk, and I don't want to hand the baking off to someone else." With my chin tilted up, I ignore the twisting in my gut at how foreign it feels to assert myself.

He pouts, but wraps his arms around my waist. "Someday, right?"

"Yes, someday." I mentally high-five myself for not completely folding under pressure. Once things are more established, I'll be happy to hand over some of the less rewarding parts of running a business. But I get to call the shots on how and when that happens.

"I hate that our schedules conflict so often these days. We need more time together." Brad drops a kiss on my cheek, reminding me of the sweet boy that won me over all those years ago. "I'm glad I got to see you, even if it was only for a few minutes."

And just like that, he ruined it. It's on the tip of my tongue to remind him he was the one who showed up almost an hour late. I press my lips shut, resisting the urge, reminding myself of our life plan. One we came up with while cuddled together under the stars during our freshman year of college. I open my coffee shop and he makes partner by the time he's thirty—providing us financial stability and the foundation to get married and start a family together.

His goals support my goals. I repeat the mantra in my head as I push up on my toes to give him a kiss goodbye.

"You have fun schmoozing." I wipe the lipstick off his cheek with my thumb and grab my food from the bar top—my bed calling my name.

CHAPTER 10

DUNGEON SUITORS

FLASHBACK - THREE YEARS EARLIER

Looping through the park, my feet eat up the trail as I run back towards downtown. My lungs burn with the exertion of pushing myself hard. Just because it's the All-Star Break doesn't mean I need to be useless. The gossip mill is rampant with rumors that I'm not in the headspace to be impactful to any team. Add in the fact that I'm joining the Bandits mid-season and I have to prove myself to a lot of people—to myself—that I am worth the trade. I have to show the fans that I will deliver now, when their team needs it the most. Not to mention I need to show the St. Louis Commanders that trading me was a mistake. And I need to prove to Jarrett that I can live out this dream for both of us.

I slow to a walk once I hit the six-mile mark and take a quick break to stretch out my legs before returning to my new apartment. Maybe I'm prolonging this run to avoid going back there, but I'm still not used to walking in the door and not finding his shoes scattered across the mat.

Leaving behind St. Louis, and the house I shared with my younger brother, Jarrett, was one of the many difficult things I did this year. There's nothing wrong with Denver or the apartment, I just never expected to be here. This was supposed to be the year that Jarrett and I got to live out our dreams. Instead, I moved across the country, alone.

My team-mandated therapist suggested I look at this trade—and move—as a fresh start after everything that happened in St. Louis. The move has helped, despite feeling out of my element. Being out of the space we shared while I played baseball for the Commanders, and he played for the local affiliate team, has helped me start the healing process.

Lost in my thoughts, the mouthwatering scent of coffee hits me when the door in front of me swings open. Two women dressed for work in the plethora of office buildings in this area step onto the sidewalk with extra tall coffees in hand. I look up and see the words *Buns & Roses* scrawled across the windows in white script.

If there was ever a sign to procrastinate, this is it. The memory of meeting Delilah at Sabor a few weeks ago flashes through my mind. Before I give it too much thought, I pull the door open and step inside.

Plants line the wide wood shelves behind the counter and there's a jukebox in the corner playing the song "Peaches" by the Presidents. The décor is trendy, with white subway tile and a handwritten chalkboard menu. The personal details, like the hula doll on the register add a little quirkiness to the atmosphere.

"Be with you in just a minute," a sweet voice, that I instantly recognize as Delilah's, calls from the back. She sounds lighter than she did that night, and I wonder if it's because this place makes her happy. Or because she's not stressed about her dickhole of a boyfriend being late.

Delilah walks backward through the doorway, carrying a tray of baked goods. Her lush hips shimmy to the music. Her long blonde hair is piled on top of her head, revealing her slender neck. Cut-off jean shorts encase her heart-shaped ass and highlight her toned legs. She's short—just a couple of inches over five feet, if I had to guess.

The last time I saw her, she wore that purple dress like a second skin. She looked like she stepped out of a magazine with her blonde hair curling down her back. But I think I like this version even better. She looks comfortable here in a way she didn't at Sabor—like this is home.

When she turns around, her plump lips stretch into a smile. Setting the tray on the counter, she wipes her hands on the folded-over apron, cinched around her waist, accentuating it. Her maroon shirt has a pair of cinnamon rolls right across her chest. As if my eyes weren't already drawn to her perfect set of breasts, now I'll have to put in extra effort not to stare at them.

"Can't handle any more corner store coffee?" she asks while she moves the scones and pastries around in the bakery case to make room for the ones on the tray.

"The smell of coffee lured me in." Everything about her shop is welcoming, but the chance that she would be here made fighting the pull pointless.

"Fabulous, my evil plan is working." Delilah wiggles her eyebrows, which should look ridiculous, but she's so carefree that it's adorable as fuck.

"Is your plan to lure attractive men into your clutches with a siren song of coffee and keep them here forever, feeding them baked goods? Where do you keep them all?" My eyes peer around the shop like I'm searching out a hidden trapdoor. "Is there a dungeon in the basement?"

Her mouth falls open in a dramatic gasp. She pauses her work and stands to her full height, one hand coming to her hip as she glides her eyes over me. The shirt I'm wearing is plastered to me from my run—clinging to my upper body and consequently showing off all the work I put in to be at the top of my game as a professional athlete. My ego swells at the way her gaze slows as she surveys my upper body.

"Did one of them escape and spill my secrets?" The confidence in her voice wavers as she brings her eyes back up to my face.

"No, I'm just wildly observant. You might look sweet and innocent, but I'm on to you. Only someone truly diabolical can make coffee and baked goods that look and smell this mouthwatering."

She steps over to the bakery case to continue refilling it. I am help-less to do anything but follow her. I lean forward to rest my elbows on the counter, watching her work. For the first time in months, the air around me feels a little less heavy. Everything is a bit easier in her presence.

Maybe because she doesn't know about my past, there's no pity when she looks at me. Unlike my teammates, she knows nothing about Jarrett, or what I have been through. I noticed it that night at Sabor too—she calms the storm that's been raging inside me.

"The asado negro you suggested was delightful. I think that means that I owe you a recommendation as repayment. What's your guilty pleasure?" Her hand sweeps out toward the bakery case.

"Pleasure never makes me feel guilty, Hermosa."

Pink stains her chest and blossoms across her cheeks. Leaning in further, I crowd her as she works, trying to pull another reaction out of her. I know I shouldn't, but I can't seem to help myself. Flirting with her is fun and she makes it so damn easy.

"I have a weakness for caramel and cinnamon," I say, my gaze flicking down to her shirt before I look back up and find her eyes wide. "I'll try a sticky bun and an iced coffee."

She tries to hide her smile with a downward glance as she plates the treat. Our hands brush when I grab it from her, sending a jolt of desire through my body. Delilah freezes for a moment before dropping her hand, shaking it at her side and getting to work on my coffee. She's flustered and I can't get enough of it.

The ice clinks against the cup as she shakes my drink—her eyes fixed on what she's doing until she slides the drink to me. This time she doesn't hide her grin.

Maybe I should feel wrong flirting when I know she's with someone else. But in the few minutes I spent with her and Brad, it was obvious he's not good enough for her. Who leaves their girlfriend waiting in a bar for them and then doesn't even have the decency to put away his phone long enough to greet her properly?

As soon as the flavor of the cold coffee hits my tongue, I regret waiting this long to stop in. This is good. Better than good—it's the best coffee I've had in a long time. Just sweet enough without being too much. "I can't believe I've been drinking that sludge from the corner store this whole time, instead of this. I hope you're ready Delilah, you just became my new best friend—I'm going to be here every day."

Her genuine laugh fills up the distance she created between us. Delilah, with her head tipped back and her blue eyes twinkling, is the most addictive sight. *That's it, Hermosa, give me more of that sweet sound.*

"I'll believe it when I see it. You'll be sick of me in no time," she says, returning to her work behind the counter.

"Mhmmm . . . you don't know me yet, but if I say I am going to do something, I do it. I'm also competitive as hell, and that sounded like a challenge." Her eyes drop to the Bandits logo across the front of my shirt.

"The same could be said for me. I can be cutthroat when the stakes are right." Her eyes pass over me in another drawn out sweeping motion before she adds, "By the way, you never told me what brought you to Denver."

"I play baseball for the Bandits. I was traded here from St. Louis."

CHAPTER 11

COFFEE TALK

FLASHBACK - THREE YEARS EARLIER

The bell above the door to the coffee house chimes, interrupting my flawless rendition of "No Scrubs" by TLC. I set the bowl of brownie batter I'm mixing aside and head to the front of the store, where I find Cruz with his hip resting against the counter as he stares down at the phone in his hand. Dark curls fall forward over his furrowed brow. His knuckles are white from the hold he has on the phone.

Alarm bells ring out in my head. We've gotten close over the past month and I find him perched against my counter at least once a day, without fail, when he's not on the road. We talk while he sips his drink or eats his sticky bun. Our conversations have covered countless topics—some fun, others more serious.

I pause in front of him, taking him in for a moment. He's wearing a pair of black joggers with a fitted Bandits warm-up shirt with a black hat.

It's his uniform for practice. His hair isn't wet so he must be heading to the stadium.

Not wanting to startle him, I gently lay my hand on his arm. When he looks up from his phone, there's pain etched into his features. I see the same stormy look moving behind his chocolate eyes that he had on when he told me how he lost his brother earlier this year. His gaze flicks to where my hand is on his arm and back to my face.

"What's wrong?" I stroke my thumb over his forearm, back and forth over his pulse point.

Brushing it off, he slides the phone into his pocket. "Just some news. It's not what I was hoping for," he says, downplaying it and retreating from whatever has him looking heartbroken.

"I'm sorry to hear that. Is there anything I can do?" I try again, hoping that he'll give me a glimpse of what's got him so twisted up so that I can help.

His hand comes down on mine, squeezing my finger for a beat. "Do you have any new treats back there that need some taste testing? That would help."

"I was just making a batch of s'mores brownies, but they aren't done yet. Can I interest you in a sticky bun instead? They're not new, but I know they're your favorite." Maybe some sugar will help him open up.

"You can never go wrong with sticky buns. They remind me of the golfeados my mom makes for my dad's birthday every year." He gives me a tight smile, but I know it's fake. There are no dimples framing his straight white teeth. When he's truly happy, those little divots shine brighter than any star in the sky. I want to ask him again what's really going on, but he's shut down, so I settle for feeding him.

"I'm not sure how someone with such a sweet tooth can be in as good of shape as you are. The rest of us mere mortals look at treats and end up absorbing the calories through osmosis. I think you get a new muscle every time I see you. Are you carrying a hammer around that I'm not aware of,

Thor?" Moving to the opposite side of the counter, I grab a plate for his pastry before I slide it to him.

Cruz arches an eyebrow and smirks at me before his eyes sweep over me from head to toe. "I'm not sure you're ready to know about my hammer. But, does that mean you've been checking out my muscles?"

My cheeks flame with heat, the way they always seem to when he's around. His eyes burn a trail across my body as they slowly rove over me. Before I can speak, he grabs my hand from where it's frozen on the plate.

"For the record, Delilah, your body is perfect. Treats and calories be damned. Anyone who tells you differently needs their ass kicked and their eyes checked."

Noted.

Cruz looks down at his hand and drags it back to his side, shaking his head. "Delilah, I'm sorry. I hope that didn't make you uncomfortable. You're my friend. My gorgeous friend but, I didn't mean to overstep. It's been a weird day."

"It's fine. It was nice to hear. You just caught me off guard." Brad's been so busy with the acquisition he's working on that I could walk into the room without a stitch of clothes on and I'm not sure he would even look up from his email long enough to notice. "Tell me about your weird day. Let me help. That's what friends do, right?"

"Friends." He echoes before lifting his hat and pushing his hands through his curls. When he replaces his hat, I see the same pained look in his eyes again.

"It's my brother. When he—" Turning away, he looks out the window before blowing out a deep breath and continuing on. "There's a lot we don't know about the night of Jarrett's accident. The detective in Miami is not having any luck. They aren't closing the case, but there's not much more they can do without a new lead. He suggested I work with a private investigator. He gave me the name of one that used to work in the precinct and moved to St. Louis." His face twists like it's physically painful for him to say the words out loud.

"Oh, Cruz." Going to him, I wrap my arms around his waist, hoping to give him some solace. He stiffens for a minute before giving in to what I'm offering. His massive arms drape around my shoulders, pulling me into him and bringing my head against the hard plane of his chest.

"The detective was trying to work with the club on getting players and staff to talk, but without criminal charges, they're out of options. He cautioned me that I may never get the answers I'm looking for." The pain in his voice makes my heart split open for him. I can't begin to understand how it felt for him to lose his brother and best friend so unexpectedly. But not knowing how or why just amplifies everything.

"What are you going to do?" Without moving from his embrace, I crane my neck to look up at him. I'm relieved to find him looking somewhat less tense.

"I don't know. My parents would flip out if they knew I was digging into his death. They want to 'mourn their son in peace.' Those were my dad's exact words. When I brought up hiring a P.I., they were concerned about how it would impact me emotionally to keep looking for answers when the police weren't able to find any."

"Can you let it go and move on without making sure you've tried every-thing to get answers?" Cruz has told me enough about his family to know that he doesn't take going against his fathers wishes lightly.

He cares a great deal about his approval, but the bond he shared with his brother was unparalleled. Even though they played the same sport at a high level, and were both fiercely competitive, they only ever drove each other to be better. They were each other's biggest fans.

His nostrils flare, looking tenser than I have ever seen him. "No. He deserves to have peace and we do, too. And for me that means finding out what happened."

"Then I think you have your answer." The door dings behind me. Cruz drops his arms and steps back, putting space between us. I look over my shoulder and see Brad standing just inside the door.

"Hey, Brad." His greeting is flat. "Can I get this to-go? I'm going to eat it at the stadium," he asks, his tone softening when he turns his attention back to me.

"Sure. I'll grab you a container."

"Dee, did you ask Cruz about next weekend?" Brad asks, clearly not picking up on the mood in the room. My eyebrows pull together in annoyance that he can't tell now isn't the time.

"No, I told you I wasn't going to." I try to hide the frustration in my voice. Cruz doesn't need this on top of his already shitty morning.

"Ask me what?" Cruz questions, taking the to-go box from my hand.

"I told Dee we should try to get to a game next weekend," Brad says as he leans across the counter to give me a kiss on the cheek. "But she didn't feel comfortable asking."

Cruz raises his eyebrow at me. He's offered me tickets before, but I have always turned him down.

"I didn't want to put you out." Fighting this battle is pointless now that Brad has brought it up. But there's no way in hell I am going to let Brad steamroll him just because he knows Cruz will do it for me.

"I have an allotment of tickets, it's fine. Hell, you can come to the game tonight too."

"See Dee, I told you he'd come through," Brad says, holding out his hand to Cruz for a fist bump. When Brad realizes that's not going to be returned, he drops his hand with a shrug. Completely unfazed.

"Of course. Saturday night's game? You need two tickets?"

"Thanks, you really—"

Brad cuts me off before I can finish my half-hearted protest. It's half-hearted because even though I haven't taken him up on the offer, I do want to watch him play.

"If we could get four tickets, that would be perfect. One of the partners at the firm and his wife wanted to come along."

And *this* is precisely the reason I wasn't going to ask. This isn't about me going to a game to watch my friend. It's an opportunity for Brad to rub elbows with his boss and throw around clout since he bragged that he's friends with Cruz at happy hour last week.

"It's not necessary. We can get tickets from the box office like everyone else. I don't want to take advantage." It's a last ditch effort to keep Cruz from feeling obligated.

"Stop. Seriously, it's fine. I'll have them at will call for you. Along with tickets for tonight, if you can make it." Cruz pushes off the counter and heads toward the door. "It was good to see you, Delilah." He smiles at me looking a little less haunted than when he walked through the door. "Later, Brad."

"Sure, later," Brad says without looking up from his phone.

When the door shuts, I toss a rag at Brad hitting him on the side of the head. "What the hell was that?" My voice is filled with irritation. I'm not sure I could hold it back if I tried, seeing as the barely contained rage is vibrating through my body. "I told you I wasn't going to ask. Cruz doesn't need you using your connection to him to get ahead at work. And you didn't even say thank you. How rude!"

Brad just shrugs, stalking across the shop towards me and pocketing his phone. "He was in a position to help, so I asked. Todd is a huge Bandit's fan, this is going to make me look so good."

"I can't believe you did that." A smug smile crosses his face as I slap at his chest.

"Don't be mad, baby," he says, wrapping me up in his arms and peppering kisses on my face. Brad's approach has always been to ask forgiveness instead of seeking permission. It drives me crazy and has been the catalyst for many arguments over the years.

When he layers the affection on like this afterwards, the guilt for how I reacted tries to rear its ugly head. I have to force it back down. Reminding myself I'm entitled to my feelings. He blatantly took advantage of my friendship with Cruz for his own gain. I know he will just argue that he's doing it for us to build the future that we always dreamed of. That thought softens the edges of my anger marginally.

"I wish you wouldn't have done that. Cruz is my friend, and it wasn't your place to ask him for a favor after I already said it made me uncomfortable." I shrug out of his hold and grab a rag to busy myself cleaning, putting space between us.

CHAPTER 12

POPPY CALLS

PRESENT

As I attempt to do inventory from home today, all I can think about is the fact that it's been just over a week since the impromptu movie night at Cruz's and the team is finally back from their longest road trip this season—a whole eight days.

That's eight days too long.

Especially since the last time I saw Cruz was when we woke up to a mess of tangled sheets and limbs.

If it were just the slumber party in his bed, maybe I wouldn't have spent the last eight *freaking* days obsessing over it, but it wasn't. There was one other very large, hard detail that we both just pretended to ignore. God, the way he hovered over me, I know I wasn't imagining the heat in his eyes when he adjusted himself.

I groan out loud, wondering if Buzz Lightgirth is charged or if the battery is drained from excessive use this week. Taking the edge off before Cruz comes over tonight is probably the best idea I have had all day. Maybe it will keep me just sane enough to keep from doing something stupid, like jumping his bones before we discuss what the hell is going on between us.

No, I shouldn't do that. I shake off the idea.

It's a conversation that's overdue at this point. The tension between us has been building for years and it's to the point that I don't think either of us can avoid it any longer. Big, life-changing conversations are never easy, but this one has me unraveling from the inside out. I grumble to myself in Spanish. It's a habit I've gotten into when I'm alone to help me learn. The idea of being able to surprise Cruz and be able to speak in full sentences has been pushing me to practice more lately.

My phone vibrates on the coffee table next to me and I set my laptop aside. The inventory spreadsheet for *Buns & Roses* is open, but I've barely touched it, trapped in my head overanalyzing what I'll say tonight when Cruz comes over after the team plane lands.

CRUZ:

We should be on the ground in 30 minutes.
What do you want me to pick up for dinner?

DELILAH:

You choose. Decision fatigue is real. I have been staring at my inventory for so long it's gone all haywire. It's like my brain is blurry.

CRUZ:

I'll be there soon and promise to take your mind off numbers.

When he says that, why do I automatically jump to dirty thoughts? God, I'm in so much trouble, my willpower to resist this pull between us is nonexistent. It's a dangerous position to be in. He's the best thing that's ever happened to me. My best friend. A constant positive force in my life. Why does that make me even hotter? I pull my shirt from my chest, fanning myself with it. The knowledge that I could quickly take care of this with a quick trip to my toy box nags at the back of my mind.

My feet are moving, carrying me to my nightstand before I even accept that I've made the decision. I freeze when my fingers wrap around the knob. I'm really about to do this, again? The drawer squeaks as I pull it open like it's taunting me.

Eyes roaming over my modest collection I grab Buzz and toss him on the bed leaving the lube in the drawer. It's completely unnecessary because I'm already dripping from the buildup my mind created. *Traitor*.

Tearing the duvet down and tossing the decorative pillows to the side I plunk my ass down on the bed and lay back, my fist wrapping around the purple vibrator. Maybe if I just wait it out this feeling will fade.

Who the fuck am I kidding my nipples are tight and achy against the fabric of my oversized crop top.

My free hand slides up my stomach, cupping my breast and brushing over the hard tip of my nipple. I bite down on my lip to stop the groan working its way up my throat, but I'm too far gone. There's no stopping the pulsing between my legs which is getting worse the longer I deny myself. Giving in I sag into the mattress when my thumb and pointer finger roll the stiff peak as I bring the toy in my other hand to life with the click of a button.

Slipping it under the waistband of my terry cloth shorts I let it drag over my swollen lips a few times before I get frustrated and shove the bottoms that are only getting in my way down my legs, kicking them free from my feet. I'm making a mess but that's a problem for future Lilah, because right now I can't see beyond the need that's taken over my body for my best friend. What the hell is wrong with me?

My forearm drops to my face, covering my eyes as I circle the entrance of my pussy with the humming toy. Jesus, there's not even a hint of resistance when I press it inside my soaked pussy. I've never been this turned on by just the thought of someone, but every single time I fantasize about Cruz my body responds this way.

I wish I could say that it's just a physical release, triggered by the fact that he's got the hottest body I've ever laid eyes on. Toned muscles covered in flawless tan skin, and those dark curls that I'd give anything to sink my fingers into right now and hold on to while I ride his face. Even as the filthy image of his fingers digging into my back side as I hover over his face, soaking his as he devours me, fills my mind there's something else there too.

My body responds like this for him, even when he's not actually here because he's my person. Cruz makes me feel cherished in a way I've never experienced before, he always has. No one has ever given me the same sense of security. He's been a steadfast force in my life for years.

The sound that leaves my body when I circle my clit with my fingers is unhinged. I feel feral for my best friend, out of control with need as my back arches off the bed seeking more. More pressure from my fingers on my clit, just fucking more everything. More Cruz. That realization has my whole body shaking as my spine snaps tight and I come, his name echoing through my bedroom.

A black haze clouds the edges of my vision as my lungs work overtime, still recovering from the powerful release. I switch off the vibrator as the weight of what I just did settles over me like a heavy blanket. Things have changed, there's no way around it, but the odds against us feel impossibly high.

What if we screw it all up? I'm not sure what I would do if I lost him.

Since the night of the Bandit's Gala, maybe even before, but definitely after that night, there was no denying that my feelings for him were not-so-platonic. The way he was so attentive and kind—his eyes never left me, and he doted on me all night, making sure I felt beautiful and desired, without crossing the line our friendship had drawn in the sand.

I bury my face in my pillow, almost missing the sound of my phone on the night stand where I abandoned it earlier.

CRUZ:

Sabor it is. A double order of asado negro and pork arepas to-go.

Of course, that's what he picked. I close my eyes, remembering that first night we met at Sabor. Cruz might look every bit the rugged athlete on the outside, but I know he's a fluffy, sweet marshmallow on the inside. With one quick interaction, on a night where I was feeling less than great, he made my life just a little bit better. Something he's done time and time again since.

I sigh, it's time for future Lilah to get her shit together and clean up this mess, the one between my legs and my trashed bed before the man who inspired my recklessness knocks at my door.

I've barely gotten a grip on myself when that exact thing happens a short time later. "Come on in!" I holler toward the door. My stomach flutters with the anticipation of seeing him. Setting aside my laptop before I push off the couch and head to the connected kitchen.

When he steps into the apartment, Cruz looks back at the doorknob, his brows drawn together.

"Unlocked, Delilah? You're killing me. Anyone could have walked in here," he says, handing me a box. "This was on your mat. It's addressed to the Velvet Lounge, but it has your address. Is that the swanky new speakeasy down the street?"

Oh. My. God. I'm going to murder Poppy—after I thank her. But *then* she is dead. She's the only person who would send something to my "Velvet Lounge." I snatch the box out of his hand and hide it behind my back.

You have precisely zero chill, Lilah.

"Ah—I have no idea." It's a lie, one I'm sure he can see right through, but maybe the unlocked door will distract him from the fact that I'm hiding a vibrator behind my back.

He shakes his head and sets the food down on the counter next to the door, stepping across the small entryway and right into my space. His hand softly raises, cradling my jaw. "Is everything okay? You looked flushed?"

Jesus, of course, I'm blushing. I nod jerkily, not sure words are my best bet right now.

My best friend has a body that's built for sin, add in the southern accent that comes out when he's flirting, a few affectionate words in Spanish, and my Velvet Lounge is weeping for a go at him. He's the entire reason I need whatever self-love contraption Poppy deemed necessary. I wish this floor would open up and swallow me whole.

"Don't make me worry about you. Lock it? Please, Hermosa," Cruz says, brushing his thumb across my cheekbone and pulling me out of my embarrassment spiral.

"I will from now on. Promise," I assure him as he retrieves the food and brings it to the kitchen. While he's busy with that I discreetly open the coat closet and toss the box inside like it might self-destruct, sending dildo shrapnel everywhere.

"It smells so good. You can't go wrong with Sabor." I busy myself with the work of grabbing plates from the cupboard to give myself a second to get it together.

Cruz appears behind me, causing me to inhale sharply as he brushes against me, lighting up every part of me. Reaching up to grab the dishes from me. "I picked up a bottle of your favorite wine." He nods toward the paper bag on the table. "I thought we could have a glass with dinner and then talk."

"Jumping right to the elephant in the room, you're not even going to ease me into it," I say, setting the wine glasses and utensils down before sliding into my seat next to Cruz.

"I've been easing you into it for a while now." He raises his eyebrows while his hands work to uncork the bottle. And I can't stop staring at his veins bulging with each move. *Focus, Lilah.*

"Is that what movie night was? I hardly call waking up with your morning wood staring at me easing into it," I tell him as I pour a healthy serving of wine into both our glasses. We're going to need it.

Cruz's eyes bore into me, waiting for me to elaborate. I swallow the dread in my throat before I set my fork down and drop my head into my hands. I suck in a big breath, steeling myself for what I'm about to say. When I peek up at him through my fingers, he's set his fork down and has his elbows perched on the table as he waits.

"We should probably talk about—" My sentence is cut off when my phone rings. Poppy's name flashes across the screen—she never calls. I look up at Cruz. "It's Poppy. She's supposed to be on her date with Hen right now." I bite my lip, unable to shake the feeling that something's wrong.

"Hey, Pop—"

"Lilah," she cuts me off, her voice broken with emotion.

"Poppy, what's wrong?" I ask, standing from the table and pacing the length of the table. Cruz's hand shoots out, and he takes my hand, squeezing.

"I need—can I come over?" Her voice cracks as she asks.

"Always. Is everyone okay? No one's hurt?" I ask, as I see Cruz go stiff next to me. My hand aches from the tight grip he has on it as the sound of Poppy's distraught voice carries through the phone. I focus on erasing any alarm that I might be showing to help ease the painful memories of Jarrett's death that are being triggered for him right now.

"All—physically fine." She sniffles on the other end of the phone. "Even if I'm so mad at him, I could be capable of inflicting physical pain at this point. I'll explain when I get there," Poppy says before disconnecting.

Cruz's grip on my hand eases as he pulls me into him. I let him tug me between his legs as he sits at the table. My hands go to his hair, scraping my fingernails across his scalp, gently combing through his dark wavy locks. He rests his forehead against my stomach, dragging in a ragged inhale.

"It's okay. Everyone's okay," I tell him softly as I tilt his face up to me. "It's okay." I run my fingers through his hair, trying to ease the anxiety that I know must be surfacing for him. Any late night, unexpected calls tend to set him on edge, and my reaction probably didn't help things.

He pulls me into his lap. "We have a lot to talk about, but it can wait. I'll wait with you until Poppy gets here and then you can focus on her. We still need to finish this, but you get a pass for tonight."

I drop my head to the crook of his neck. "I missed you, Cruz."

"I missed you too," he tells me before picking up his fork and sharing the food from his plate while we wait.

A few quiet minutes later, Poppy crashes through my door in a flurry of anger and sadness. "Your friend is an asshole," she rants the second she walks in the door. When she kicks off her shoes and pauses for a second, her eyes focus on how we are sitting at the table, sharing one seat and one plate, her eyes soften.

"Fuck . . . guys, I'm sorry. You two are supposed to be"—she flaps hers around gesturing towards us—"hanging out tonight. I ruined—"

Cruz stands, holding me by the hips, so I don't topple over. "It's okay. I'd wait forever for this one. " His thick arms band around me, hugging me to his chest as he kisses me on the top of my head—making me dizzy with the swell of emotions I feel over the sentiment

Poppy steps into the kitchen, heading for the living room. "Call me later?" I say to Cruz as he steps away to slip his shoes on. I want to pull him back to me, ask him to stay, figure out what this is between us but my friend needs me.

"I will." Then he slips through the door with a glance over his shoulder.

I join Poppy on the couch, handing her my untouched glass of wine as I drink from Cruz's. She twists her red hair around her finger as tears well in the corner of her eyes." I'm going to have to kick his ass, aren't I?" I threaten, looping my arm around her shoulders.

"I'd do it, you know, march over there and . . . and kick him right in the shins. With pointy shoes."

"The shins?"

My head bobs up and down and I try my best to come up with a plan to inflict maximum pain, but it's not my forte. "I'm going to kick him square in the shins. Hard enough to really bruise so that every time he has to run the bases or jump for a ball, the impact hurts."

Her laugh comes out more of a snort because she's still fighting tears. "That's an innovative punishment. But you don't even know what he did."

"Doesn't matter, you're my girl, and anyone who makes you this upset deserves a beat down." I stand from the couch, but she tugs my arm, pulling me back down.

"I appreciate that more than you know, but he's not worth it." She lays her head in my lap and my fingers sift through her soft hair, massaging her scalp.

"If Hendrix thinks I'm going to make him coffee, he will be sorely disappointed. Maybe I'll even print a sign that says, 'I reserve the right not to serve twat-waffles, aka Hendrix James.'"

"Now that's the kind of karma he deserves. Deprive him of the best coffee in Denver." She lifts her head and looks up at me from where she's snuggled in. "I'm sorry I interrupted your night. You guys had a lot to talk about."

"I blame Hendrix."

Poppy sighs, dropping her head to my shoulders. "Still, you two looked pretty cozy when I walked in. Did you get anywhere?" I guess we are using my problems as a distraction from her own.

"No, we were just chatting when you called. He hadn't been here for long and we never got to talk about what happened at movie night." I remember the package he found when he arrived and add, "I'm not sure if I should thank you for the gift or slap you upside the head. Cruz found it."

"He did not," she says, picking her head up and biting her cheek. "Well, did you like it?"

"I haven't opened it, I tossed it in the coat closet to hide it from him the moment I realized what it was." Standing from my spot I retrieve the box from where it landed on top of my winter boots, carry it back to the couch, and open it.

"Woody will be very pleased to join his friend in the toy box." I suction the curved white and black dildo to the table and give him a flick testing the grip. "Impressive."

"He's a beaut. Do you know how hard it was to find a cow print dildo with any kind of length and girth to it? And he vibrates. You hardly even need a man."

That's doubtful. I don't think anything could erase my need for Cruz after today. There's too much history there and now, with him invading every part of my life in a new way, it feels like it's only a matter of time before the sexy baseball player becomes so much more than he already is.

CHAPTER 13

YOU'VE GOT GAME

FLASHBACK - TWO YEARS EARLIER

The perfectly trimmed grass is spongy under my cleats as I step over the crisply painted foul line and jog to my spot on the field. When I look around the stadium it's not the crowd noise or the bright lights that have my attention. Instead, my eyes immediately weave up and down the rows of fans, decked out in their black and teal. Scanning the crowd for the head of blonde hair, all piled up on top of Delilah's head. When I find the seats I set aside for her, disappointment settles over me.

She didn't come.

I remind myself not to take it personally, but that's easier said than done. It's been a long time since anyone has shown up at a game for me. Even before Jarrett died, my parents didn't travel to games often. My dad still works twelve-hour days, and now that they don't have kids at home, my mom has taken to mothering the staff at the screen-printing business they own in San Antonio—where I grew up. Both of them are first-generation Americans and the ultimate example of what hustling looks like. My mother's family moved from Mexico and my father's from Venezuela. The two of them were inseparable from the moment they met in elementary school, forging their way together as they adapted to life in a new country.

After seeing their parents struggle, they felt strongly about blazing their own trail. Watching them raise a family with two active boys, while running a thriving business, taught my brother and I how to apply that same dedication to the game. My dad felt so strongly about ensuring that we found similar success, that one of the conditions behind his support of our baseball careers was that we had still had to finish college before going into the draft. I'm not sure I would have been successful in achieving my dreams of making it to the MLB without their example. The last time I had someone show up for a game to watch me was the week before Jarrett's accident. He had a rare day off that coincided with my home game and could come watch.

Every moment of that day is etched in my memory.

As a player on the Commanders' farm team, he was allowed to spend the entire afternoon watching batting practice, warm-ups, and listening to Coach's pregame talk.

He was so giddy at the prospect of being called up and playing on the same team that he couldn't wipe the smile off his face. And he was so close to achieving that dream. A week later, he was gone.

Blinking away the stinging sensation behind my eyes. I have to force myself to refocus on the diamond in front of me as I fire a ball across the outfield to the right fielder, warming up my arm. The New York Knights come at us hot-out-of-the-gates and have me working hard to keep up with the deep balls to the outfield.

After getting the third out, we head to the plate for our turn to hit. I pull my batting helmet down tight over my head and lean against the railing, looking out over the field as I wait for my turn in the lineup. Against my better judgment, my eyes are drawn to the section of seats where Delilah would be sitting if she'd shown up.

When my gaze sweeps across the section, they catch on a head of blonde hair decked out in a Bandit's shirt. I stare in disbelief as she sips from her beer, watching the game. The seat next to her is empty. I can't fight the grin that takes over my face. She came, and she's alone. That fact shouldn't make me happy, but it's typical with her. There are so many things that I feel about Delilah that I have no right feeling—like the posses- sive urge to see her sitting there in my jersey for example.

She's here for me, and fuck if I don't want everyone to know it.

"Cruz, you're on deck." Our team captain, Lincoln, nudges me with his elbow bringing my focus back to the game.

I step up to the plate, looking at the stands one last time before I etch a 'J' into the dirt in front of the plate with my bat and step into the box. It's a reminder to play this game and live my life to the fullest—the way Jarrett did. Like I promised him I would the day I held his hand and said goodbye. Playing with my whole heart is the easier part of that deal. It's life outside the walls of this stadium that I haven't figured out how to do without him.

When the ball leaves the pitcher's hand, I know it's mine. Time slows to a stand-still as I watch it until it's right where I want it. My grip tightens on the end of the bat and I swing with everything I have. The crack of the bat reverberates through my hands and up my arms as I watch it fly over the outfield wall. Jarret would be proud of that one. For a pitcher, he had one hell of a swing.

When I round second base, heading toward third, I see Delilah jumping up and down with her hands in the air as she goes nuts over my home run. We make eye contact and I point at her, letting her know I see her cheering for me.

When I rejoin the team in the dugout, Lincoln slaps the mangy teal and black zebra print cowboy hat down on my head—a Bandits tradition—as the team claps me on the back. But once the fanfare has died down, I grab the usher's attention and point out Delilah with instructions to make sure she can find me after the game and request an extra jersey be sent to the locker room for me.

♥

I've barely cleared the threshold of the locker room door when Delilah launches herself at me, wrapping her arms around my neck and grinning up at me with pride shining in her cobalt blue eyes.

"That home run was unbelievable and that catch in the seventh? Do you need a getaway driver? You robbed that guy," she rambles wildly as players and staff weave their way around us. Her attention is only on me and there's no better feeling. "Who knew you were so good at baseball?"

"You had doubts?" I raise my eyebrow at her as she drops her hands from my neck and steps back.

"Men have a reputation for embellishing their attributes."

"I can't speak for all men, but I can tell you I always live up to the hype."
Shit. Fuck. Damn.

I mentally chastise myself for letting the flirting slip out. It tends to happen when your best friend is also one of the most stunning women you've ever met. But I've been trying to curb it and keep our friendship rock-solid, without crossing any boundaries. She and I are firmly in the friendzone for a multitude of reasons.

The main reason being I'm a train wreck, and she is in a relationship with someone else. Someone she plans to marry, I remind myself, regardless of the fact that I think Brad is an entire bag of tools.

Delilah raises her eyebrow and laughs. Every time I hear that sweet sound some of the darkness clouding me clears. I've come to crave it over the last month and I'll do just about anything to hear it.

"Good to know, Slugger." She loops her arm through mine as we walk toward the player's entrance. "So, how do you usually celebrate a big win?"

"Dinner to-go from Sabor, and a documentary on Netflix. Lame, right? I haven't gone out with the team much since the trade." It's not that I don't like my teammates, the appeal of going out just isn't there right now. Jarrett definitely wouldn't approve. I'm surprised his spirit hasn't shown up to drag me out of my self-imposed isolation. This is the part I haven't figured out yet, how to move on and keep my promise to him.

"Remember who you're talking to? I'm usually in bed by 9 p.m. so I can make sure everyone gets their sticky bun fix. Your nights sound wild to me."

Guilt gnaws at me. She stuck around to see me when she probably should have gone home to sleep right after the game.

"We should get you home so you can bake with those beautiful blue eyes *open* tomorrow. I would hate for you to mix up your savory and sweet because of me." I hold the door for her as she steps into the players' parking lot. "Did Brad come with you? I didn't see him in the stands."

She rolls her eyes, but she's smiling like it's just another day in her life, which makes me want to punch him in the face. "Dinner with a client. It came up at the last minute."

I let it go, since she doesn't seem overly annoyed. As close as we've grown over the last month, I'm not sure she would tolerate me speaking my mind about the way Brad treats her. Even if it's because I can't imagine a situation where I wouldn't put her first if she were mine.

She bounces on her toes, rubbing her hands together, excitement rolling off her. "I actually don't have to bake in the morning. I got enough prepped tonight before I walked over for the game. So this girl gets to sleep in tomorrow. Lucky, right?" Her lips tilt up as she looks at me through her lashes. "What do you say we get you out of your comfort zone and let the documentaries rest for a night?"

"Did you have something specific in mind? The guys go to Draft after the games. Or we can go somewhere a little more low-key if you don't feel like hanging with the team," I tell her, setting my backpack—containing the jersey I made the usher fetch—in the backseat of my car. "I'll even drive you."

The inconspicuous dig at Brad just slips out. Either Delilah doesn't notice or she lets it slide.

"Let's go to Draft. It's been ages since I was out at anything but a stuffy restaurant," Delilah says, moving around my car to slide into the passenger seat. "This ride is cushy." Her hands smooth over the supple leather seats on either side of her legs. She's rocking her favorite pair of cut-off jean shorts. Delilah's a tiny thing, but she packs a punch with her pint-sized body. Right now, with the emotions of her showing up for me, and the post game adrenaline, I'm having a hard time ignoring the way the line of her thigh muscle disappears under her tiny shorts in the dimly lit car.

Gripping the steering wheel tightly, I look ahead and start the car instead of leering at my friend like a creep. Fuck. I need to get laid. My hand just hasn't been cutting it lately, but making my sex life a priority feels trivial when I can't even hang with my teammates. Jarrett is probably getting a kick out of the fact that he can even cockblock me from the grave.

I ease the car forward and pull out of the parking lot, focusing on the drive to Draft. For the first time since we've met Delilah doesn't fill the silence with chit chat. And from the covert glances she keeps throwing my way I can tell she's concerned, but giving me the space I need to process as I weave through downtown. When we park, I turn toward Delilah, ready to face the question that I know is on the tip of her tongue. She's been patient but now that she's got my attention she's studying me carefully.

"Is everything okay? You were quiet on the drive," she finally asks.

I'm not sure I can express what it felt like to have her watch me in the stands without losing the slippery grasp I have on my emotions right now. She doesn't know that she gave me a sense of normalcy I haven't had in months. The simple joy of seeing her there, cheering for me, cracked me wide open and left me a little raw.

I look back at her, taking in the concern in her eyes. Her hands fidget like she's just a little nervous about what might come out of my mouth. I can't blame her. I enjoy keeping her on her toes. You never quite know what I might say.

I blow out a long breath and run my hands through my hair, letting my curls sift through my fingers. "Thank you for coming tonight. It's the first time I've had someone in the stands for me since—" I can't stop the way my voice breaks.

"Jarrett?" she finishes for me, saving me from myself. Her small hand reaches out, wrapping itself around my larger one. The pad of her thumb rubs a circle on the back of my hand, assuring me she's here.

I nod in response. Thankful, yet again, that she knows how hard talking about this is, and is trying to take some of that sting away. Delilah gets me even when I don't always understand how to navigate my grief. She gives me the space and time I need to work through it, knowing exactly what I need before I do.

It's part of the reason I made the impulsive decision to get the jersey for her. She's always showing up for me the same way my brother did. I want her at my games, watching with my name across her back. Plus, the idea of her at a game with Brad, while wearing it, does a little something to my ego.

I reach into the back, grabbing the jersey from the backpack.

"Having you there tonight was the highlight of my season. Thank you for being there for me, tonight and so many times over the past few months. I—um." I swipe my damp palms on my pants. Delilah's become my closest friend and as sweet as the treats she makes. She'd never make me feel silly for something like this. "I got you a jersey. So you can wear it to the games you come to." Flipping the jersey around so she can see the back. "*My* jersey, I want everyone to know you're there cheering for me."

"I think the way I pointed at you screaming, *'That's my bestie'* probably gave that away tonight, but this is even better. Now no one will doubt me." Her words are light and bubbly, but when she takes the jersey from me, I don't miss the way her fingers trace the letters of my last name. This time her words are soft. "Thank you. I can't wait to show it off. You deserve to have someone there cheering for you, Cruz."

We haven't been at Draft for more than a few minutes and Delilah has already won over everyone. She marched right in and charmed them with her wit and bright smile. Lincoln seems particularly interested by the way his eyes keep flicking over her. The catcher and I are going to have to have a little chat about the way he's looking at her.

"You tell us 'no' every time we ask you to come out, but a pretty girl asks you, and here you are. I see how we rank," Lincoln says, looking Delilah over.

"She is much nicer to me than you all are, and makes the best coffee so I have to stay in her good graces," I say, dropping my hand to the small of her back as I steer us from the bar to one of the high-top tables.

When Delilah excuses herself to use the restroom I level Lincoln with a glare, stepping into his space. "Don't even fucking think about it. Not only is she seeing someone, but she's not some cleat chaser that you can use to get your dick wet and kick out in the morning. She's my friend and if you make that shit awkward for me you might find yourself benched on the IL with a broken nose."

His hands come up in front of his chest and the self-satisfied look that crosses his face does nothing to tame my annoyance. "Message received, hands off the bestie. For the record I never kick them out without a good-bye orgasm. Morning sex is my kink—we both part happy."

"Keep your eyes to yourself too while you're at it," I grumble as Delilah bounces back up to us cheerfully oblivious.

"It was nice to meet you, Delilah. It's like Cruz is a brand new man with you around," he tells her with a smirk.

Delilah frowns at me and I know we are going to dive deeper into the reason for that later. She looks back over her shoulder at Lincoln. "You can call me Lilah. You'll be seeing me at more games. I had forgotten how much I loved watching baseball in person."

When we get to the table, I set our drinks down and take advantage of the more private setting. "Do you prefer Lilah?"

Her head tilts to the side, and she nibbles on her plump bottom lip before replying with, "I like when *you* call me Delilah. No one else really does, but it feels right." She pauses for a second. "Is that weird?"

"Not at all. It feels right to me too. I like Lilah, it suits you, but to me, you're Delilah. That's how you introduced yourself when we met and calling you Lilah seems too casual, like you're just an acquaintance."

"But I'm not, I'm your bestie." Her smile lights up her face, making her ocean blue eyes twinkle under the bar lights.

"That you are," I tell her, tilting my beer to my lips. "So, you really want to come to more games?"

Her brows pull together. "Yes. What's not to love? I get to be there for you, plus there are hot guys in tight pants and all the popcorn and beer a girl could dream of." Her demeanor shifts to something more serious. "My dad and I used to go to games together before they moved to Hawaii. Going to games makes me feel close to him."

"Remind me to thank him for fostering your love of baseball. I'm not sure we could stay friends if football was your favorite sport," I tease, drawing her brilliant smile back out.

CHAPTER 14

(FOUND) FAMILY DAY

FLASHBACK - TWO YEARS EARLIER

"Are you coming to Family Day next week?" Lincoln asks as I pack my bag up after practice. I pause, thinking about the email the team coordinator sent us earlier this week. It's an annual party at the ballpark to recognize the sacrifices the players' families make for the team.

When I got the email, that hollowness in my chest that's been slowly easing over the past two months came roaring back—leaving me angry all over again that my brother isn't here for these moments. Then a text came through from Delilah with a funny meme of a dog with his head out the car window, saying, *"Can you imagine, isn't he the cutest?"* There was still that ache in my chest, but it felt a little less empty. Like maybe it was slowly healing—little by little, slowly stitching itself back together.

"Yeah, I'm going to ask Delilah to come with me. My parents can't make the trip this time," I explain, slinging my bag over my shoulder.

"Is her boyfriend okay with that?" He raises an eyebrow at me.

"He'll probably encourage it. Brad is all about making connections. He'll love that she's spending time with the team, because he can claim he knows players by association." The look he gives me tells me exactly what he's thinking: *He may as well have Craftsman stamped across his forehead.*

"Speaking of hanging out with the team, I'm glad to see you are doing more of it. We're lucky to have you, even if the circumstances of your trade sucked," he says as he squeezes my shoulder.

It might be my first season in Denver, but I know that the days that it'll be warm enough to walk to and from the stadium are numbered. Patting Lincoln on the back I head out of the locker room to meet up with Delilah at the coffee shop.

The scent of cinnamon floats in the air when I get to *Buns & Roses*. The whisk in Delilah's hand scrapes against the metal bowl as she whips up the glaze for her sticky buns. Her newest hire, Mikey, runs coffees out to customers, making small talk and laughing with them like he's been here since the start.

"Is this your new work station?" I ask, stopping in front of her at the counter where she's mouthing the words to the '90s pop song playing in the background.

"Not a chance. I like to bake in the back where I can really belt out the words while I mix ingredients." She sets the bowl down and brushes a strand of hair off her face with the back of her hand before picking it up and resuming her work. "I'm out here so that I can help Mikey when he has questions. He's catching on fast, I'll be relegated to the back of the house by the end of the week."

"Any chance he'll be ready for a solo shift by tomorrow?"

"We can probably figure it out or I can have one of my part-timers come in to help. Why do you ask?" Her nose wrinkles in concentration while she mixes the ingredients together. Holding the whisk up to test the thickness of it. It's then that I notice the grated cheese in the small dish next to the bowl.

"Are those golfeados?"

I've seen Delliah blush more times than can count but never this red. She peeks up at me through her eyelashes looking almost guilty. "Don't get too excited, this is my first time making them. I'm sure they are nowhere near as good as your mom's."

My heart stutters in my chest and any lingering disappointment I had about my parents not coming fades.

"It's family day at the stadium. There are activities before the gates open for the players' families. I wanted to see if you would come." The words come out in a rush. I feel uncharacteristically sheepish asking her. Delilah freezes in place, glaze dripping onto the counter.

She sets the bowl aside and looks up at me, her normally plump lips pulled tight. "That's the most nervous I have ever seen you. Did you really think I would say 'no'?"

"Not really, but I know that you're busy training, Mikey, and it's not always easy to get away. It's a lot to ask." I look down at my feet before meeting her eyes. I hate feeling vulnerable, even though I know she would want to be there for me. She already has one guy in her life that expects her to drop everything for him.

"What kind of activities are we talking about?" Delilah asks with a mischievous smile. "Is there a dunk tank?"

"There might be." Her teasing tone is already helping loosen the knot in my chest. "I heard there's a three-legged race, complete with a trophy," I say, as she pours the mixture over the warm pastries.

"Oh, it's on like Donkey Kong. You better be able to keep up." She reaches under the counter for a plate and slides one of the freshly made pastries to me. "Stop eye-fucking my buns and eat one. Lord knows you'll just turn it into more muscles."

My lips tilt up in a smile. "You love my muscles. All the better to haul your pocket-sized ass across the finish line during the three-legged race."

"I think you forget I ran track in college, you clown."

"How did I not know this?" It makes sense for someone so petite. Delilah's got the kind of curves that men crave. Her short stature only enhances the mouthwatering peaks and valleys along her hips and waist. Plus, she's not the kind of girl that talks about herself much, and she definitely doesn't boast, so I'm not surprised that the topic hasn't come up. She would rather celebrate everyone else's achievements than brag about her own.

I watch, stupefied, when she dips her finger into a puddle of filling and syrup that have dripped out of my golfeados onto my plate and brings her finger to her mouth, sucking it off. "There's a lot you don't know about me."

What the fuck was that?

I stand there gawking as she crosses the space to the sink and washes her hands, completely off-balance from her teasing. Maybe it's a good thing Dellah and I can't be more than friends, because one little innuendo and I'm totally at a loss for words. She looks over her shoulder and smiles, a blush staining her cheeks.

"What time does it start tomorrow?" Just like that, she pops the ill-advised lust bubble we've found ourselves in, bringing us straight back to the friendzone.

"Noon. They will have food and games, then there's a break for the crew to clean up and the players to have some downtime before our game," I say, trying not to stare at her ass as she dries her hands and failing. "I can meet you here and we can walk over."

"A man with a plan, I like it. You better bring your A game, Tellez," she jokes, using my last name like the guys on the team do. Her ridiculous, competitive streak is a pleasant surprise and just one more thing that makes me admire her.

I push through the door of *Buns & Roses* the next morning to find Delilah bent over a pan of brownies, dusting them with powdered sugar.

For a moment it looks like she's only wearing her apron, her tiny black shorts and tank top barely peeking out.

Then she straightens up, giving me a look at her face. A rough laugh bursts out of me before I can stop it. Delilah's face twists in confusion as she wipes her hands down the front of her apron, leaving white streaks from the powdered sugar. "What's so funny?"

I cross the coffee shop in a few quick strides, so I'm across the counter from her. Wordlessly, I lift my hand to her face, cupping her jaw in my palm and brush the pad of my thumb over her cheekbone, where she has a generous dusting of powdered sugar.

"You're so sweet you're turning into one of your desserts," I tell her, and, because I can't help myself after the way she tortured me yesterday, I hold eye contact with her while I lick the sweet powder off my thumb. Delilah's pupils dilate and her hands comes up, covering the spot on her cheek I just touched. I smack my lips as my thumb leaves my mouth, breaking her out of her trance.

Clearing her throat, she grabs a rag, wiping the leftover mess off her face. "Let's see if you still think I'm sweet when I'm yelling at you to run faster during the three-legged race."

"You know I'm a professional athlete, right? I think I'll be able to keep up." She just looks at me doubtfully before setting the brownies aside, untying her apron and slipping it over her head to reveal a barely-there outfit that shows off her tight body.

Jesus Christ, is she trying to kill me? I knew the shorts were tiny—they're also molded to her, leaving nothing to the imagination. But it's the damn tank top that almost pushes me over the edge. It's teal, strappy, and cropped, showing off a few inches of skin. It must have some sort of bra built in because her round tits sit high on her chest and are trapped so tightly in the top that they barely move.

She's your best friend. Stop looking at her tits and ass, Cruz.

"Mikey, I'm heading out," Delilah says, hanging her apron up. Squatting, she grabs her jersey and purse from under the counter. Talk about conflicting emotions. I'm pretty certain I can hear my dick weeping and yelling *"STOP"* as she slides it up her arms covering her tempting body, but every other part of me is rejoicing at the sight of my name across her back. It makes the cracks in my heart start to fuse back together.

I follow her out the door, holding it as she passes, not wanting to look away from the seven letters stitched between her shoulders until I have to.

When we step out onto the field at the stadium, it's a maze of people. Players, staff, and spouses are chasing giggling kids and corralling them toward activities. Some of the younger guys have brought siblings or parents and are congregated by the food and drinks. The atmosphere is a lot like a carnival—if you transformed a baseball diamond into a midway. There's a face painting table teaming with kids who are hyped-up on cotton candy. Not far from that, Coach is sitting in a dunk tank while some of our rookies are lined up to take their turn dunking him.

Wren, our team coordinator, walks over, presenting us with teal cotton candy and a schedule of events.

"Hey, Wren, this is my friend Delilah."

"Nice to meet you. Welcome to your first Denver Bandits Family Day!" she says, excitedly. "Your schedule has all the activities here, and there's a map on the back. Let me know if you have questions." She flips it over, pointing to the map.

"Can you tell us about the competition for the three-legged race?" Delilah bounces on the balls of her feet next to me, her face schooled. It would be ridiculous if it wasn't cute as hell.

"Lincoln and his brother have won it three years and counting," she says with a dreamy look in her eyes.

"Well, their luck is about to run out. Anyone else we need to be on the lookout for?" Delilah asks as Wren looks between us, trying to figure out if she's serious.

"Watch out for Coach and his wife. She's feisty and has been gunning after the trophy for years. Between you and me, she's not above tripping."

Delilah's face hardens into a stoney expression. "Thanks for the heads up. I respect her drive."

Wren nods politely and walks over to where Lincoln just walked in with his brother. Pain blossoms across my sternum seeing them here together. Growing up my family was inseparable. Even with the hours my parents put into building their business, they never missed a game. When college recruiters started showing interest there was no question that Jarrett would follow in my footsteps and join me at University of Texas. That was my mom's condition, we stay together and pick a school in the south so we could come home for holidays, and they could visit as much as possible

Delilah pulls on my arm dragging me out of my memories. "We can totally take them. I'm way more agile than either of them. Do you think we will get a practice run?" She's looking up at me and peering around to check out the competition every so often. Her face is so fucking serious that I can't help but smile.

"Come with me." I take her hand, leading her off the field to an empty hallway outside the clubhouse. "Wait here for a minute."

I duck into the locker room and grab a belt out of my cubby. When I get back into the hallway, I hold it up for her to see. She claps her hands excitedly.

"Why do I feel like this is where your villain origin story starts?" I hand her the belt so she can do the honor of strapping us together. I'd be lying if I said seeing that belt in her hands didn't give me some highly inappropriate thoughts about my best friend. But like always, I bury the filthy thoughts, focusing on the task at hand.

"Stop, you love it. You are just as competitive as I am." She stoops, lining her leg up with mine. When she bends to tether us together, it's clear how poorly matched we are. I'm almost a foot taller than her. Running tied together is going to be a spectacle.

She loops the belt around our legs, just above the ankle, and stands, beaming up at me. "Please don't fall on me. You're huge and I'm just a little thing."

Damn right I am. "I promise to sacrifice myself not to hurt you. But let's try to stay upright." I wrap my arm around her waist, pulling her tight to my side. She does the same to me.

"I think we want to try to move swiftly, but in sync. It's not all about speed," she explains before we take a step, testing it out.

"Maybe we need a count to keep us on tempo with our steps."

She snaps her fingers. "I love it. Let's try it. Outside foot, on one. Inside foot, on two."

Delilah starts the count, and we successfully make it about five feet before we are tangled and leaning against the wall, both of us clutching on to each other as our bodies shake with laughter. When we pull it together and line back up to start again, we make it about twice as far.

"Let's go again. I feel like we are getting a rhythm down," I tell her before we take off down the hall like an overtired toddler—if toddlers had four, poorly matched legs that were tied together.

"That wasn't too bad. Maybe we should quit while we're uninjured," Delilah says, bending to unstrap her leg from mine.

"I feel good about our chances. Let's go see what kind of trouble we can find before we kick some ass."

The smell of funnel cakes surrounds us when we step back out onto the field. Booming cheers carry across the diamond from my teammates as Russ, the Bandits owner, takes Coach's spot in the dunk tank. Delilah sees it too and weaves through the crowd, leading us to the back of the line. When it's our turn, I hand her a ball and step back as she cocks her arm to throw. She misses the first attempt, but just barely.

"That was close. Make sure you follow through on your throw," I explain, coming behind her and wrapping my hand around hers to show her the motion from start to finish. "Just like this."

Her small body relaxes into mine, letting me lead her through the movements and she looks over her shoulder at me, nodding her understanding.

Her blue eyes are steeled with determination when she takes another ball from me and steps up to the line. Her arm comes forward, following the exact motion I showed her, and hits the bullseye with a *thud*. The sound of Russ splashing into the tub is drowned out by the roar of my teammates cheering as they look on. Lincoln's front and center, cocking his eyebrow at me in a look that says, *You're fucked*.

Delilah leaps, wrapping me in a hug. "I did it! That was so fun."

Her spirit and enthusiasm is contagious. It's hard to be anything but happy when she's enjoying herself this much. She dulls the sharp pain of missing my family.

Maybe it should concern me that I feel so comfortable with her. I know better than anyone that nothing is guaranteed, and the way I crave having Delilah around is dangerous. But I can't bring myself to care about how needing her could backfire. Right now, Delilah and baseball are the only good things in my life.

"Yeah, you did! What's next?" I survey the other games and activities looking for one she might enjoy.

Delilah steeples her fingers turning in a circle as she takes in her options like a nefarious, but adorable, cartoon character looking for her next victim. Her arm extends in front of her pointing at the strong man game, the kind where you have to swing a sledgehammer hard enough to send the weight up the pole to ring a bell. "Let's go win me a Bandits stuffed animal." If that's what Delilah wants, that's what she gets. I'll swing that sledgehammer until the first pitch if I have to because this feisty version of her only makes more want to give her anything she asks for, more than I already do.

"Piece of cake." I take the hand she holds it out to lead me towards the game, her miniature legs eating up the grass in front of us.

Thanks to my batting average, it only takes three tries before Delilah is picking out a large teal and black Bandits Mascot. Lincoln might be right, but being totally fucked is worth it when she's beaming up at me like I just gave her a new car, not a carnival prize.

The music around us fades and Wren's voice blares over the sound system making it crackle before her voice comes through. "If you have signed up for the three-legged race, please report to the first baseline."

Delilah's eyes light up and she takes off toward first base, her stuffed Bandit's Mascot clutched in her other hand. She stops in front of Wren, handing over the stuffed animal. "Guard this with your life while we crush these fools."

Wren takes it from her with wide eyes. "Okay, well, you two can line up over there and a volunteer will be over to help you get ready before I go over the rules."

The volunteer comes over and ties a thick strap of fabric around our legs, securing us together. Delilah tests it tentatively, her forehead scrunched with concentration as she tries to wiggle her leg around.

"Does it pass the test, partner?" I ask, when she bends to smooth the fabric where it's wrapped around her lower calf.

"I think so. Does it feel good to you?"

I have to bite my tongue to keep from telling her that anything that ties her to me is better than good. "Yeah, I think it'll work."

The volunteer moves down the row—securing Lincoln to his brother and Coach Wright to his wife. There are a few other staff members and teammates lined up to compete. When everyone is ready, Wren's voice echoes through the stadium again to go over the rules.

"The moment you all have been waiting for, the legendary three-legged race. Make your way to the outfield to see if Lincoln and Braxton Hayes can defend their reigning championship. The competition is fierce, with past contenders and fresh, blood-hungry ones hoping to knock them off their throne. The prize might be a trophy, but we all know everyone's after the bragging rights."

The outfield fills in as everyone lines up to watch us race. Wren continues to go over the rules. "No tripping your competitors. No trying to carry your partner." She clears her throat performatively. "I'm looking at you Lori Wright. Coach needs to pull his own weight. Lastly, trash talking is encouraged but keep it clean or quiet enough so the kids can't hear. The first team to round second and make it back to the start will be our winner. Contestants, take your mark and go on the air horn."

A crowd is buzzing as we all shuffle forward toeing the line. My arm comes around Delilah, gripping her waist. "Ready?" I sneak a glance at her face which twisted in concentration, her slender arm mirrors mine, fingers twisting in my shirt as we await the countdown.

"I was born ready. Outside on one, inside on two." The words are barely audible, blending with her nervous exhale as she repeats the pep talk to herself.

We crouch forward, taking an athletic starting position—well, as athletic as we can be tied to each other.

"On your marks, get set—" The blast of the air horn trumpets through the infield. It's chaos for a moment while everyone finds their rhythm.

"One, two, one, two . . ." I block out the cheering and noise from our competitors, hearing only the sound of Delilah's voice. Her petite body is molded to mine as we steadily waddle toward second base. To my side, I see Lincoln and Braxton lumbering alongside us. They have no rhythm but their combined size and athleticism seems to be working in their favor.

"Come on Delilah. Take the base counterclockwise and then we need to turn the jets on."

Her arm tightens around me, and she increases the tempo of the count as we approach the base. She's impressively fast, easily keeping me up with me. But they're still right there with us. I can hear them bickering under their breath.

We take off back toward first, but the turn makes us lose our cadence. It's the opportunity the competition needs to catch up. Lincoln and his brother take the lead and the Wrights are gaining on us.

"I can go faster. Don't hold back on me Cruz," Delilah barks and then increases the pace of her count again. We quickly make up the lost ground on the Hayes brothers. Pulling ahead of them with about fifteen feet left.

"Son of a bi—biscuit," Braxton yells from behind us.

"Hurry the heck up, Frank," Lori yells at Coach, before there's a shout and a thud behind us. "Did you just trip me? You did that on purpose, you turd."

"Chill out Lori. I'll make it up to you later."

"You bet your sweet a—apple you will," she huffs out.

The finish line is right there. I can hear the footsteps right on our heels, but we cross the finish line just in time. Delilah wraps her other arm around my waist, squealing in delight.

"We did it! We won!" She's trying to jump up and down, but it's more of a bounce since we are still connected.

I grip her hips tightly, trying to anchor us because I'm afraid this little celebration is going to take us down to the ground. I am about to ask her to stop because I don't want her to get hurt, but a volunteer rushes over and undoes the fabric tie.

As soon as we are free, I lift Delilah, spinning us around. Her hands wrap around my neck, and she giggles into my shoulder. "Yeah, we did. You were awesome, bestie!"

"Nice job, guys. You better watch it. We are coming for redemption next year," Lincoln says, patting my back when I set Delilah back down on her feet, face beaming with pride.

"Bring it on," I tell him as Wren walks over with our trophy. It looks as absurd as you'd expect a three-legged race trophy to look.Two flailing bronze figures ambling towards nowhere. But Delilah clutches the heavy statue to her chest like it's her prized possession.

"Congratulations guys. I look forward to the rematch next year," Wren says as she hands me Delilah's Bandits stuffed animal.

CHAPTER 15

THE TALK

PRESENT

Anytime Delilah's not at work, she's been hovering over Poppy. It's been that way for weeks. Her need to nurture, combined with two, short, away trips, means we haven't spent more than a few minutes together in almost two weeks. But she just texted me to let me know she'll be at the game tonight, and better yet, she's going to come out to Draft with us afterward.

While she's been tending to Poppy, I have been stewing over how much my feelings for her have grown and changed over the last three years. I know she feels it, too. I could see it when we woke up together after the movie night. The way she looked at me when I had her pinned down, her pulse jumping in her neck. The flare of her eyes when she dragged her gaze over me, settling on where I was so fucking hard for her. There was a heat there that you don't feel for a friend, and she was so close to admitting as much before Poppy called needing her.

I want to show her how perfect we can be together, but mostly I want her to understand that our friendship will always come first. If we decide to be together and fail spectacularly, I will still be there for her as a friend. I know I need her in my life more than anything, and I'll take her anyway I can get her.

My excitement about seeing Delilah tonight propels me through one of my best games of the season, ending with a walk-off grand slam to win the game against the Chicago Comets.

I'm riding that post-game high when we walk into Draft. She's tucked under my arm, texting Poppy. She crooks her fingers at me and cups her hand around her mouth. The bar is buzzing with noise from hyped up fans after the game. I strain to hear her over the crowd. "Poppy's going to meet us here. She's locked herself up in that apartment for long enough."

"You'll have both your besties reunited," I reply, bringing my lips to the shell of her ear. Nothing can bring my mood down. I have every intention of getting Delilah alone tonight. We are finally going to finish the conversation we started the other night before Hendrix and Poppy imploded.

The reserved area at the back is much calmer thanks to being removed from the crowd at the main bar. Delilah settles into the chair next to me at a table with a few of the guys. Xavier, Dom, and Dean are out with us tonight. We are only missing Hendrix from the crew. He wasn't in the mood to come out. He's been a grouch since everything went down between him and Poppy—even more so in the last few days, since he's been verbally accosted by all the women in his life for acting irrational.

"You were a beast tonight, Cruz. A monster on a rampage with a bat," Xavier says, pulling out the seat across from me.

"Did you eat an entire box of Wheaties this morning?" Dom echoes, pouring himself a beer from the pitcher.

I sip from the beer I'm nursing. "Nah, just feeling it today. You know how it goes. Some days you're just hot." I play it off like it's no big deal. I'm not about to tell them that my hot bat tonight was due to how psyched I'm to see Delilah tonight. They would never let me hear the end of that, and it would embarrass the shit out of her. The last thing I need is to freak her out before we have time to talk.

Dom eyes me skeptically. "Whatever it is, I want some of it. Did you change up your routine? You get laid today?" If he doesn't stop talking right this second, I'm going to be short a teammate due to justifiable homicide.

Delilah tenses next to me before she stands up to go wait for Poppy by the hostess stand so she can come back to the reserved section when she gets here.

Dom flinches when she walks away. "Sorry, Lilah. I'll be on my best behavior, promise." He says to her back as she walks away.

Wading up my napkin, I throw it, hitting him right in the nose. "You're a fucking moron. You know that, right?"

He pushes his hand through his floppy hair, looking remorseful. "Yeah, in hindsight, that wasn't my best moment."

Poppy and Delilah return to the table, and Dom keeps his word, but it's too late. My girl sits next me with her back ramrod straight—keeping a very platonic distance between us.

I'm dying to pull her aside and tell her it's not that. Assure her that Dom's just a dumbass and that there's no one else—there hasn't been for a while. I want to spill my heart until she understands *she's* the reason I played so well tonight.

Instead, I sling my arm around the back of Delilah's chair and run my pinkie finger along her shoulder. My touch seems to ease her into relaxing, her shoulders drop, and she melts into me. Everyone's enjoying themselves, talking about their plans for the next day off and the TV shows they are currently binging—until Delilah freezes next to me. I follow her hardened gaze across the bar and see Hendrix leaning against the bar, watching Poppy and Dom with barely contained rage on his face. It's the first time they've seen each other since their falling out.

Fuck that noise.

Hen might be my closest friend on the team but, there's no way I will let these two and their problems get between Delilah and me again tonight.

It's our time now. I'll haul my girl out of here over my shoulder while the world burns down around us with their drama if that's what I need to do.

Hendrix stalks over to the table. Both Xavier and Dom push away from the table and make themselves scarce out of self-preservation. Delilah is a statue next to me, muscles taut and mouth twisted like she could tear into Hendrix at any second. I drop my hand to her knee under the table. It's enough to distract her from Hendrix for a moment. My hand coasts up her thigh and back down to her knee several times. Coaxing her into dropping her shoulders before her hand finds mine and she threads our fingers together.

Poppy asks Delilah about her search for another employee at *Buns & Roses*. She's worked so hard to get here and loosening the reins didn't come easy for her. But I know she's ready to start enjoying her life outside of work.

The conversation flows, almost like it did before Poppy and Hendrix imploded. But it doesn't last long. Hendrix says something stupid, and before we know it, they've both taken off. Leaving Delilah seething in the seat next to me.

I stand and hold out my hand for her. "Let's get out of here. I'll walk you home."

Her blue eyes find mine filled with heat and the unspoken question between us, *Is this it?* Her fingers cover my palm and I pull her from her seat to lead her through the crowd and out onto the sidewalk. I keep her close to me as we weave through the downtown crowd and I'm sure she can feel my heart beating through my rib cage. She's leaving with me and not hiding from the conversation we need to have.

We walk the three blocks to her place in silence. By the time we get to her door, the tension between us is buzzing like electricity in the air before a storm. Facing me she lets her head fall against the door frame, her lip trapped between her teeth. She's fidgeting with her keys, twirling the key ring in a slow circle. Her eyes slowly lift from where she is watching them spin to me.

Even with the uncertainty swimming in her blue orbs, she looks so fucking pretty, and I'm dying to kiss her. Delilah's not shy, but she seems a little unsteady right now. She's wearing a pair of frayed black jean shorts that hug her hips and make her legs look longer than they are. My Bandits jersey is unbuttoned over a tiny white tank top, with a healthy amount of cleavage on display. She tilts her head up and wets her lips. It almost feels like a dare.

When I prop my forearm against the wall next to her head, she clears her throat. "Do you want to come in? Talk?" It comes out all rushed and squeaky, and I have to quell a laugh.

"Are you nervous?" Her eyes widen. If she thought she hid that from me, she's mistaken.

She nods her head. "No—yes. For fuck's sake. Just come inside."

This time I don't bother stopping the laugh. "Would you feel better if I told you I was nervous too?"

Her blonde hair shifts around her shoulders as she shakes her head. Wordlessly, she turns and opens the door to her apartment. "Not really. I was hoping one of us knew what the hell we were doing."

I have walked through this door with her more times than I can count, under all kinds of circumstances, at all hours—day and night. But this time feels markedly different—like this space isn't large enough to contain the air that's buzzing around us. It's only magnified during the time since we left the bar, reaching the point where it feels explosive. One spark and everything will ignite.

Our admission that both of us are anxious did nothing to calm the situation. Delilah drops her keys and purse on the counter as I follow her into the kitchen from the entryway.

"Do you want anything to drink?" She pulls a glass down from the cupboard.

"Water is fine." Delilah pulls down a second glass and moves to the sink to fill them both. I stand back, watching her as she moves, tracing the lines of her body with my eyes.

I've wanted her for so damn long, and my stomach flips at the thought that I might be on the precipice of getting just that. That hope is immediately followed by the dread that always comes after. What if, by taking this step forward and changing our relationship, we fuck it all up? What if I lose her?

I rub the ache that thought causes, trying to loosen the knot at the center of my chest with my knuckles as I follow her to the living room. When she drops onto the couch, I sink down next to her, shifting my body so I'm turned toward her.

Delilah looks at me tentatively, that bottom lip rolling between her teeth again. I want to kiss it and pull it between my teeth every damn time she does it. The realization strikes me that, if I get through this conversation, maybe I can do just that.

One of us has to start or we'll just sit in this awkward limbo forever. I clear my throat before saying, "You feel it too, don't you? The way things have changed between us? Slowly, our friendship has morphed into something more. Neither of us has openly acknowledged it or acted on it yet, but we both feel it a little more strongly each day. Like we are inevitable at this point."

CHAPTER 16

LAST FIRST KISS

PRESENT

Nothing comes out when I open my mouth to speak—the words stick in my throat, which is bone dry from the adrenaline and nerves. My hand wraps around the icy glass, bringing to my lips. It's a stall tactic as much as it's a necessity as Cruz's words bounce around my head. They hit their target dead center. Whether we've admitted what we both feel, and said the words out loud or not doesn't really matter because everything has already changed. He's no longer just my best friend, that was true as soon as I admitted my feelings to myself.

It was easier to ignore when I was with Brad and in the aftermath when I was healing. I tried to bury it, scared of how deeply I was beginning to feel that tug towards something more with him—but now it's undeniable. I'm still afraid. Fucking terrified, actually, but I can't keep ignoring it. The need to know what we could be outweighs my fears.

Cruz sits next to me on the couch with his large frame turned toward me. God, he looks good. I love how he looms over me. I'm tiny, but there's something about knowing he can wrap me in his embrace that really gets me going. His half-lidded, chocolate eyes rake over me as he waits for me to continue. Having his attention focused on me tonight feels raw, like we have stripped away the protection our friendship offered us and now everything is exposed.

"I've felt it for a long time, too. It scares me." I search his face for a reaction before I continue. "Terrifies me, actually. I don't want to—No, I *can't* lose you. What if we try this, and it doesn't work?" My voice cracks, and my throat burns as it tightens with emotion.

Cruz's hand comes to my cheek. He sweeps the rough pad of his thumb over the apple of my cheek. "Delilah, I will never let that happen." His voice is staunch with conviction, but he continues to stroke my cheek, softening the delivery. "I can't lose you either. But what if we do this, and it works? What if it's the best thing we've ever done?"

His thumb sweeps across my face again. This time catching a tear that I hadn't even realized had fallen. "How can you promise me that? Neither of us knows what the future holds. Even if we both have the best intentions, things can go wrong."

I don't need to tell him where my head goes. Cruz knows exactly how badly Brad hurt me. He was there, picking up all the pieces and helping me put my life back together.

"You're right, life is unpredictable. Things can change in an instant. But I will never hurt you the way he did. If this doesn't work out, I will still be in your life. I can't give you up. If that means we go back to being friends, I'll do that." He looks almost as fiercely determined as he does when he steps up to the plate.

There's no doubt he believes every word. In my soul, I know he would never intentionally hurt me and that he would try to salvage our friendship. But does he understand how much that is asking of both of us?

"What is this, Cruz? We keep dancing around it, but I need to know we are on the same page."

"I've wanted you for so long, maybe even since that first night when we met. But I wasn't in a place to pursue anything, and there was Brad." His name rolls off his tongue, dripping with disdain. "Regardless, even then, I thought you were beautiful."

"You called me, *Hermosa*."

"You remember?" His dimples pop like they did that first night. I thought he was cute then. But now that I know him, cute doesn't even begin to cover my attraction toward Cruz.

"I came home and googled it. I had to know what it meant. It was the first time I googled something in Spanish." I leave the rest unsaid. It's not the only thing he's said that I've translated. Slowly, over the course of the last few years I've picked up several phrases from him. Earlier this year I downloaded an app and started learning Spanish. When I'm baking in the morning I use my earbuds to practice it, conversationally. He has no idea and it's not something I'm ready to share just yet. "You say you want me. What does that even mean? Dom said—"

"Dom's an idiot. He has no idea what he's talking about. There hasn't been anyone in a long time."

"What do you mean there hasn't been anyone?"

"I think you know what I mean."

"I'm not willing to make any assumptions where this is concerned." I wave my hand between us as my heart gallops in my chest at the meaning behind what he's suggesting.

"There hasn't been anyone else I wanted. For the last two years you're the only person I've shown any kind of affection. I haven't wanted anyone else since I realized that my feelings for you are more than just physical attraction, and are anything but friendly."

"No one? Not even a hook up on the road. Because you want me?" I repeat, trying to wrap my head around the implications of what he just said. Cruz scoots in closer before he grabs my legs and pulls them over his lap. His arm comes around my shoulder.

"No one else. If I wasn't clear enough, I want to date you, and *only* you. If you let me, I'll make you mine in every sense of the word, Mi Cielo."

"Mi Cielo. That means my heaven. I heard it someplace the other day and looked . . ." A sense of déjà vu overtakes me. Visions from my dream infiltrate my subconscious. Cruz's eyes go wide. "You've never called me that, have you?"

"Where did you hear it?"

"You first. Have you called me that before?" I'm not sure why I'm pushing it. It's silly, but I feel like I have heard it somewhere other than my dream.

"Movie night with Poppy and Hen when you fell asleep in my bed. I whispered it in your ear."

My cheeks heat, and I know I'm caught when Cruz's lips tilt up in a sly smirk. I shake my head. "That's not the first place I heard it. You said it to me in a dream the night before movie night."

Why did I admit that to him? Way to jump the gun. Your best friend admits he wants to date you, and you up the ante with a sex dream confession.

The hand that Cruz has wrapped around my shoulder tangles in the hair at the nape of my neck. "What was I doing in the dream when I called you that?" He leans in closer, ducking his head to run his nose along the column of my neck before burying it in my hair and whispering, "Tell me, Hermosa."

I shiver—fucking *shiver*—at the command in his voice. But I shake my head, needing to hold on to that piece of me for now.

"No?" He pulls back, and his expression is steely.

"Nope," I tell him, shaking my head wildly. Loving the new side of him he's giving me a glimpse of. I've seen it before, but never like this, where it's aimed entirely at me, with this much intensity behind it. Usually, it takes on a more playful quality with us, like after movie night when he pinned me to the bed. That was hot as hell, but this is on a whole other level. My thighs clench together trying to stem the desire settling low in my belly.

Cruz pointedly looks down at his lap where my legs are and groans before looking at me again. "That isn't playing fair. This is your warning, I've got one more thing to say, and then I'm going to pull you into my lap, and kiss you until you can't remember anyone that came before me."

I blink at him. Once, twice, and then nod, waiting for him to continue. Although I'm not sure I'll be able to hear anything over the rushing of the blood in my ears.

"Here is how I see this going." He laces his fingers through mine. It's sweet compared to all the heat he's been throwing off. "We're going to date. Publicly. I want everyone to know you are mine, and I'm yours. I'm going to take you to dinner, movies, concerts, anything you want. When I'm on the road, we'll video chat. Now that you hired Willa—once you get her trained and you're comfortable—I would love for you to join me on an away series."

"That sounds a lot like what we do now," I muse out loud.

Cruz's hand tilts up my chin. "I wasn't done, Hermosa. There's going to be kissing. So much fucking kissing. I've waited too long to get a taste of you."

"Is that all?" I ask, raising my eyebrow.

He shakes his head. "You want more?"

I bite my lip. Cruz brings his thumb to my lip, his eyes dropping to it as he pulls down, freeing it from my teeth.

"It drives me crazy when you bite that lip." His forehead rests against mine. "When you're ready, there will be more. I want every piece of you. Are you going to give it to me?"

As I nod, he graps me by the hips and shifts me into his lap, so I'm straddling him. An unexpected laugh bubbles out of me. Even with the warning, I'm still taken by surprise.

"A nod isn't gonna cut it on this one. I need to hear the words. Tell me you want me too. That you want to be mine, and that I get all of you."

"I want you too." I rest my forehead against his. "I want you to be mine as much as I want to be yours. I'm still scared, but I think we could be great together. I need you to swear I won't lose you." But even as I make him say it, I know it's not a promise he can keep.

"Never. I swear you will never lose me. As long as I'm here on this earth, I will be yours in whatever form. Lover, friend, whatever you need from me."

"That's all I needed to know. Make me yours, Cruz."

His lips are on mine as soon as the words are out of my mouth. I gasp in surprise before I melt into him. His strong arms band around my waist, pulling me to him as his soft lips move against mine. They blaze a path from my mouth down to my neck, layering kisses across the sensitive skin there before returning to where he started.

This time I'm ready for him, and I kiss him back. His lips part for me, and my tongue sweeps against his. His answering groan only makes me greedier. The fear is still there, but it's buried so deep under the yearning that I almost forget about it.

My heart punches my ribs as his curls slip through my fingers. Nothing about kissing my best friend feels the way I thought it would. It's the best kiss of my life. And I have a startling thought that I hope it's my *last* first kiss. It's the one thing about giving into my feelings that doesn't scare me at all.

My hips rock searching for any friction they can find because he was right, that kiss did its job and I can't remember anything but him. I immediately find what I'm looking for when my pelvis tilts forward, rubbing against where he's hard. His hands ghost up my back, wrap around the base of my skull holding me tight. An instant later he breaks the kiss, our chests heave brushing together.

"Not today, Hermosa."

"You don't want—" My words die on my tongue. He lifts his hips, brushing the apex of my thighs.

"There's nothing I want more. But what we want, and what we *need* aren't always the same thing. That kiss changed everything, and we both have fears and insecurities about what this means for us. I want to take it slow and make sure that we work through those things first."

"You're bossy, and I'm not sure I like it." That's a lie. It's inconvenient that he's using logic to put a stop to the fun my body was begging for but I can't deny I like that he takes charge here.

"You fucking love it, and you're going to love it even more when I'm bossing you around in bed." His lips flutter softly against the sensitive skin making my brain short-circuit, and a moan slips past my lips.

"It's time for me to go," Cruz announces, unprompted. Kissing me on the forehead before standing and lowering me to the ground.

"You're serious?"

"As a heart attack." His arm wraps around my waist, holding me to him as I look up at him. "I meant what I said about taking this slow. It's too important to fuck it up by rushing into this. If I take you to your bedroom right now and fuck you the way I want to, you're going to spiral as soon as it's over. You'll go into a tailspin of panic and overanalyze everything. I won't risk us like that."

My forehead thuds against his chiseled chest. He knows me better than anyone, and if my reaction to the sex dream I had is anything to go on, then his prediction is spot on. It doesn't make me want to keep being greedy with him any less.

"Fine," I grumble, looping my hands around his neck and pulling him down. "But I need another kiss to ease the rejection I'm feeling."

"Don't tease me. This isn't that, and you know it," he says, pulsing his hips forward, letting me feel how his hard length presses against the front of his jeans. "You do that to me, Hermosa. Only you. Feel how utterly crazy I am for you—how much I need you."

"I feel it, alright." There's no ignoring how hard and thick he is. "You're not making this any easier. So how about you shut up and kiss me."

He does just that. His lips descend on mine. Plunging his tongue into my mouth as his fingers tangle with my hair, tipping my head back and commanding my mouth. His kiss steals all the air out of my lungs, and I can't believe this is what we have been missing out on all this time.

When my hands fist in his shirt, pulling him tighter to me, he breaks the kiss. "I need to go. My willpower can only handle so much." His voice is gravelly and low as he takes my hand and pulls me to the door.

"Fine, be that way. You should know the only regret I have is waiting this long to kiss you."

"You weren't ready until now."

One more kiss that starts chaste and turns to more, and he's gone. Leaving me struggling to wrap my mind around the fact that kissing my best friend has left me breathless and desperate for more of him. More of us. I hope like hell he's right and I'm ready because the way I'm craving him now makes me question my sanity. Kissing my best friend has made me unwell.

CHAPTER 17

LET THE DATING BEGIN

PRESENT

The scowl on my face is burning as bright as any lighthouse, warning my teammates away as I storm up the stairs of the team plane. I plow down the aisle, earbuds in, eyes down, heading toward the back, where no one will bother me. Right when I get everything I want, and finally tell the girl I've wanted for three years how I feel, I have to leave for a trip.

Should I be crabby? No, but I can't help it. After kissing Delilah and convincing her to give us a chance, all I want is to be with her, but instead I'm on my way across the country to Boston. I have only been able to see her once since the other night, and it was a quick visit to the coffee shop on my way to the stadium before practice this morning.

You wouldn't think it would be a big deal, but I waited so damn long for those few kisses. Getting her alone and exploring the rest of her body is the only thing I can focus on. It's almost enough to make me kick myself for holding back when Delilah was pushing for more. So here I am, stomping around the team plane like an oversized baby, drawing looks from everyone on board.

My phone vibrates in my pocket as I sit alone in the back, my leg bouncing in place. I glare at it before I look around the plane to find the culprit.

HENDRIX:

Is it safe to come sit by you?

He's smiling at me from his seat like my sour mood is amusing, which is ironic because he's just as much of a grump as I am these days. He may as well join me—misery loves company and all that bullshit.

I lift my hand, waving him over. It's for the best. If I had to deal with Dean or Dom right now, I'd probably lose my shit and shove them out of the emergency exit. Those two are so carefree. They float through life, enjoying it for everything it's worth, and right now, that alone is enough to annoy me.

He slides into the seat across from me, pulling his headphones off and letting them hang around his neck.

"This morning when you walked into the stadium you were like Mary Poppins, whistling and smiling from ear to ear. What changed between now and then to turn you into"—he gestures toward me—"this?"

He's not wrong. I was on cloud nine after I left *Buns & Roses*. Delilah grabbed my hand and practically dragged me into a small storage room before leaping into my arms and kissing me senseless.

She claimed her brain needed the reminder that we made the right decision to stop it from falling into an overthinking death spiral. I kissed her until she was soft and pliant in my arms, her eyes glossed over with lust. When I set her down, she declared, "Much better," before making my coffee and kicking me out, so I wasn't late for batting practice.

"I kissed Delilah," I finally admit.

"I'm not sure I see the problem. Isn't that what you wanted? Did she not like it?" He's scratching his jaw and looking at me like I'm a caged animal about to pounce.

"She loved it. It was some of my best work."

"Are you sure? You seem agitated for someone who just got everything they want."

"Yes, I'm fucking sure. I changed my mind, go back to your seat," I grumble as Hendrix cracks half a smile. It's the closest I've seen him get to losing his perma-scowl since he and Poppy broke up.

"Just trying to remind you that whatever's got your panties in a twist probably isn't that bad if you finally convinced Lilah to give you a shot."

"I got my shot, and now I'm on a plane to Boston. While she's over-thinking everything in Denver, I can't be there to remind her in person why it's a good idea."

He rubs his hands down his face before looking at me like he's about to regret the words coming out of his mouth. "You need some tips on how to keep her interested on the road?"

I blink at him. I'm not sure what he and Poppy got up to over the short time they were together before it all went to shit, but I know her too well for him to give me any suggestions.

"Nope, I can handle it on my own. Thanks."

A smirk pulls across his face. "Are you sure? I'm happy to help." As much as I want to be annoyed, I can't be. Hendrix joking with me is an improvement over mopey Hendrix. "I'm going to find another seat. You text your girl and work that magic." He stands and turns to leave, but then his steps flatter, and he glances over his shoulder. "She is your girl, right? You were smart enough to lock that down, right?"

I grit my teeth before I respond. "Yes, but we are taking it slow. I'm trying not to freak her out."

"Well played. Text her, but try not to get hard on the plane. It's uncom-fortable for everyone."

I want to comment that maybe he should focus on his relationship or lack thereof, but I remind myself that he's trying to help. Hendrix slips out of the seat and I tap on the screen of my phone, opening my text thread with the one person I want to talk to.

CRUZ:

I'm glad I got to see you this morning.
The guys aren't nearly as pretty.

DELILAH:

Not even Dom?

CRUZ:

Nope, no contest.

DELILAH:

What time do you get in?

CRUZ:

Late. It's a four-hour flight.

DELILAH:

That's past my bedtime. Call me tomorrow?

CRUZ:

Just try to stop me. I hate that I had to travel right after I finally got to kiss you.

DELILAH:

Why's that?

CRUZ:

Now that I know what it's like to have you, all I want to do is be with you.
Learn all the ways I can make your pulse race. Take you out and show how good we can be together.

DELILAH:

...

CRUZ:

God damn it. I scared you away, didn't I?
I should have taken Hendrix up on his offer.

DELILAH:

...

CRUZ:

Delilah?

DELILAH:

Sorry, I went into a temporary sugar
coma from all the sweetness.

CRUZ:

Oh, you got jokes.

DELILAH:

I blame Poppy. She's rubbing off on me.

DELILAH:

Just so you know, I miss you too.
Kissing you is my new favorite hobby.
My mouth is very bored without you.

The flight is long and boring after I say good night to Delilah. The documentary I watch on the Inca Trail is just background noise. When I realize I've zoned out for half of it, I flip through some pictures of the two of us before falling asleep for the rest of the flight.

The next day, we win an afternoon game against the Boston Marauders. The game goes long, and we get into extra innings before our closer finally shuts them down. Coach pulls me from the field for media after the game.

Luckily, they stick to asking about the game, and no one asks about Jarrett. It's been almost three years and I still get questions from the media about him around the anniversary. Maybe this is the year that they stop poking at that wound, leaving me flayed open on the dais after each game.

Delilah's missed call is waiting for me when I get to my locker. After the world's fastest shower, I hurry out of the locker room without a word to my teammates for the quick walk back to our hotel to call her back.

"Come on, Delilah, pick up," I chant under my breath, buzzing with the need to hear her voice.

"I'm here," she says as I push through the door and drop my gear bag on the bed. I turn the phone to speaker as I change out of my jeans and slide on a pair of basketball shorts. Once I'm changed, I flop on the bed, soaking in the sound of her voice and letting it wash over me.

"There's my girl. Tell me about your day. Willa started today, right?" I jump right in, not wasting a minute of the time I get with her before life pulls us in opposite directions again.

"She did! I'm so happy I found her, she'll make it so much easier for me to give up some of my control over the day-to-day stuff. She picked up on everything I showed her and had some suggestions about how to move things around, so the flow behind the counter is better when it gets hectic."

"You built this dream from scratch. If you want to step back and enjoy your life a little more, that's okay. But if you need more time, that's okay too. You've worked hard to get to this point, and I'm proud of you either way."

"I'll never completely step away. I want to be there baking and talking to customers. Having her will free up some time to focus on other parts of the business, and it would be nice to travel once in a while," she says with a laugh. "The last time I traveled was right after Brad and I broke up and crashed your family trip to Telluride."

"Those fucking beavers tried to kill us one dam at a time when we went hiking that weekend."

"It wasn't all bad. I got to meet your parents. Your mom was so sweet. Making me tinga de pollo to warm me up. The stew alone made it worth closing *Buns & Roses* for the weekend."

"She fell in love with you on the spot that weekend. But then you refused to sit and helped her make the stew instead. It's safe to say you earned a fan for life."

"Mhmmm . . . I think that's the moment she started plotting for grand-kids," Delilah says with a light laugh.

She's not wrong, but I don't want to scare her away, so I change the subject. "What's on your travel bucket list now that you have more help?"

"Someplace warm, with a beach and a drink. Maybe in the Caribbean." She sighs wistfully.

"Just a beach and a drink, that's all you need? You can't think of anything else?" I press the button to switch the call over to video.

"Now that you mention it, I'd love for Poppy to be there," she says as her face comes into view on my screen.

"Poppy? That's how you want to play this."

"Mhmmm, she's fun, looks hot AF in a swimsuit, and will get couples massages with me." She's twirling strands of her blonde hair around her finger, looking off into the distance, but the corner of her lip twitches as she teases me.

"I guess when I plan my time off in July and the postseason, I can see what the boys are up to—since you'll be traveling with Poppy." I prop the phone on the pillow and reach for the hem of my shirt, pulling it over my head and discarding it. I'm not beyond using my body to remind her what she would be missing. I readjust my position on the bed, grabbing my phone and tilt it, giving her a full view of my naked torso—flexing my abs in the process.

"I—I guess it would be nice if we had someone to fetch us our drinks. Maybe someone with broad shoulders. So that they could carry multiple drinks without issue, of course." Her eyes trace the lines of my body.

"Of course. It's just too bad you don't know anyone like that."

"Actually . . ." She taps her lip with her pointer finger. "There was this customer the other day. He was pretty flirty with me and, if I remember correctly, he had a nice set of shoulders on him."

"Delilah. Think carefully about what you're about to say." The idea of anyone else flirting with her makes me want to break someone's face, but the way her pupils dilate at my tone tells me she's enjoying this game.

She likes it when I'm bossy and demanding. I file that under fun facts I've learned about my best friend this week. Right next to how her moans sound when we kiss and the way her pulse flutters under my palm when my fingers are sifting through that hair at the base of her skull.

"I'm not feeling very cautious right now." She shifts, so she's on her back on the couch with the phone held above her. She's not wearing a bra and her tits sit high and round on her chest in this position.

I lick my lips, weighing my options on how to play this. How far to push her. I meant it when I said I wanted to take things slow but. . .fuck.

"It's not a threat if it turns you on, is it?" I watch as she rolls to the side.

"I suppose not. It's more like foreplay." She bites her lip.

"You think you're ready for that? You're not going to push me away and overthink it?"

She nods her head. Her blonde ponytail bounces behind her. "No more fighting this. I'm not going to push you away."

"Tell me about the dream, Delilah." Her eyes go wide. She thought I forgot that little tidbit, but it's burrowed its way so far into my brain that it's never leaving. In fact, it's playing a starring role in all my daydreams about her. Especially the ones in the shower with my fist wrapped tightly around my cock.

She shakes her head again. "I can't—not like this."

"You want to tell me in person?"

"No—yes. Gah. I'm not sure. I wish I wouldn't have said anything." Her hand comes up to cover her face, one blue peering out at me. "Can you just forget I said anything? Wipe it clean. Use brain bleach."

"Not possible, Hermosa. I haven't stopped thinking about it since you mentioned it. There's nothing you can tell me I haven't already imagined."

"You've imagined it?" she asks softly, peeking out from between her fingers.

I nod. "Will you tell me about it when I get home? I want to know what you think about when you dream of us together."

She covers her face with her hands. "God, you're really going to make me—"

"Delilah, I'll never make you do anything you're uncomfortable with."

"I know, and I'm not uncomfortable. It's been a long time since I have been with anyone, and Brad—it was never—he was pretty vanilla. He wasn't vocal like you."

"What do you mean?" I push away the anger that comes along with hearing his name. Even if it fucking kills me to hear about her with another man, I want to give her everything she needs. Anything she tells me I'll use to make sure it's so mind-blowing with me that she never thinks about anyone else.

"Are you sure you want to hear this?" She sighs, her lips pulling down into a frown.

"I do. I know you better than anyone else in many ways, but you never shared this part of yourself with me. Giving into our chemistry is new, and I want—no, I need to know where your boundaries lie, what you want, what you don't like."

"That's the thing. I'm not sure I have any boundaries—not with you. I trust you more than anyone else. With you, I crave it all." She blows out a breath, like she's gearing up to say something that makes her nervous. "But to answer your question, yes, I'll tell you about the dream." The words leave her mouth in a rush and hang in the air like a bomb. If she were here instead of across the country, there is no way I could hold myself back after that.

I look at her for a minute before I speak, taking time to figure out how to respond. Her cheeks are rosy, and she has that damn lip trapped between her teeth. I wish I were there to do something about it. Before I can second guess myself, I tell her exactly what it makes me want to do to her.

"Delilah, whenever you trap that pretty pink lip between your teeth, it drives me crazy. It makes me want to kiss the two little dents your front teeth leave there—sooth them with my tongue before I nip at it."

She whimpers as it springs free from her teeth. "No one's ever bit my lip before."

"No? I'm going to be the first?" She nods, and I really fucking like the sound of being her first anything. "I bet we can find some other things I can be first at. Does that sound like fun?"

"I'm not sure if I will ever get used to hearing you talk to me like that. You're still my best friend, but suddenly I get this whole other side of you." She pauses like she's not sure how much she wants to say, and it makes my skin prickle with anxiety. My girl is careful with her words. She's empathic, almost to a fault. Over the years since we met, she's gotten better at putting herself first. For a moment, I'm afraid she's trying to figure out how to tell me that this is all too much and let me down easily. "I like it. No one has ever turned me on with just words like you do."

Her praise goes straight to my head—both of them. All the blood rushes to my cock, which is only a problem because when I slipped off my jeans, I didn't put underwear on with my Basketball shorts. With how I am laying on the bed holding the phone, my cock is barely contained in the waistband of my shorts, and I know the moment Delilah notices.

She licks her lips as her eyes flick from my face to the bottom of the screen, where my crotch is barely in the frame.

"Your words affect me just as much." The color that is staining her cheeks crawls down her neck and chest. "Look at you blush for me. I can't wait to see you turn that pretty shade of pink for me in person. I'm going to make it my life's mission to discover all the things that make you flush like that. I bet you do it when you come, don't you?"

"Jesus, Cruz. I praise you for your dirty mouth, and you crank it all the way up. I thought you were going to take it slow."

"This is me taking it slow, Hermosa. I have been holding back for years. Does that scare you?"

"No. I'm not scared of how much you want me or how I feel the same. The only thing about being with you that scares me is the thought of losing our friendship if things don't go as planned."

"You can trust me to keep our friendship safe."

"I know you want that, too. But you can't possibly promise that. Neither of us can. If this ends and I lose you, I will never get over it. The last time I had a broken heart, you put me back together and made me stronger."

"Nah, you did that all on your own. I just stuck by your side. Besides, you did the same for me when I was at my lowest point. We both have a lot to lose here. But the thing is, we both have even more to gain. Don't write us off before we even get started."

"I'm not, I promise." Her eyes flick down. "God, I know how to take the sexy out of a conversation."

"Don't do that. This conversation is more important, and this thing between us isn't going away anytime soon." I slip my hand under the waistband of my shorts, adjusting myself in case she has any doubts about how much I still want her. "Nothing is happening between us until I get home, and I know you can handle everything happening here."

"Oh, I can handle it, alright."

"That's what you say now." I give her a wicked smile that makes her breath hitch. "Now let's talk more about this hypothetical vacation that you're going to let me take you on."

CHAPTER 18

SWAMP BEAVERS

FLASHBACK - 1.5 YEARS EARLIER

"Where the hell did the trail go?" Cruz stands in front of me scratching his head as he looks around. There's murky water everywhere and the next trail marker is all the way on the other side of the log littered bog.

"Are you sure this is the right way?" I ask, looking warily at the map on my phone, trying to make sense of it. Maybe if I turn my phone to the side? Nope. Still doesn't make any sense.

Everything about this trip is outside of my comfort zone. From closing *Buns & Roses* for the weekend so I could be here, to the hiking day trip that Cruz planned. Cruz has been a constant presence since I found Brad and Bridget in bed together—quickly changing from acquaintance to earning his spot as my best friend. It was his idea for me to join his family on their weekend trip to Telluride.

Despite our current predicament, it's been exactly what I needed. His family has taken me in like one of their own and being in the mountains, getting fresh air, has been like a salve for my wounded soul. God, I feel like a fool for even admitting this, but he's taken better care of me in the last six months than my ex-fiancé ever did.

"Yes, this is the right way, but these fucking swamp beavers are trying to ruin our day." His back muscles tense as I come up behind him on the last bit of dry trail.

"Don't let the beavers get you down. We'll figure it out."

Cruz glances down pointedly at my feet. He was relentless in trying to convince me to let him buy me hiking boots before the trip. But I insisted that my running shoes would work just fine. Looking at all the nasty water in front of us, he may have had a point. There's no telling what's lurking under the muddy surface.

"You don't need to gloat," I say, testing the log in front of me with my foot to see how stable it is. "It'll be like playing *The Floor is Lava*. We came out here looking for adventure, well, here it is." I transfer some of my weight to the rotten log, feeling it give a little under my foot.

"And what happens when you fall in?" he asks, his hands landing on my hips as I step up onto the fallen tree. "Who's going to save you?"

"I can save myself, thank you very much," I say, not feeling quite as brave as I sound when I step out of his grasp and the log tilts.

"Yeah, you can," he says. When I look back over my shoulder, he's looking at me with so much admiration that it makes me lose focus and I almost end up covered in the putrid smelling puddle at my feet.

Once I've successfully made it across the first log and found a stable stump to wait on, Cruz teeters his way across. "You're impressively nimble, Slugger."

"It's like you forget I get paid to be athletic."

"That's because I do. Most days, you're just my sweet friend. Not . . . all that." I wave my hands in his general direction, careful not to lose my balance.

We leapfrog through the giant mess the beavers have created taking turns leading until we get to the dry trail marker only to find more swamp.

"Jesus Christ," Cruz says, taking his hat off his head and pushing his hair back. He glances at his watch and looks up at the sky. This is really slowing us down. The trail we picked is a loop at this point, our only option is to keep going or tack on extra miles by backtracking. Neither option is ideal with the dwindling daylight.

His brow furrows as he looks around. "Hop on my back. This section doesn't look too deep. I can carry you through and save us some time. My boots are waterproof, but you'll end up with soaked feet if you try.

"Don't be ridiculous, I'll be fine." I brush him off taking a step forward. Large fingers wrap around my wrist and when I turn around and see the look of concern etched in his brow, I cave instantly. "Okay, we'll do it your way, but put those puppy dog eyes away, you used your one allowance of them."

He squats in front of me and it takes me two tries before he hoists me up like I weigh nothing. Big hands wrap around my thighs holding me tight to him as he starts his slow trudge towards the next trail marker.

Trying to make this as easy on him as possible I mold myself to his back so I don't throw us off balance which results in my face being buried against the side of his neck. Rather than turn my head away, I inhale the scent of him—leather, grass, and a salty tang from the day's exertion fills my nose. It's become a staple in my everyday life, and after the last six months one whiff and I instantly feel at ease—steady.

Just like he is now, putting me first. I bite my lip and hug him tighter.

"You good back there?" he asks, treading carefully as we approach a rickety looking log bridge.

"The best. Thank you," I say thinking about everything he's done for me this weekend alone. Having his parents around has been an unexpected perk. I was nervous about meeting them, but with my dads so far away the parental attention was exactly what I needed.

He slowly lowers me to the ground.

"Let me go first," I tell him, not waiting for the argument I know is coming and stepping up onto the log. Rickety as fuck, it flexes beneath me. "I'm smaller, it makes sense," I add before I gingerly shuffle to the other side.

Once I'm safely on the other side, Cruz slides his feet across the slippery surface. He's almost there when his front foot loses its grip and his arms windmill wildly, but there's no recovering. He lands with a splash, dotting my legs with brown mud.

I lunge forward, but he holds up one slimy hand. "Don't . . . trust me." The sulfuric fumes fill the air around me and I stop in my tracks.

"Oh, that's bad," I say pulling my shirt up to cover the lower half of my face.

He pushes off the ground, not bothering with the log anymore. He's covered in a thick, shit-colored mud that drips from him with each step. I roll my lips together and he gives me a warning look.

"Oh, my god! You look like the Swamp Thing," I finally say, unable to hold back. "Come on, the lake should be up here after this incline. Let's get you cleaned up. You stink."

"No, Delilah," he argues as I kick off my shoes and follow him towards the edge of the much cleaner water in the lake. "It's an alpine lake, it's going to be freezing."

"I can handle it, and it will be faster if I can help you." He's fully dressed, but there's no way I'm hiking back with wet clothes. I pause, letting him think I've given in. When his back is turned, I push my shorts down my legs and pull my long-sleeve shirt over my head, leaving me in only a black sports bra and boy shorts.

I follow him into the water before he can stop me, startling him when I come up behind. My teeth chatter as I scoop water in my hands to help with his back.

"Fuck, Delilah." His jaw twitches, and I know he wants to yell. He's never lost his cool with me, but I am afraid I might have pushed him too far with this one. His protective streak is fierce.

"J—just let me help so we can both get out of here faster." I try to hide my shivering, but it's impossible. I really didn't think it would be this cold. The chill goes all the way to my bones making them ache as I work to scrub his shirt clean. Tugging on it with shaky hands, I try to pull it up, but my fingers are barely working. "Ta—take it off. Faster to clean." I breathe out.

Thankfully, he doesn't argue. His eyes drop to me as he hands me the shirt. The heat in his gaze might be enough to warm me up if I wasn't turning into an ice sculpture.

He does the same to his pants. "Stand in front of me," he demands roughly. The soft look of concern returns to his face. I do what he asks, and he wraps his body around me, trying to give me some of his heat as we work quickly, scrubbing the fabric of his clothes together under the surface of the water to get the heavy mud off them.

"That's good enough. Get out of the water and get dressed," he says right before he ducks under to get the rest of the mud off his body.

I stand on the shore, my entire body shaking so hard that I can't get my feet in my shorts. Dropping his soaked clothes on a large rock near the water's edge Cruz strides over to me dropping to one knee to pull them up my legs for me.

"I'm good." I tell him, pulling my shirt on much more quickly. I'm not any warmer, but I'm motivated by the look of worry covering his features. If he thinks I'm okay he'll take care of himself.

Grabbing his pants he shoves his legs into them, not bothering with his shirt. There's a fire ring from an old campsite in a clearing off to the side of the beach. Gathering a few logs scattered around and some kindling, I watch as he works to build a fire using the emergency matches he had in the daypack he was carrying.

I grab his wet shirt and bring it over hoping the fire can help dry it.

"Come here," he says as I hang his shirt from a nearby branch. When I'm close enough, he pulls me to him, wrapping his arms around my back and rubbing his hands all over my upper body.

I sag against his chest, letting him warm me the best he can as I shake in his arms.

"Jesus, Delilah. You shouldn't have done that. You're freezing."

We stay like that until the fire dies out and we are in danger of a very dark hike back. Cruz doesn't let me get out of reach as we make the hike back. When we get to the cabin, he insists I take a hot shower, which I don't fight because I'm still cold.

Feeling achy but warmer, I join everyone in the kitchen, my mouth waters when I get a smell of onions and chicken cooking.

"Go sit by the fire, cariño," Cruz's mom, Analia, says as she works at the stove, a cutting board of tomatoes next to her on the counter.

I ignore her, walking over and picking you up the knife. "The stove puts off heat. Why don't you teach me about the dish you're making so I can make it for Cruz when he misses home?"

The spoon in her hand stops its circular motion. Her eyes crinkle at the corner, and she gives me a loving smile. "That sounds like a wonderful idea. This is my mother's recipe for tinga de pollo. Will you halve those tomatoes? They'll need to simmer in that saucepan."

Later, when we sit around the table for dinner I feel like part of the family, warmth radiating from head to toe.

CHAPTER 19

FIRST DATE

PRESENT

The morning the team flies back from Boston, I'm working on inventory in the lobby of *Buns & Roses*. Even over the sound of my Airpods playing the Spanish language learning app in my ears, my eyes shoot to the door every time the bell jingles. Only to be disappointed each time I look up, expecting to see him walking in, and find a stranger instead. I'm about to give up hope when it jingles during a lull before lunch.

Glancing up from what I'm working on, I find Cruz leaning against the doorframe, staring back at me with those hauntingly beautiful brown eyes. I can't help the squeal that escapes me as I jump out of my chair and head straight for him. His powerful arms wrap around me as I crash into his hard body.

"I could get used to a welcome like that," he says, kissing my forehead. "Think you can get out of here for a little while?"

I look around the coffee shop. It's slow, and I'm all caught up on baking. The only thing that needs my attention is inventory, but it can wait until this afternoon. It wasn't getting one hundred percent of my attention with my mind on seeing Cruz anyway. I'll be able to focus better when I get back, or at least that's how I'm justifying it.

"What did you have in mind?" My smile is so big my cheeks ache as I look up at him.

"I thought we could go on an impromptu date. I promise not to take up too much of your time. Give me an hour, tops." The way he tacks that last bit on warms my heart. He recognizes I can't just bolt and hand everything over without notice—something Brad never understood.

"I can spare some time for you. Let me just clean this up," I say, nodding toward where my computer and notepad are spread out. I pile everything up in my arms and carry it to my desk in the back, the one I never use because I would prefer to sit in the front when I can.

When I come back up front, Cruz is leaning against the wall waiting for me with a smile that tells me he's got something up his sleeve. "You look pretty sure of yourself over there."

"I have plans for my girl that I think she'll enjoy." My heart rate picks up, causing my cheeks to flush, and I'm not sure if it's because he called me his girl or that he planned something for us to do today. "Such a pretty shade of pink. I have been looking forward to seeing it in person since our call the other day." His knuckles skim across my cheek.

My eyes drift closed and I lean into the touch. "Where are you taking me?" I ask when he grabs my hand and leads me out the door and down the sidewalk.

He looks down, giving me his brightest smile, complete with panty soaking dimples. "Have a little faith in how well I know you. Would I plan something you don't love?"

"No, but I would be a little more patient if I had gotten a kiss before this surprise," I grumble as we turn toward the park.

"You'll get your kiss. When you see what I've planned, you aren't going to be able to help yourself."

My feet skid to a stop right there in the middle of the sidewalk. The abruptness takes him by surprise and he tugs on my arm, not realizing I've stopped moving. He turns to face me, looking puzzled as I cross my arms under my chest. "*Cruz Tellez,* I'm not taking another step until you kiss me."

His forehead creases at my sudden attitude. But I can't help it. I want to kiss him; I'm a heartbeat away from stomping my foot on the sidewalk like a toddler if he doesn't get over here and give me what I want.

Cruz looks me up and down before his eyes shift from teasing and playful to concerned. He steps into me, pulling me into his arms and using his finger to tilt up my chin. "What's wrong, Mi Cielo?"

"I missed you. Whenever someone walked through the door this morning, I was looking for you." My voice shakes. "I was ecstatic to see you, but you didn't kiss me. It's making me question things—did you change your mind?" I try to look away, afraid of what his answer might be.

"Hey, no. Look at me." Cruz nudges my chin again, so I'm looking up at him. Onlookers walk around us with curious looks. I'm sure more than a few have realized who Cruz is, but thankfully no one stops or pulls out a cellphone. "There's nothing that could change my mind about us. I'm sorry I didn't show you that. I was just really excited about our date. Will you let me kiss you now?"

I bite down on my lip. I really want him to kiss me, but now I feel ridiculous for making a big deal of it.

Cruz's eyes drop to my mouth. "*Delilah.* You can't bite your lip like that in public."

"I can't?"

"That depends. How okay are you with public displays of affection?" His dark eyes bore into me with an intensity I'm not used to. Cruz steps in closer, crowding me.

"I think I could deal with a little PDA." His lips crash into mine, stealing my words as he devours me. If he didn't have his arm wrapped around me,

I would tip over. The moan that escapes me is obscene when he sweeps his tongue past my lips. Definitely not suitable for public consumption, but I give myself over to the kiss, letting him show me exactly how much he missed me.

This is the kiss I was craving earlier and then some. I twist his shirt in my hands, matching his intensity before he pulls back just enough to rest his forehead against mine as we both let our breathing return to normal.

"Wow . . . I'm fucking stupid. I should have done that the moment I saw you."

It takes me a second to find my words, and I make my dad proud. The people pleaser in me wants to tell him not to worry about it, but I feel a little feisty after that kiss. "Don't let it happen again."

Cruz chuckles, and the sound vibrates through me, setting off my laughter. "I think I learned my lesson. Ready for our date now? We should hurry. Our guests are going to be very anxious to see us."

"Our guests?"

"Yep, our guests."

"You're testing my faith today, Tellez."

Cruz threads his fingers through mine as we continue toward the park. My mouth drops open when we take the path around the corner into the green space. Right there, in the middle of the opening, is the bench where we spent my birthday three years ago.

Next to it is a woman wearing a Saving Paws volunteer shirt and holding two leashes. On the other end of those leashes are two very excited puppies. They both have long hair in shades of gray, black, and white. As soon as they spot us, their tails wag, excited at the prospect of new people. And if that's not enough, there's a canvas tent decked out with pillows, snacks, and a cooler.

"This is our first date?" My voice is barely a whisper. I look at him in awe. He made it more romantic than Brad's proposal, but Cruz has always spoiled me. So it shouldn't surprise me that he excels at planning dates.

Cruz tugs on the back of his neck, looking wary. "Is it too much? We haven't been to the shelter in a while, and time was tight today. I figured we could walk puppies before lunch, and then I can walk you back to *Buns & Roses*."

"Too much? This is the most thoughtful thing anyone has ever done for me. And so very *us*. What more could a girl want? There are puppies, food, and you."

"Puppies are first. I couldn't make them wait. Look how excited they are to see you," Cruz says, leading me to where the dogs are excitedly jumping at the end of their leashes. "Hey, Simone. Thanks for coming to us today."

"I think you donate enough that walking the dogs a few blocks to spend time with you two wasn't a big deal. We appreciate all the support, Cruz," Simone says as she hands us each a leash. "I'll be back to collect them in twenty minutes. How does that sound?"

"Sounds perfect. Thanks."

I drop to my knee and give the smaller of the two some ear scratches, which quickly escalate into belly rubs. "What's her name?" I ask when Cruz joins me to give his pup some attention.

"That's Leia, and this is Han."

"Look at that. You have two different colored eyes. Aren't you handsome?" I croon to Han as Cruz rubs his back. "And you remind me of my old friend Bella. Such a pretty girl. Are you two ready for a walk?"

"They would probably rather get belly scratches all day, but let's get them some exercise before we have to return them."

When I stand, I step into Cruz and push up on my tiptoes—placing a quick kiss against his lips. It's the first time I've kissed him so casually, and it feels right. "This is the best surprise. I'm sorry I gave you such a hard time about the kiss."

He grabs my hand as we walk. "Don't apologize for communicating what you need from me. We know each other really well in a lot of ways. I might know the reason you love baking is that it reminds you of your grandma, and that your favorite food to eat when you're stressed is home-made caramels. Or that there's nothing you love more than the feeling of taking your bra off at the end of a long day—how you make that contented little sigh when you're talking to me on the phone and you can finally be free of it. But I don't know how to be everything you need in a boyfriend, *yet*." My heart stutters in my chest at the way he tacks that on the end. "I screwed up when I didn't kiss you. I want you to keep telling me when something isn't working for you so we can figure it out together."

"I have some questions. First, do I really sigh when I take it off? Second, boyfriend?"

"You really do, it's this little whimper-hum hybrid and it's adorable as fuck." Cruz looks over at me. His eyebrows knit together as we walk alongside the riverbank on the trail, both dogs ahead of us with their noses to the ground. "That's how I think of you—as my girlfriend. But we haven't actually talked about labels, so maybe I should have checked first."

"Consider this my endorsement. There's nothing I want more than to be able to call you my boyfriend. Look at me, on my first date with my new, very sexy, boyfriend."

We loop the trail while Cruz tells me about his trip to Boston. When we approach the bench at the end of our walk, Simone is waiting there, ready to take the dogs off our hands. I'm sad to let them go, but I'm ready to have Cruz to myself.

Crouching down, I give Han and Leia some snuggles before they leave. "Thanks for walking with us today, guys. We promise to come to visit again soon. Hopefully, you two will have found homes by then. If not, you might come home with me."

When Simone leaves with the dogs, I follow Cruz to the tent. Once inside, he unties the fabric strap holding the door open, and it falls shut, giving us privacy for the first time today.

CHAPTER 20

TENT IN THE PARK

PRESENT

The flap to the tent falls shut with a quiet *whoosh*. I finally have Delilah alone and I'm antsy as hell to lay her down in this tent and kiss her until it's time to walk back to *Buns & Roses*. It would be so easy. The tent floor is layered with pillows, and Delilah is stretched out next to me, reclining against the large bolster pillows.

Her long blonde hair is braided down her back today. A tiny pair of white shorts give me a view of her legs that makes it hard to concentrate on anything but how badly I want to run my hands up them and over her hips to where her shirt is knotted at her waist. The urge to push her to the floor of the tent and explore her flawless body is pressing in on me.

If I were anything like Brad, I'd be selfish and ask her for more time, so I could do just that. But I won't. I understand how much her dreams mean to her. So the exploring is going to have to take a backseat to lunch and talking.

Just as I'm about to suggest we eat, Delilah shifts next to me. Her hand comes to my face, cradling my jaw as she leans forward. "Thank you for today, Cruz. It was an amazing first date. But you know what I want more than anything right now?"

Delilah is looking at me like she wants to eat me for lunch, and I'm not going to be strong enough to say no to that.

"You promised me some firsts while you were in Boston, and that kiss earlier was fantastic, but it missed the mark in one way." Delilah's eyes drop to my lips before she bites hers. *She's trying to kill me.*

"I had plans, Delilah. I was going to feed you, maybe talk about that trip to the Caribbean some more. You are making it really hard to take things slow."

"Yeah, about that. I've already told you I'm not interested in taking it slow." Delilah moves toward me again, pressing against me and peering up at me sweetly.

Well, I can't say no to that.

I pull her to me so she's pressing up tight against me and lean down, all my focus on the bottom lip that's extra puffy from how she was just nibbling on it. Delilah's eyes widen in surprise right before I bring my mouth to hers. She's going to see that I'll live up to all my promises where she is concerned.

My tongue glides over her bottom lip before I nip at it, biting down just enough that it stings. Her hold on me tightens and when I finally slip my tongue past her lips, she's molded to me like even a millimeter of space is too much. I have to remind myself that we are in a tent in a very public park. I let the kiss go a few beats longer before I pull back.

"Hermosa, I heard you when you said you don't want to take things slow, but we are in a tent at one of the busiest parks in the city, and I need to get you back soon. I'm trying to do the right thing here and you're not making it easy."

She huffs out a sigh and pushes to sit with her legs crossed next to me. "Fine. I'll be on my best behavior, but I don't like it. Now, feed me sandwiches while you tell me about this plan for the All-Star Break."

"Is going away with me on the break something you would consider? Are you comfortable leaving *Buns & Roses*?" I ask, moving the tray of food in front of us. There are sandwiches, cheese, and an assortment of fruit. The cooler is packed full of all her favorites, root beer, seltzer water, and lemonade. Delilah points to the lemonade, and I grab it, twisting it open before I pass her the frosted glass bottle.

"I'm not sure 'comfortable' is the right word. For years it's been something I'll do someday, when it's a little more established, when I have a staff I trust, when I can step away more. I don't take time just for me very often, and that's okay because I love what I do. This is the first time I've wanted to make the space in my life to do these things." Delilah brings a strawberry to her mouth, biting the end off before continuing. "Even when I was planning the wedding and honeymoon, I didn't want to be away from the shop. That's something I should have been over the moon about."

"And you weren't excited about those things?"

Delilah tilts her head to the side as she studies me, her blue eyes searching my face. "I thought I wanted the life Brad and I dreamed up. But once it was over, all that was left was this sense of relief." She takes a drink of her lemonade. "Not at first. You saw how devastated I was. But after you helped me put myself back together, I was grateful I didn't end up married to him. The life we planned was all about him. It put me second in every way. I never wanted to take three weeks off to travel after the wedding. He pushed my concerns aside. Our marriage would have slowly sucked that life out of me."

Everything she said makes my blood pump hot through my veins because I remember watching him chip away at all the pieces of Delilah that make her special. "He didn't value your dreams because he didn't see the same things I do when I look at you."

"What do you mean?" Delilah asks, pausing another strawberry just inches from her mouth.

"Brad saw you as an extension of him, and not in a sweet way. Like you were a tool that could help him get where he wanted to be—craft the life that would make him look good. Maybe he loved you in his own way, but it wasn't the love you deserve. He looked at you and saw how you helped him do better, achieve more."

"It didn't feel like that at the time but I can see that now." Her eyes narrow as she watches me, skeptical about where I'm going with this.

"When I look at you, I see all your dreams, and my first thought isn't the convenience of those dreams, it's how I can help you achieve them. How hard you work to reach your goals is a turn on for me." I toss a blueberry into my mouth. "You're built for so much more than to be someone's arm candy. If you tell me right now that you can't take time off over the break, we will have a staycation instead. You make me a better person, always have, and all I want is to do the same for you."

Her mouth hangs open with the strawberry just dangling between her fingers. Reaching out, I pluck the juicy fruit from her hand and pop it into my mouth with a smile. Delilah stretches her legs out in front of her. My hand falls to her knee, just holding it. "Stunned silent?"

"Absorbing. There's so much that hasn't changed between us, but then you say things like that, and it's like I have to get to know this whole other side of you. You're still my best friend, but now you say things like that and"—Her body vibrates with a shiver and her eyes hood—"make me not want to take it slow in this tent."

"Don't stop on my account. I love hearing what I do to you."

"You have always been sweet, but hearing you talk about our future. It does things to me."

"I'm going to need a little more than that, Delilah. What kinds of things?"

"All good things. Like right now, I really want to spend the rest of our time kissing and take these sandwiches to go."

"I like the way you think, Hermosa," I tell her, shifting so I'm hovering over her. I desperately wish we were someplace more private than this tent and had more time together. And now that she has told me several times that she isn't interested in taking things slow, my whole-body aches to make her mine.

I brush my lips across hers, tasting the strawberries and lemonade. Delilah drops back against the pillows lining the tent floor, tugging on my neck and forcing me to follow her. Not that I have any desire to resist.

Soft light filters through the tent's canvas walls, making her look almost ethereal, with her blonde hair and bright blue eyes standing out against the colorful pillows. I could stare at her like this for hours, but she's not having it.

Her small hand sweeps up into my hair, gripping the strands and anchoring me so our noses are brushing. Those blue eyes disappear behind her lids as she arches up and licks at the seam of my lips. There's always been a balance of give and take in our relationship but I've taken the lead when it comes to the physical side and pushing the boundaries of our friendship. Her seizing control right now is the hottest thing.

My hand drops to her waist, burrowing under her shirt, searching out the feel of her skin against mine. Everything about Delilah is a contrast to me. She's soft where I'm hard. Her skin is creamy and smooth. Mine is a rich bronze color with calloused hands from years of baseball. She's petite and shadowed by my larger body, yet we fit together perfectly like this.

When the pad of my thumb brushes against the underside of a lacey bra, I swallow up her drawn-out moan. The sound alone is almost enough to make me lose control completely.

My dick takes notice and perks right the fuck up. Making sure I know he's ready and willing. "Fuck Delilah, that was the prettiest sound I've ever heard. I can't wait to hear the way you scream my name the first time you let me inside you."

"God . . . yes, please. Let's do that." Delilah pants against my lips as her legs fall open.

The temptation to slide my leg between hers and let her use me to get off before going back to work is strong, but then an idea strikes.

"After my game tonight. Come over."

"Done. I'll be there."

"Oh, my eager girl. I wasn't done, but I love the initiative." I chuckle, brushing my thumb over the swell of her breast again just for the reaction, and she doesn't disappoint. Delilah sucks in a jagged breath and shudders under me. "You're going to go back to work and try to make it through the day, even though all you're going to think about is how badly you want me." I grind my hard cock against the outside of her leg. My greedy girl likes that. She squeezes her eyes shut and nods. Her fingers tug on the hair at the base of my skull, trying to pull me back down to her, but I stay right where I am.

Not so fast.

"Then you're going to go home and get ready for the game. You'll be tempted to get yourself off. Carrying around this tension all day is going to make you ache for relief." Delilah's eyes snap open, and her breathing picks up. She's searching my eyes, looking for something, maybe trying to gauge if I'm serious or how far I'll take this. "But you're not going to touch yourself. Not with your fingers or your toys."

Delilah freezes in my arms. Yeah, she has toys. I may not have seen them, but she's been single for a long time, and is far too sensual not to have something to help her take the edge off. I bet she has several, but there's that one that hits her just right. One she uses when she's desperate and throbbing, like she will be tonight. I just smirk at her wide, blue-eyed expression of disbelief.

I run my nose along her jaw, breathing in the way she smells like coffee and caramel. "You'll come watch me play and then go home with me, where I'll take care of your pussy, the way no one else can. How does that sound?"

Delilah swallows before she looks up at me through her dark lashes. "And what happens if I don't?"

I pull back, a little stunned but not at all disappointed. The fact that she pushes back is an even bigger turn on than if she had bitten her lip and wordlessly nodded her understanding.

"If you don't, what? Come over? That's entirely up to you. I would never pressure you if you weren't ready."

"Nothing is going to keep me away." Delilah's fingers twist in my hair as she pushes up into me. "What if I don't wait for you? What if I get rid of that ache on my own? You won't even know." Her lips tip up in a smug smile. One that tells me the way we are toying with each other is right up her alley and that the punishment holds just as much appeal.

I shift so that I'm straddling Delilah. Two can play this game. I drop my hips down, giving her the pressure right where I know she needs it the most.

"I'll know. By the time I get you back to my apartment, you'll be so needy for me that you'll be dripping. Every brush of your thighs together is going to remind you how empty you are. How badly you need me to fill you up."

Delilah's mouth falls open in the most adorable little, "Oh."

"Yeah, 'oh.' Can you be a good girl and wait for me?"

Delilah nods, swallowing as her eyes drop to my lips. But I shake my head. *This is going to be so much fun.* Pushing up off the pile of pillows, I hold out my hand.

CHAPTER 21

DANGEROUS GAMES

PRESENT

His hand? He's giving me his hand after the most erotic speech I have ever heard?! I'm tempted to slap it away, but I give in, allowing him to pull me to my feet. I study his face, trying not to get lost in his deep brown eyes.

He's got that same determination that serves him so well on the field written across his stupidly handsome face, except right now there's a bit of arrogant mischief there as well. Cruz really expects me to go back to work and then sit through his game after *that*. And now that he's planted that seed in my head, he knows damn well all I'm going to think about are the things I can't do.

"You think you're so clever? This is a dangerous game you're playing." My fingers climb up his chest before I push up on my toes and lightly kiss his jaw. I lean in slightly, ensuring my hardened nipples brush against his chest. I might not have a clue how I'm going to torment him, but I'll figure something out.

"There's nothing you can do to me that's going to be worse than having to wait as long as I already have for you," he says with a cocky grin as he grabs the plate of sandwiches and holds it out to me.

I swipe the turkey and cucumber sandwich, ducking through the opening to hide my bluff and wait as he follows me. Leaving behind the serenity of our lunch date, his large hand warms the small of my back as we stroll through the park.

"Is Poppy coming to the game with you tonight?"

"She said she was yesterday, but I haven't heard from her today." Cruz pulls me to his side, making room for a runner to pass. He stiffens beside me unexpectedly, and then I hear the song blaring from the approaching runner's phone. It's one I know well—he plays it when he misses his brother.

I step in front of Cruz, my arms going around his neck and pulling him to me. "Cruz, look at me." He stands there frozen for another second before his arms come around my waist and he rests his chin on my head.

"I haven't heard it in a while. It took me by surprise. God, I miss him. I can't believe it's been three years. And still no answers. No one has come forward with anything to help us figure out what happened before he was found on the beach. No one's been held responsible. Just a gaping hole in the world where Jarrett used to shine."

I comb my fingers through his hair, trying to comfort him. I don't know what it's like to lose a sibling. Or not have any closure on why they were taken too soon. I know there's nothing I can say to ease his pain. I'm not even sure that finding out what happened or who was to blame will help. Cruz clutches me tight to his chest, almost like he's afraid if he lets go, I'll slip away. "What can I do?"

"Just let me hold you for a minute." So, I do. Right there on the sidewalk in the park with my sandwich dangling from one hand and the other burrowed into his hair, massaging his scalp. When Cruz's grip on me loosens, he keeps me tucked tight against his side as we walk back.

"I'm sorry, Delilah," Cruz tells me when we stop in front of the coffee shop.

"Never apologize for your grief. You have every right to those feelings. I'll always help you through them, no matter when and where they creep up. The middle of the sidewalk, at the stadium, in a restaurant. It doesn't matter. I'll stop and hold you."

"What would I do without you? For years, you've been the unfailing light that guides me from my darkness." His chin rests against the top of my head before his lips tenderly skim across my forehead. "I'll see you tonight?"

I nod up at him. "I'll meet you after the game. Are you going to be okay?"

"I'm good now. I just needed a minute. It's easier when I'm holding onto a reminder of all the good things in my life." His arms contract around me, looking down at me with softness reserved for me.

Pushing up on my toes, I link my hands behind Cruz's neck and pull him to me for a kiss before he walks back toward his apartment. Before I've even tied the knot on my apron, my phone vibrates with a text.

CRUZ:

Don't think I forgot about what I told you at the park. Hands off. That pussy is mine.

His words hit their target as a dull pulse starts between my legs. I pocket my phone without responding. My retort needs to set him on fire. And right now I'm so flustered my fingers can barely form a bow to tie off my apron. Getting used to this bossy, uber-sexy side of him is going to take me a minute, but I'm not mad about it. Not at all.

The words he said earlier replay in my head, *"Carrying around this tension all day isn't going to feel good, but you're not going to touch your-*

self." He's right, I'm not going to. He painted quite the picture of how delicious that build up will be when I finally get him alone tonight. Cruz might not realize it, but he's unlocked a part of me I didn't know existed.

Since I was a child, baking has been something that helped me clear my head. As early as I can remember, my gran came over, without fail, every Sunday and we spent the morning baking while my parents went out for a day date. She passed away when I was fourteen and Pops stepped in to fill her shoes, helping me launch the early version of *Buns & Rose* from their kitchen. Back then, I only baked treats for friends and family. The one thing that has never wavered is how at peace I feel in the kitchen. Whether I'm making a favorite recipe or experimenting with something new. There is nothing serene about the way I feel right now.

Mikey has called me out more than once for the far-off look in my eyes, scolding me for drooling. It's pointless. I shift gears, giving up any hopes of perfecting the "Everything but the kitchen sink" cookie bars I was working on and turning them into regular old cookie bars with the addition of M&M's.

"What did you do with your hunky baseball player while you were gone? You have that glazed over lusty look in your eyes."

"Do not." My protest is so weak, not even I'm convinced. I caught sight of myself in the reflective surface of the espresso machine earlier. Mikey's right, I so do. There's no denying my dazed eyes and slightly parted mouth. It's been this way all afternoon.

Heat crawls up my neck as I recall the way Cruz spoke to me earlier. I knew he had a filthy mouth, but I didn't expect him to take it this far. Not that I'm complaining, it's the best kind of torture.

"Okay. Whatever you say. You're thinking of him now, aren't you?" Mikey says with a laugh as he wipes down the counters. "Yeah, you are. That man has big dick energy and you're ready to ride."

"He does, doesn't he? How come I never noticed it before?" I wonder out loud, completely ignoring his very accurate innuendo.

It's a mistake. Mikey loves gossip, and he's like a dog with a bone, unwilling to let it go.

"You know how race horses wear blinders, so they can't see anything but what they're supposed to be focused on. That was you with Cruz. He was your friend, and you refused to see anything outside those boundaries. Like how hard he's been pining for you all these years."

"What? Pining for me? No, that's not right."

"For. Years. Delilah," Mikey says, drawing out the words and tossing his rag down with a dumbfounded look.

The door to the shop opens and Willa walks in. Looking adorable as hell in a pair of comfy bike shorts and an oversized concert shirt. She's taking a shift tonight to prep for the morning. Which means I don't need to be up early because Mikey is opening, and she'll have all the baking done.

"Willa, help me out," Mikey calls dramatically. "What vibes do you get from Cruz?"

Willa looks between us for a moment nervously. "It's fine. You can say what you think." I reassure her. I can't imagine she expected to walk into this tonight.

"Daddy vibes."

My mouth falls open. That is not what I was expecting to come out of her mouth. "Um, what now?"

"And who are they aimed at?" Mikey asks, putting Willa on the spot.

"Lilah, you really don't see this?" Willa asks, her head tilted to the side. She may have been reluctant initially, but she's all in now.

"I do now, but I didn't before."

"That man has been after you for years. All that sexy energy has always been aimed at you. Think about it, babe. He makes sure you have someone walking with you to the stadium for games. Does he ever let you walk home alone or even take an Uber?"

"No, but that's because of Jarrett."

"Maybe that's why it started, but he's possessive of you. He's always got a hand on you when you're together. Like being within arm's reach keeps you safe. It's not a bad thing, but it is probably heightened because of his past," Willa chimes in. When she met him and asked me how recently he had lost someone. She's incredibly observant as a grad student pursuing a master's for counseling with hopes to open a practice that focuses on kids dealing with loss.

"Do you think he's still struggling more than he lets on?"

"I can't answer that. I don't know him well enough to give an opinion, but I think you probably know the answer."

I think back to earlier when we heard the song in the park and the way he froze up. Losing Jarrett was devastating. He lost his brother, his best friend, and his future teammate. They had big plans together. Then to have no answers about what exactly happened that night and how Jarrett ended up in the hospital. It messes with his head especially this close to the anniversary. There's no closure.

"How did we go from me blushing about you two calling him daddy, to this?" I drop my head into my hands.

"Loving Cruz isn't going to be the hard part. There's still a lot of pain buried in there under that fun, sexy, best friend package. Not everything with him is going to be easy," Mikey adds. He's known Cruz almost as long as I have and spends enough time with him around *Buns & Roses* to have some perspective.

"Who said anything about love?"

"Um, your heart eyes," Willa declares with a laugh.

She's got me there. I have been flitting around the coffee shop like a lovesick teenager after every encounter with him since that first kiss.

My phone chimes from where it's plugged in behind the counter. I grab it off the wood shelf it's on and unlock the home screen.

CRUZ:

Can't stop thinking about seeing you tonight.

Included with the sweet message is an image that is anything but sweet. It's a selfie of Cruz taken in front of the mirror in the weight room at the Bandits stadium. He's got a massive dumbbell resting on his knee and his phone in the other hand as he sits shirtless on the bench. It's not like I haven't seen him without a shirt before, but the smoldering look in his eyes should come with a warning label.

That coupled with the light sheen of sweat covering his caramel skin and how he's sitting with his back curved, making every single valley and ridge of his toned stomach stand out. Well, it's enough to make a girl drool, and both Willa and Mikey notice rushing over to see what's got me staring at my phone with an awestruck look.

"Hot damn."

"Jesus, girl. You are in trouble."

They both hum in appreciation.

"Hey, that is not for your eyes," I scold, locking my screen quickly.

"What's tonight?" Mikey asks with no shame at all that he's continuing to poke around.

"Um. He asked me to come over after the game."

"Mhmmm. So much trouble." He cackles, and it's downright villainous. He's enjoying that I'm thrown completely off axis. "Are you two together now?"

"What is this, an interrogation?" A nervous laugh escapes me. I know he called himself my boyfriend, but that label doesn't feel quite right. He means more to me than any boyfriend ever has. It almost feels like a step backward for us. "We are, but it's new."

"Is it time for me to clock out? I need to go find Mitch?" Mikey whines dramatically as he hangs up his apron.

"Yes, please. Go home to your husband. I can't deal with any more of your nonsense right now." I bump his hip with mine playfully. We're friends, and he could say pretty much anything without offending me. But their combined attention and questions about my relationship with Cruz has me feeling a little exposed and nervous about tonight.

After Mikey clocks out, Willa and I spend a little time brainstorming a few fresh additions to the bakery case. She eventually kicks me out, claiming there's no way she'll be the reason I'm not primped and prepped "within an inch of my life" for my night with Cruz, so I head back to my apartment to do just that.

As I'm unlocking my door, my cell phone rings and I slide it out of my back pocket. Cruz's name lights up the screen along with a picture of the two of us after a hike together last summer. It's one of my favorites. Cruz's wide smile is prominent, and it makes me happy every time I see it.

"Hey, Cruz," I say as I pull the door shut behind me. I lock it because I know he would scold me if I didn't.

"Hermosa, you left me on read all afternoon. I hope you weren't busy breaking the rules. That would be very disappointing." He tries to play it off like this is all fun and games, but I can hear the edge of worry in his voice that I didn't text him back for another reason. It's barely detectable, but it's there.

"I've been a good girl, but I just got home, so anything is possible." I'll let him keep this playful for now, even if I know we'll have to have a deeper talk about how he's doing soon. "You weren't playing fair with that photo earlier."

"I only recall setting one rule." His voice is rich and deep. I can imagine how it would rumble against my skin if he was here holding me.

"And does that rule go both ways?" I walk through the apartment toward my master bathroom. Setting the phone on the vanity counter, I pull my shirt over my head and drop it in the hamper. My fingers work the button on my shorts free just as Cruz answers.

"Of course. I wouldn't expect you to do it if I wasn't going to participate."

A plan forms in my head. I swipe out of the call and open my camera, propping the phone against the mirror. "And where are you now?" I ask to be sure he's not in the team lounge surrounded by teammates. This is a private show.

"At home. I have to meet Hendrix to walk over in a while."

"Good to know." My voice is infused with an innocence that has no business being there, given what I'm planning. With the button popped open on my shorts, I remove my bra and click the timer button. One arm crosses over my chest and the other dangles the lacy teal bra over the hamper. I let the timer expire, capturing the photo. Before I can think too hard about it, I navigate to our text thread and send it.

I know the moment it comes through.

"Fuck, Delilah." Cruz's voice is rough and when he says my name like that, I fear my plans may have backfired. That thrumming pulse that's been plaguing me all day intensifies, but I'm too invested to stop this now. This time I hit the button and turn around, looking over my shoulder as I push my shorts down my legs. Another text sent and a sharp inhale on the other side of the phone.

I think I have him right where I want him when my phone rattles against the vanity with a message from him. When I open it, I find a picture of Cruz in bed shirtless with the camera held low against his thighs, giving me a view of his hard cock covered only by a pair of tight black boxer briefs. I saw him like this the other night, but we were still toeing the line of our friendship and I didn't soak it in the way I am now.

Trepidation washes over me and I'm split between hoping it's the angle of the camera creating an optical illusion and hoping that things are exactly as they appear. Everything about the morning after the *Avengers* movie night is a little hazy. That's bound to happen when you wake up with your best friend's impressive morning wood knocking on your backdoor. I swallow, but it doesn't help. When I speak, the words come out huskier than I expected.

"Mikey is opening tomorrow, and Willa is taking care of all the baking. So, I won't turn into a pumpkin at nine o'clock tonight."

"That's good, because I wasn't planning on getting much sleep tonight. You're staying over tonight, right?" His tone slips back from commanding to uncertain with his question.

"Mhmmm. But first I need to shower the smell of coffee and sticky buns off me," I tell him, hoping to refocus on my plan.

Sliding my matching underwear down my legs, I drop them on the top of the rest of my clothes and send that picture.

"Don't even think about touching yourself in that shower. That pussy is mine tonight."

"I wouldn't dream of it, but Cruz, I'm already soaked for you," I tell him as I turn the water on and strategically prop the phone up on the ledge in the shower. I click the timer button one last time and duck under the water. Getting creative with the angle, I run my hands up my body, so my fingers are threaded through the hair at the base of my neck, which covers my chest while leaving my ass on display for him. "Good luck with that hard on. I'll be waiting for you after the game." I disconnect and send the last picture before resting my head against the tile, letting it cool my heated skin.

My whole body is tingling with anticipation and probably a little adrenaline. I have never been that bold with anyone, but Cruz has always made me feel like the best version of myself. Beyond that, he makes me feel safe in a way that doesn't compare to anything else I have ever felt. The way he speaks to me and looks at me fuels my confidence and makes me feel sexy.

And do I ever feel it now. Never has a shower called for a little sexual self-care more than this one does. If I gave in, I know it would be his name on my lips, his face starring in my fantasies, his hands stroking my skin. I'm flushed with heat from head to toe as I grab the shampoo and turn the water temperature down, allowing it to cool me.

As I wash my hair, even the beat of the water against my skin is over-stimulating and not at all the touch that I need right now. How the hell am I going to sit through a game like this with Poppy? She's going to pick up on this right away and she's never been shy about saying what's on her mind.

I groan aloud while I rinse the suds from my hair and move on to conditioning. While the conditioner sits in my hair, I quickly use my body wash, being careful to avoid any areas that are just going to push me closer to the edge. Thankfully, my fine blonde hair means shaving this morning will hold me over because I need to get out of this shower before I do something I'll regret.

By the time I'm done rinsing my hair out, the thought of a towel touching my skin is almost unbearable. I wrap the towel loosely around me and pat myself dry quickly.

I haven't looked at my phone again, fearing that any response from him will make me crack. As good as that sounds right now, there's no denying the payoff will be better if I play the game. By the time I get him alone tonight, my body will be begging for him and I'm certain that he will feel better than anything I can give myself right now.

Once I'm dry, I grab a pair of frayed gray denim jean shorts and my black and teal Bandits jersey with Tellez spelled out across the back. That was the easy part. Shifting through my drawer of lingerie is a bit more challenging. I run my fingers over the mesh fabric of a teal bralette and the matching underwear. I try to picture Cruz's face when he sees me in them, the way his dark eyes widen and how he might run his hand over his jaw as he takes me in.

Grabbing them, I slip them on before I dry my hair. Once that's done, I apply a little makeup and retrieve my phone from the bathroom. I frown when I grab it and see only a text message from Poppy.

POPPY:

I have a lot of things to tell you.
See you at Buns & Roses.

CHAPTER 22

UNDER THE LIGHTS

PRESENT

When I push out the door onto the sidewalk, my phone vibrates from my pocket. Pulling it out, there's a text from Cruz.

CRUZ:

Do you know how uncomfortable it is to wear a cup when you've been hard half the day? It's not great, Hermosa.

That makes me snort out loud. I should probably have a bit more sympathy for his predicament, but I feel giddy that I did that to him after wrestling with self-doubt. Typing while I walk toward the coffee shop to meet Poppy, I feel the lightness from earlier return chasing away all the anxieties that I wasn't enough.

DELILAH:

I can't say I know that specific feeling, but I'm sure it's a lot like drying off with a towel when your nipples are tight and achy.
Every brush of the soft fabric was torture.

CRUZ:

That visual didn't help.

DELILAH:

Wasn't trying to, novio. You started this and you'll be just as much of a mess as me later.

When I look up from my phone, I see Poppy leaning against the brick wall, waiting for me with a dreamy smile gracing her pillowy lips. She's also wearing a jersey that looks new. It's in the team's current black and teal design, matching mine, which is unexpected because she hasn't been to a game in weeks and still isn't speaking to Hendrix.

"Turn around," I say, twirling my finger in the air, indicating I want to see her back. That look on her face and the new jersey. It's clear something changed overnight. She brushes her braid over her shoulder and turns to the side, showing me her back while she beams at me over her shoulder.

"That's a recent development. Hen must have done some serious groveling to earn another chance with you."

Poppy gushes as we start our walk toward the stadium.

"He did. He apologized for being a colossal idiot and explained something about his past that made him think the worst of me. I get why he jumped to the conclusions he did, especially after he told me about his ex and all the ways she messed him up. And that's not all, Janet is his Nana."

That makes me stop on the sidewalk. "Seriously? I didn't see that one coming. We had her pegged all wrong," I confirm, picturing the older women Poppy and I befriended a few weeks earlier. She joined us for a night of drinking wine and watching baseball. But I never would have guessed she was Hendrix's infamous grandmother.

"Our new friend and fairy godmother is Hendrix's grandmother," Poppy asserts with a chuckle.

"I pictured his grandma as this sweet old lady. The way he always calls her at night and the fact that she brings him plants. I pictured someone a little less vibrant and youthful."

"For some reason, I kept picturing Grandma Tala from Moana."

I snort out a laugh at that visual, personality wise it's not far off. "I'm glad he finally listened to reason and apologized. Do you think you guys can make it work this time?"

"I do. I missed him even though I was angry with him. He's the first guy since Paul to make me want to try, and that's gotta count for something. How are things going with Cruz since the kiss?" Poppy glances over at me with one coppery eyebrow raised at me.

"Um . . . He took me on a date this morning. He had Saving Paws bring over some puppies to walk and had a cute canvas tent set up for lunch so we could have some time alone during a quick break from the coffee shop."

"That's the sweetest thing I've ever heard. I'm impressed that he came up with such a cute first date. Wait, that's what it was, right, a first date?"

"Yeah . . ." I pause, debating if I should tell her about the not-so-sweet parts. But I need to talk to someone about this. "Is Hendrix a dirty talker?"

That elicits a surprised snort from Poppy. "Yeah. That first road trip after we met, the things that came out of his mouth over the phone were almost enough to get me there."

See, now that doesn't surprise me. But apparently I've done a bang-up job of being willfully ignorant to my best friend's charms.

"What aren't you telling me?" Poppy eyes me suspiciously.

"That sweet date turned not-so-sweet fast. Like in the blink of an eye." I walk her through the date and how it escalated from Cruz pinning me down and kissing me, to when I asked for more and how he made me wait.

I leave out most of the details because I want to keep those just for myself but give her enough to paint the picture.

She fans her face dramatically. "I'm a little jealous. That's like, super genius dirty talk. God, you must be wound so tight right now. I'll be careful not to brush against you. Cruz would never forgive me if I accidentally made you go off after all that work he put into getting you primed for tonight."

I laugh dryly because it's too true to be funny. A light breeze in the right place would be enough at this point.

"I'm honestly not sure how I am going to survive this game."

When we get to the stadium, we stop to grab a beer and have a quick chat with Betty, our favorite concession worker. "A small one for me tonight Betty," I tell her when she grabs the large cup.

"She needs to be sober for her evening with Cruz tonight. He's laid the groundwork for a very exciting night together," Poppy jokes and Betty gives me a wink.

"I got you, girl. I'll give you one for the nerves now. Better to have your wits about you with a man like Cruz."

"Why does everyone keep talking about him like that?" I grumble, taking my beer from Betty and bringing it to my lips for the first sip of cold lemony goodness. "I know I had stupid friendship blinders on, but really, it's been years and I still missed the signs?"

"How that man looks at you is enough to set the world on fire," Poppy comments before Betty adds.

"That combined with all that rizz. I hope you are prepared."

"Rizz, really?" I give Betty a questioning look. She's cooler than me, but her use of the word surprises me.

"I heard some frat-looking college guys saying it at a game. I made them explain it to me," Betty says with a shrug of her shoulders as she finishes pouring Poppy's equally tiny beer.

"Why is mine small too?"

"I see that James jersey. You're going to need to be on top of your game tonight too, aren't you?"

That makes Poppy's cheeks flame pink, but she nods. "Good thinking, Betty," she says, and slips a twenty into the tip jar as I swipe my card to pay for our drinks.

As we turn to walk away, Betty calls out to our backs. "I expect an update at tomorrow's game, and both of you better be limping."

The guys are heading back toward the dugouts from warmups as Poppy and I take our seats in the outfield. When Cruz and Hendrix get to the railing, they both lean against the padded barrier. Cruz is the first to glance up at the seats. He nudges Hendrix with his elbow, nodding toward where Poppy and I are both wearing big goofy smiles.

"Those freaking baseball pants," I whine, as Cruz nods with a devilish grin, acknowledging that he saw me and he knows the state I am in.

"I think I'm gonna make Hendrix wear a pair for me one of these times."

"Seriously. Can we talk about anything else? No sexy talk. I can't deal with it right now."

Poppy throws her head back and laughs at my discomfort. "Okay. I'll try to keep myself under control. It's hard with all this." She waves two floppy hands towards the dugout. *Trust me, I know.*

The Bandits come out strong and take the lead from the first inning. When Cruz takes the plate, I watch anxiously as he traces a "J" in the dirt. Right before he gets into his stance, his eyes zero in on me and he winks, looking far too pleased with himself. It works. That cocky self assured attitude only makes me want him more desperately than I already do.

The first two pitches are balls and Cruz sits back waiting for the one he wants. When the third one is a fastball that comes in right over the plate, Cruz loads and swings with a speed and precision that is impressive, sending the ball sailing right up and over our heads into the second level.

Poppy and I are hoarse from cheering by the sixth inning when Dom dives for a catch in center field that looks impossibly out of reach but by some physics-defying miracle it sticks in his glove like a snow cone, and he comes crashing to the ground. Cruz is right there with him, ready to back up the play. He calls out and Dom flips it to him so quickly that I almost miss it. Cruz has the advantage of being on his feet to make the throw into third just in time to get the runner out. It's a beautiful play that's sure to end up in the highlight reel for ESPN.

I let my loudest whistle loose, earning me a smirk from Cruz as he and Dom celebrate. This is my favorite part about these seats. Sure, the WAG section he's always trying to get me to sit in has impeccable service and is closer to the dugout, but out here I can act like a fool cheering and heckling my best friend on each night.

There's a levity to Cruz as the outfield comes together to celebrate. The grin that explodes across his face is brighter than the stadium fireworks. I love seeing him like this. Free from worry, it's a rare but beautiful sight. He hides it well from everyone else, but I see the grief he carries with him daily and the way it makes him fear for all the people in his life. This is the life he deserves, on the diamond with his best friends, looking untroubled.

The game is fast-paced and exciting, with the Bandits leading the entire time. It's enough that I almost forget about the achy need sitting low in my core. That is, until the 8th inning when Cruz jogs into the outfield, points right at me, and mouths, *"You're mine."*

Shots fired, woman down.

I can't even tell you what happens for the rest of the game as I'm reduced to a fidgeting puddle of need. I know the Bandits kept their lead for the win, but that's almost wholly because of the fireworks going off at the end of the game.

Poppy tried talking to me a couple of times and I remember nodding and agreeing to which she laughed. Other than that, I was so lost in my thoughts about Cruz and tonight that I basically blacked out—both the excitement and the nerves taking over.

As we walk through the tunnels under the stadium to meet the guys, I'm wringing my hands. Am I really about to sleep with my best friend? Even though neither of us has said it, we both know that's where tonight is leading.

"Lilah, stop for a second," Poppy says, grabbing my elbow and pulling me off to the side of the concrete tunnel. She leans against the off-white wall with the teal Bandits logo emblazoned on it. I mirror her stance, facing her with my shoulder against the cool brick. Poppy's bright green eyes shine with concern as her brow wrinkles with worry. "Talk to me. What's going through that pretty blonde head of yours?"

I sigh, not sure where to start. Dropping my shoulder, I let my head rest on the wall. "I don't know. I can't get out of my head."

"Are you having doubts about being more than friends?" she asks, toying with the ends of her red braid as she searches my face for any clues about how I'm feeling.

"No." My answer is immediate and certain. "That's not it. I know I want this. It just all feels very real. I haven't been with anyone I care about since Brad, and even the casual encounters have been few and far between."

Poppy nods, letting me continue with my thoughts. We are close enough that she knows how guarded I have been with that part of my life for the last few years. It's something we have in common. After her ex betrayed her trust in a completely different way, she shut out the possibility of finding someone until Hendrix.

"You know what it's like to hold that part of yourself back. Now that I'm opening myself back up, and with my best friend of all people, tonight feels monumental. Like it's going to change everything."

"I know it does. Can I give you some advice?"

"Please," I practically beg, "because I feel like a floundering mess. He's going to take one look at me tonight and decide I'm not ready. He'll try to get me to wait, and I don't want that. I am ready—so freaking ready." My laugh comes out a little high-pitched and manic.

"Try not to focus on the big picture. Just stay in the moment. These guys, with their singular focus on us—it's consuming, and it's easy to get caught up in that. Let him sweep you up in the moment and don't focus too much on what it might mean. You'll get lost in your head."

"I think I can do that."

"Good, but know you don't have to. That man only wants what's best for you. He'll go at whatever speed you need."

"I know, but I want this. No, I need it. It took us years to get to this point. I don't want to wait any longer." Saying the words out loud just makes me realize how true it is. This is the path we are meant to be on—the two of us together, I'm sure of it. Pushing off against the wall, I squeeze Poppy tightly. "Thanks for the pep talk."

"Anytime, now let's go get your man," Poppy says before throwing her arm around my shoulder and walking down the tunnel toward the family waiting area with me.

When we get to the area where friends and family wait, the players are trickling out of the locker room.

"Are we going to see you guys at Draft tonight?" Dean asks. He's got that clean-cut look with a little bit of a broody personality that drives girls crazy. He's a bit more reserved than Dom, even though the two are practically attached at the hip. But there's a definite difference—Dom is the playboy ready for a good time, while Dean tags along. He's not as light-hearted. It's obvious that he prefers to be in Dom's shadow in social situations.

"Not tonight," Poppy answers, looking at the door for a moment before looking back at Dean and Dom. "Hendrix and I are going to grab dinner, just the two of us." A smirk crosses her face before she looks at me, waiting for me to respond.

"Nope. Cruz and I have plans." That's all I'm willing to say. I don't know what he's told the guys, and I'm already too on edge to have that conversation right now.

Dom has a knowing look in his eyes and when he opens his mouth with, what I'm sure would have been a smartass remark, Dean backhands his stomach, causing him to double over and wheeze.

Thank you, Dean.

Dom is known for the way he lives life to the fullest and that extends to his mouth. He will say anything that pops into his head, no matter how brazen. With the way I'm teetering between eager and nervous, I don't need his commentary on Cruz and me.

When the door swings open this time, it's Cruz and Hendrix walking out of the locker room, both laughing and looking content after a stellar game. Before Hen has even cleared the door, Poppy takes off toward him, throwing her arms around his neck and long legs circling his waist. She peppers his face with kisses in a display that puts movie night to shame.

"Hey there," Hendrix says, holding her tight to him. "Are you ready for our date?"

"I think that's pretty obvious," Dom says sarcastically as he nudges Dean with his elbow. "Ready to get out of here? I don't want to catch what they have."

Dean just grunts, but from the look on his face, I'm not certain that it's in agreement.

"You just wait." Hendrix shoots back, lowering Poppy to her feet but keeping her pressed up against him. "It's coming for you, and you might not realize it now, but you'll welcome it with open arms when you meet the right girl."

Poppy beams up at Hendrix, but my attention is pulled away when I feel Cruz step up behind me, his hand finding my waist. My skin tingles with anticipation as he leans in. *"And are you ready for me, Hermosa?"* His voice is gravelly and laced with double meaning, the term of endearment rolling off his tongue in a way that makes me clench my thighs together.

"Later guys, have fun," Dean says with a knowing look on his face, but thankfully he stops there, which might make him my second favorite Bandit. The two very unattached and happy-about-it teammates head off to see what shenanigans they can get into tonight. With those two, the possibilities are endless.

"Remember what we talked about," Poppy says, leaning in, so her voice doesn't carry as Hen pulls her toward the exit.

"I'm about to change your life with these tacos, babe," Hendrix says as they walk away.

"If the tacos are the highlight of her night, you aren't doing your job!" Cruz shouts at his back, earning him a middle finger from his teammate as they disappear into the parking lot.

When the door swings shut behind them, I'm distinctly aware that it's just the two of us alone in this hallway. I focus on the advice Poppy gave me and stay in the present instead of getting sucked into the meaning of it all.

Turning to Cruz, I run my hands up the hard planes of his chest. "Let's get out of here." The words make his dark eyes seem even deeper, his pupils expanding so there's barely any of the chocolate color I love so much.

CHAPTER 23

DTF

PRESENT

When Delilah asks me to take her home, it's music to my ears. She's peering up at me with those big blue eyes wearing my jersey. She's come back to my place more times than I can count over the past three years, but this is different, and we both know it.

Her golden hair is down in waves, drawing my fingers to it. I push a piece that's fallen forward behind her ear. She wore her hair like this the other day, and I told her how much I liked it. "Did you wear your hair like this for me?" The question makes her blush and I fucking love that I can do that to her with a simple question. "Don't get me wrong, I fucking love it. I can't wait to have my hands in it later, but you don't have to change a single thing about yourself for me. I want you whether your hair is piled on top of your head at *Buns & Roses*, styled to perfection like it was at the Gala a few weeks ago or long and loose just waiting for me to wrap it around my fist."

That makes her swallow roughly as she steps closer, sinking her fingers into the curls at the base of my skull. "Cruz, please get me out of here." I can see the pulse in her neck beating rapidly and when her hardened nipples brush against the ridges of my stomach through her jersey, I groan. She's just as turned on as I knew she would be after the little game we played earlier.

Lacing my fingers through hers, I pull her toward the parking lot. Thankfully, I had the foresight to drive today. The walk to my apartment is short, but not nearly quick enough for how badly I want her.

I adjust my hardening cock before I push through the door, praying that the fans and photographers have left for the night. Luck is on my side. They have all cleared out, giving Delilah and me some privacy as we walk silently to my Bronco.

Keeping Delilah tucked against me, I lead her to the passenger side door. But instead of opening it, I back her up against it. A surprised look crosses her face just before I slant my mouth over hers. She opens up for me like she needs this kiss as much as I do. Her fingers twist in my hair when I sweep my tongue inside her mouth. Remembering that we are still in public and there's a genuine possibility of being caught, I slow the kiss and bring my forehead to hers.

"I needed that before I have to keep my hands off you during the drive."

"Thank god it's a short one. I need more of that, and I'm not feeling very patient tonight, but I suppose that is your fault."

"Oh yeah, were you a good girl for me? Did you keep your hands off my pussy when you showered?"

Delilah's back arches off the door of my truck as she tugs on my neck. When her lips are right next to my ear, giving my lip a playful bite. "You'll find out soon enough. Think you can drive or is this going to get in the way?" she asks, slipping her hand between us and cupping me through my pants.

I hiss through my teeth, loving her brazenness. "Let me be very clear Delilah, there's nothing that'll stop me from getting you back to my place tonight as long as that's still what you want."

"I'm not sure there's anything I have ever wanted more."

"That's my needy girl. Now get in this car so I can get you home safe. Because make no mistake, when I get you there, I'm going to absolutely ruin you."

I step back just enough for her to turn around so she's facing away from me while I open the door. My hand drops to her waist, and I guide forward so we are sheltered from anyone walking past. I can't deny us both one more for the road. My fingers tighten, digging into the soft flesh as I drop a searing kiss on her neck. When my lips suck on the delicate skin below her ears, she shivers and lets out a long whimper.

She was right. I'm just as greedy for her. Not afraid to give it right back, she presses her ass against me and I almost lose all sense, right here in the parking lot.

I lift her into the passenger seat, deciding we better get out of here before I bend her over the front seat of my truck and bury myself so deep inside her I get lost. Leaning in, I brush my lips across hers as I pull the seatbelt across her lap and tug to make sure it's secure. Stepping back, I shut the door and practically sprint to my side, where I slide in and turn the key silently.

When I pull out of the parking lot, I look to my right to check for traffic and see Delilah staring at me. Her eyes, appraising, like she's never seen me before. "What's going through that pretty head of yours? You're looking at me like you haven't known me for years." She bites her lip and I reach across the center console, swiping my thumb across her bottom lip, tugging it free from her teeth. "Not while I'm driving, Hermosa."

"It's different now. I see you in this entirely new light. Even though I've always been attracted to you, now I notice things I didn't before."

"Like what?" She looks away, turning toward the window before she looks back at me.

"Like the golden flecks in your eyes. I have always thought they were this beautiful shade of brown. This deep chocolaty shade that reminds me of the cinnamon in the center of my sticky buns, but when you lean your forehead against mine and the light hits them just right, I can see that there are lighter flecks of gold around your pupils."

"What else?" Delilah rolls her eyes at me. She might think I'm teasing, using her words to stroke my ego. And they do, but hearing her talk about me this way does something to me. Delilah is just catching up to the feelings I have had for years. I check my blind spots, making sure that there are no cars around, and then reach for her hand, entwining our fingers and pulling it onto the console. "Tell me."

Her face softens, and she continues, "The way your dimples are the deepest and most pronounced when you're flirting. They're always driving me crazy, but when you are laying on the charm with me, they stand out."

"That's because I'm never happier than when your attention is on me. It makes me feel like a king. When you look at me like you want me, I feel like I could do anything," I admit quietly and Delilah squeezes my hand in response.

We ride in silence for another minute until I pull into the underground parking for my building. When I turn off the engine, I hear Delilah let out a shaky exhale. "Hey. Delilah, look at me." Using my finger to lift her chin toward me, I tell her, "Nothing has to happen tonight."

Her small hand wraps around my wrist and ghosts up my arm. "Cruz, trust me, that's not it. This all just feels freaking surreal. You've been my person for years and I have been fighting these feelings for a while. This is happening—it almost feels like a dream."

"Kind of like an out of body experience. Speaking of dreams, don't think I forgot about that. Are you ready to tell me yet?"

"Mhmmm, I'll tell you, but can we go inside first?"

"You wait right there," I tell her as I unbuckle and then make my way around to her door. When I open her door, she's waiting with her seatbelt off.

"This is extremely unnecessary. I can get out on my own."

"I know you can, but now that you are mine, I want to do it for you. Just let me." My hands bracket her waist and I lift her out of the truck, setting her in front of me, but I don't let her go far.

I wrap my arm around her shoulder and walk her toward the building entrance. I keep her there as we ride up the elevator and step onto my floor. When we get to my door, I look over at her, trying to read how she's feeling. She told me repeatedly that she's ready for this, but I want to make sure there's no doubt there. She looks up at me and her eyes are shining with lust.

Delilah steps into the apartment first. I stand in the doorway, just waiting to see what she does. I want her to take the lead, at least for now. She looks over her shoulder as she walks through the dimly lit kitchen. Her hands disappear in front of her as she turns down the hallway that leads to the bedroom.

I shut the door behind me, locking it and then double-checking it before I follow her through the apartment. She crosses the threshold to the bedroom just as I round the corner to the hall. Her feet move a few more steps into the room and stop at the end of the bed. When I walk through the door, she turns around, her eyes finding mine right away. *Oh, fuck.*

Delilah's hands are busy working on the buttons on her jersey, *my* jersey.

She's standing at the end of my bed on display for me. The unbuttoned jersey reveals a teal mesh bra that meets in a deep V in the valley of her breasts. The jersey still covers most of her, but I can tell that as soon as she lets it fall from her shoulders, this bra won't hide anything. I can see the creamy white skin and the swell of her breast right through the mesh fabric.

I run my hand over my mouth as I watch her in disbelief. "You are a fucking vision, Delilah—seeing you in my room, just waiting for me in my jersey. Tonight I want you bare so I can see every beautiful fucking inch of you." I step closer, needing to close some of the space between us. "But someday soon I'll have you in nothing but my jersey as I devour you." One more step and I can almost reach out and touch her. "You look like a fucking dream come true." I don't even consider the words I use as they pour out of me.

Delilah chuckles, but the sweet sound is frayed with nerves. "You just can't wait to hear about my dream, can you?"

"Shit . . . I didn't. I meant it, Delilah. I wasn't even thinking about that when I said it. You don't have to—"

She shakes her head, rolling her lips to hold back her laughter. I'm a rambling mess, but there's no blood flow left to power my brain. "Shhhh. I'll tell you. I want to." When I try to move closer, she shakes her head again. "No, stay there. If you come closer, I won't be able to get the words out."

I watch as her finger slowly traces over the curve of her collarbone. "The first thing I remember is you touching me here." Her mouth falls open slightly as her fingers trace a path across her flawless skin. "You were so gentle, but each caress stoked a fire inside me. You told me how badly you've wanted me since that first night. And how hard it was to fight it all these years."

Afraid to interrupt and derail this masterpiece in front of me to confirm that everything she's said is true, I dip my head, encouraging her to continue. Her hand crosses the front of her body and pushes the jersey down the opposite shoulder, letting the fabric gape open just enough to give me a glimpse of her perfect tits.

Her hand slips under the fabric of the jersey, kneading her breast. My hands tighten into balls at my side. It's an effort not to reach out and replace her hand with mine.

"You were wearing basketball shorts, and I could see how hard you were for me. Everything was so vivid, I could feel the heat of you pressed against my center. Then you touched me here." Her fingers ghost around the outline of her beaded nipple. Showing me how I touched her, kneading her breasts and toying with herself until a needy moan slips past her lips. Her lashes flutter closed as she loses herself to the memory. She's flawless as she tortures both of us, reliving her dream. I flick the button on my pants loose and tug my zipper down. Giving myself a reprieve from the painful confines of my jeans.

"When I told you I needed you and pulled my tank top off, that's when you told me, *'Fuck, Mi Cielo. You are so beautiful.'"*

She rolls her shoulder back, and the jersey slips off. Her hand comes up, sliding it off the other side, so it's split all the way open. I can't take my eyes off her. Never in my wildest dreams did I think we would end up here. "And then"—she freezes for a moment before she steps forward slowly, and removes the jersey, dropping it to the side. When she stops in front of me, she looks up at me and grins—"you dropped to your knees in front of me."

I do just that, but keep my hands to myself. I want to see where my fiery girl takes this.

She bends at the waist, running her hands along my shoulders and down my biceps. Before lifting my hands to her hips. "You put your hands here before you worked my bottoms down my legs so that nothing was left between us."

My hands quickly work the button on her shorts and I guide them down her legs, mapping the curve of her hips with my fingers. My hands run back up her legs and I look up, waiting for permission from her.

"I think we've both waited long enough." Her voice shakes as my fingers toy with the waistband of her matching underwear. The sound of my pulse echoes in my ears as I strip them away to find that she's already soaked for me.

When my hands land back on her hips, she covers them with her own and pulls them around to grip her ass, tilting her pelvis forward. "Fuck, Delilah. Tell me I eat this pretty pussy in your dream." I think I would die if she told me this is where she woke up and I didn't get to taste her.

I look up, waiting for her to say something. Anything. But she just smiles down at me for a beat, eating up how much of a mess I'm for her. On my knees, begging for her to tell me what's next. She threads her fingers through my hair, holding me so that I can't do anything but watch her.

"You used your tongue, and it felt so good. Better than anything I have ever felt in real life." Her grip on my hair loosens, giving me the freedom to move.

I lean forward and pull her to my face, running my tongue along her seam. She tastes like heaven. "Like this?" I ask against her center before I repeat the same motion with my tongue.

"Yes. Just like that and then you used your fingers." Her voice breaks when I suck her clit into my mouth.

I run my lips along the inside of her thigh. "How many? One?" I ask, sinking one finger into her tight heat.

"No." Her legs tremble as I crook my finger inside her.

She's so fucking tight and wet. I circle her clit with my tongue, keeping my lips pressed against her as I ask, "Two?" I add another finger and her knees buckle.

"Yes—just like that."

"And then what, did you come for me like a good girl?" I pump my two fingers in and out, focusing on the spot that makes her knees lock as I suck her clit back into my mouth.

"I did. I came so hard." Her fingers twist in my hair as I feel her core pulse around my fingers. She's close, but I want to hear the rest of this dream, so I slow my movements, keeping her right on the edge.

"Tell me the rest. What happened after you came all over my fingers and face, Hermosa?"

"You fucked me, but not until I asked for it."

"Now that sounds like fun. I'd love to make you beg for my cock. How did you ask for it?"

She whimpers as I continue to flick her swollen clit with my tongue while my fingers work her right back to the brink again. I never want to come up for air again. The way she tastes and the sounds she makes are enough to sustain me. My bank account is big enough to retire both of us right now. We could spend the rest of our days doing this and I wouldn't have a single regret.

"Cruz please, I need to come," she begs, but it's not what I'm looking for.

"That doesn't sound like asking to be fucked?" I *tsk*, pulling my mouth away from her core, and looking up at her. She still got that teal bra on, and I can see the outline of her nipples poking at the fabric. I've fantasized about this moment, but Delilah falling apart for me is more beautiful than anything my mind could conjure. "Say the words and I'll make you come so hard it will put your dream to shame."

She gasps as I latch back on to her clit, sucking it hard and pulling my fingers out, so they barely brush her entrance.

"Cruz, I want you to fuck me." I take directions well, fucking her with my fingers. Pulsing them in and out until she is fluttering around me again. My tongue flattens against her clit, giving her the pressure she needs right as she crumbles, my name on her lips.

"Cruz—oh fuck."

"That's it, Hermosa, give it to me. You sound fucking perfect when you come for me," I praise as she works through her tremors, gently crooking my fingers as she squeezes me until she's pulling my head back. "Did I fuck you before you woke up?" I look up at her, chest heaving as she looks down at me with the post-orgasmic haze in her blue eyes.

She shakes her head. "I woke up as soon as we started. You bent me over the couch and rocked into me." I lay a kiss on her mound and she shivers between ragged breaths. "That's when you said, *'Mi Cielo, you feel like heaven'* and I woke up."

CHAPTER 24

DTF

PRESENT

"There's *no way* that's happening," Cruz says, his mouth still shining as he looks up at me with a grin, those dimples on full display. My heart plummets at his words. Did he change his mind? I'm about to ask what he means when he continues.

"Well . . . maybe later, but not the first time. You're gonna look so pretty with your lips swollen from my kiss. There's no scenario where I give up the chance to see you crumble under my touch with my cock buried deep inside you." I blink several times, his meaning sinking in. He still wants this. Still wants *me*.

Reaching behind me, I unclasp the mesh bra I'm wearing, letting it slide off my shoulder before dropping it to the ground next to Cruz. I watch as Cruz's eyes rake over me—up and then back down again. He rests his head against my stomach, letting his lips graze my hip bone, and then gets to his feet.

My hands find his unbuttoned jeans and push them down his chiseled legs. I have no idea when he undid them, but knowing he's as eager as I am only feeds my growing need. You would think after the earth shattering orgasm he gave me I would be temporarily sated. But that is not the case. He rids himself of his shirt just as eager to get himself naked as I'm to see him that way. Standing there in only those black boxer briefs, it's my turn to take him in. I say a silent prayer thanking the patron saint of Calvin Klein because these underwear are doing god's work.

He's marvelous—broad shoulders and corded muscles running over his entire chest. My fingers twitch at my side, ready to test how he feels. Dropping my gaze to his stomach, a dark trail of hair starts right above his belly button, splitting the ridge of his stomach. My eyes follow it to where his black boxer briefs are barely containing his hard cock.

I swallow roughly. This isn't the first time I've seen him like this. But knowing that he's about to be inside me for the first time, that bulge looks more intimidating than I remember.

Cruz picks up on my hesitation, cupping my face with his hand. "Don't worry, Hermosa. I'll make sure you're ready to take me. And you're going to take it so well." Stepping into me, his large hands grip my hips as his mouth slants over mine. My knees hit the back of the bed and let gravity do the rest pulling him with me.

Hands circle my ankles, holding me in place when I try to scoot toward the headboard. Tugging me back to the edge his dark curls bounce on top of his head as he kneels at the side of the bed. "I got a taste of you, but it wasn't enough, and I definitely didn't get a good enough look at you. No, I need you spread out in front of me for that." He pushes my knees apart, but it's not necessary. I let them fall open without an ounce of uncertainty.

Warm breath tickles my thighs as he kisses his way from the inside of my knee. I suck in a shocked gasp as his hands slide under my thighs pulling me right to his mouth. He doesn't take it slow this time and soon as his mouth makes contact with my still-sensitive clit, I'm gripping the sheets.

"Cruz, it's too much. I can't—not so soon. I've never come back to back like this before."

"Looks like we found another first for me. You can, and you will. Let me get you ready to take me."

"I am. I'm so ready. Please—" My words are cut off when he slides two fingers inside me, and a moan slips out.

"That's it, Hermosa. Give me another one. I know you need it after today. It was so hard not to touch yourself all day, wasn't it?"

"Yes. It was all I could think about." I slide my hands up my body, cupping my breasts. They're heavy and aching just thinking about how turned on I was all afternoon.

Cruz peers up at me from between my legs and the sight alone makes me whimper. His free hand covers mine, giving my tight nipple the attention it needs. And that whimper turns feral and the bite of pain turns to pleasure.

"It's okay, I've got you now." He adds another finger, stretching me as he grazes his teeth over my clit before lapping at me. I feel so full like this, and I know it's nothing compared to him.

"I'm close. I'm ready. Please." My voice is frantic, my words coming in short bursts as I beg him for what I need.

"Please what? I want to hear you say it like you did in your dream."

The pressure builds until I'm at risk of splintering in half. Cruz twists his fingers inside me and slides his large hand up my chest so he is holding my neck. He doesn't squeeze but just holds it there, owning every inch of my body. He's relentless, using his thumb to work my clit as he pumps his fingers. My vision clouds at the edges and I barely register him moving up the bed to capture my nipple in his mouth sucking hard. Determined to give me all the pleasure I can handle.

The ceiling above me bursts with stars and I come apart on his fingers, but he doesn't stop. He stays like that, slowing his movements as the aftershocks rock through my body wringing every last bit out of me.

"Fuck Delilah. You are so goddamn beautiful when you come for me."

A garbled string of curses mixed with his name come flying out of my mouth as my orgasm crests. It's too much and not enough at the same time.

"It's okay baby, say the words and I'll give you what you need."

"I need you to fuck me now."

His fingers slip out of me, leaving overwhelming emptiness behind. Cruz covers my body with his, pulling me up the bed with him. My hands slip to his waistband, but I can't think straight and getting them over his hips is a chore. He laughs and helps me out by sliding them down his legs.

I'm useless to do anything more than tug him to me and kiss him hard, letting our tongues tangle as my hands trace over his body. Using any leverage I can find to drag him closer, in a feverish need to be connected. When his hard length brushes my core, his chest rumbles and he pulls back from the kiss to rest his head on my shoulder.

"Give me a second. Condom." Apparently I'm not the only one struggling to hold it together.

My grip on him tightens, and I tilt my hips up, letting him slip through my heat. I'm soaked at this point and there's no resistance. It feels so good. His hot length nudges my center.

"Delilah." There's a warning in his voice, and I can tell he's barely holding back. Nothing has ever been sexier than seeing dangling off this ledge with me.

"Fuck me, Cruz."

"I'm trying." He laughs. "I'll be right back, I promise." My legs wrap around him, trapping him, so he's pressed right against my core. It feels so right with nothing between us. This wasn't my plan, but now that I have him like this, there's no way I want anything separating us.

This time, his groan is borderline wild as he looks down at me with his eyes narrowed.

"Like this. Bare." I pump my hips causing his grip to tighten on my waist. It bites but I don't care if it bruises. "We've waited so long. I want you with nothing between us."

He freezes in my arms, his dark brown eyes softening. "You'd let me inside you just like this." He moves his hips gliding against me, dragging the head of his cock over my clit, causing me to tilt my hips more, seeking him out. He's so close.

"God yes. Please, do it. Ruin me like you promised."

That's all it takes. He pushes inside me. One thrust and he's so deep that I can barely take it, but he doesn't move. His eyes close and he presses his forehead to mine, his jaw popping as he clenches it.

"Holy fuck. Your dream got one thing right. You feel like heaven, Mi Cielo."

"So do you, but right now, I need you to move. I'm so full . . . I can't . . . please move."

He lets out a shaky breath before lifting his eyes to find mine again. "It's too good. I'm not sure I can." His chest rumbles with laughter.

"You think it's funny?" I ask, shifting my hips under him, trying to get the friction I need.

He shakes his head. "Nothing about this is funny. I'm just really fucking happy. I finally have you and it feels better than I could have dreamed."

Resting on one of his elbows, he lifts my leg with his other hand, hooking my leg over his shoulder and stretching me open as he moves his hips. When he pushes back in with my leg like this, he drags across all my sensitive bits.

My mouth falls open and Cruz smirks at me before looking down at where we are joined. "Look at you, Delilah. Taking me so well, just like I knew you would."

All the pieces fall into place. Like it was always supposed to be this way. He's my best friend. There's no one I trust more, and that makes this more intense than it's ever been with anyone else. I know, without a doubt, that it will never be better than it is with him. He has thoroughly, and completely, ruined me for other men, and I'm more than okay with that.

He rocks into me again, harder this time. His face is a mask of concentration. I can tell it's taking all his focus to stave off his own release. "Tell me you're close."

Weaving my fingers through his hair, I pull him to me. "Kiss me, Cruz. I need all of you."

He grants my request, matching his thrusts with the way he kisses me—deep and hard. It feels like my entire body is consumed with him. I tilt my hips up, giving him better access, and that's all it takes. My core tightens as he drives in again, pushing me over the edge.

"So fucking tight Delilah. I love the way you squeeze me," he grits out as he swells inside me. His hips slow as he works through his release before rolling to the side, taking me with him. When we are settled side by side, he wraps my leg around his hip.

"Let's never leave this bed."

"I like how you think, but maybe expand those boundaries to include the rest of the apartment. I can think of lots of other places and ways I want you."

"Oh, yeah?"

"Yeah, right now I want to take you to the shower. Clean you up before I fuck you against the tile."

He lays a gentle kiss on my lips before he rolls to the end of the bed and scoops me into his lap. Standing with my weight cradled in his arm, he crosses the room to the bathroom.

"Oh, okay, like right now. You weren't messing around." I lock my arms around his neck with a giggle.

Flipping the water on, he sets my feet on the tile floor and grabs a clean washcloth before lowering to his knees in front of me. He runs the damp cloth over the inside of my thighs softly and with painstaking focus as he cleans me up.

With two fingers, he taps the inside of my ankle. "Spread those legs for me."

I stare down at him like this and my heart swells at the way he's so focused on taking care of me. My feet slide apart, doing what he asked.

"Jesus, Hermosa." His hand sweeps up the inside of my leg, leaving goosebumps in his wake. "This is the hottest thing I have ever seen."

My eyebrows pull together. He spent plenty of time earlier with his face between my legs, but something about the way he is looking at me now is different. "What is?"

His fingers brush the sensitive skin between my legs before he holds them up for me to see. They're coated in him. My mouth drops open. We glossed over some details earlier in the heat of the moment because we already have a foundation of trust between us. Before I can remind him I'm on birth control, his finger disappears between my legs, gently pushing his release back inside me. *Who is this man and what did he do with my best friend?*

A laugh escapes me because it's so unexpected, but it quickly turns into a moan when he licks me. "I thought you were getting me clean."

"What's the point when I'm just going to dirty you up again? The thought of filling you back up does something to me I didn't expect."

"Cruz."

"I know it's too soon, but fuck, you're my best friend. This part might be new, but I know you better than anyone else. Even though I know you're on the shot, fuck, the idea turns me on."

Cruz raises in front of me, and the truth in the statement is clear. He's unapologetically hard as his cock bobs against his stomach. I'm not ready to admit it yet, but everything he said, the idea of him putting a baby in me one day, is enough to make me beg for round two.

"Turn around and brace your hands against the wall. I haven't been able to stop thinking about taking you from behind since you said it earlier."

I do as he says, and Cruz touches my body like he's been doing it for years. Knowing just what I need by how I react. He gets me off two more times in the shower before he's groaning against my neck with his own orgasm. And at this moment I know, no matter what happens, it will never be this good with anyone else.

"Take me to bed and feed me," I tell him, shutting the water off. He carefully dries me off, wrapping the fluffy towel around my body and tucking the end in securely. Once we are both cozy in bed, he orders food from his phone and we cuddle naked, planning the trip over All-Star Break.

"Look at this," Cruz says, showing me pictures of a villa in St. John with panoramic views of turquoise blue ocean and deep green tropical forests sweeping across the mountainside.

"Cruz, that place is perfect," I say, swiping through the pictures. "Are we really doing this?"

"Why not? There's no way I would rather spend my time off than with you in a bikini or naked. That's the dress code. No other clothes allowed," he says seriously.

"There are several rooms. We could see if any of the guys wanted to join, maybe Hendrix and Poppy."

Cruz groans. "I tell you I want you naked, or in a tiny bikini, and you want to invite my teammates along. I thought you liked me, Delilah, but you're trying to kill me."

"Don't be dramatic. There's still plenty of privacy."

"Not possible," he says, rolling on top of me. "I can't do this whenever I want if they're around." He drops his hips down and grinds against me.

"I don't think they will mind us going missing occasionally." He melts into me before kissing my cheek, and I know I have him. The overwhelming feelings I have after just one night together is leaving me feeling a little frazzled. Planning this trip as a couple is more than I can cope with on top of everything else we've shared tonight.

"If that's what you want, let's talk to them. As much as I want you all to myself, it sounds like a fun way to spend the break."

Cruz's phone vibrates next to me as his lips descend on mine. "That's probably security calling about the food," he says, kissing his way down my neck as he blindly grabs for the discarded phone.

When he finds it, his forehead wrinkles as he stares at the screen. "Is it the food?"

"No, it's not. I'm not sure who it is. It's a St. Louis number, but I don't recognize it." His lips tilt down as he places the phone screen down and buries his face in my neck, holding me tight.

"Cruz. Look at me." I bury my fingers in his hair, scraping my fingernails across his scalp. "You can talk to me."

"I know, but right now I don't want to think about anything other than you naked in this bed with me. If it's important, they will leave a message. It's probably just a wrong number. There's no one in St. Louis that I need to talk to, especially not when I have you pressed against me. Tell me what you want to do in St. John's?"

I should push him to talk about it, but I don't want this lazy moment in bed with him to end. And he's giving me a pass on vacation. It seems we both want to keep living in this bubble where it's just the two of us. No outside world, past traumas, or unknown phone numbers that can ruin our night. So, I'll do as he asked and let it drop for now, like he did for me. "Can we go snorkeling?"

"We can do anything you want. As long as I get you naked in bed at least twice a day," Cruz says as he plays with the thin bracelet that he got me a few years ago for my birthday.

"I want to take you shopping while we are there and find you a friend to match this bracelet. Maybe one for your ankle. Now that you're mine, I can spoil you like that."

"Because that stopped you before?" I shove at his chest playfully, pushing him onto his back so I can cuddle against his broad chest.

"Someone had to do it."

"Mhmmm. You can take me shopping, but I'm giving you a spending limit."

This time when his phone vibrates next to my arm on the bed, it's the front desk calling to let us know the delivery is here. Cruz answers it, wrapping his arm tightly around my waist when I try to roll off him. "You can send them up. Thanks. Have a good night," he tells the on-duty security guard.

"You stay right here. I'll grab the food and we can eat in bed." Cruz slides a pair of gray sweatpants over his legs, letting them rest low on his hips.

"Can you at least toss me a shirt? I'm not eating naked." Cruz's face falls into an exaggerated frown that causes my chest to vibrate with laughter while he reaches into his dresser to grab a shirt. "Did I ruin all your fantasies?"

"Kind of. I had my heart set on feeding you cheesy fries while naked in bed. I hoped that some cheese would accidentally fall right here," he says, running his finger across the swell of my breast. "I was looking forward to licking it clean."

"Wow. What a vivid fantasy. I'm sorry to ruin that for you." I reach my hand out, grabbing for the shirt, but Cruz lurches forward, sending me soaring backward. I land flat on my back with him, pinning my hands above my head. His smile widens as he lowers his head to my chest and licks my breast. Right where he had pointed before.

I laugh and squirm underneath him as he licks at the imaginary cheese.

"Mmmm, delicious." Cruz's lips tickle my skin as he talks.

This is what Mikey and Willa were talking about when they said Cruz would be easy to love. When he lets himself be light and carefree, it's priceless and I soak up each of these moments as they come, hanging on to them for when the grief strikes.

Cruz finally relents and hands me the shirt when there's a knock at the door. "Food's here. You got lucky, I was about to lose a piece of bacon in your belly button."

"I hope this isn't a deal breaker for you, but my belly button is off limits." His shoulders shake with amusement as he walks through the door to retrieve our food order.

CHAPTER 25

UNKNOWN NUMBER

PRESENT

Watching Delilah sleep in my arms as the sun spreads across the room is the best part of my day. Her blonde hair shines in the light and her lips flutter lightly with each breath. But hands down, the part that tops it all, is how she's wrapped herself around me in her sleep.

Her leg is thrown over my hip, giving me unrestricted access to palm her ass or wake her up slowly with my fingers. She's got her arm draped over my middle, hanging on to me like she thinks I might get away from her while we sleep. She doesn't know it yet, but I have no plans to let her go, ever.

Eventually I need to get to the gym to lift before practice, but it can wait. I'm not ready to leave this bed and go back to the real world just yet. Pushing Delilah's hair out of her face, I debate whether I should let her sleep. I kept her up late last night and this is the only morning she will have off all week. The right thing to do is let her rest, especially after all of the orgasms I pulled out of her last night.

Careful not to disturb her, I reach for my phone which is lighting up on the nightstand. I sit up quickly when I see the same number from last night on my screen—the one I don't recognize from St. Louis. Even just seeing it flash across the screen again makes my palms sweat with the same panic I always feel when I think about that city, that team, and the people who weren't there for me when I needed them the most.

There's a reason I left everyone from St. Louis behind when I was traded. If they needed to reach me, they would have contacted my agent or left a message.

Gripping the phone tightly with my fist, I decline the call—pissed that whatever this is, has pulled me out of bed with Delilah. She rolls onto her stomach, her hand searching for me as her eyes flutter open. She smiles when her hand connects with my knee, but when she looks up it fades immediately.

Delilah's soft hands cradle my face as she kneels next to me, examining me with concern. "What's wrong Cruz?" she pleads, her hands running down my neck and shoulders before smoothing back up to my face.

"They called again." I look down at the phone like the device in my hands is guilty of a terrible offense.

"The same number? Did they leave a message?" Delilah's gaze drops to the phone.

"No. I'm going to call my parents to check in." I don't need to tell Delilah that my greatest fear, when I get calls like these, is that someone is hurt or injured. But that doesn't make sense because they're in Texas, and this is a St. Louis number. It's why I could mostly ignore it last night, but with another call and no message, but now, I just need to be sure.

Her hands wrap around my fist, which is still squeezing the phone. She gently runs her hands over my knuckles until I loosen my grip. When she takes it from me, she uses my code to unlock it while I just sit there like a statue. I barely register what's happening as she navigates to the missed call and then to my voicemails before pulling my mom's phone number and looking at me for permission.

"Yeah. Go ahead."

She connects the call, putting in on speaker. When the phone rings, she shifts, so she's in my lap, running her hands through my hair. It's a move that has always calmed me. I rest my head against her shoulder as the phone continues to ring. Right before it goes to voicemail, my mom picks up and the knot in my chest loosens.

"Morning mijo," my mom says, her voice warm and inviting.

"Buenos días mamá."

"This is an early call for you. Is everything okay?"

My arm snakes around Delilah's waist, pulling her tight against me. "Yeah. Everything is fine. Are you and Dad okay? I had a few calls from a number I didn't recognize last night and again this morning," I admit sheepishly. My parents have already lost one son. The idea of them worrying about the one they have left me makes me feel weak and I hate it.

"*Oh, Cruz.* Everyone here is fine." The sympathy in her voice just makes me feel like more of a burden. I wish I could be stronger for her. Closing my eyes, I fight the urge to scream in frustration. "Are you okay?"

Delilah shifts the phone away from me, bringing it to her ear and taking it off speaker. "Hey, Analia, it's Lilah. He'll be fine . . . No, I'll be here with him until he leaves for the stadium."

Delilah's cheeks pinken at whatever my mom says on the other side of the call. "I bet you are."

Her shoulders shake against me when she laughs at Mom's response. My mom is no doubt thrilled that Delilah is here this early in the morning. Her greatest wish for me, aside from seeing my baseball dreams come true, is to make Delilah my wife and fill a house with her grandchildren. She's never failed to remind me of those hopes over the years.

Delilah looks at me silently, asking if I want to talk with her. I hold out my hand for the phone.

"I'm going to hand the phone to Cruz . . . I'll make sure he's okay . . . Te extraña también." She passes me the phone and I bring it to my ear knowing that my mom is about to go full-on mama bear with worry.

"No, don't do that. I'll be fine . . . Yes, she's staying . . . Te amo, má," I tell her before I hang up—having talked her out of a trip to come check on me.

The Spanish Delilah so easily used with my mom doesn't go unnoticed and I catalog that detail to ask her about later. She shifts in my lap, changing positions so she's straddling me, but I can see by the concern in her eyes and the way she's rolling her lips together this isn't an invitation for some morning fun.

"It's okay to ask for help. Whether it's me or someone else. You need an outlet when the grief is too much, or when the anxiety creeps in from something like this."

Downplaying this with her doesn't feel right, and she would see right through me. The last thing I want is to burden her. My mom and Delilah have a lot in common in how they nurture those around them. It's part of the reason they've had an easy friendship for years.

My mom appreciates the way Delilah's always been there for me, putting me first. But I watched her do the same thing with Brad. And I want to be better than that for her. She should come first, and she can't do that if she's taking care of me all the time.

"I'll send Rich the phone number and ask him to look into it. I don't want you to worry about it, and I'm sure it's nothing."

"The P.I. you used to work with?"

"Yeah, he and I still speak once in a while. It shouldn't be hard for him to track down a number."

"This time of the year is always harder for you and with these calls and the upcoming travel schedule to play the Commanders, do you think calling him is going to be enough?"

It's been three years and I still don't have the answers I need. For the first two years, I paid a private investigator to find something that would help shed some light on the hours before Jarrett ended up in the hospital fighting for his life. The leads never amounted to anything, and about nine months ago, Rich told him he wouldn't take any more money from me.

"You'll let me know if this all gets to be too much, right? The travel, the calls?" she asks, her hands bracketing my face, so I'm forced to look at her when I respond.

"That's not going to happen, but I promise I'll tell you if it is."

I pull up Rich's information in my contacts and open our text thread. Even though he won't take my money, we check in monthly. It's mostly me asking if he's heard anything or if anyone's come forward with information, and him gently letting me down. The Miami police have kept the case open as long as there's still hope that Rich might find something, mostly as a favor to him for his many years of service before he left the department.

I hold the phone so Delilah can see what I'm texting.

CRUZ:

Hey Rich. I've gotten a few calls from a number in St. Louis that I don't recognize. They haven't left any messages. Can you look into it for me?

Hopefully, that will give Delilah some peace of mind, so she isn't worrying about me. I fucking hate that an unknown number, from a city that holds some of my worst memories, is completely derailing our morning. It's the first time we have woken up together since we admitted that there's more to our relationship than just being friends.

This is not how I envisioned it would go.

Eager to salvage what we have left, I slide my hands up the oversized shirt Delilah has on, gripping her hips before I lean forward and pepper her neck with kisses—because she always knows exactly what I need, she lets me distract myself by reaching for the hem of my shirt and pulling it over her head in one quick motion. If I thought she looked good next to me in bed with messy hair, swollen lips, and only my shirt draped over her, it's nothing compared to this—her naked, in my lap, first thing in the morning. She's the most beautiful distraction I have ever seen.

After a few minutes of heated kisses and my hands tracing over every square inch of her skin, she slides her hand between us, slipping it into the front of my briefs.

"Mhmmm, you don't have to do that." I hiss when her fist wraps around me.

"Actually, I do. You got to spoil me last night, and now it's my turn."

I let my upper body fall back against the headboard and watch as her perfect tits bounce up and down with each stroke of her hand. It's enough to make me forget my name, along with all the anxiety I was feeling earlier. At least, for now.

CHAPTER 26

MEET JARRETT

FLASHBACK - 3.5 YEARS EARLIER

Pressing my back flat against the bench, I extend my shaking arms, holding the bar above my chest when my phone vibrates against the bench from the pocket of my shorts. Racking the weight, I sit up, answering immediately when I see my brother's name light up the screen.

"Hey, Rett, how's San Diego?" I swipe my discarded shirt across my forehead, soaking up the sweat rolling off me from my workout, out of the corner of my eye I see one of my teammates walk into the St. Louis Commanders weight room.

"The sun is shining, the bikinis are tiny, and I get paid to throw base-balls. Life doesn't get much better than that." He sounds every bit the southern boy our mom raised. The accent tells me he's relaxed, but that's Jarrett. My younger brother loves life and the only thing he takes seriously is his baseball game and being a momma's boy.

"You're soaking up those west coast vibes, aren't you? If you were a state, you'd be California." The waves lap in the background, and I can picture him lounging on the beach—his brown hair flopping to the side like it always does, with his favorite pair of obnoxiously bright, pit vipers perched on his nose. Giving him the perfect cover to check out the ladies walking by. Not that Jarrett would let them just walk by—he's never met a girl he doesn't want to flirt with.

"Maybe when I get called up, we can negotiate a trade to the golden state. I bet I could find a pretty little thing to teach me how to surf."

"I don't doubt you could. Let's focus on getting you to the show before we aim for a dual trade and finding you a surf instructor." I tilt my head to Colby Miller, our closing pitcher, as he slips his headphones over his ears and heads for the free weights.

Miller was a top prospect coming out of college, but he hasn't adjusted to the spotlight well. After a promising rookie season two years ago, he's spent more time in the tabloid headlines than the sports highlights.

Like many young rookies, he'd let his game suffer and opted to over-indulge in the fame that comes with being in the spotlight. But I'm glad to see him here working. The team needs him, and if he doesn't turn things around this season, he'll be looking at a trade or being sent down.

"I'll be there right beside you soon. Well, not right beside you because I'll be center stage taking down batters and making your job boring."

"I'm sorry I didn't hear you over the sound of a big-ass paycheck hitting my account. You have one job out there. How hard can that be? Throw the ball hard. Come talk to me when you are pulling back game-changing grand slams from the wall and making throws to home." My damp curls fall over my forehead, and I push them back, catching Miller glaring at me in the mirror while he lifts.

"No thanks, man. I'll keep saving games when you all fuck it up." I hear muffled voices from his end of the line, followed by his husky laugh. "Good luck at your game tonight, bro. A friend just showed up. I'll text you later."

There's a high-pitched squeal that makes me pull the phone away from my ear.

"Same to you. Have fun with your *friend* and wrap it up." I shake my head when he disconnects the call. When I look up, Miller is still giving me the stink eye in the mirror.

What an asshole.

"Sorry man. Jarret's playing in California. We haven't had much luck getting a hold of each other with the time difference and our game schedules."

"Next time maybe take your call elsewhere so we don't all need to hear you bullshit with your *little shadow*." My jaw pops, but I keep my mouth shut. None of the other guys even seemed to have noticed, let alone cared. One thing I've learned about this guy is he's bitter as fuck. I don't envy Jarrett having to be in the bullpen with him when he eventually gets called up. Miller will see him as a threat. And that's just going to make his attitude even more unbearable.

Grabbing the dumbbells at my feet, I stand from the bench and continue my workout, using my annoyance with our primadonna pitcher to fuel me.

I tug my hat down tight on my head and squat slightly. My glove and throwing hand meet at the center of my body, ready to explode if the batter gets a hit. Miller starts his wind-up. He's been hot all night. It's almost like looking back in time to his rookie season. He's zeroed in, throwing hard and striking out batters with ease. The pitch is a fastball over the plate and the batter swings, sending it straight back at the pitcher's mound. There's not enough time for Miller to react, and the ball catches him on the elbow as he's trying to turn away, dropping him to the ground where he writhes in pain until the medical staff helps him off the field.

A short while later, when I jog off the field and down the tunnel to our clubhouse, I can hear the chaos before I see it. There's yelling and a loud crash as I push through the locker room door. In the corner, by the training table, the team doctor is working to calm Miller down while Finley, one of the training staff, cowers in the corner. Her eyes are wide as she shrinks back further, trying to put more space between her and Miller. Coach is still on the field talking with reporters and I'm one of the few players that got out of post-game interviews and made it down here.

"Hey, you okay?" I ask over my shoulder as I step between her and the commotion. She nods, but stays behind me. From the tremble in her lip and how her shoulders are turned in, I can tell she's still shaken. "Want me to get you out of here?"

"Please." Her voice is timid, but she's at least looking at me instead of the ground now.

"Let's go." I motion for her to join me as I turn around to keep myself between her and Miller. She leads the way out of the locker room as I follow.

"Thank you for getting me out of there. I don't like confrontation at all." Her voice is steadier now that she's got the physical barrier of being outside the locker room.

"Not a problem. What happened there?" Miller's outburst after his injury isn't a huge surprise. He's a loose cannon on a good day, and today was not one of those.

"He didn't like my recommendation to Dr. Saleh about his injury and recovery." When she speaks this time, she stands a little taller, finally getting some of her confidence back. "He's going to be out for a week or two to let his elbow heal and will need a stint playing in the minors as part of his rehab." She rolls her lips together like she's bracing for my reaction.

"It sounds like he needs to focus on getting better, not berating the staff for doing their jobs. I'll let the Doc know you stepped out."

"Thanks again, Cruz." She turns and heads down the hall to a set of offices the medical teams use. Once the door swings shut, I head back into the locker room where things have calmed down. Miller is nowhere to be found, and Dr. Saleh is cleaning up the mess left behind. He looks up when he hears me approaching.

"Finley went down to the offices. Everything okay?"

Shaking his head as he continues moving around the space. "Just dandy. Coach Becker came and got Miller out of here. Sent him home and told him to calm down. That kid's gonna have a short career if he doesn't get himself under control."

"You'll go check on Finley? She was pretty shaken up."

"Yeah, I'll go talk to her. When your brother gets called up, make sure the spotlight doesn't go to his head."

"That won't be a problem, Doc." Jarrett might enjoy his life to the fullest but never at the expense of others. Miller is selfish and entitled. If my brother ever acted the way he just did, I would have hauled him out of here myself. Not to mention he would never disappoint our mother like that.

Miller is wasting all his potential, and there are guys like Jarrett just waiting to get a chance on the roster. Doc isn't wrong about the direction his career is heading. Everyone, players, staff, and the front office are tired of his antics on and off the field. I get the sense his days are numbered with this team and maybe the league.

RETT:

Good luck tonight.

CRUZ:

You too. Kick some Hurricane ass. A few more games like the one you had last week against San Diego and you are bound to be called up this season.

RETT:

Geez. Way to lay on the pressure.

CRUZ:

*Don't even try that shit with me.
You're a diamond, baby bro.
Pressure makes you shine.*

RETT:

Damn right I am.

CRUZ:

That's more like it.

♥

CRUZ:

Your slider was nasty tonight!

RETT:

That homer!

CRUZ:

*Yeah, I was pretty fucking impressive
at the plate tonight.*

RETT:

*You were, but did you pitch a shut-out inning to save
the game?*

CRUZ:

Wow... Don't let that go to your head.

I'm proud of you.

RETT:

*Awe! Love you too. Just think, you're going to get to
see my naked ass strutting around your locker room
soon. I hope you don't get jealous.*

CRUZ:

I'm afraid to ask why you think I would be jealous.

RETT:

I would think that's pretty obvious.
God gave me the bigger dick.

CRUZ:

Is that what you think?

RETT:

I know it.

CRUZ:

I know you're delusional.
Good night LITTLE bro.

RETT:

There's nothing little about me.

♥

RETT:

How do you play with this guy every day?

CRUZ:

Miller? I mostly ignore him.

RETT:

What an asshat.

CRUZ:

Just steer clear as best you can.

RETT:

That's not going to be a problem.
Have a great game tonight.

CRUZ:

You too.

By the way, you need more Fruit Loops.

RETT:

You ate all my cereal? You better replace it before I get home.

CRUZ:

I guess you'll just have to wait and see.

RETT:

You have two days to replace the goods or I'm going to leave crumbs in your bed for you to find after every late-night flight from an away series.

CRUZ:

You wouldn't

RETT:

Are you sure about that?

CRUZ:

No...Alexa, add Fruit Loops to my grocery order.

♥

RETT:

What's Miller's deal?

CRUZ:

Why?

RETT:

Normally he's a surly asshole to all of us, but he's extra friendly today.
Trying to chum it up.

CRUZ:

Really? Be careful, he's trouble that you don't want to get caught up in. The front office is buzzing about how well you've been playing. And there are a lot of frustrations all around about Miller. It's not looking good for him.

RETT:

Maybe he's turned over a new leaf.

CRUZ:

This series has been a big deal for you. Don't let getting involved with him mess it up. The Commanders are trying to get rid of problems, not sign new ones.

RETT:

I hear you.

CRUZ:

Good. Listen, I'm older and wiser.

RETT:

Saggy balls and all. Love you, old man.

CRUZ:

Fuck off.

CRUZ:

Love you too. Go earn your spot on the roster.

♥

CRUZ:

What a fucking game! I'm so proud of you. Coach told me after the game that he was impressed with how well you've been playing.

Jarrett, did you end up going out? Call me.

Come on man, don't leave me hanging.

CHAPTER 27

LATE-NIGHT VISIT

FLASHBACK - 3.5 YEARS EARLIER

I startle awake on the couch. I must have dozed off after the game waiting for Jarrett to text me back. The ESPN highlights I was watching are over and there's an infomercial for a sponge playing on the screen. A sharp knock at the door echoes through the dark room. Checking my phone, I see it's almost 2:30 a.m. and there's still no response from my brother.

My stomach churns. Having someone knock on your door at this time of night is never a good thing. Pushing my hand through my hair, I make my way across the apartment we share and twist the deadbolt before I pull the door open.

Coach is standing there, casually dressed in a pair of jeans and a Commander's hoodie. When he looks up from where he's staring at the floor, the pity in his eyes is undeniable. I know whatever he's about to tell me isn't good news.

"Coach?"

"Cruz, can I come in?" There's a deep V creasing his forehead as he looks past me into the apartment.

"Um, sure. What's going on?" That churning in my gut is a fucking wave pool now. He doesn't just show up at a player's house for no reason.

"Let's take a seat for a second." He points toward the couch, and I follow him but don't sit. I can't. Instead, I pace the floor, waiting for him to speak.

"Coach, I'm freaking out. Can you tell me why you're here?" I'm nearing full-on panic. My heart is beating so rapidly that I can barely hear my own words over the rhythm, and there's a coppery taste in my mouth that's setting me on edge. Nothing about this feels right.

"There was an accident tonight in Miami. Jarrett was injured. I don't have a lot of details yet, but I've spoken to your parents. They're on a plane down there now. I'm going to take you to the airport where a plane is waiting."

"Jarrett was hurt? What happened? Is he okay?" I fire the questions at him, barely taking a breath between them as I search the room, looking for my phone.

"We can talk more on the way to the airport. I don't have a lot of information, but I can tell you what I know. Do you want to grab anything?"

I shake my head. "Just my wallet and I need to find my damn phone."

Coach places his hand on my arm. "Where's your wallet? I'll grab it for you. Your phone is in your hand."

I look down, my hand is wrapped so tightly around my phone that my knuckles are turning white. "Bedroom, end of the hall, on my dresser." My voice sounds like it's off in the distance. Coach Becker stands, looking hesitant to leave my side for a moment before he turns down the hall.

Robotically, I move to the door, shoving my feet into a pair of shoes while I wait for him to return. When he returns, he hands me the wallet and grabs the keys from the hook and places them on top of my wallet.

I follow him out of the apartment and into the elevator without a word. When we get to the lobby, he leads me out front where his car is parked, with the hazards blinking, in a loading zone. I stop short at the passenger side door.

"Coach? Is he going to be okay?" He fucking looks away, staring down the road before he looks back at me, and I can see it in his eyes. They're filled with sympathy.

"Let's get you on the plane so you can be with your family, Cruz."

On the drive to the airport, I try calling Jarrett first. It takes several failed attempts before I move on to my parents. Their phones just ring to voicemail as well. Coach looks over at me as we take the exit to the private terminal.

"They're probably still in the air."

"Well, what the fuck do you expect me to do here? Huh?" I'm yelling at my coach. It's something I've never done before, but the fear and frustration are overruling everything else. "You show up and tell me my brother is hurt, but nothing else. It's obviously bad if you are flying me out in the middle of the night, but you won't tell me a goddamn thing." My voice breaks. "So what the fuck am I supposed to do?" He keeps his eyes on the road, but I can see his hands twisting on the steering wheel. It's not in his nature to allow a player to speak to him like that. Not that I give a fuck right now.

He slows to a stop at the curb before turning to look at me. "I wish I could tell you more, but I can't. You need to scream at me? Fine. But right now, your family needs you and I'm trying to get you there. The doctors will give you more information."

Only that doesn't turn out to be true. After the longest flight of my life, I arrive at the hospital where no one can tell me a fucking thing. When I give them my name at the front desk, it takes the nurse what feels like hours to get me directed to where my parents are waiting.

"Cruz!" my mom cries out when I enter the private waiting area. The agony in her voice when she says my name is a sound I never want to hear again. I cross a small, barren room in a few long strides before I have her in my arms. Any strength she was hanging onto when I entered the room dissolves and her body trembles violently as she sobs.

I smooth my hand over her hair, looking at my dad, desperate for guidance, strength, information, fucking anything. But he's as wrecked as my mother. He's slouched over in a corner chair, his elbows resting on his knees, as he cries silently into his hands.

My mom's tears soak my shirt, as I try soothing her. "Shhhh . . . Mamá, va a estar bien." It's an empty promise. I don't know if it'll be okay, but I'm not sure what else to say or do. I'm crawling out of my skin, not knowing what is going on, but until I calm her down, she won't be able to give me any answers.

My dad stands sniffling as he wipes his tears with the back of his hands. He wraps my mom and me in his embrace. "It's bad, hijo," he croaks out, looking at me with so much pain in his eyes over my mother's head.

We all stay like that for a few minutes before my dad speaks again, his voice steadier this time, "Come sit."

"What's going on? No one's told me anything."

They know about as much as I do: Jarrett was hurt, and he's in surgery—brain surgery. He sustained a head injury and they are working to assess the damage. By the time they're done explaining to me what they know about his condition, and how he got here, we all look as weary as we feel.

"What do you mean, he was dropped off? Why wasn't he in an ambulance?"

"We don't have those answers. I wish I could give you more information. He was dropped off and the driver said he found him like that."

What the fuck. In my tired state, I'm having a hard time processing what I'm hearing. I'm not firing on all cylinders right now, but something is not adding up. He usually goes out with teammates. Did he end up going out on his own?

"Found where?"

"They said something about a beach. Police are questioning the driver, but that's the last I've heard." I can see the toll each question is taking on my dad. The circles under his eyes are a deep purple. He's used to being the one in control, knowing all the answers—having so many unknowns, when his youngest son is fighting for his life is destroying him.

There's a soft knock at the door before the doctor steps into the room. My mom lifts her head from where it's resting on my dad's shoulder. My need to know what's going on overrides my exhausted body. I cross the room to meet the doctor, simultaneously nauseous at the thought that this news could be bad, and desperate for it to be good.

"Jarrett suffered a serious head injury. When he came into the ER, his CT scan showed significant swelling. We worked to relieve the pressure on his brain, which we hope will help the fluid drain." The doctor looks between us, waiting for any questions before he continues. "Right now, he is medically sedated and has a breathing tube. It will need to remain in until the pressure in his brain has improved. Keeping him sedated will prevent unsafe increases in pressure and allow him to heal. The next twenty-four hours are going to be critical and may give us a better understanding of his prognosis."

"Can we see him?" my mom asks, sitting stiffly next to my dad.

"Soon. He's still in recovery. A nurse will come get you when he's in his room."

"When can we expect him to wake up?" Dad wraps his arm around my mom's shoulder and pulls her to his side.

My eyes pinball between the three of them. It's the most hopeful I've seen my dad look since I arrived. The doctor tries to keep his face the same stoic mask it was earlier, but he lets it slip momentarily before his lips turn down and there's an almost imperceptible shake of his head.

"He is going to wake up, isn't he, Doc?" My fists open and close at my sides. He doesn't need to answer, it's written all over his face. The way he can't quite meet my eyes tells me everything.

"It's too soon to say. The swelling was extensive, and we know very little about how, or even when, his injury was sustained. Right now, we need to focus on getting him through the night without further complications."

I sink back into the chair next to my mom, prepared to wait. The doctor clears his throat, stepping further into the room. "There is something else you should know. Jarrett's tox screen came back positive for GHB."

"That doesn't make any sense." Jarrett doesn't mess around with drugs. During the season, he has a strict limit on what, and how much, he drinks. "There's no way he would take any banned substance. He has too much to lose."

"There was also alcohol in his system. Not a lot, but enough that it could have caused the effects of the GHB to be amplified. Combined, they can cause dizziness, confusion, and disorientation."

"Nothing about this makes sense." I stand and pace in front of the doctor, whose lips are drawn into a tight line. Anger and confusion mixes with all the pain and I just want to wake my brother up and ask him what the hell is going on.

When the doctor leaves the room, we wait in silence for the nurse to come take us to see Jarrett. All of us are too drained to speak. And with the bomb the doctor dropped about his toxicology report, I don't think any of us even know what to say. There are so many questions we can't answer.

Jarrett's room is even more bleak than the waiting room. Red bruises mar one side of his swollen face and there are so many machines. Machines breathing for him. Machines buzzing and beeping that are doing God knows what. Machines pumping medicine into his eerily still body. My brother is never still. He is always full of life. He even fucking talks in his sleep. Seeing him like this is wrong on so many levels, my stomach sours. Lurching towards the trash can, I heave into the bin, my already empty stomach cramping until I can finally breathe through it enough to regain control.

The room spins around me as I struggle to breathe. My dad takes my arm, leading me to a chair. He kneels in front of me, checking to make sure

I'm okay before he goes to my mom's side. She's hunched over my brother's body, clutching him like she can hold him to this earth, while the tears stream down her face.

The nurse takes pity on us and lets us stay much longer than we are supposed to before she makes us leave in shifts to eat and take a break, but he's never alone. It's an unspoken agreement we made that someone will always stay.

Jarrett makes it through the first twenty-four hours with no changes, which seems encouraging, but when there's no change for several more days the doctors come in to talk to us about what's next. They use words like cognitive impairments, brainstem reflexes, ventilatory drive, brain function, and irreversibility. All of the medical terminology blends together and the only thing that's clear is how dire his situation is.

They do physical tests for everything. Jarrett is wheeled in and out of the room more times than I can count for testing. There are tests for blood flow within his brain, repeat ultrasounds, CT scans, and MRIs, along with countless other tests.

Later that afternoon, the team of doctors comes into the room looking weary. They patiently explain the tests and results as we ask question after question. I look over at my parents and then at my brother, who looks less like himself every minute.

"You don't think he will wake up?"

My mom whips her head toward me, looking like I slapped her. I need to hear them say the words. They have already told us as much, but we are just refusing to listen. She buries her head in my dad's chest and he wraps his arms around her like a shield.

"No, the tests indicate that there's no brain activity. The damage was too severe. Jarrett is brain dead."

"If he had been brought in sooner, could it have made a difference?" We still don't know more about what happened than we did that first night. It's eating away at me a little more every day. The police cleared the driver that brought him in but didn't uncover any new leads. They've moved on to speaking with his teammates, but either no one knows, or no one is saying where, and what, his plans were for the night of his accident.

"It's possible. Brain injuries respond best to treatment within the first hour, but we have no way to know for sure."

"What's next?" my dad asks, still clinging to my mom as she shakes with silent sobs against his chest.

"The machines are keeping Jarrett's body alive, but he's gone. Take some time as a family to discuss it and decide whether you want to continue life support. I know this is incredibly difficult. If we thought he would wake up, we wouldn't be having this conversation with you."

Those words make me crumble. The façade I had in place while I asked questions earlier evaporates and I fall apart for the first time since Coach showed up at my door. Once I got off the plane and saw my parents, I knew I needed to be strong and hold things together while he got better, but that's not happening. My brother is not waking up.

That's what they're telling us, they're preparing us to say goodbye, to accept that Jarrett won't come back to us. I fold over in my chair and try to fill my lungs, but suddenly the room feels like a vacuum. It's a hundred times worse than when I walked into the hospital room for the first time.

A hand comes down on my back, rubbing circles rhythmically and I hear chatter in the distance, but nothing makes sense until her concerned voice breaks through the fog.

"You don't need to be strong for me, mijo. It's okay to fall apart with me. Ven aquí, Cruz." It's the same voice she used when we were boys and she was comforting us. Her arms tug on my shoulders, urging me into a sitting position.

I let her pull up from the chair and wrap me in her thin arms, her sweater absorbing my tears. At some point, the medical staff leaves the room, giving our family the space we need to say goodbye.

The next few hours are a blur of medical personnel coming in to talk to us about what's next, but every time the door opens, I leave. I can't hear them talk about the process of ending my brother's life. My parents sign countless forms before we all take turns with Jarrett alone.

"Rett, what the hell happened? How did you end up here, like this?" I ask when I take the seat beside his bed.

His normally bronze skin looks almost gray. His thick brown hair is all wrong. Instead of flopping to the side, it's hanging over his forehead. I can't help myself. I half stand from the chair and brush his hair to the side, but it's still not right. The strands are dull and flat against his head.

"I wish you could tell me—or fuck, if we are making wishes here, I would do just about anything for one last game of catch with you. Or how about going back in time and this never happened? I want to wake up to you talking in your sleep back home. Hear you laugh and watch you toss my fruit loops into your mouth. That's really what I would wish for." I feel the heat of the tears on my face and drop my head into my hands, trying to stop the flow, but it's no use.

"I'm not sure how to do this, bro. How am I supposed to go back to St. Louis and walk through the door of our place without you? Go back to the ballpark and play without you? You were supposed to be there with me. We had plans, we were doing this together, and I don't understand how it all went so wrong."

For a second, I foolishly hope with everything in me that this is the moment he proves the doctors wrong. I close my eyes, scrunching them closed tight, and wish for his eyes to open. For him to tell me what happened. Then I watch for anything, any sign that he's here with me. A change in his breathing, a twitch in his hand, a blink of an eye, but there's nothing.

"I promise you I'll figure this out. I'll find out what happened to put you here." I know, deep down, this wasn't just a random accident. There's more to this story, and I need to know. Reaching forward, I take his hand in mine—something I've avoided to this point. "I promise to make you proud. I'll play the way you do, with love for the game, and live my life the best I can without you." Wiping my tears with the back of my hand, I stand and bend over the bed, wrapping him in my arms the best I can as I silently say goodbye to my best friend, my teammate, and my little brother. I hold him to me as I cry. I have no idea how much time passes before my parents are at my side, joining in on the hug and walking me away from the bed.

A short while later, the medical staff comes in as I numbly sit between my parents while they do their thing and Jarrett slips away. Just like that, he's gone. The promises I made give me something to focus on besides the pain, but I know it will be a long time before I can make good on them. Nothing is going to feel right without him by my side.

CHAPTER 28

MODERN DAY BEAST

PRESENT

"Cruz, check my pulse. I think I've died and gone to heaven." I raise the back of my hand to my forehead dramatically and wilt in his arms. The Bandits played an afternoon game and don't play again until tomorrow evening, so we all took Ubers from the stadium to Dean's penthouse.

The guys have been giving him a hard time because he's got this killer penthouse and he never hosts. I'm not sure what they did to convince him, but my little baker's heart is in heaven. This kitchen is a dream, with its enormous marble island and one of the nicest ovens I have ever seen in person. It makes me want to dig through his pantry and see what I could bake in here.

"Careful Dean. Next time you come home, you might have a squatter in your kitchen. Lilah looks like she's ready to move in," Indie teases. She flew in to visit Poppy—her childhood friend—for the week and the two of them just got back from backpacking in Breckenridge.

Cruz's arms stay wrapped around my waist as Dom pulls a handful of beers out of Dean's fridge and starts passing them around. "Are you ready for a cold beer after all the nature, Wild Child?" Dom asks, dangling Indie's beer in front of her. His eyes flick over the jersey she's wearing and I swear I see a flash of jealousy over the fact that Dean's name is stitched across the back.

Her hand shoots out, and she snatches the beer from him, rolling her eyes at the nickname. "Do you ever just stop and turn it off?"

"Nope," Dom says, popping the "P." "You'll find it takes some time to acclimate to me, but eventually I'll win you over."

Indie raises the beer to her lips, taking a sip before responding, "I doubt it. I know your type. Been there. Rode that ride. Got the t-shirt. Last time I was lucky enough to walk away without a rash." Her eyes crawl up Dom's body, her red lips twisted in a sneer.

The door opens and more of the team filters in, stopping to say hi before Dean leads them into the living room where they spread out and kick back on the couch.

Nodding my head towards the corner of the kitchen where Hendrix has Poppy caged in, looking broody as he whispers something in her ear I say to Cruz, "Those two seem to be doing well now that they've figured things out."

Cruz's husky laugh tickles my ear as he leans in over my shoulder. "Yeah, they look like they are about to tear each other's clothes off."

I glance up at him over my shoulder. "I know the feeling."

"Hmmm . . . now that you've got me, you can't get enough?"

My chest vibrates against his arms. "You're ridiculous. You know who you sound like when you say shit like that?" I ask, tipping my chin to where Dom, undeterred by the exchange in the kitchen, is listening with rapt attention as Indie tells him and Dean a story.

"Take it back." Cruz turns me around so I'm facing him.

"I said what I said," I tell him with a shake of my head.

"That mouth of yours is going to get you into trouble, *Mocoso*."

Big hand trails up my arm, trailing a path over my shoulder until he's cupping my neck. My skin heats when he ghosts his thumb over the swell of my bottom lip, looking down at me with dark eyes.

How the hell does he do that? A few words and I'm ready to drop to my knees right here and let him wreck me. The image fills my head. It's something we haven't done yet, but now it's all I can think about.

"Should we go see what the others are up to?" he asks, releasing his hold on my neck and leading me through the living room to a game room where most people seem to have congregated.

"Su—sure." My head is reeling. This man melts my brain cells and turns me into a puddle of stupid. It's unnerving. Is it always going to be like this? More than anything, I want to turn the tables on him. Make him feel as out of control as I feel.

Cruz lets my hand drop to say hello to Xavier—pulling him into one of those one-armed hugs, before pulling me right back to him, draping his arm over my shoulder as they talk about the game.

"I am going to find the girls," I tell Cruz, ducking out of his hold. His fingers close around my wrist, pulling me so that I bounce off his chest before he wraps his other arm around my waist and lowers his mouth to mine in a searing kiss.

"That's better," he says before pressing one more sweet kiss to my lips. "Have fun with the girls."

I wobble when he releases me, still dazed from the kiss. I find Indie and Poppy in the living room—each with a bottle of beer in hand, sitting cross-legged on the massive sectional.

This place is designed for entertaining. It makes me wonder why Dean bought it when he never seems to have people over. I know his family is wealthy and that, even without baseball, he'd never have to work a day in his life.

"This place is nuts. We should come here after every game," Poppy says as I sprawl across the oversized ottoman that's nestled into the center of the sectional.

"You could always talk Hen into a place like this someday," I muse, looking around the room.

"No, thanks." Her mouth twists to the side. "It's nice to visit, but I don't want to live here. It's too cavernous. I'd rather have something more . . . cozy."

"Given this some thought?" Indie asks with a raised eyebrow.

"I meant, in general, you brat." Unfortunately for Poppy, there's no hiding her true feelings as her cheeks blaze with color.

"Not even a little?" I ask because I can see it—the two of them finding a place outside the city. Nothing huge, but with enough space for her to have an office and room to spare for Janet and Mia when they visit.

"Well, maybe a little daydream here or there. But we just got to a place where we are great, so that's a long way off."

"Mhmmm . . ." Indie hums, hiding her smirk behind her beer bottle. "Don't act like I didn't catch you gazing at the houses in Breckenridge dreamily, like you could picture spending the offseason there with Hen and your two and half babies."

"Two and half? What is wrong with you?" Poppy shakes her head and Indie just shrugs.

"You had that glow about you. I thought maybe daydream Poppy was pregnant."

"Not that watching you two spar isn't riveting, because it is, and I want more of this in my life"—I gesture between the two of them—"but I need your help right now. I'm just going to declare it more urgent than Hendrix and Poppy's unborn children."

"Thanks Lilah, I think you just secured my spot as godmother," Indie says, holding up her beer to me.

I clink my glass against hers. They'll understand when they hear my plea. Besides, I'm fairly certain that title was already going to be hers. "Cruz has all the power, and I want some." What I don't tell them is that I'm desperate for some control over my feelings and this is the only way I know to do that. Everything with Cruz is so intense—physically and emotionally. The panic wells up in my throat if I think too hard about the way I feel for my best friend.

"Are we talking about the same Cruz?" Poppy asks with a blank expression on her face. "He would literally walk through fire for you. I think that means *you* have all the power."

"I am not talking about *that* power."

"Are we talking about those 'yes, sir' vibes he gives off?" Indie asks, far too loud for my liking. All the guys might be in the other room, but they could come out here anytime.

"Shhh . . . what are you talking about?"

"He looks like the kind of guy that could get a girl to say 'yes, sir' in the bedroom." Indie gives me an appraising look. "He is, isn't he?"

"I changed my mind. This isn't helping," I say as my neck prickles with heat at the thought of me on my knees in front of Cruz saying those exact words. It only makes me want him more, but the physical intensity I can handle. I crave it because it's like nothing I've ever had. It's everything else that scares me, the thought of falling so hard and losing what we have— losing my best friend.

"Knock it off, Ind. You're making her get all worked up," Poppy says, but she can't hide the snicker. "What do you need help with, Delilah? We will be on our best behavior."

"Um. I actually might need you on your worst behavior for this."

"I like where this is going. I know what you need to do . . ." Indie starts.

"You haven't even heard the problem yet," Poppy cuts in, looking between the two of us. Before taking a drink from her almost empty beer.

"Doesn't matter. I know the solution. She needs to suck his dick."

Jesus . . . again with the loud voice.

Poppy's hand flies to her mouth just in time to keep the beer from spraying all over. It dribbles out between her fingers.

Indie passes her the napkin she has wrapped around her bottle and continues without missing a beat. "That's how you get the power back. Suck it right out of him. Works every time."

I nibble on my lip. She might have a point, but it's been a long time. "It's like riding a bike, right? I can do this."

"Yeah, you can!" Indie cheers, poking her cheek with her tongue and holding her hand up for a high five.

"Do what?" Dom asks, as he walks back in with Dean trailing behind. His eyes roam over Indie, openly checking her out as he stops behind where she sits on the couch looming over her.

She tips her head back to look up at him. "Wouldn't you like to know? Sorry Domino, girl talk."

"*Domino*?" he silently mouths down at her. Indie gives him a smug look but doesn't offer an explanation.

"A little help with the beers?" Dean hollers from the kitchen, where he's pulling them out of the fridge. "She's not into you, buddy. Which is probably good because she looks like she'd chew you up and spit you out."

"Fuck, yes! And I'd love it," he says almost wistfully.

"You should listen to your friend," Indie chimes in with a wicked smirk on her face as she looks right past Dom, her heated gaze finding Dean before abruptly turning back to me. "You got a plan, Lilah?"

"Maybe?" I say. I have an idea, but I'm not sure if I'm brazen enough to pull it off. "Let's go see what's going on in the game room."

The guys are finishing up a game of arcade style shuffleboard when the girls and I walk back in. "Dean, this place is incredible. Tell me you have a movie theater?" I ask, eyeing the elaborate set-up.

"No movie theater, but there's a library. Cruz, take your girl on a tour. You remember where everything is?"

"What do you say? Want a tour?" Cruz says, hugging me from behind as the guys set up another game of shuffleboard.

"Sure." He takes my hand and leads me out of the game room. "So, what's the story? His mom is a lawyer?"

"His mom, sister, and brother—grandpa too. They own the largest law firm on the east coast. His brother and sister will take it over at some point when his mom and grandpa retire."

"I wouldn't have guessed. He's so down to earth. A little brooding when he's not being dragged into Dom's nonsense, but he doesn't come off as a trust fund kid."

He leads me through a doorway and the lights turn on automatically. It's a state-of-the-art gym with some sort of electronic batting cage in the corner. "Fancy. Do you guys ever workout here?"

"Not really. We have a few times." He points toward a large screen and netting in the corner. "That's a VR batting cage. It's pretty cool. I'll have him set it up so you can try it next time."

Leading me by the hand, we weave our way through the gym to the attached balcony. There are several seating areas and tucked in the corner looking out over the city is a hot tub.

My hand brushes over the cover, imagining all the filthy things I'd like to get up to with Cruz in it.

"This is his favorite part about the penthouse. I think it might be the only thing aside from the library that he likes about it."

"Really, why?" I ask, leaning against the railing to take in the sweeping views of the mountains.

"It's complicated. This place was a gift from his grandpa. I don't know the whole story, but there's some tension there."

"Library next?"

"Lead the way." Butterflies take flight in my stomach and I have to fight the urge to fidget as Cruz leads me back inside the penthouse and down the hall further.

When he walks through the last door on the left, I quietly pull the door shut behind me. "Wow, this is impressive. He's a talking clock away from being a modern day beast locked up here in his castle." Opposite the long wall of books there's a sitting area with a small couch in cognac leather and matching armchair.

The shelves are filled with classics and some newer thrillers. My fingers dance across the spines, temporarily distracted from my plans.

"It's funny. He's got this whole library, but he reads on his phone when we travel. I have never once seen him with an actual book."

I spin around to find Cruz sitting in the armchair, his gaze crawls down my body as I stand in the middle of the darkly lit room. My feet carry me towards him, the nerves I was feeling earlier turning to an ache that radiates deep within me. This isn't just about feeling a sense of control over this crazy longing I feel for my best friend.

He's made everything about *me*. He's been unwavering in his pursuit to make *me* feel good, and I want to do the same for him. When I stop in front of him, his hands grip my hips.

"God, Delilah. You're so fucking stunning. It kills me that I've waited this long to tell you that whenever I want."

Does this man even know what he does to me? He's been the most important person in my life for years—the one I go to for everything. Just being his friend has made my life infinitely better. I cup the side of his face and straddle his lap. "You have me now and I'm not going anywhere."

Our kiss starts out sweet, but after his tongue slips into my mouth, I melt into his body. Molding against him as he bands his arms around me and tugs me closer. When I thread my fingers in his hair, tilting him back to give me better access, he hums against my lips.

His thick length hardens between us as the kiss intensifies, and I let my hand drift down his chest and torso before my fingers find the button on his jeans. With a deftness that impresses me, given how flustered I felt earlier, I pop the button loose and scoot back on his lap so I can drag his zipper down.

The sound it makes seems to echo through the room. My skin tingles at the prospect of getting to taste him, letting him fill my mouth.

"Hermosa." The word is a rough moan as his chest heaves up and down. Eyes widening when I back all the way off his lap and kneel between his spread knees.

"Mhmmm." I'm too focused on the heavy erection in his pants to say anything more. Moving my hands up his strong thighs, I push them further apart, giving myself room to work as I slip my hand inside his open zipper and palm his thick cock through his boxer briefs.

"What are you doing?" His voice is measured, but when I look up, I find a soft expression on his face.

"It seems pretty obvious to me. Since this mouth was getting me into trouble earlier, I figured I would put it to use in another way."

"Oh yeah. You're going to wrap these pretty red lips around my cock right here? Where anyone could walk in?"

I hadn't really thought about that. It shouldn't make me want this more, but it does. I clench my thighs together, the pulse there ratcheting up to the next level.

My hand slides under the elastic of his waistband, pumping him with my hand before I pull him out.

"You better get to work then, before someone walks in and finds you on your knees choking on my cock like a greedy girl." He cups the side of my face with a gentleness that contrasts his words.

With my free hand, I tug on his jeans and he lifts, pushing them down for me as my hand moves up and down his length languidly. When a bead of pre-cum glistens on his tip, I dip my head and kiss it away.

"Don't tease me, Hermosa. If someone walks in and sees you like this, I might have to punch them in the face and I'd rather not—"

His words are cut off when I bring my tongue to the base of his shaft and lick him before circling the tip with my tongue.

"Like that?" I ask, letting my lips flutter against him as my hand pumps.

"Yes, fuck. Delilah, you could blow on my dick and it would feel good. The fact it's *you* is enough to make it amazing."

"What if I did this?" I ask before I suck him deep into my mouth, taking him as far as I can manage.

His hands fly to my hair, pushing it off to the side and gathering it up. I can feel his thighs tense underneath me, like he's holding back as I pull back and take him further this time. I know I said I wanted the control but the thought of him taking control and owning my mouth has me moaning around his cock as it bumps the back of my throat.

The hand Cruz has my hair wrapped around tightens. "I can't decide if I want to watch you swallow down every last drop of my cum or bend you over the arm of that couch and fuck you from behind."

I suck harder, his filthy words spurring me on. I want both of those things, but this isn't about me.

"Fuck, Hermosa. I'm close." He gives my hair a gentle tug, but I shake him off. Twisting my hand at the base as I bring him deep, hollowing my cheeks.

Cruz stifles a groan as his body tenses and his cock pulses against my tongue before he spills down my throat.

"You did so good." His voice is raw as I release him from my mouth. My pulse beats wildly against my eardrums. Never once has giving a guy head made me so needy. He tucks himself into his pants as he pulls me off the floor and into his lap.

"We should get back before anyone comes looking for us," I tell him as he hugs me against his chest, his heart still thundering under my ear. It's the last thing I want to do, but it's going to be obvious if we don't get back soon.

His lips move against my neck. "And let you walk around all night with wet panties and that ache between your legs? I don't think so."

It doesn't sound fun when he says it like that. We haven't been gone that long. A few more minutes won't hurt . . . right?

Cruz makes the decision easy when he cups me through my shorts and whispers into my ear. "Stand up and hang on to the back of the couch."

Yes, sir.

Moving from his lap, I stand to do just that. Cruz follows me to the couch, crowding me from behind as his hand comes around to work the button on my bottoms free. "You're going to need to be very quiet. If you can't do that, I won't let you come."

I nod eagerly. I'd bite my tongue off right now if it meant he would touch me. When he works the zipper down and snakes his hand into my underwear, I shudder. Cruz bites down on my shoulder lightly.

"Just fucking drenched. Having me in your mouth did this?"

It really fucking did.

"God, yes. I love your cock." He circles my clit with his finger before he withdraws and pushes my shorts down, leaving them around my ankles. His hand glides up my thigh and over my hip before he pushes down between my shoulder blades.

Leaning over my back and letting his hand drop to my hip before his other hand slides up the inside of my leg. Just the brush of his hand has me biting back a cry. I suck my teeth to keep quiet as he dips one and then two fingers inside me. Being on my knees for him has me so close already, each touch from him taking me higher.

My hips push back, forcing him in further as his grip on my hip tightens, keeping me from being able to ride his fingers the way I want to.

"So impatient. You had your fun. Now it's my turn." A whimper slips free and Cruz stills behind me. "Shhh, I would really hate to stop now when we are just getting started."

I drop my head to where my hands grip the couch as my back bows when Cruz adds a third finger. "You're gripping me so tight with this needy pussy. It makes me wonder what it would be like if I slid a finger into this hot little hole?" His thumb slides up, putting just enough pressure *there* that I can feel it. "Fuck, you like that. Has anyone ever touched you here?"

I look over my shoulder at him, my eyes half open from all the lust coursing through my body, and shake my head. "You'd be the first."

"Fuck, you don't know how much I love that." When his fingers leave me, I almost cry out, but he doesn't go far. They slide up, coating me with my release. He repeats the movement again. My grip on the back of the couch is so tight that there will probably be permanent marks from my nails digging in. "Say the word and I stop."

"Don't you fucking dare." My knees nearly buckle when his fingers slide back inside my pussy. The way my heart is thumping against my ribs from anticipating what he's going to do next, it might actually burst. He runs his thumb along my seam, coating it before it slides back up and massages my tight bud.

"So fucking tight, you need to relax. Rub your clit for me."

Cruz takes advantage of the rush of pleasure that surges through me while my fingers work over the bundle of nerves, sliding his thumb inside me. I groan into the crook of my arm at the unfamiliar sensation.

"I can't wait to take this ass. That's it, squeeze me. Show me how much you like that idea."

"Yes," I huff out as my spine tingles, building my release up block by block, getting closer to tipping with every caress. Cruz pushes his thumb in further until I am pushing back against him, riding his fingers as I make tight circles over my clit. I didn't even know it was possible to feel this full. It only makes me want more. More of him, more of this—of everything.

"That's it. Shatter for me, Hermosa."

I bite down on my arm as my orgasm rips through me, causing my knees to buckle, but Cruz is there to catch me before I sag to the ground, looping his arm under my hips and kissing the side of my neck.

"Jesus. That was so fucking hot."

I nod, still resting my head against the back of the couch as I fight to catch my breath.

"You did so good staying quiet for me." Once my legs are under me again, Cruz drops to his knees behind me and shocks the hell out of me by running his tongue along my slit without warning. His hands work my shorts up as he chuckles at the way I shudder at the unexpected assault.

"Warn a girl," I huff out, pushing up off the back of the couch and turning to face him as he rises from his knees.

"Where is the fun in that?" Cruz pulls me to him, nipping at my bottom lip before slanting his mouth over mine for a kiss.

It's short-lived, now we've actually been gone way too long. On the way back to the party, Cruz ducks into the bathroom and I head back to the game room where everyone is distracted by the Mario Kart battle happening between Hendrix, Poppy, Xavier and Dom.

When Dean saddles up beside me, he's got a smirk on his face. "Just tell me his bare ass wasn't on any of my furniture."

"His bare ass wasn't on any of your furniture," I say without taking my eyes off the large projection screen where the intense match up is happening.

"Hmmm . . . Why don't I believe you?"

I shrug just as Cruz comes back into the room looking content with a serene smile on his face. Dean just shakes his head at him, but it doesn't matter. Neither of us would change a thing.

CHAPTER 29

ANNIVERSARIES SUCK

PRESENT

Sorrow washes over me as soon as I wake up. Even having Delilah wrapped around me like a sexy Koala doesn't help. My sleep was fractured last night, as I spent most of it tossing and turning, dreading the sunrise because it's been another year since the accident. After all this time, I still can't fulfill either of my promises to Jarrett.

I wrap my arms tighter around my beautiful best friend, in awe that I can call her mine now. Careful not to wake her up, I bury my nose in her blonde hair, letting the scent of cinnamon and vanilla ease the ache in my chest. It took me this long to go after what I wanted with Delilah. That doesn't scream living life to the fullest to me.

Having her this close helps combat the uncontrollable feeling that I've let Jarrett down. I'm still no closer to knowing what happened to him than the night coach showed up at my door three years ago.

"Cruz! Wake up, pretty boy. It's my birthday and we start celebrating now!" Something wet runs down my face. "Let's go, Hermano. Rise and shine." Another stream of water hits me. This time on my chest.

I crack an eye open to find Jarrett leaning against the doorframe of my bedroom, water gun in hand, finger posed over the trigger.

"I knew it was a mistake inviting you out for the weekend," I grumble, tugging the blankets up. I played a late game last night, and it went into extra innings. I'm not ready to be awake yet, but we have places to be this morning. Namely, a surprise brunch with my parents. Jarrett has no idea that they flew in last night and are meeting us this morning. "Okay, I'm up, but put down the weapon or there are no gifts for you."

Jarrett's hands shoot up above his head. "You wouldn't."

"I would. Where did you even get that thing?" I ask, sliding out of bed.

"Picked up yesterday with some essentials for the weekend." His lips tilt up in a smirk.

"I'm afraid to ask." I make my way past him to the shower, only for him to squirt me in the back. "Give me twenty minutes and I'll be ready for your big day."

"Estas son las mañanitas, que cantaba el Rey David, Hoy por ser día de tu santo, te las cantamos a ti Despierta, Jarrett, despierta, mira que ya amaneció,Ya los pajarillos cantan,la luna ya se metió." My mom's voice rings out from the private room that I rented, which she's decked out in colorful banners as part of our little celebration today.

"Well, you're a sneaky fucker, aren't you?" Jarrett says under his breath, his grin wide making his dimple pop. Where I got two dimples, he only has one on his right side.

"You can thank me later, when you're stuffed full of mom's tres leches."

"If you squeeze me any harder, I might pop," Delilah says in a tender way that tells me she understands exactly why I'm clinging to her like she's my only lifeline. "What were you thinking about?"

"Am I hurting you?" I relax my arms, giving her room to push back, but she doesn't. "Just a memory. Jarrett's 23rd birthday. It was the last time we were all together."

"Don't you dare let me go. There's no place else I would rather be." Her hand snakes up to my face, and she cups my cheek. "Take whatever you need from me today."

"I just need you to be here." Looking into her loving blue eyes like this, I'm not sure how I would have done this without her by my side for the last three years.

After the doctors told us there was nothing else they could do for Jarrett, I went back to St. Louis, but everything had changed. Not just life without my brother and best friend, or the crater-sized hole in my heart left behind, the Commanders' organization refused to answer questions about what happened that night. It created an unmendable rift that ended in my trade.

Things didn't get easier when the police couldn't find any information and claimed it was just an unfortunate accident. I refused to accept that. I could feel in my soul that they were wrong, so I hired Rich at the recommendation of the lead detective in Miami. Like me, he thought there was more to the story, but they were at a dead end and no one was willing to talk. His minor league teammates claimed they didn't know what Jarrett's plans were that night—not Miller, who was traveling with the team for rehab, and not Coach Becker, who got the call from the hospital.

The cab driver who took him to the hospital wasn't any help either. He was called to the address for a pickup but found Jarrett instead. The number that called the taxi company was untraceable because of the volume of calls and the fact that the caller took steps to block the number.

"Cruz, did you hear me?" Pillowy lips along my jaw pull me from my thoughts. Fuck, I need a distraction. I shift in bed, sitting up against the headboard.

"No. Sorry, what were you saying?" Delilah frowns at me, her brow creased with concern.

"After the game, do you think you'll be up for the sunset boat ride with Poppy and Hendrix? We found a local marina that rents out boats."

"Yeah. I was just thinking I needed something to take my mind off things, and that sounds perfect." I promised Jarrett I would live my life to its fullest, that I wouldn't let his death break me. Spending time with friends was what he loved the most outside the ballpark and family.

Delilah settles into my lap and drops tender kisses along the side of my neck. "Maybe I can offer you another distraction in the meantime. How long before you have to get to the stadium for strength and conditioning?"

"It doesn't matter. I'll make time for whatever you have in mind." It'll be worth getting fined if I'm late. Her fingers grip my biceps desperately as she slants her lips over mine. Kissing me with everything she has right from the start.

I return the kiss with a matched need. She's offering herself up as a distraction and I'm going to fucking drown myself in her because both of us know she is so much more than that.

Wait, does she know that?

"*Delilah*, hold on for a second," I mumble against her lips. It takes effort to pull myself away, but I need to say this because I swore I wouldn't hold back.

"Yeah, I don't want to do that." Her voice is husky as she kisses down my neck again.

Oh, fuck, give me strength.

"Hermosa. One second, *please*." Her lips stay connected to where she was kissing her way across my sternum, but she tilts her head up, pausing her progress. "Don't get me wrong, stopping you right now is painful. I just need—" Kiss. Taking a deep breath, I tug at her shoulder, trying not to laugh as she pouts when I move her back up my body. "You're not making this easy."

"I'm trying to be *very* easy." Delilah flutters her eyelashes at me, and I have to stifle my laughter. "Fine, out with it," she finally grumbles, resting her head against my shoulder and giving in.

"I told my brother I would always live in a way that made him proud and part of that means telling the people in my life what they mean to me. I need you to know you're not just a distraction to me."

"Cruz, I know that."

I shake my head, not quite finished. "It's been three years and you've been there helping me through it for most of that time. I was at my lowest point when I met you and, piece by shattered piece, you helped me to rebuild my life. You didn't even know you were doing it. You did it by just being you." I push a strand of hair away from her face so I can see her eyes. "He would have loved you, Delilah. The two of you would have been insufferable together, ganging up on me, but God, I would give anything for just one day of that, for him to know you. You're not a distraction, Mi Cielo. You're everything."

My thumb swipes across her cheek, catching a tear that I'm not sure she even realized had fallen.

"Is it my turn to talk? Although I'm not sure I want to follow that. Talk about sweeping a girl off her feet." Her nervous chuckle makes me smile.

"Sure, but you know you don't have to. I didn't tell you that because I expected anything in return. I just couldn't keep it in, not today."

"Cruz, shut up for a second. Please." She has the nerve to roll those big blue eyes at me and it has the same effect as when she bites that damn lip.

My fingers slide across my lips as I flatten them into a line. When she seems satisfied that I'm done, she lifts her head, so she's looking right at me. Her hand wraps around the base of my skull and stops when her fingers are threaded through my hair.

"I think sometimes you forget all the ways you've helped me over the years. When I was lost and broken after—everything—you protected me.

From myself. From *them* that day at lunch. You refused to let me feel worthless after they betrayed me. Without you, it would have destroyed me. You showed me all the things I deserve." She rests her forehead against mine. "Being with you still scares the shit out of me. I can't fathom how much it would hurt to lose this, but as much as I try, I can't deny it. I want to keep being your everything, just don't break me because there will be no one to pick up the pieces."

"Never, Delilah."

She brings her mouth to mine, picking up right where she left off.

"What a fucking bomb!" Hendrix shouts, slapping me on the back when he joins me in the dugout in the ninth inning. "He'd be proud of you. You're one hell of a teammate and captain. Not to mention you carry him with you every day with your passion for the game and your devotion to your friends."

"Thanks, man." Hen means well but I can't help feeling that I failed my brother by not finding out what happened. That thought has my fingers twitching to text Rich and ask about that number again.

Hendrix can't wipe the stupid grin off his face as we sit through the post-game breakdown with Coach Wilson, and I can't say I blame him. Playing under the lights has the spectacle and glory, but right now, none of that compares to the fact that I get to spend my night with my favorite person after winning the game over the Chicago Comets.

"Aren't you two cute, with your matching heart eyes?" Dom throws over his shoulder as he walks to the shower with his towel slung over his shoulder and his hand cupping his junk.

"Hey, moron, you could wrap your towel around your waist like the rest of us instead of strutting around, ass out," I retort, grabbing what I need to clean up.

"Don't pretend like you don't love my ass. Have you seen this cake? It's the source of all my powers." Laughter rings out through the locker room when Dom grabs a handful of ass cheek while winking at me.

"Jesus, let's just shower and get to the girls. It's too bad the water can't wash that image out of my brain," Hendrix comments standing from the locker room bench.

"He's not wrong. He's got a fucking dump truck on him. Did you see the way it bounced when he grabbed it?" Dean blinks slowly like he's scarred by the whole interaction.

Hendrix shakes his head and walks back to the shower, picking the stall furthest from where Dom is currently singing, "Too Much Booty in the Pants."

"I would have thought you were more of a 'Rump Shaker' kind of guy," I tell Dom, taking the stall between them.

"Good call. I can sing that one for you next," he says over the top of the stall with a wink.

"Please don't," Dean remarks when he walks in. "You two are going to get him all juiced up and then leave me to deal with him while you enjoy your evening with your girlfriends."

"You almost sound jealous. Sick of playing wingman to Dom and ready to find someone?" I ask.

"Not a fucking chance. I've seen how that works out in the long run."

"So, you're never planning on being in a relationship." Hendrix pauses with his sudsy hands in his hair, looking at Dean with a raised eyebrow.

"Pretty much."

"I can't wait to watch you fall flat on your face for some girl." Hendrix grins over the stall before rinsing his hair and grabbing his towel—leaving me to fend for myself with Tweedledee and Tweedledum.

"This is amazing. Hendrix, this was the best idea ever," Poppy says from where she plastered against his side with her arms around his waist.

Delilah and I are seated on the other side of the boat. There's enough room for both of us to have our own seat but I'd rather share. She's pressed against my side with my hand gripping her knee where her legs are thrown over my lap. Our friends chartered this boat for the night, claiming we were overdue for a double date, but I know they did it to keep me busy and distracted today. They even made sure the marina could provide a driver so we could just kick back and enjoy the picnic dinner the girls packed.

"That's right, because I'm a very smart man."

"Speaking of great ideas. We found a place in St. John for the All-Star Break," I say, not wanting to focus on why we are on this boat. Next to me she excitedly pulls out her phone, opening up the link for the house, and passes it to Poppy.

"This is amazing, but it's huge." Hendrix's head tilts to the side in question.

"It is. Someone wants to turn a romantic getaway into a group trip."

Without warning, she smacks my chest, her face twisted in faux annoyance. "You're going to throw me under the bus like that?"

I lift my shoulders innocently. There's a reason she's not ready to go on vacation as a couple. I haven't called her out on the fact that she's letting her fear keep her from being all in. She'll find her way there. I just hope it's not too much longer.

"So, this would be a group trip, not just the four of us?" Poppy asks, swiping through the pictures.

"We haven't worked it all out yet, but there's enough room to invite some of the guys."

She nudges Hendrix with her shoulder. "Should we see if your sister wants to come? It will be right after her next book release. I bet she'd love a break."

"This is your master plan. What did you think?" He gestures to Delilah and me.

"I love it! I have heard so much about Mia and am dying to meet her in person when we go to St. Louis. Can we invite Indie too?" Delilah claps her hands, thrilled that her plan is coming together.

The suggestion to have her childhood best friend join the trip makes Poppy's smile widen. "That's perfect. We had talked about planning a girl's trip, but this would be just as good."

"You're just a little troublemaker, aren't you?" Hendrix pokes her in the side, causing her to squeak.

"Don't pretend like you don't want to sit back and watch her get Dom and Dean all twisted up again like she did last time she came to visit," she says, trying to shift away to avoid any more fingers to the ribs.

Hendrix's eyes are narrowed at Poppy when he says, "The only thing I'm interested in on this vacation is you strutting around in a hot little bikini and then crawling into my bed."

"Yo! There's an audience here, buddy," I remind him before they get too carried away.

He raises his eyebrow at me as if to ask, really you aren't thinking the same thing about Delilah?

"So, we have the four of us, Dean, Dom, Indie, and Mia. What about the other guys?" Delilah takes control of the conversation, steering us clear of any further discussions about how we want to spend our private time on the trip.

"Xavier always goes home to visit his parents, and the other guys are either playing or already have plans," I explain.

"That's it then, the eight of us?" Hendrix asks, looking at his girlfriend before glancing back at us.

"I like it," Poppy declares, putting her stamp of approval on the plan. "Does that work for you, Lilah?"

"Yes, and I'm so excited." When she tilts her head up to me and her lips find my jaw, I'm not even a little annoyed that the trip has turned out this way. Making her smile like this is my favorite pastime.

The captain slows the boat and turns in his seat so he's facing the four of us. "This is the best spot to anchor and watch the sunset. If you want to sit at the bow, I'll hang out back here to give you some space."

The boat is only twenty-five feet long, but I appreciate his attempts to make it feel like it's just the four of us out here.

I thread my fingers through Delilah's as we move to the front of the boat where the girls stashed the food earlier. The sunset has painted the sky a breathtaking mix of pink and orange hues.

"Wow. It's so beautiful," Delilah murmurs in awe as she ducks under my arm to stand next to me, looking out over the water.

The view in front of us is straight out of a painting with the mountains and sunset mingling over the calm surface of the blue water, but that's not what has me captivated. It's the woman at my side, and the way her blonde hair shimmers with the late day sun, or the way she tilts her chin up to the sky, taking it all in. Delilah is more beautiful than any sunset or mountain range. "The most stunning thing I have ever seen." My lips brush the crown of her hair as I pull her closer. Her answering smile ignites a light inside me brighter than any star in the sky. There's nothing I wouldn't do to see her this happy every day.

"Babe, take a picture! Look how cute they are," Poppy whisper-shouts, bursting our bubble.

Delilah buries her face into my chest and turns in my arms so she's facing the two of them, dragging me with her.

"Yeah, Hen. Take a picture." My girl eggs him on and I do what any good boyfriend would do. I snake my arms around her waist and smile for the photo.

"Make sure you send me that," I tell him over my shoulder as Delilah leads me to the table hand in hand. I finally have the girl I've wanted for years and you're damn right I am going to print that picture. It might even have to travel with me while on the road, but not this upcoming road trip because I've got something better.

The real life version is coming along for the trip.

CHAPTER 30

THE ONE WHERE I ALMOST GOT HIM BENCHED

PRESENT

The elevator dings as the door slides open. Checking my room key for the third time, I step out onto the twelfth floor. My suitcase trails behind me as I follow the signs to the room Cruz and I have for this part of the road trip. The team plane flew in earlier and Cruz has to leave for the stadium soon, so this is a quick stop to drop off my bags before Poppy and I grab food ahead of the game with Hen's sister—Mia—and his nana—Janet.

There's a rush of air when the door opens before I swipe my key. Cruz's hands grip my hips, hauling me forward. My hands flatten, bracing against his hard chest as a high-pitched squeal leaves me.

"What were you doing? Looking out the peephole to watch for me?" His stubble scrapes the sensitive skin of my neck as his lips pepper me with kisses. He drags my discarded suitcase into the room, letting it tip over before the door clicks shut and his lips find my neck again.

My head tilts back, allowing him more access. "I heard you coming down the hallway and wanted to get as much of this in before I had to leave for the stadium." His lips hover against my skin as his hands slide down my back and over my ass. Without warning he lifts me, walking me through the hotel room towards the bed.

When we fall to the bed, he bounces beside me. "You're nuts. You know that, right?"

"You love it." His lips seal over mine, stealing the response from my mouth. He kisses me like it's been weeks since he's seen me, not less than twenty-four hours. "I missed you, Hermosa." Then he's on top of me, pinning my arms to the mattress, as his lips drop blistering kisses down my neck.

"Do you have time to show me how much?" The smile he gives me makes me melt into the mattress. Has my best friend always been this hot?

"Coach can bench me tonight for being late and I wouldn't care if it meant being inside you right now." My hands slide down the back of his joggers and right into his boxer briefs, and he doesn't resist when I pull his hips towards my center.

"We're gonna have to do something about all these clothes between us."

Cruz stills above me, pushing up on his forearms. I swallow roughly when I see the look on his face. He's looking at me like he's got the best kind of bad idea. His dark eyes sweep down my body before his tongue darts out to wet his lips. "Strip." His voice is rough like sandpaper when he rises to his feet, leaving me star-fished across the bed.

I look at him for a beat. Part of me wants to say no, just to see his reaction, but I like this side of Cruz. More than I ever would have imagined, having him take control in the bedroom is the biggest turn on. He stares me down from where he stands at the foot of the bed, both of us refusing to break eye contact. *"Yes, sir."*

My words have the desired effect. His jaw ticks as he palms his length through his pants looking like he wants to fuck me until I'm too sated to give him any sass.

Leaning up on my elbows, I shift up the bed and swing my knees under me. Taking my time, I reach for my shirt, tugging it over my head before I let it drop next to me. Cruz steps in closer so his knees brush against the bottom of the bed, but he doesn't reach out or make any other move towards me.

"I know I said I'd get benched for this, but I didn't think you'd take that as a challenge. Someone's feeling feisty."

My hands lower to the button on my shorts and push them down my hips, watching as Cruz's chest starts to rise and fall more quickly. His hands are balled tightly at his sides like it's taking all his restraint to hold him back. Somehow, I free them from my legs without tipping over.

As I kneel there in just a pale pink sheer bra and matching high rise thong, goosebumps pebble my skin, I'm not sure if it's from the air conditioning or the way Cruz makes me feel when he looks at me like this. "Was it worth the wait?"

"You're always worth the wait. Did you think of me when you picked this out today?" He leans forward, placing his palm flat on the mattress. In this position, he's more imposing than he was towering over me.

The way he phrases his question with such certainty makes my pulse thrum between my legs. The scrap of fabric between my legs is soaked, and he's right. Not only did I pick this out for him this morning, but I ordered it online the other day, desperate to see his reaction to it. "And what if I did?"

When I push the strap down my shoulder, a low groan works its way out of his chest. "That would deserve a reward for thinking of me this morning after I left."

"And if I didn't?" My heart rate speeds up at the thrill of challenging him.

"I would be disappointed to know that I wasn't on your mind when your fingers ran up your legs as you pulled this on."

"But no reward?" I slide the other strap down my shoulder as Cruz places a knee on the bed, getting just a little closer. I'm dying to see how far he'll let me push him.

"No reward. As a matter of fact, I'd need to find a way to make sure that next time you were thinking of me when you picked out something this sexy."

Fuck, is it hot in here? I have to bite down on my bottom lip to stop myself from moaning at the visual that just popped into my head of all the ways he could accomplish that. Would he spank me, or maybe he would keep me on edge for hours, tie me up? And why do all of those things turn me on so much? I've never done any of them. There's no way Brad would have ever—No, he doesn't belong here.

"What's that look for, Delilah?"

"Hmmm?"

"That look? Your eyes got all glazed over and your cheeks flushed to the perfect shade of pink. What were you thinking about?"

"All the ways you could make sure you were on my mind every time I pulled on a pair of lacy underwear."

"I'm listening. What was in that brilliant mind that had you so worked up, Hermosa? I told you I would figure out all the ways to make you blush. So, I want to know what you were thinking." His voice is measured and controlled as he reminds me of that promise.

I can feel the heat return to my chest and racing upward to my face. If I tell him, will he actually do those things to me, and do I want him to? Will I like them? Or is it just the idea that gets me hot? Everytime we are together I learn something new about how mind-blowing sex can be when you have a partner you trust, that enjoys giving you pleasure more than just receiving it. It makes me ravenous to try everything with him.

Cruz studies me like he's got the key to my mind and with a simple twist of his wrist, he can unlock it and see right inside. "Are you nervous? Remember who you're talking to. I was your best friend long before we ever slept together. Nothing you tell me will change the way I feel about you."

"Well, the opposite of reward is usually punishment. I was thinking about what you would do to me if I told you I hadn't been thinking of you when I ran my hands over this set before I pulled it on and studied myself in the mirror this morning."

His other knee comes up onto the mattress. He's so close, but he keeps his arms at his side, and it makes me want to scream out and beg for his touch. I continue hoping that it'll be enough to drive him to action.

"I was blushing because the idea of you punishing me turned me on. Would you spank me or keep me from coming? Bind my hands and tease me until I couldn't take it?"

"Jesus—Fuck, Delilah." His chest heaves and I can tell he's so close to losing control and I can't help myself when I want to see what happens when he does. Reaching behind me, I unclasp my bra, letting it fall down my arms to the bed in front of me. "Is that what you want? Did it make your skin match that sexy underwear because you are embarrassed? Or because it makes you soak through those panties?" His finger gently trails up from the swell of my breast to my cheek, and my shoulders quiver with a shiver.

"Yes." It's the only answer I have for him because while I was pushing him, something inside my head snapped and the brain-to-mouth connection broke.

"Turn around."

"What?"

Cruz holds a single finger up in the air, twirling it in a tight circle. "Turn around. Let me see all of you."

Still on my knees, I spin around on the bed and find him over my shoulder as he continues to watch from the foot of the bed. "Like this?"

"So good at following directions." His palm presses between my shoulder blade as his other hand grips my hip. As he lowers me to my hands and knees, his voice is like sandpaper. "Now, tell me what you were thinking when you put on this pretty little ensemble this morning?"

"How dark your eyes would get when you saw me in it. If you'd like it." It comes out one long string of words. Stupid brain, you weren't supposed to admit that yet. My eyes find him, and I can't bring myself to be mad about my admission. Pushing him was exhilarating, but the way his face softens at my admission is worth all the sexy fun that I might have just sacrificed.

The hand on my hip drags towards where I want him the most, tracing the line of my underwear with his fingertips. A deep hum leaves the back of his throat when he brushes over the drenched spot between my legs.

"Is this all from thinking about me punishing you?"

His fingers sweep over me again. "Mostly. But it's also because I was remembering how I felt this morning when I picked this out for you—picturing the way you would react to me in it."

His thick fingers hook into my panties and tug them to the side. "I'm not sure I can punish you when you have been so good to me. Not this time, at least." He sinks two fingers into me without warning and I collapse to my forearms, back arching from the pleasure that rockets through me. "Besides, Hermosa, I have to leave for the stadium soon, and that's not something I want to do when I won't be here to make sure you're okay."

The softness in his voice takes me by surprise, but I don't get time to think about it as he slides his fingers out and then back in.

"You are a fucking sight like this. I wish you could see how you look with your ruined panties pushed to the side, riding my fingers."

"Cruz." His name is a plea for more.

"I suppose it's not a punishment if you want it this bad?" His hand connects with my ass and I gasp, clenching around him tightly. Behind me, he chuckles.

"Are you—did you just laugh after you spanked me?"

"You're just so fucking surprising. Every time you show me something new, I want you even more." His words are sweet, and his hand comes down again. This time on the other cheek. "Fuck." His hand smooths over the spot, soothing the sting.

"Again," I beg, pushing my ass back towards him.

"Last one. We'll do more another time." When my eyes find him, his forehead is creased in concentration. He studies me like he's worried that this is more than I can handle. "You're dripping all over my hand at just the thought. Who would have thought you'd be such a dirty girl?"

His fingers hook inside me, hitting all the right nerve endings as his palm comes down one more time, causing me to cry out a garbled string of nonsense.

I feel him shift behind me on the bed and his fingers slide further between my legs to find my clit. I'm about to protest the loss of his finger when he brings his mouth to my center. He works me with his mouth like I'm the only thing he needs to survive for the rest of his life. Humming deep in his throat as he laps at me from behind.

My hands grip the sheets as my upper half melts into the bed, unable to hold myself up any longer with the heat coursing through my veins. Cruz pinches my clit, and it sends me tumbling into a black hole.

There's no time to recover before he shoves his joggers down, freeing himself and entering me from behind. My hips push back into him, chasing the aftershocks of my release and drawing it out.

"Harder, Cruz."

"That's it, Hermosa. Take what you need." He praises me as I continue to meet him thrust for thrust, the tingling feeling already building again at the base of my spine.

Cruz covers my back with his chest as one arm wraps around my front, gripping my breast with his large hand. He holds me tight to him, dragging me so we are both upright. The other hand travels up the curve of my waist and between my breasts before he wraps it around my throat. Just holding it there. And holy fuck. The rush of bliss that cascades through my body is like nothing I have ever experienced before.

Leaning in, Cruz's lips graze my ear. "I wish you could feel how wet your pussy just got. My cock is fucking soaked. I knew you'd like that. Such a filthy little brat for me."

"I fucking love it. Please don't stop." My hand covers his. Holding him there as I frantically chase my release. When Cruz lowers his mouth to my shoulder and bites down just enough to cause a slice of pain, I clench around him, coming harder than I thought I could.

"You're so perfect when you come on my cock," Cruz croons as he pulls out, flipping me so I'm on my back and thrusts back in without missing a beat. "Perfect for me." He gives me everything he's got as he races towards his own release. My name comes out in a hoarse shout when he seizes inside of me, letting himself go.

I'm in a daze when Cruz presses a sweet kiss to my lips. "You're unbelievable. Let me get you cleaned up."

"I'll just be right here trying to figure out if there are still bones in my body or if you fucked them all out of me."

The smirk he throws my way as he disappears through the bathroom door does nothing to calm my still racing heart. The sound of the sink running penetrates my foggy brain and then he's back at my side, causing the mattress to dip when he lowers himself to the bed.

Cruz is at my side, a warm washcloth gently swiping between my legs, and he hovers over me with creases lining his forehead. "Was it too much?"

"Not at all," I say, shifting to my side so we are face-to- face. "Everything with you is better than the last. If you weren't about to be late I'd be on my knees begging for more." My hand comes up to cup the back of his head as my lips slant over his.

"Now that's something I want to see." He ducks his head kissing my forehead. "I wish I didn't have to leave. You're sure you're okay?"

"Better than okay. I promise. I'd tell you if it was too much."

"I don't like the idea—"

"Listen to me carefully." The last thing I want is for him to think that I can't handle what just happened. If he takes this away from me, I might cry. With him I feel more alive than I ever have. "I love how considerate you are, but in this case, it's unnecessary. I've never been with anyone that makes me feel as confident and comfortable as you do. You didn't do anything that I didn't ask for, but if you don't like it or it's too much for you, then we won't do it again."

"Fuck, no. Mi Cielo, you were a goddamn fantasy. I just don't like the idea of leaving you right after. That was intense."

"I'll be with the girls, not alone. As soon as that game is over, your ass better be back in this bed with me, giving me more amazing firsts."

"Well, now I kind of feel like a piece of meat." Kissing me one more time, he pushes off the bed to dress and leave for the stadium. "But I think I can live with it."

Cruz peels me off the bed and drops one last kiss on my lips, followed by an overly pat on the ass for motivation to get ready for dinner with the girls.

I'm in seventh heaven watching Cruz play in St. Louis. Despite the fact that this city holds some of his worst memories, he's having a stellar game. He hasn't said it, but I know that me being here for this road trip has helped him keep his demons at bay. When the team takes the field at the start of the fifth inning, his eyes find me while he runs out to his spot in the outfield. And because my best friend is as goofy as he is sexy, he wiggles his fingers at me in an adorable wave.

The Bandits continue to fight back against the Commanders even though the home team ties it up going into the sixth. His next turn up to bat Cruz steps to the plate with Hendrix already at second. The team needs this hit desperately if they want to break this tie.

Although his pitching has been steady tonight, Miller looks decidedly off-kilter right now. He keeps shaking off the signs from his catcher. And the way he's glaring while he gets settled in the batter's box is unsettling. I wipe my damp hands on my shorts before I lock Poppy and Mia's hands in a death grip as he gets into his stance.

Cruz's face is twisted in contempt as he waits for him to pick his pitch. There's no love lost between the two of them and the arrogant pitcher is a big part of the reason Cruz was okay with a trade to Denver. I can hear the blood pounding in my ears as I wait for the pitch, impatient for it to be over.

As soon as the pitch leaves Miller's hand, my stomach sinks and rage takes over as I push to my feet. It happens so fast that I don't have time to turn away. A blood-curdling scream leaves my body as the ball hits Cruz in the side of the head.

Poppy's arms band around me, locking me in place to keep me from turning towards the field. My breath is coming too fast and Mia rubs my back in circles, trying to calm me down. I can tell by how eerily still the stadium gets, it was as bad as it looked. In my ear, Poppy chants, "He's going to be okay. You hear me? He's going to be okay." I keep my face turned away, trying to not to think the worst as time seems to slow to a stop.

The murmurs surrounding us grow and Poppy's grip on me loosens enough to let me turn to the field. Hendrix can't leave the bag, but he's crouched down with his hands in his hair under his helmet, helpless as he watches the medical staff help Cruz to his feet—one trainer on each side to steady him.

"I need to go. Get me to him." I look at Janet, her wrinkled face etched in concern and her pale blue eyes watery. Hendrix grew up here, and she comes to every game in St. Louis. She knows the stadium better than any of us. Her thin hand wraps around mine as she uses her mom voice to clear the aisle and pulls me behind her.

I follow her as she hustles us through the stadium at a speed that's impressive for her age. The hallways and corridors are a blur as she leads me to the lowest level where we find a security guard that takes pity on me and probably fears for his safety if he denies Janet with the way she commanded that I be let back to be with Cruz.

When he opens the door, she hugs me tight. "Go take care of him."

CHAPTER 31

SPONGE BATH THREATS

PRESENT

There's no stopping the tears that pour down my face when security lets me back to see Cruz. All things considered, he looks okay. If it weren't for the clammy, grayish sheen covering his skin and the far-off look in his eyes, you wouldn't even know he was hurt.

"Is she riding along?" The paramedic that's preparing for the transport to the hospital asks the team doctor. He looks down to where my knuckles are turning white as I clutch Cruz's hand and then to where he has his bicep wrapped around the thigh closest to him on the exam table.

"It looks like it." The older gentleman's lips twitch before he gets back to work assessing the injury. "I'll follow you to the hospital and speak with the doctor treating you here in St. Louis."

Cruz nods, but the move causes his teeth to clench as he grimaces. "Sounds good. The sooner we get there, the better. I could use something a little stronger for this headache." His voice is strained, like every word requires extra effort.

I shake my hand only now realizing I have pins and needles in my fingers from the death grip I had on his hand during the ride from the stadium. Once we get to the hospital, I wait alone in his room while the staff wheel him in and out for imaging and tests. As soon as the doctor leaves his room, he's waving me over from the chair I'm sitting in with my knees tucked to my chest.

Those deep brown eyes I love so much are hidden behind his closed eyelids when I crawl into the bed next to him, careful not to jostle him. Blindly, his arm raises to allow me to slide closer. Once he has me tucked into the crook of his arms, he hisses through his teeth and relaxes against the pillow. They've given him some medicine to manage his pain, but it hasn't kicked in yet.

"How are you doing?" I try to keep my voice calm, but a sniffle escapes me, giving me away. I feel my control slipping and bury my face in his chest, hoping to stem the tears before they start falling again.

"Shh . . . I'm okay." He drops his lips to my forehead. "The meds are starting to kick in. My headache is almost completely gone."

"You scared the hell out of me. I thought—god that was so dirty. Your injuries could have been so much worse. The ball hit you so hard your helmet came off. It looked awful." He cups my cheek, brushing away a tear with his thumb. My phone buzzes in the pocket of the hoodie I grabbed out of Cruz's cubby before we left the locker room.

When he saw me shivering from the adrenaline, he refused to get in the ambulance until I put it on. Even in that state, he was more concerned about me being warm than he was about his own head injury.

"It's Poppy checking in. I'm sure Hen is losing his mind," I tell him, typing out a response to her.

"We can call them in a little while. The game should be almost over."

"That doesn't seem like a good idea. Your doctor said to rest and avoid stress. Maybe you should just try to get some sleep."

"I'm feeling much better. We need to call my parents. I'm sure they're freaking out. Can you grab my phone for me?"

"I'll call them for you," I protest, sitting up so he can see I'm serious about this.

"Hermosa, my parents are going to want to hear from me. I know you're trying to help, but after Jarrett, I wouldn't be surprised if they were already on the way to the airport. I should have called them before I even left the stadium. If you won't help me. I'll get the phone myself."

As soon as he says Jarrett's name, my stomach twists with guilt. His mom and dad are probably beside themselves. I was so worried about him that I never even considered that they would have watched the game on TV and seen him go down.

"Don't you dare. Keep your ass in bed." I glare at him until he settles back against the pillow. Padding across the hospital room, I grab his backpack and find his phone. The screen is littered with texts and missed calls.

Sure enough, both his parents have been trying to reach him. I'm about to return to bed when another notification from earlier in the day catches my eye. Biting my thumb, I glance over my shoulder. Cruz has his head tipped back on the pillow with his eyes closed. Making a split-second decision, I swipe the notification clear and open the app to clear the red circle.

My stomach churns with guilt, but the doctor was very clear. His concussion is severe, and he needs to rest. That means avoiding physical activity, screens, and stress so his brain can heal. He has every right to know, but it can wait a few days before we deal with Rich and the unknown caller.

My heart races as I cross the room back to the bed. Cruz's health has to take priority, but I'm unsure if that was the right decision. I swear to myself that I'll tell him about the calls as soon as we get home and he's had a few days to heal.

"Do you want me to call your mom or your dad's phone?" I ask, sliding into the bed next to him.

"Mom. She'll be sitting at the kitchen table waiting for a call." I unlock his phone and find Analia's number dialing on speakerphone.

"Cruz, mijo. Are you okay?" she answers before either of us can say hello, the slight tremble in her voice is unmistakable.

"Sí, Má. I'm fine. Sorry, I didn't call sooner. The doctors just left."

"Where are you now? The hospital? Your dad and I will come out to St. Louis."

"Calm down. I'm only here for observation but should be discharged in the morning. Delilah and I will fly home in a few days."

"She's there with you, can she hear me?"

"I'm here, Analia."

"Menos mal!" She huffs out in relief. "How's my boy doing? Don't sugarcoat it like he would."

"He's okay. His concussion is severe so he'll need to take it easy and it will be at least seven days on the injured reserve. The doctor thought it would be closer to two or three weeks before restrictions would be lifted."

"Lilah, dear. You'll be staying with him when he gets home, right?" I feel my cheeks flame. Cruz and I haven't talked about what happens beyond flying home when he's feeling well enough.

I glanced at Cruz to see his reaction. If I thought he would bail me out of this conversation with his mom I'm sorely mistaken. His eyebrow is cocked at me in amusement.

"Um, we haven't really talked about that yet. I can—I mean . . ."

Cruz takes the phone from my hand. "Má, Delilah's had a hard enough day without you instigating. It's up to her, but I'd rather have her stay with me than hire a nurse to take care of me. I'm sure she'll give me a much more thorough sponge bath." The pain meds must be in full-effect because he drawls the words out in the thickest Texas accent I've ever heard from him. It's not the time to get turned on but that silky smooth voice soaks right into my skin making me break out in goosebumps. His eyes shift to me, as if he senses the change and his mouth tilts up in a teasing smile.

Talk about stirring shit up. If he didn't have a head injury, I would slap him upside the head. "You asshole," I mouth to him while his mom howls with laughter on the other end of the line.

"I'll come to stay with you, but just for that, I'm calling in Dom to assist with all your bathing needs."

"Don't think I've forgotten that neither of you has admitted that you are finally together? Once that brain of yours heals, we are going to have a conversation about why it took you two so long to figure it out and how we make sure that my son doesn't screw it all up."

My insides churn with guilt, knowing that I'm already jeopardizing everything by not telling him about the missed call from the private investigator. He has to understand. Cruz would do anything to protect me, and this is the only way I know how to protect him right now.

"Hey, you okay?" Cruz asks, his lips a whisper from my ear.

I nod woodenly as I swallow down my guilt. "Just tired. We still have to call Hen and Poppy. You should get some rest." I go to stand up, but Cruz holds me in place and shakes his head.

"Má. We are going to let you go. I need to check in with Hendrix and then Delilah insists I get some rest."

"That's my girl. I know you'll take care of my boy. There's no one better for the job, mija." My heart swells at Analia's words. I know she would support my decision to give her son a chance to heal before he deals with whatever is waiting on his voicemail.

"Buenas noches, Analia. I'll text you my number so you can check on him while he heals."

"I'd appreciate that. Thank you, Delilah." Her voice is filled with sincerity. I know it must be emotional for her to have her only remaining son in the hospital after everything they went through.

"Of course."

"Love you, Má."

When we hang up the phone, I let my head rest on Cruz's shoulder. "You up for one more call? We're going to keep it quick. Poppy's been texting non-stop. Hendrix is a mess. You should have seen him when you went down."

"He was on second, wasn't he? Man, that's a front-row seat. I'm impressed at his restraint not to charge the mound."

"I think he would have, but his concern was for you at that moment, not revenge."

Using my phone, I find Poppy's name in my contacts and call her on FaceTime. She answers on the first ring with Hendrix right over her shoulder like she's in his lap. Cruz shifts next to me so he is in the frame, but I only let him talk to them for a few minutes before I make them wrap it up.

Sitting up, I swing my legs off the bed. Cruz needs his rest, and that means I'm banishing myself to the chair for the night, so he gets a decent sleep.

"What do you think you're doing?" His voice is flat, and when I look over my shoulder, he's slumped against the pillows. His unfocused eyes find me through the drooping lids he's struggling to keep open.

"Moving to the chair so you can sleep." He squeezes his eyes shut as he winces when I stand, making the bed shift. Shit, he overdid it. I never should have let him call Hendrix. I could have just texted Poppy like I did with Dean and Dom.

"If you want me to sleep, get back in here." He cracks one eye open at me. "Don't fucking argue with me about this. I'm injured and you're the best medicine."

"I didn't know that cheesiness was a side effect of the meds," I say, carefully sitting on the edge of the bed.

"Oh, it's not. That's all me. But it's true. I'll sleep better knowing you're next to me and not sitting in that god-awful chair all night. And take that bra off too, I know you're dying to." He picks on the remote for the bed. "Now get in here before I press this call button and demand that they bring you a bed. That's going to take a while and it'll probably wake me up," he says weakly before tugging on my arm to pull me closer.

"Even concussed, you're insufferable."

"You love me." His voice drifts off and his breathing evens out.

I don't respond with words. Instead, I lean over him, careful not to wake him as I kiss his lips. He's not wrong. I have loved Cruz for years at this point. It's not the first time he's said those words, but this feels different. Now, it's not just that I love him. Now I'm falling in love with him and it's a bone-deep, forever kind of love. One that doesn't touch anything I've ever felt before, and I am pretty sure he feels the same.

CHAPTER 32

HOME SWEET HOME

PRESENT

Loud voices in the other room wake me up, but thankfully the raging headache I had when I laid down has faded to a dull ache. The flight home from St. Louis was a bitch. Flying with a concussion is not for the faint of heart.

I slip out of bed and make my way towards the bedroom door, pausing when I hear Delilah's voice over the others. "Dominic Duran, sit down and shut up or I'll kick you out."

"Lilah, don't be like that. I said I was sorry. I didn't know Cruz was asleep. I'll be on my best behavior." He's using the voice he uses on the cleat chasers after games. Usually it gets him whatever he wants. He infuses that charm into it and the ladies fall at his feet. It's not going to work this time. Delilah was over the top protective the entire trip home. Trying to make sure I was okay and as comfortable as possible. If he thinks he can waltz in and charm her into letting him do whatever, he's going to find out quickly that her claws are sharp.

"If you get us kicked out, I'll be in line right behind Lilah to kick your ass," Dean chirps at him in a much quieter voice than Dom was using.

"Hen, can you keep these two out of trouble while I go help in the kitchen?" Poppy's rich voice comes through next.

The team flew home from Chicago this morning and I'm not surprised that I was their first stop. Delilah's been reading me the text messages they've sent since I'm still on technology ban per the doctor's orders. They've been checking in daily to see how I'm doing.

Pushing off from where I am leaning on the door frame, I make my way into the kitchen. Delilah's got her back to me and Poppy's helping her load up a tray with snacks and drinks for the guys in the living room.

"You know they can grab their own shit, right? The last thing they deserve is you serving them when they so rudely woke me from my nap." I say, startling her when I sneak up behind her and wrap my arms around her waist, kissing her neck. "Hey, Poppy."

"Hey Cruz, you're looking better."

"Thanks, I've had excellent care." Delilah squirms in my arms, trying to turn around, but I know she's just going to scold me for being up and moving around, so I hold her where she is bringing my lips to her ear. "I'm fine. I would've gotten stiff lying around for any longer, and not in the fun way."

Poppy snorts beside me, and Delilah slaps my arm.

"Ouch, Hermosa. I'm injured. Take it easy."

"Sorry, Cruz, I tried to hold them off one more day—Hendrix too, but they wanted to come see you and wouldn't let it go until they did."

"Children," I say with a shrug because sometimes it feels that way with Dom and Dean. They are a couple years younger than Hendrix and I. Dom has the personality of a golden retriever puppy and Dean is a bit of a puzzle. To an outsider, he seems just as carefree and fun-loving as Dom, but he doesn't let many people into his inner circle. Even though I consider him one of my closest friends, there is a lot I don't know about him.

"I'll get the kids their snacks before they revolt." Poppy takes the tray from Delilah and leaves the two of us in the kitchen.

"We can ask them to leave anytime. If you need a break, just let me know and I'll kick them out," Delilah says, turning in my arms.

"I love this protective streak you have. So hot. You're going to be such a sexy mama bear someday." I kiss each of the worry lines on her forehead before adding, "I feel much better than yesterday. Let them stay for a little while. Don't tell them, but I've missed their goofy asses."

The lines on her forehead smooth as she melts into my embrace, looking up at me with those blue eyes that make my heart beat faster every time they're on me. "I know you do. They can stay as long as they are on their best behavior. If not, I can't be held responsible for any maulings that happen."

"By 'they' do you mean Dom?" That makes her smile warmly. He's been on the team since his rookie year last season. Lilah's never been shy about putting him in his place. She treats him like an annoying little brother. Both of them like to see how far they can push each other.

"Of course. Every group has their problem child," she says with a roll of her eyes.

"Just one thing before we go out there." Her face falls, and then I lower my head and take her mouth. Kissing is all she'll let me get away with right now. She hums against my lips and then opens, letting me sweep my tongue inside.

"Oh look, another couple in love and kissing." Reluctantly, I pull away from Delilah and find Dom standing against the counter watching us with faux annoyance.

"Oh look, it's the asshole who woke me up," I toss back.

"Ouch man, that hurts. Lilah, you're going to let me stay, right?" He brings his hands together in front of his chest, giving her his best puppy dog expression.

"I don't know. Can you act like an adult?" Delilah asks as she steps out of my arms and leads me to the living room where everyone is waiting.

"I think we should tar and feather him," Dom says, out of nowhere, as he drops onto the couch next to Dean. "Like they did in your day, gramps." The tips of Dean's ears turn red next to him, but he restrains himself from making a scene.

"What are you talking about?" Poppy asks, looking as confused as the rest of us with her head tilted to the side.

"Miller, we should tar and feather him. Tell me I'm wrong," he challenges clapping his hands together. The sound echoes and makes me wince.

"I am going to tar and feather *you* if you don't stop clapping," Delilah tells him with a glare that is enough to scare even me.

"Miller's going to get what's coming to him. He's been on thin ice with the league for years. After that stunt he'll be lucky if anyone wants him when his contract is up with the Commanders this season," I say.

"Always wearing that captain hat. Take it off for a minute. Be irresponsible with us. We can come up with another way for revenge. Let's hack his Instagram and post a dick pic, but make it super tiny. Hit him where it hurts," Dom says excitedly.

"There is something truly wrong with you," Hendrix comments from the other side of the room where Poppy is perched on his lap.

"I actually like that one. If you can figure it out, I fully support it," Delilah says to Dom. Who replies with a silent but very animated fist pump. "But you need to find the pictures. I'm not taking on that task."

"That shouldn't be a problem for him. Just dip into the folder of dick pics you've sent your road hookups," Dean says, taking us all by surprise. I choke on a laugh. The best thing about his humor is it takes you off guard because he's usually the quiet one.

"Please tell me you don't." Hendrix levels Dom with a serious glare.

"You know I'm not actually an idiot, right?" Dom fires back hurt flashes in his eyes.

"Just checking, man. I don't want to see you trash your career with one bad decision." Sincerity coats his words.

Poppy and Hendrix are the first to leave. She has a meeting with an author about recording the audiobook for their Christmas novella, but I get the feeling they were ready for some alone time. They came back from Chicago looking extra in love.

"Dom, we should get out of here and give these two some space. I am sure Lilah wants to get him back to bed," Dean says with a straight face, but he's got that look in his eyes like he knows exactly what he did.

Normally someone else making Delilah blush the way she is right now with pink creeping across her delicate cheekbone would make me want to punch them. I'm supposed to be the one making her cheeks turn that rosy shade, but I can't even be mad at Dean. She's smiling after days of her looking at me with worry. I'll take it however I can get it.

"I like that plan. What do you say? Join me in bed for a nap?" I pull her to me as we walk Dom and Dean out. It only makes the pink on her cheek crawl down her neck and disappear under that oversized t-shirt she pulled from my closet this morning.

"Take it easy on him. We want our captain back on the field," Dean says from the door as he slips on his shoes.

"The locker room is chaos without you there to keep us in line," Dom adds as Dean pulls the door open.

"You mean keeping *you* in line?" Delilah retorts as Dom slips through the door after his friend with a shrug.

"I am who I am," he shouts back as the door shuts, leaving the two of us alone in the kitchen. When I look down at her, she's staring up at me with her lips parted.

"What's going on in your gorgeous head?" I ask, stepping into her more so that she's flush against me.

"Seeing you around the guys like this—how much you mean to them— it got me thinking about the day you found out you were made captain." Her smile is stretching her face now. It was a good day. She teamed up with

Lincoln to surprise me after practice with a giant sticky bun. Across it she had scrawled "Captains Get the Biggest Buns."

"That was a great day. I got the sticky buns of my dreams delivered by the girl of my dreams," I say.

"I wasn't the girl of your dreams back then, just your friend." Her voice is low as she looks up at me through her lashes.

"You've always been the girl of my dreams, Hermosa." She licks her lips and gives me that same shy smile I saw in the hospital when she didn't think I was looking. She feels it, she's just not ready to say the words out loud, and that's okay, I can keep waiting.

Delilah clears her throat. "The sticky buns of your dreams? Is this something you dream of regularly?" Her arms come around my waist.

"It's part of the regular rotation. *You*, hitting home runs, *you*, catching fly balls, *you*, and sticky buns." I lean in close, dropping my mouth to her ear. " And lately there's been dreams about my other favorite dessert and the sweet sounds that come out of your mouth when I eat that pretty pussy." Her next breath comes out as a gasp and when I kiss her cheeks, they're warm and I know without looking they'll be glowing.

I eat that shit right up. It was me that made her blush this time. And I get to crawl in bed with her, even if it's just to take my mandatory nap. Because she's mine finally, and I'm never going to let go.

CHAPTER 33

SNEAKY SPANISH

PRESENT

I'm so fucking bored. All athletes deal with injuries at least once in their careers and it always sucks, but this is worse. All my other injuries have allowed me some level of activity. Not this one. The worst part is Delilah is taking it seriously. Since we returned from St. Louis last week, I haven't gotten anything more than a brief kiss from her.

I'm losing my goddamn mind. She's sleeping in my bed, looking sexy as fuck in my shirt every night and she won't let me touch her. The morning after the game in St. Louis, when the nurse came to discharge me and was going over care instructions and restrictions, she asked specifically about sex.

The nurse, who must have been close to retirement, just cocked an eyebrow at me before telling me that she hoped sex fell under strenuous activity. Then added insult to injury by pointing out that if it didn't, there was no way I was keeping a girl like Delilah.

When the nurse left, Delilah damn near fell out of her chair laughing. I couldn't even fault her because she gave my girl a much needed break from all the worry.

Once I was discharged, we spent two more days at the hotel so I could rest before flying home. In the overreaction of the century, I was forced to wear an eye mask and earplugs for the flight even though Dean sent his grandpa's plane and pilot to get me home.

And here I thought the first time I got her on a private plane that I could convince her to join the mile-high club. Not a freaking chance. Six days later and she's still ducking me.

My follow-up appointment is tomorrow and you better believe it's going to be my first question.

"Hey, I'm home—er back." Delilah shouts as she closes the door behind her. I hate that, she corrected herself, but the fact that she called it home makes my heart hammer in my chest.

"In here," I call from where I'm laying on the bed with my back propped against a stack of pillows. My eyes are closed and I have a documentary playing on the TV. I have worked my way up to one hour of screen time, but I'm desperate to get cleared for regular activity, so I'm listening instead of watching.

"What are we listening to?" Delilah asks, crawling across the bed with an overabundance of caution. Her concern for me is borderline comical, but sweet. When she's within arms reach, I pull her to me.

"*Cruz!* Have you lost your mind?" Her voice comes out high-pitched as she places her hand on my chest, trying to soften the impact when I tug her on top of me. Which is ridiculous because she's tiny and I'm not.

"It's possible. I'm going crazy stuck here with nothing to keep me busy." I tilt my head back, looking at the ceiling as I hold her snug to my chest. She's given in and is laying across me. It's not Delilah's fault I'm in the situation. Her concern for my health is heartwarming and I appreciate everything she's done for me, but I'm ready to get back to my life outside this apartment—back to the stadium and my team.

"I have an idea to get you out of here. I even called the doctor to make sure it was okay. They wouldn't release any medical information to me, since we aren't married, but gave me a hypothetical answer to my question." She props herself up, so she's looking at me and the way the tips of her ears turn red when she talks about being my wife has me swallowing the laugh that's trying to escape.

"I'm listening," I say, sweeping a piece of blonde hair that's fallen loose from her bun behind her ear.

"How would you feel about going over to Saving Paws to walk some dogs? I'll drive."

"And here I thought you were going to propose so you had access to all that medical information. But sure, walking dogs sounds fun." I pull her to me, kissing her on the lips hard. She relaxes against me. It's the first time she's given in this easily since my injury. Slipping my tongue into her mouth, I take full advantage of her willingness. "You taste like caramels. So sweet," I whisper against her lips.

"There may have been a little snaccident on my walk home."

"I can't say I'm disappointed about it." I deepen our kiss, chasing the high of having her like this.

She moans into my mouth when my hands tangle in her hair, holding her in place. Sweeping my tongue against hers, every cell in my body sparks back to life. She's held me at arm's length for far too long.

Delilah's hands trail up my chest and when they cup the side of my head, she freezes. With a sigh, she pulls back, touching her forehead to mine. "We should stop. There are puppies waiting," she says with a sigh, but doesn't make a move to distance herself from me.

"I might be a sucker for puppies, but I'm not that easily distracted. Let me kiss you a little longer. I've missed this."

"Siempre tratando de tentarme."

I pull back, caught off guard by her use of Spanish in a full sentence. She buries her face looking guilty. Raising my eyebrow I ask, "What was that?"

Peering up at me with tentative blue eyes she nibbles at the cover of her lip. "I've been learning Spanish using an app for a while."

"Why didn't you tell me? I would have taught you." I brush a strand of blonde hair from her face.

"It seemed like something I should do myself. Besides, I wanted to surprise you. But with everything that's happened. I didn't want to keep it from you." Guilt that seems misplaced crosses her face.

"So many missed opportunities for dirty fun quizzing you on vocabulary. Say something else," I demand, needing to hear more. Does she realize how much this means to me? These days I pretty much only speak Spanish to family and a few close friends. There's never been a doubt that she owns my heart, but this is more that I could have ever imagined.

"Eres mi mejor amigo y no puedo imaginar mi vida sin ti."

"You'll never have to worry about that. I'll always be your best friend and I'm not going anywhere. You're stuck with me." My lips brush across her forehead. "Not to sound pathetic, but you still want this, right? Nothing's changed for you?" God, I sound like such a pussy, but I need to know that she still wants me as much as I want—no, need her. Delilah would do anything for the people she loves, and that includes staying here with me while I recover even if her feelings had changed.

She flinches like my question caused her physical pain. "Why would you think that?"

Shit. I didn't mean to hurt her feelings. "Hey, Hermosa, look at me," I say, cupping her cheek so she can't turn away. "This is hard for me. Not being able to do the things I want to. It makes me feel completely useless. And you're stuck here taking care of me."

"Stuck here? Is that what you think? That I'm not strong enough to tell you no? I'm here because I want to be here. The single most important person in my life was hurt, and it scared the shit out of me. Do you really think that I would want someone else here with you?" She tilts her chin up and squeezes her eyes shut.

She's pissed. "Single most important person, huh?" I ask, to defuse her anger. "I like the sound of that."

"Are you mocking me right now?"

"Maybe? Not about the first part." I sigh. "Remember who you're talking to. I know you better than anyone else. You would do anything for me and I just wanted to make sure that you are still feeling the same. Since we got home, things have been different. This isn't exactly what you signed up for. Things got real, fast. I don't want you to have any regrets."

"My only concern right now is making sure you get better. I want this big dumb brain of yours to heal so we can get back to being us. Watching you take that hit was the scariest moment of my life. If it feels like things are different, it's because I need you to be okay."

"So, no regrets."

"Zero. You're my person, concussed or not. Every decision I've made is about keeping you healthy and safe."

"So you still want me?" I ask, tucking my hands behind my head as I look up at her hovering over me. Her expression flips from concerned to disbelief.

"You're impossible. I can't believe I just poured my heart out to you and it goes straight to your ego."

"That's not the only place it went." Look pointedly down at my crotch. The outline of my erection, visible through my gray sweatpants.

"Un-fucking-believable." She laughs when she follows the path of my eyes.

"I know. It's pretty impressive. Want to take it for a ride?" She leans in close, wetting her lips, and it makes my pulse flutter in my neck.

"Mhmmm, but what I want more is for your brain to heal so that you remember all the ways I want to be fucked when the doctor releases you for physical activity." She walks her fingers up my chest before playfully tapping the side of my face. She's oh-so-gentle. As much as she might pretend otherwise. "I was hopeful it would happen tomorrow, but now I'm thinking you could use another week. You obviously are having a hard time making smart decisions if you're baiting me right now."

"Feisty. I like it. And don't you worry, there isn't a single thing you told me about all the firsts you want to try with me in the hotel room that I've forgotten." Her pupils flare as she melts into me. "I hope you're ready because when I get cleared tomorrow I'm going to tie you to this bed and spend hours worshiping your body—eating that perfect pussy until you can't stand it anymore."

"Is that so?" Her voice is breathy.

"You want that too, don't you? You miss the way it feels when I make you fall apart. Being close to me." I wrap my arms around her waist, shifting her so she's on top of me.

"Cruz." My name comes off her lips like a prayer.

Gripping her hips, I move her over my cock. *Fuck.* I've missed this. Delilah braces her hands against my chest, rocking over me as her head tips back. "You're so pretty when you use my cock. Let me make you feel good. You've been so busy making sure I'm okay that you haven't taken care of yourself."

"Cruz, we can't. You're still supposed to be resting."

"Then do all the work for me. Take care of yourself and use me to do it." My hands grip her thighs, letting her take over. I'm going to have a wicked case of blue balls, but if it means I get to watch her come apart, I'll survive.

"But you—"

"Uh-uh, this is about you. Give me this. Let me watch you get off. It's the least I can do with how well you've taken care of me."

She rotates her hips, grinding down as her pace picks up.

"Tell me how it feels. You like how hard I am beneath you?"

"So good. I want more." Her hands come up to palm her breasts over the black tank top she's wearing.

"Take your top off. So you can play with those tits."

Her shirt and bra come off in record time and she's pinching her nipples, tugging them as her mouth forms an "O."

"That's better. I love watching you like this. One of these days, I'm going to make you show me how you use your toys to take care of yourself when I'm not here. Then I'm going to use them on you."

"Would you let me use them on you?" Her voice breaks, barely able to get the question out.

"There's not much I wouldn't do for you. You know that."

"Fuck. Keep talking. I'm so close."

"I can do better than that." Shifting up, I sit against the headboard and drop my head to her breast, sucking her nipple into my mouth. I give the other side equal attention as she rocks over me. Her breath is coming fast now. "That's it. Come for me, Hermosa," I tell her before sucking hard on her nipple, scraping over it with my teeth. That pushes her over the edge. She clings to me and her movements stutter as she topples over the edge.

Watching her let go is almost enough to get me there, but I keep it together. Tilting my chin up, I bring my lips to hers, kissing her softly as she melts into me.

"I can't believe I let you talk me into that. Are you okay?"

"I'm more than okay. That was the highlight of my entire week."

She bites the inside of her cheek as she assesses me.

"I promise I'm fine. You did all the hard work. Give me five minutes to take a cold shower and then you can drive us to the shelter to walk some doggies."

CHAPTER 34

PUPPY TIME

PRESENT

"I can't believe you made me drive this thing. We could have taken my car," I complain as I round the front of Cruz's Bronco after we pull up to Saving Paws.

"That would have been a waste of time. Your car is at your place. This was much faster," he says, turning to look back at me as he opens the door to the shelter.

"You just wanted to see if I could handle it," I say as we stop at the counter to check in. "Hey Simone. How've you been?" She greets him with a beaming smile when she looks up from the pile of adoption applications in front of her. After years of working with the rescue she's developed a soft spot for Cruz.

"Hey guys! I gotta believe I'm better than you. How's the head?"

"It looked a lot worse than it was." He shrugs like the fact that he took a ninety-eight mile per hour ball to the head is no big deal.

"He was lucky. I've never seen someone so stir-crazy. Thankfully, dog walking is on the list of the doctor approved activities or there might've been a mutiny."

"Glad we could avoid that. Want to take Han and Leia for another spin?" Simone asks, standing from the desk.

"They're still here?" I ask around the tightness in my throat.

"We thought we had found a home for them last week, but they changed their minds. They decided they only wanted one dog and we just can't separate them."

"Poor babies! That makes me so sad that they're still waiting to find someone to love them," I say, leaning into Cruz as Simone goes to grab the two dogs.

"I'm sure they will find a family soon." A big goofy grin takes up residence on Cruz's face and his shoulders relax as he stands next to me, uncharacteristically serene.

"I hope so. They're so sweet," I say, as we each take a leash from Simone and head out the front door, turning down the sidewalk that leads to the park.

Cruz is giddy next to me as we walk, chattering with the dogs about how good they are. It's the happiest I have seen him, aside from just earlier at the apartment in almost a week. "What are you thinking about over there? You have a big goofy grin on your face."

"Do I?" He tilts his head as he looks over at me.

"Yeah, it's a lot like the one you make when you catch me on my walk from the shower to your closet but with less—intensity." We walk past our bench in the park and continue down the path.

His hand comes up to scratch the stubble that he's let grow out on his jaw. "I was daydreaming about what it would be like if we could take them home with us."

My feet come to a stop as I take in his words. It's on the tip of my tongue to tell him: *Yes, let's do that. Now, please!* But my mouth opens and then closes the words stuck. "You . . . you were?"

"Don't you know by now? You're my favorite daydream, with the four of us were hanging out in the living room. There were tall floor to ceiling windows that overlooked the huge backyard with a view of the Rockies."

His piercing eyes look back at me as I slowly resume walking beside him. "That sounds pretty perfect."

"I think so." Cruz reaches out and takes my hand, completely enveloping it with his much larger one. "Someday I'm going to make it into a reality." His voice is filled with sincere belief in our future.

"Is that so?" I want that future with him so badly but if it slipped through my fingers it would cause unimaginable pain. So I hold back that piece of me and don't give voice to the part of me that's screaming *yes*, begging to grasp on to this dream with both hands.

"You're not going to make me wait too long, are you?" His phone vibrates in his pocket, saving me from a response. He hesitates, looking apologetic for interrupting our time together.

"Hey, Rich. How are you doing? It's been a while since I heard from you. I'm hoping that means you have an update for me?"

My blood runs cold, and lancing pain pierces my heart as soon as I hear him say Rich's name. I still haven't told him about the missed calls or voicemail. It wasn't my intention to keep it from him for this long. It all just got away from me.

He insisted that I go back to work right after we got home, and I did. When I haven't been at *Buns & Roses*, I've been helping with everything from groceries and cooking to laundry. Anything I can do, so he focuses on resting.

"I don't think I got any voicemails. Hold on. Delilah, did you take any calls for me while I was in the hospital?"

Bile rises in my throat and I have to force myself to swallow it down. My gaze darts to Cruz's eyes as he stands there waiting for a response.

"There was a voicemail that night in the hospital. When we called your parents. I'm sorry I didn't tell you." My voice trembles as I wrap my arms around myself, dropping his hand in the process.

"Sorry Rich. I didn't see that you had called. What's going on?" He's watching me out of the corner of his eyes but his expression is unreadable. There's no choice but to wait with a heavy stomach as Cruz listens intently. "The calls were coming from Colby Miller's ex-girlfriend? What did she want?"

I replay my decision to clear the notification from his phone back in my head. I was just trying to protect him, give him a chance to heal. There was still so much uncertainty around his injury. The doctor's felt strongly enough about it to take the precautions of keeping him overnight and gave us a laundry list of things that could still go wrong. My decision to remove that stressor felt like it was the right thing to do at the moment. Now I'm not so sure. How did I let it get this out of hand?

"Hold on. She what?" Cruz's face blanches. Running his hands through his hair he looks at me with a vacant expression. "Why would she say that?" His voice cracks and the sound breaks me.

Oh god. I can see the grief closing in around him. Taking the leash from his hand I wrap him in my arms. His heart is hammering in under my ear. I would give anything to take his pain away.

He's silent as he listens to Rich on the other end of the phone. Nodding every so often.

"Thanks Rich. Let me know when it's set up," Cruz says, before he ends the call.

He slides the phone back into his pocket and I lead him back towards the bench. He drops limply onto the metal seat letting his head fall to his hands. I crouch in front of him, my hands on his knees.

"Miller's ex-girlfriend was the person that kept calling from St. Louis. She thinks he had something to do with Jarrett's accident that night."

"Wh—what?" I say, scrambling to understand what's happening. "Did you know her?"

He shakes his head as he looks to where the dogs have settled at our feet. "No, I think they had just started dating at that point. We were never close."

"How'd she get your number?" It's an odd thing to fixate on, but I'm struggling to wrap my head around what's happening.

"She worked at the stadium and had access to everyone's information. She held onto it, they broke up recently and she told Rich she didn't feel right not telling someone her suspicions."

"Did she tell him what she thought happened?"

His eyes find mine for the first time since he hung up the phone. "Rich is going to set up a meeting with her. If she seems credible, then we will figure it out from there. It could be going back to the police. He couldn't say for sure without hearing her side of the story."

"Why don't we take the dogs back? I'll drive you home and we can talk more if you want to. Or I can leave."

"Leave? Why would you leave Delilah?" he asks, covering my hands with his.

"I thought—you're not mad? I kept this from you. I didn't tell you about the missed call."

He cups my cheek with his hand. "I'm confused, a little shocked, but not mad. I'm sure you had your reasons. You've never done anything to hurt me and I don't think you'd start now. Let's go home and you can tell me what happened."

"Okay." I stand on wobbly legs, fighting back the tears that are building behind my eyelids. Cruz reaches over, taking the leashes from me and tucking me under his arm as we walk back to the shelter. "These guys kind of got the short end of the stick. That wasn't a very good walk."

"I think they'll manage. Besides, I have a feeling they'll find a home soon." He kisses my temple and I feel him smile but it doesn't reach his voice. He just sounds drained and I hate myself for the role I played in that.

CHAPTER 35

WHAT NOW?

PRESENT

We drop the dogs back off and thank Simone before I drive us back home to Cruz's apartment. As soon as we get inside he takes my hand and pulls me towards the couch. Without letting go he sits, tugging me into his lap.

"We should heat up some dinner," I say, letting my head drop to his shoulder. I'm procrastinating the conversation I know needs to happen. But I don't make any effort to leave my spot cuddled against his chest.

"We will. But tell me what happened at the hospital. I have a feeling you need to tell me more than I need to know."

Cruz has always made me feel safe. He would do anything for me and his trust in me might just be the greatest testament to how accepted I feel with him. My chest loosens and I breathe easier than I have since his phone rang earlier this evening.

The words just start to pour out of me. "There were a bunch of notifications after we got to the hospital and the doctor had just finished telling us all the things that could still go wrong and why they were keeping you for observation. I was terrified that you weren't really out of the woods yet. I just wanted to buy you a little time before you had to deal with anything." He listens intently, rubbing my back as I tell him everything. "There was a voicemail from Rich that caught my eye. I cleared the notification and planned to tell you about it once things were more certain with your health. I knew if you saw that he called, you wouldn't be able to drop it."

His voice is calm; there's no judgment or accusation in it when he says, "You were trying to protect me from myself. Why didn't you tell me about them when we got home?" There's that word again. Home. There hasn't been a moment since we got back from St. Louis that I've missed my place or wanted to leave his side.

"It just got away from me. Today was the first time I thought about it since we got home. I've been so focused on making sure you're okay that it got pushed to the side. When I cleared out the notification, I left the voicemail. I wasn't trying to hide it from you, I just needed you to be okay before you focused on whatever Rich needed to tell you. I'm really sorry, Cruz."

Guilt eats away at me when I think about what that voicemail was about. My finger twirls a strand of hair that came loose from my bun. When I look down at my lap Cruz's hand tilts my chin back up.

"Don't do that. This changes nothing, Delilah. I would have done the same thing if I thought it would keep you safe. You've done nothing but think of me for the last few weeks. Every step of the way you have put me first." His gaze stays fixed on me. "Thank you for telling me." His lips press against mine. His kiss is tender like he's trying to reassure me that everything he just said is true.

CHAPTER 36

TIED UP IN KNOTS

PRESENT

"So I can practice and start workouts again this week?" Delilah's grip on my arm tightens.

"That's not exactly what I said." The doctor's eyes crinkle at the corner as he laughs. He's in his late fifties and I'm pretty sure he's seen and heard it all at this point. Dealing with a team of professional athletes, none of us are eager to ride the bench for any reason, let alone being sidelined with a serious injury.

"We are going to ease you back into it and see how you respond. Light aerobic exercise like low effort running for short periods of time while gradually increasing time and intensity over the course of the next two weeks. If there are no setbacks, you'll be back right before the All-Star Break."

I glance over at Delilah, who's biting her lip as she listens to the doctor's treatment plan. "So, he should continue to avoid stress for the next few weeks as much as possible."

"Speaking of, let's talk about stress relief." Delilah freezes in place, anticipating my question. The topic was unavoidable this morning when I woke her up with my hard cock nestled right up against her perfect ass. "If I can run, sex must be safe at this point."

"Sex is fine, just don't exert yourself more than you would running. If your dizziness or any other symptoms return, we will need to reevaluate. But to answer the original question, you should avoid stress as much as possible. It will only help to speed up your recovery."

"Got it. Sex is good. Stress is bad."

"That's what you got from that conversation?" she asks, tilting her face up to look at me.

"Essentially."

The doctor goes over a few more details like driving, paperwork for the team, and what the next stage of recovery looks like. It'll be about a week before I return to fielding drills and batting with game play following shortly after.

When we leave the office, I snatch the keys out of Delilah's hands. I appreciate all the sacrifices she has made since I got hurt, but I am ready for some independence back.

"You really couldn't help yourself back there, could you?" she asks as we approach the truck.

"I'm not sure what you are talking about." I feign innocence as I open the door to the Bronco for her, leaning into her space to kiss the corner of her mouth before I pull back and shut the door. "Are you going into work this afternoon?"

Her hand comes up to her throat and her voice is raspy when she says, "No. I was hoping to spend the rest of the afternoon with you."

I snap my seat belt into place and pull out of the parking lot, my tires squealing with my eagerness to get her home. The air in the Bronco is charged as we ride back. The short drive to the apartment seems to take forever. Out of the corner of my eye, I see her shifting in the seat. She's as desperate for me as I am for her.

The elevator slides open with a ding that sounds like a fucking gong interrupting the maddening silence. Delilah and I walk through the hallway hand in hand. Pausing when I reach the door I use the grip I have on Delilah's hand and back her up against the wall. My ego swells at the sight of her chest rising and falling as I step into her. She still wants me.

"You remember what I said I was going to do to you when I was cleared?" I ask, brushing my nose along her jaw.

"I am not sure I could forget, even if I wanted to." Her back arches off the wall and into me as I slip my keys out of my pocket.

"When I open this door you're going to go into our bedroom and take all these clothes off. I want you waiting naked on the bed when I come in. Understand?"

She nods her head as I slot the key into the lock and turn. When it opens, she slips through the door in front of me, but not before my hand catches her ass cheek in a sharp slap. "That's my girl. See you soon." I watch as she retreats into the apartment.

I want her dripping for me, so I take my time removing my shoes and drop onto the couch. My cock was half hard by the time we left the doctor's office. Now it's fucking painful knowing that she's naked and waiting.

Aching for some relief, I grip my cock through my joggers and tip my head back into the cushion. I want to wait her out for a few more minutes, but fuck, I need her. Going a week without sex shouldn't be this hard. For fuck's sake, I went two years before I convinced Delilah to give me a chance, but now that I have her, it's never going to be enough.

Images of her naked and waiting in bed for me flood my mind. Pushing to my feet I eat up the space between the living room and bedroom with long strides making the large apartment feel much smaller.

Slowing when I reach the open door, I pull my shirt over my head and step into the room. My hand comes up to my mouth, dragging over my jaw when I see her. I let my shoulder lean against the doorframe, giving myself a second to take her in.

Fuck, she's gorgeous. But I have always known that. It's why I called her *Hermosa* that first night. But seeing her like this it's something else entirely. This woman is my perfect match. She's hardworking and loving. She knows what I need, like it's a sixth sense for her. In my darkest days, she was the only thing that kept me going.

"Mi Cielo, you are fucking stunning. I can't wait any longer to show you how much you mean to me."

Delilah turns her head, letting her eyes explore the expanse of my chest. I love the way she still looks at me like it's the first time she's seeing me like this. Despite my words, I don't go straight to the bed. She told me what she wanted and there's no way in hell I'm not going to deliver. I walk around the bed to my closet and return with the tie I wore when I took Delilah to the Bandits gala.

When I turn back towards her, it's all bright blue doe eyes looking up at the tie in my hand. Recognition sparking as her lips turn up in a sweet smile that makes her nose crinkle.

"That's the tie you wore to the gala. You're going to use that to tie me up?"

"Just your hands, if you still want that?" Her eyes flutter closed, and she nods. "I knew that night that there was no way I could keep ignoring my feelings for you. But you weren't ready yet. So I waited, but now that you're mine. I don't want to keep waiting to live this life with you. I want it all with you. The early morning kisses before you leave for work, coming home from an away game to you in our bed. I want the house, the babies, and the dogs."

"Is that all?" she asks with an eyebrow raised.

I can't contain the laugh that rumbles free. "If I didn't know you better, you mocking me might hurt my feelings. I pour my heart out and that sassy mouth just can't wait to chime in." The thing about waiting so long is that I've got the patience of a saint. Delilah's right there with me, it's written all over her face. Her slightly parted lips and the little hum that left her mouth right before she teases me.

"I only see two problems with this." Her hands move from where they're on the bed by her sides to her stomach. She slides one up to her breast and the other moves down her body, cupping her mound. "You're too far away while I'm here naked in bed and so horny."

"That sounds like one problem."

"Does it? I couldn't tell you because the only thing I can think about is that silky tie in your hand and how good it's going to feel against my skin when you wrap it around my wrists."

Stalking forward, I kneel on the bed, coming down on my forearms so I am over the top of her and drop a kiss on her forehead. "Arms above your head."

Her nipples pucker into tight pink buds at my words, and she slowly lifts her arms without taking her cobalt blue eyes off mine. Looping the black fabric around her wrists, I secure it to the headboard. Delilah tests it by wiggling her hands and tugging.

"Anytime you want out, all you have to do is tell me," I say, kissing her forehead.

"I don't think that's going to be an issue."

It takes all my strength to pull myself away from her. Not being able to be with her this last week has me strung tight. Every instinct in me is telling me to sink into her now. I want to kiss her and cover my body with her, but that's not what I promised her.

And if I am being honest, I am just as excited about seeing how much I can make her squirm. Pushing off the bed, I come around to the foot of the bed. Her long blonde hair is down around her shoulders as she lays stretched across the bed. The position makes her full breasts sit higher on her chest. My gaze travels down her body to where her curves flare out at her hips and my hands twitch to grip them. "Spread your legs for me. Show me how much you want this."

A whimper escapes her mouth, but she doesn't immediately do as I ask. "Promise me you'll stop if it's too much. The doctor said you need to listen to your body if it's too hard or you start to feel dizzy—"

"Hermosa, nothing about eating your pussy is hard, and if I get dizzy, it's going to be because of how badly I want you. Are you going to make me ask again? Or are you going to spread those legs for me and let me have my fun." I drop my hands to her ankle, smoothing up the creamy skin of her legs as she lets them fall open. Giving me a perfect fucking view of her glistening center. A groan vibrates through me from deep within my chest at the sight of her.

"Look at you, so swollen and wet for me. You did such a good job waiting for me. I bet it was hard not to touch yourself while I left you in here alone and stripped bare for me." Her breath hitches in her throat, catching as I use my thumbs to spread her. "How badly do you want my tongue right here?" The pad of my thumb brushes upwards. The contact is painfully light and short when it caresses her clit.

I can't look away when her hips twitch and her head tips back. "Yes. Please—I need you to touch me."

My cock is throbbing at the breathy way she's begging for more. Shifting up the bed, I lower my head, kissing just above where I know she wants me the most, and continue my path north until I get to her chest.

"I think I'll start here." I trace her nipple with my fingertip before moving to the other side to do the same. I can feel her heart pounding under me as I lower my head to suck one pert bud into my mouth.

"Oh god," she cries out as I release her nipple with a soft pop. My gaze catches on where her fists are balled tight, gripping the black tie that's keeping her at my mercy. Dipping my head again, I give the other side equal attention. Alternating back and forth as she writhes underneath me. "Cruz." My name is a plea for more and it makes me even harder.

Lifting my head from her chest, I look up at her where she's looking back down at me with her eyes at half mast and strands of her golden hair stuck to the side of her face. She's a beautiful mess.

"What's that, Delilah?" I ask, trying to keep my lips from curling upwards in a smile. "Did you want me to stop?"

"No. Never." Her blue eyes soften as shakes her head side to side, not able to do anything else.

"Never is an awfully long time." My finger traces lazy circles across her chest and up to her face where I sweep the strand stuck there aside.

"I don't care. There's no such thing as too much with you." She stretches her neck to kiss my chin.

"If you weren't going to ask me to stop, what did you need? Use your words and I'll give it to you," I ask against her lips, letting my hand wander back down to tweak and pull at her nipples.

"Give me more. You promised me your mouth."

"Like this?" I ask, right before I sweep my tongue into her mouth and kiss her hard. It's filled with all the promise of what I am about to do to her. She hums into the kiss, pressing up into me and giving back as much as she can.

"Or like this?" My lips find the skin at the juncture of her neck, the hallowed out spot that I know drives her crazy. Below me her chest starts rising and falling faster.

"Not quite, but you're getting warmer."

"How about here?" I ask, marking the skin at the swell of her breast.

"Fuck. That was good but, no. Lower."

When my lips connect with her hip bone, her stomach hallows out. Goosebumps decorate her torso as I position my body between her legs.

Letting my lips skim the inside of her thigh, I hear the audible breath she sucks in. "Keep going."

My hands grip her legs, spreading her wide for me. If I thought she was wet for me before, it's nothing compared to now. I push my hips into the bed, trying to soothe my aching cock and blow out a hot breath, letting it hit her center. "Where to start?"

"Anywhere—just fucking do something." Her eyes go wide, surprising herself with the demanding tone in her voice. She doesn't have to ask me twice. I have held off for as long as I can stand.

"I love hearing you beg for it." Fucking finally, I let myself bring my mouth to her center, licking the length of her before I suck her clit into my mouth. The moan that comes out of her is loud enough that all of Denver can probably hear it. Her panting becomes muffled when her thighs close around my head. "Keep them spread for me or I'll stop." I hum against her core as I continue lapping at her.

Her legs fall back open and I take advantage of the access, letting my fingers glide through her slit, gathering up her arousal. "Look at how soaked this pretty pussy is for me." Her eyes darken to almost a navy blue as I hold them up for her to see. "But it doesn't just look pretty, you're so fucking sweet. I am addicted to your taste. Suck yourself off my fingers and see why I can't get enough of you."

Stretching up towards her, I bring my fingers to her mouth, letting them run over her lips before she sucks them into her mouth. "Jesus. Delilah, you are incredible."

"Cruz, I want you to untie me." My stomach sinks at the thought that maybe I pushed her too far. "Please, I need you now. I don't want to wait any longer." A harsh breath leaves me and my hands shoot to the knot on the tie, working it free.

"Thank fuck. I would have done that for as long as you would have let me, but I need to be inside you so bad it hurts."

"Another time, maybe when I haven't had to sleep next to you without touching you for a week. Now lose the sweatpants and get on your back. I want to ride you like I did the other day, but this time without the clothes between us."

She's not going to get an argument from me. I slide the joggers and my boxer briefs down in one movement and take the spot she just vacated in the center of the bed with my back propped against the headboard. Reaching for her, I pull her to me and she straddles my lap.

I'll play any games Delilah wants. If something turns her on, it turns me on. But this, having her warm heat gripping my cock with her mouth right there for me to take, is all I need. "Ride me, Hermosa. Show me how good you can take me when you're in control," I tell her as she lifts her hips and positions me at her entrance.

When she sinks down, taking me all at once, I don't even try to stop the rasping groan that comes out. My head falls back resting against the headboard, while my fingers sink into the flesh at her hips to help her move along my length. "I wish you could see how beautiful you look like this. Nothing—no one has ever turned me on like you do."

Delilah takes the lead and brings her mouth down on mine in a searing kiss, lifting up until I am almost all the way out and then dropping back down. As the pace of her kiss picks up, so do her movements.

Pulling her to me, I flip us over so she's under me. She opens her mouth to argue. I shake my head and cup the side of her face, bringing my forehead to hers. "I'm fine, I promise. Now let me show you how much you mean to me."

Propping myself on my elbow and finding her clit with my other hand, I thrust into her. "You did such a good job riding my cock. But it's my turn to give you what you need. Just like you did for me last week." I look down to where we are joined and the sight of my cock disappearing inside of her is almost enough to make me come before she does.

When her legs start to tremble around my hips, I give her deeper thrusts, rocking my hips to hit her where I know she needs it. I can feel my own orgasm rocketing down my spine. I have to grit my teeth to keep myself in check. "That's it. Let me make you feel good. You're my heaven. Let me be yours."

Delilah clenches around me, letting out a moan. "Always, you always make me feel good—Cruz," she says as her body seizes, locking down on my cock. There's no holding back once she lets go. Her release tips me over the edge. But I don't stop moving until we're both lax and covered in a sheen of sweat. I roll onto my back, tugging her with me so she's laying across my chest. "Thank you, Delilah."

"For that? Anytime," she says around the deep breaths she is still sucking in as she recovers.

"You know that's not what I mean." I brush back the hair that's fallen into her face. I want to see her eyes right now.

"The way you put me first last week. You've had my back since the moment we met. Being together is new, but there's nothing about us that feels that way. You're it for me, Delilah. I meant what I said. I want it all with you someday, Mi Cielo. "

"Cruz, I will always be there to take care of you and I want all the same things as you. I know you're excited to be cleared and I am so thrilled for you, but I need you to take care of yourself so we can have those things. That future you talked about means nothing if you're not there to see it. Can you do that for me?"

CHAPTER 37

BREAKING RULES & HEARTS

PRESENT

The comforter is in a pile on the floor and I'm sprawled across Cruz's chest as we recover from another round. He was the big spoon to my little spoon as he thrust into me from behind. I can't get enough of him today, or any day. The position was a compromise because I was afraid he would overdo it. When we left the hospital we got a long list of things to watch out for that could indicate post-concussion syndrome.

As an athlete this was not the first time Cruz has suffered a concussion, but the risks are greater each time. I was holding back before because I was afraid to lose my best friend if we didn't work together. That fear has multiplied with that thought that I could lose him to an injury.

He insisted he was fine and didn't need a less adventurous position, but there were no arguments from him when I backed my ass up into him and tugged his hip over mine. After dragging the head of his cock over my center a few times, he was more than happy to bury himself deep inside of me for a leisurely session that felt a whole lot more intimate than anything else we've done together.

Cruz's fingers shift through my hair as we lay together in silence when, somewhere on the floor, his phone vibrates.

"There's no part of me that wants to move to answer that right now." He groans, his arms banding tight around me.

The phone goes still and I relax back into his chest. Tomorrow he'll resume workouts and I'll go back to my regular work schedule. This lazy day in bed together won't happen again for a while. And I have every intention of enjoying it to its fullest.

The humming starts again, and I roll off to the side. "It could be important. They wouldn't have called twice if it wasn't."

His gaze darts to the floor and back to me before he pushes off the bed. I should probably be ashamed of the way I openly gawk at his thick thighs and round ass as he walks to where the blankets are in a pile on the floor.

It only takes seconds of sifting through the blankets for the phone to tumble to the floor with a thud. Cruz clears his throat before he looks up at me. "It's Rich. He wants me to call him right away."

Tugging the only blanket left on the bed to my chest, I sit up and pat the spot next to me. Cruz has seen every inch of me up close and personal, but something about this call has me feeling the need to have that barrier.

The bed sags as Cruz joins me, sliding under the blanket. I grip his free hand, letting him know I am here. His eyes lower from the phone in his hand to our linked hands. "I'm here. Whatever happens."

"Hey Cruz," the gruff voice greets us.

"Hey, I take it you've got news for me?"

"I met with Victoria today. This is what we've been looking for." There's a long sigh on the other end of the line. "She's got a lot of dirt on Miller to make me believe he was involved."

"You're sure she's not just an angry ex?" Cruz's eyebrows pull together. He's been skeptical that this would lead anywhere. His reluctance is partly protective, so he doesn't get his hopes up after all these years.

"She ended the relationship. There's details about the case she shouldn't have been able to share and she knew them. She seems credible to me."

"Why did she wait so long to come forward?" Cruz asks, the air whooshing out of him. My grip on his hand tightens. He manages a weak smile in return and tucks me into his side. I run my hand up his chest to cup the side of his face, feeling his pulse hammering under my palm.

"Are you okay?" I mouth at him when I pull his face towards me. He nods, but I don't buy it—he's barely hanging on.

"What did she say?" Cruz's voice comes out detached.

"Are you sure you want to do this before we go to the police and get the entire story?" His rough voice softens. He's worked with him long enough that he knows how hard this is for him and it's clear that Cruz is more than a client to him. It makes me wish I could hug Rich.

"I've waited three years. Give me something." I can see the pleading in Cruz's dark eyes as he looks blankly down at his lap.

"According to Victoria, he was angry the night of the accident. He wasn't pleased with how he played. Afterward, he called her and they fought. She remembered because he was really paranoid and complaining about how well Jarrett had pitched. He claimed Jarrett was trying to make him look bad."

"Did she know if they were together that night?" Cruz asks, blinking rapidly. Seeing him like this is enough to break me, but I can't let that happen. He needs me to be strong for him, so I steel myself for whatever is about to come.

"She couldn't confirm. She knew Miller went out but not where. Over the course of their relationship, she's put some pieces together from drunk ramblings and his state when he came home from Miami."

"So what happens now? Does she have anything that the police will actually be able to use because this sounds like a lot of speculation?"

"Maybe. She knew the details about where and how he was found on the beach, down to the fact that he was found near a damaged pier."

Cruz's head snaps up, looking at me with pained eyes. "The exact location was never released to the media."

"There's more, but Cruz, we need to see this through and pursue the proper channels." Rich clears his throat on the other end of the phone. "Are you alone?"

"No. My girlfriend is here with me." A pang of sadness hits me that the first time he's calling me that is under such shitty circumstances.

"You may want to take me off speaker for this," he says, careful to temper his tone.

"It's fine. There's nothing you could say that she can't hear." For the first time since he answered the phone, some of the tension leaves his body.

"Cruz—"

"It's fine, just tell me." Suddenly, he sounds so exhausted. The wariness in his voice amps up all my protective instincts. "Please."

"Victoria has a bottle of GHB she found in his luggage after the trip to Miami."

The phone slips from his hand, dropping to the bed. I'm caught off guard, not sure what GHB has to do with Jarrett's death, but I don't have time to figure it out because Cruz is crumbling in front of me.

My heart breaks as I watch him bring his balled hands to the side of his head before he curls in on himself and lets out a strangled cry. It's the most heart wrenching sound I have ever heard.

"Cruz." Rich's sharp voice is muffled by the sheets as he calls out in concern.

I grab the phone and shift so I am in front of Cruz. "Rich, it's Delilah. I've got him, but I'm going to hang up now. I'll have him call you later."

"There's no rush. I can handle things on my end. Take care of him."

I don't bother saying goodbye before I end the call. My hands smooth up Cruz's arms, covering his tight fists with my own and lowering my head so I am eye level with him. As soon as our eyes connect, he pulls me into his lap. My arms loop under his and hold him tight as he buries his head in my hair. His body shakes as he struggles with his emotions.

"I've got you." I have no idea what to do for him other than to hold on tight and let him know I'm here. "I'm right here."

"He did this. That fucker took my brother from me." I've never heard his voice like this before. It's filled with a vengeance that sends ice through my veins. Not because I'm scared of him, but I'm afraid *for* him. I can feel the way this is taking over stealing him from me.

I blink back the tears brimming my eyes and fight every instinct I have to tell him he needs to calm down. It's the last thing he needs to hear, but his doctor just reiterated his need to avoid stress. Maybe it's selfish, but I need him here and whole for me.

And so does Jarrett. He promised his brother he would find out what happened. He can't do that if he ends up back in the hospital.

My hands make circles on his back as I hold on tight, hoping that the motion will do something to calm him. Eventually, his breaths become less ragged and the tight hold he has on me starts to loosen. The first words out of his mouth are a bucket of ice water over my head.

"I need to pack a bag." He shifts me off his lap. His movements are almost robotic as he moves towards the closet and pulls a pair of clean boxer briefs up his legs.

"A bag?" My mind races, trying to catch up. I pull the bedsheet with me, almost tripping over it as I follow him to the closet.

He's already lugging his suitcase out when I get to the closet door. He breezes right past me, dropping the suitcase on to the bed before returning to the closet and pulling things off hangers.

"Cruz, slow down." Fuck. Where are my clothes? I look around for anything I can put on before this sheet gets wrapped around my legs again. I grab his discarded t-shirt from last night and slip it over my head.

"Can you grab my charger for me? I'll need to talk to Coach about starting rehab from St. Louis."

"St. Louis? Can we talk about this for a minute?" My arms come around my stomach as I stand in front of him, trying to get him to stop moving long enough to talk to me.

"Uh huh, sure, just let me book a flight."

"Stop. Please," I say, dropping to the bed between him and the suitcase.

"I have to go. Three years I've been waiting for this, I promised him I'd figure this out. I owe him that much."

"What about you?" My voice breaks on the last word and part of me really wants to ask, *what about me*? I silence that thought. I don't want to stand in the way of what he needs to do for his brother, but he just got cleared for some activity today. Two weeks ago, I sat by his side in St Louis while he was recovering from a head injury.

This seems like too much too fast. What if he has complications or his symptoms return? I need him. The turmoil rages inside me as I fight to lock it down tight.

"Me? I don't matter. This is about him."

Those three words "I don't matter" hit me square in the chest, cracking it open wide. My throat thickens as I push the words out.

"You matter to me. *This* matters to me." My hand gestures between our bodies, desperate to break through to him. "I need you Cruz. You're my future. I—I don't think you should go. Not right now. Give Rich a few days to figure things out. See how you're feeling. Let your brain heal a little more." My stomach knots itself into a mess that I'm not sure I'll be able to untangle as I try to plead with him to stay. But I can see on his face it's not going to make a difference. He needs to do this, but I am not sure how I'll be able to standby and watch him put himself at risk.

He winces like my words are a punch to the gut, but I can't take them back. I wouldn't even if I could. When I kept the voicemail from Cruz in the hospital, I did it to protect him. This is the same thing. I remember the way he was when he first came to Denver. He tried so hard to hide his pain, but it was there. Every single day. Cruz was a shell of the person he is now and he's worked so hard to get his life back.

He needs this closure and I would never stand in the way of that because not only is Cruz my best friend, but he's the man that's stolen my heart one piece at a time until he owned the entire thing. My future is his future. And he's just well enough to run for short distances again. Nothing about a trip to St. Louis to track down the man he thinks causes his brother's death fits into his recovery.

If he refuses to protect himself, then I'm going to do everything in my power to protect him from himself by reminding him what he's risking: his health, our future. Flying across the country on a whim to track down your brother's killer is about as stressful as it can get.

Cruz drops to his knees in front of me while I sit at the end of the bed, tilting my chin up so that he's looking me in the eyes. I try to pull my head away to wipe my tears. I am so fucking scared for him. I don't want him to see that weakness, but he grips my chin, not letting me look away.

"Get Willa and Mikey to cover at *Buns & Roses*. Come with me." His voice is barely a whisper and I can hear the uncertainty in it even as he asks. He knows what he's asking is a lot. I just got back to work. It was the longest I have ever been away from the shop, but that's not even the problem. I trust my employees, and I want to be there for him, but not if it means standing by and watching him put himself in a harmful situation.

"I can't." The heat from the tears burns as they roll down my cheeks. Wiping them away now is pointless, they are coming too fast.

"Can't or won't?" Cruz asks, still not letting me look away. The sadness in his eyes is enough to break me. I'm making this harder for him, and I know it. But why does he need to leave right now? He has no idea where this is going to go. He could stay here and wait for Rich.

"Can't. I can't watch you put your health at risk like this when you don't have to," I finally admit—the words tasting bitter on my tongue.

"And I can't stay." His grip on my face tightens, pulling me to him. When his lips meet mine my heart feels like it might stall in my chest. Normally his touch makes my heart beat right out of my chest but this is different. He pulls back still cradling my face and I can see the same heartbreak swimming in his eye. This feels like goodbye. His hands drop from my face and he lowers his head to my lap, hugging my waist. "You know I can't, right?" The words are muffled as he hugs me tight.

"I know you think you can't, but that doesn't mean I like it. I'm scared, Cruz." My tears fall into his curls, but he doesn't look up from where his head is resting on my thighs.

He's never held me like he's not sure when he'll see me again. It cracks my chest wide open. Logically, I know he won't be gone long. He's got a contract with the team that requires him to be back to play.

But that doesn't matter, because I don't know what version of Cruz will come back. This feels like this could change everything for us.

My chest feels like it's been cracked open, my heart carved out and packed in his bag as I repack the suitcase I brought with me when we left for St. Louis so I can go back to my apartment for the first time.

When I walk back into my apartment I collapse onto my bed, calling my Dad and Pops. I sob to them through the entire story. How we finally got our shot and how it might already be over, about my fear for Cruz. I admit that I've been holding back because I knew how much it would hurt, but I was wrong, it's worse. Being without him hurts more than I could have imagined.

Right now I would give anything to erase the ocean between us so they could wrap me up in their arms and comfort me in person. But that feels as selfish as asking Cruz to stay. They earned their retirement in Hawaii and I know they would give it all up if I asked. They would move back to Colorado. Raising a little girl as two gay men wasn't easy, but they gave me the very best family. So I suck back my tears and promise them I'm okay. That I'll lean on the girls and call the second I need to talk.

CHAPTER 38

FLYING THE LONELY SKIES

PRESENT

It takes me a minute to talk myself into turning off the engine of the Bronco when I pull into the parking spot in the private terminal at the airport. Nothing about this afternoon is sitting right with me. Rich dropped a bomb on me today and I need to see this through, not just for Jarrett but for me.

I'm not blind, I know that my life has been tied to his death for the last three years. I need this closure. Delilah might think I'm risking our future and my health by doing this, but I don't see it that way. I need to do this for us. She deserves a man that is fully present. Not one that's got one foot in the past.

As far as my health goes, I know the risks I'm taking, but I also know what a slippery slope grief is. One wrong step here and I'll slide right back into the black hole that I was in when Delilah and I met.

This is the right thing to do, for both of us, even if it feels like I just ripped us apart.

God. I wish she was here. This would be so much easier with her by my side. The irony that she asked me to stay and I walked away is not lost on me.

Sliding the keys free of the ignition, I pocket them and step out of the Bronco. There weren't any flights available, so I called in a favor with Dean. My offer to pay his pilot's fee to get to St. Louis tonight was brushed off. Luckily he was able to help because I knew if I stayed any longer I'd let Delilah talk me into waiting it out.

Nothing can slip through the cracks, we are too close to getting answers. And I want to be where I can get updates from Rich as we figure out what the hell happened with Miller and Jarrett before his accident.

Pulling my suitcase behind me, I walk towards the small private plane. I still need to call Coach, but I'm not released to practice yet, only light activity. As long as I continue to workout and go to follow-up appointments in St. Louis, I don't expect any problems.

My phone vibrates on the seat next to me. For a second, I find myself hopeful that it's Delilah telling me she's on the way, but it's fleeting. It won't be. She wants this to be the closure I am looking for, but she meant it when she said she couldn't watch me put myself through this. I get where she's coming from. She already picked up the pieces of my shattered soul and put them back together once, one coffee and pastry at a time. Still, I wish she was here.

Reaching across the arm rest I pick up the phone. Hendrix. Of course. Delilah would have gone right to Poppy after she left.

"Please don't give me a hard time," I answer without a greeting. This day has left me so drained I don't have the patience to listen to him try to talk me out of this.

"I'm not going to. Just checking in. Are you okay?"

"Um . . . I'm not sure." I feel numb but broken. It's not a feeling that's easy to describe. "I just need to get to St. Louis so I can talk to Rich face to face—understand what's next. Miller needs to pay for his role in Jarrett's death. Whether it's his fault or he knew what happened this whole time—I owe it to Jarrett to find out."

"Yeah, you do. Have you talked to Coach yet?" he asks cautiously.

"Not yet. I am going to call him after I hang up with you." I push my hair off my forehead. All the adrenaline that was roaring through me before has faded and my energy is waning. I can feel the crash coming.

"If there's anything I can do with him or the team to help let me know. I've got your back." I can hear the sincerity in his voice.

"Thanks, man. I don't think it will be a problem as long as I am back in the next two weeks." My muscles feel like they have turned to lead, so I push the button to recline my chair. There's no way I can make it through this flight without conking out.

"We've got your back. Whatever you need."

"I will—"

Hen cuts me off. He's not going to let me dismiss his offer to help.

"I mean it. We want you back here in one piece. All of us. Me, Poppy, the team. Delilah was wrecked when she called and she's not the only one worried about you. This is a lot to deal with."

"I know. I know." He isn't saying it to make me feel guilty. Hendrix gets it. He fought to get Poppy back, and he was a miserable asshole the whole time. After almost losing his person, he doesn't want me to lose mine.

And I really hope I don't. I'm counting on the fact that Delilah will be there waiting for me when I get back because there is no way I could choose between getting justice for my brother and her. The choice alone would tear me apart.

Hendrix and I hang up on a promise to check in with him every other day. If I was capable of feeling anything right now, his concern would be heartwarming. But I'm numb and struggling to keep my eyes open by the time I finish talking to Coach. He's supportive, but like Hen, he wants me to check in to make sure I am prioritizing my health—mental and physical. The conversation also came with a stern warning that if I was released to practice, his hands would be tied on how lenient he could be before fines would start.

The plane's descent into St. Louis wakes me with a start. When I open my eyes, the plane is dark. The crew is seated in their jump seats and I'm just fucking lonely. It has me questioning my decision to leave Delilah behind. She was right. It would have been possible to do this from Denver.

Every cell in my body was telling me that I needed to be here. That this was finally it. Jarrett was going to get his answers. After all this time, I couldn't ignore that. So why does it feel like a limb has been ripped away?

CHAPTER 39

ST. LOUIS (AGAIN)

PRESENT

When I open my eyes early the next morning, there's no hair ties on the nightstand and the pink AirPod case I'm so used to finding beside my phone is missing. These sheets don't smell like caramel and coffee beans either. It makes me want to close my eyes and roll back over and pretend this is all just a bad dream.

My screen is littered with notifications, but the notification I want to see the most is nowhere to be found. I'm not sure why it bothers me. I hadn't really expected a text last night.

Naively, I had hoped that we would stay in the same blissful state we were in before I left, and even though it's been less than a day there is a noticeable rift. She's protecting her heart by pulling back because she's terrified for me, but I'd hoped she might reach out this morning.

Instead, there's an obnoxious number of texts from the guys in our group chat starting at 3 a.m.

DOM:

GIF of Will Ferrell streaking

DEAN:

Don't even fucking think about it. Coach will have your ass if you get caught.

DOM:

Fine Grandpa. I'll just go to bed.

DEAN:

Stop calling me that.

DOM:

You're such a crotchety old man.
I'm not sure what else to call you.

DEAN:

I said no to going out one time.

HEN:

This is how chat's end up muted.
GO TO SLEEP!

DOM:

Hey! It's Hen. Are you going to come streaking with me?

HEN:

Are you drunk or just dumb?

DOM:

Neither. Just bored. All my friends are tied down or elderly.

DEAN:

I'm not fucking elderly. I'm the same damn age as you.

DOM:

You should see a doctor for that.

DEAN:

We need to find you a girlfriend.
Someone to settle you down and keep you occupied so the rest of us can sleep.

DOM:

I'm plenty occupied. I just kick them out before they fall asleep.

DEAN:

Not always.

DOM:

Shut your mouth.

HEN:

I like the direction this is heading.

DOM:

DEAN!

DEAN:

Go to sleep and stop calling me old man or I'll spill my guts.

DOM:

You wouldn't!

Thank fuck Dean talked him out of streaking. Once I'm caught up on the texts that I thankfully missed last night, I tap out my reply, not even hesitating at the time difference. They were okay with texting me in the middle of the night. I have zero guilt giving them an extra early wake up call with the time difference.

CRUZ:

You all know I'm supposed to be getting rest to heal right?

DOM:

CRUZ! My man, did I wake you?

CRUZ:

No, because I turn this chat on mute at night for a reason.

DEAN:

That's smart. How do you have so much energy?

DOM:

Because I am not elderly.

DEAN:

...

DOM:

Before you do anything rash, I only agreed to stop calling you "Old man."

DEAN:

You're lucky I'm terrified of her.

HENDRIX:

Terrified of who?

DOM:

Nobody, you can't trust his memory.
The advanced years are setting in.

Suddenly Dom's not so talkative, ruining the only thing that was distracting me from the fact that I'm here, alone, with no word from the one person I want to talk to more than anything.

The hotel I checked into last night has one perk, the location. It's close to Rich's office in downtown St. Louis and has a decent gym. After a quick shower I walk the two blocks to the gym. The staff set me up with a pass for the week, and while my workout is boring and doesn't do shit to take the edge off, at least I'm moving.

The glare Rich gives me tells me just how happy he is to see me when he rounds the corner and finds me waiting outside of his office at 7:55 a.m. He stops in front of me, muttering under his breath with a pinched expression and shake of his head. I don't catch it all but it sounds an awful lot like, *"Dumb kid," "should be home,"* and *"hospital."*

When he finishes unlocking the door, he finally stops and looks up at me. "You're an idiot, you know that, right?"

"I'm fairly certain you're not the only person in my life that thinks that right now." When I called him back after packing and watching Delilah walk out my door, I didn't have the fight left in me to tell him I was coming. He would've tried to talk me out of it, and I wasn't sure if I was strong enough not to let him. It's the same reason I didn't tell my parents. My mom would've lit me up. I can practically hear the swear words rolling for her tongue in Spanish.

"You piss the little lady off?"

"I'm not sure pissed is the right word. Delilah's not angry. She's too good to be angry. Scared and hurt is more accurate," I say as I toe the sidewalk in front of his office.

"I like her. Make sure you don't fuck that up beyond repair by being here." Rich sweeps his arm out in front of him. "You may as well come in."

I walk into the office ahead of him. "I'm not letting her get away. She's my best friend and the only person I want a future with."

"I don't have any updates for you. So I'm not sure why you flew halfway across the country."

"Didn't expect you to, but I want to be here when you do. I think I've got at least a week before I have to be on the field—"

With a scowl that would put my dad's to shame, Rich cuts in. "Don't think I don't know about your injury. I saw that hit and I know you're supposed to be recovering from a concussion, not playing detective with me." He drops his eyes to the picture frame on his desk. "But I also know why you came. I'll do everything I can to get you answers, but these things take time."

"I've waited three years. We are so close I can feel it. Miller had a part in this. He's always been a bitter asshole. He was bitter about Jarrett rising to the top when his career was slipping away from him. I don't know how he was involved or what happened, but he knows something."

"We need to be careful how we handle this. If you want a real shot at justice for your brother, it needs to be airtight."

"So what's first?" I pace across Rich's office as he watches me from his chair with narrowed eyes.

"There's no way I can talk you into going home to your girl and resting?" He shifts in his chair, crossing his foot over his knees.

"Nope," I say, popping the "P" and dropping into the chair across from him.

With a heavy sigh, he pulls out his phone, scrolling through it before he looks up and continues. "I have a meeting with Victoria at 11 a.m. to secure the bottle of GHB as evidence, along with her journals." He scratches his jaw, pausing like he's not sure how much to say. "Those probably won't be admissible, but I'll study them to see if there's anything we can use. She also has an old phone that I'll have my tech guy scrub for any other evidence."

"When do you talk to Miller?" My knee bounces rapidly as I roll my shoulders, trying to loosen the tension that's settled there. It doesn't work and I'm not sure anything will.

Rich tilts his head to the ceiling like he needs to gather his patience before he speaks to me again. I know I'm pushing my luck, questioning every step of the way. "I might not. If we get enough evidence, the case will get turned over to the police and they will bring him in."

"How long before—"

"You need to let me do my job. I promise you, I'm going to do every-thing in my power to help you get justice for Jarrett. If I have to explain each decision, or update you on every detail as it happens, it's going to slow this down."

My head drops to my hands. "I know, Rich, but I need to be here. I'll try to give you space to work."

"I get it. Let me meet with her this morning. Then, give me some time to look over her journals and the phone. I'll update you tomorrow on what's next. I don't want to keep you in the dark, but if we are going to nail Colby Miller, I need to be focused on that."

"Okay. I'll get out of your hair." I push up from the chair and head towards the door, leaving it in Rich's hands.

"And you'll go back to the hotel and rest." The tone in his voice tells me not to argue with him. A memory of the way Delilah looked when she was begging me not to leave flashes in my mind.

"Yeah. I'll go back and take it easy," I concede before opening the door to leave.

CHAPTER 40

CRYING OVER STICKY BUNS

PRESENT

When I wake up in my apartment, nothing feels right—and I'm not just talking about the empty bed or the scratchy, swollen eyes. Both suck, but it's the hollow feeling inside my chest for the last five days that still takes me by surprise each morning.

Being away from Cruz isn't new. He's traveled since we first met and I've been through road trips since I started to have feelings for him, but this is different. I don't just miss him because he's not here. I hate the way we left things. There was so much we didn't say to each other. I let him go, not forever, but for now, and until he comes back, I don't think I'll feel whole.

When I walked out his door, I may as well have left my heart in his suitcase.

It's still dark outside when I step out of my apartment to open *Buns & Roses*. I don't bother to turn on my radio during my short drive. The coffee shop has always felt more like home to me than my apartment or anyplace else. But when I step inside the space and flick on the lights, the luster is gone.

There's no humming or dancing. I can't bring myself to work on my Spanish while I bake either. I've just been going through the motions, opening up the shop and getting ready for the day. Time seems to stand still as I do it. Each minute that passes, knowing he's alone in St. Louis and I'm here makes the tightness in my chest a little more acute. When I pull the sticky buns out of the oven, I can't stop the tears from falling. Willa's been making them for me but we ran out yesterday so I needed to make them first thing this morning.

The service door creaks open and I frantically swipe at my face, trying to cover the sadness with a forced smile. Willa steps flatter when she walks into the shop and sees my puffy red face still damp with tears. Dropping her keys and phone to the metal prep table as she rushes to my side. "Oh, honey. What's going on?"

"It's nothing. I'm fine." That's a bold-faced lie. I'm so far from fine right now, everything's a mess. I'm crying over sticky buns because they remind me of Cruz. I asked him not to leave, and he went, but that's not why I feel like my stomach is tied in knots.

"It's very clearly not fine, Lilah." Willa takes my hand and leads me over to the desk chair in the corner. "Is this about Cruz?"

"How'd you know?" I ask through short breaths as I try to rein in the tears.

"For starters, you're in love with the guy. So when I find you sobbing over his favorite dessert, it's not a reach to assume it has something to do with him."

Her words catch me off guard. I thought I knew what love was when I was with Brad, but what I feel for Cruz is nothing like that. It's more. Deeper. Organic. The way I feel about him spills over to every part of my life and every part of my being. He's a part of me that can't be left out. And I would never want him to. It would be like sticky buns without caramel—

incomplete and nowhere near as sweet. Is that why it hurts so bad, because I'm missing a piece of me?

The door to *Buns & Roses* chimes and before either Willa or I can get to the front to see who it is, Poppy's voice sounds through the quiet space.

"Lilah, you back there?" Poppy's red hair appears around the corner of the open doorway that connects the kitchen to the lobby. She's wearing a pair of spandex bike shorts and a cropped tank with her running shoes. Her hair hangs in two long braids that swing side to side as she rushes back when she sees the state I am in.

"You were doing so good when I left last night. What happened?" Poppy's arms come around me, pulling me into her body, holding me tight like maybe she can keep me from falling apart with her arms.

"The sticky buns set me off, they're his favorite. I know it's silly. He's not leaving me. He needs to do this for himself, but I am just so scared for him. And not just because of his head." I squeeze my eyes shut, trying to fight off the tears. "He wants this to be it. To get the answers he's been fighting for all these years. It's going to crush him if it's not, I'll have to watch him break all over again."

"No one wants that, but if it happens, you'll put him back together and you won't have to do it alone. You'll have me, Hendrix, Dean, and Dom. The Bandits are a family. We won't let you or Cruz fight this alone."

"God, why am I such a disaster?" I ask, pulling back from her hold and pacing the narrow space between the prep table and the sinks.

"Do you really not know the answer to that?" Poppy asks with a tenderness that tells me she thinks I do.

"Should I have gone with him?" I avoid her question. I've asked her the same thing each day since Cruz left. Her response hasn't wavered.

"I can't answer that for you, but I think I might have a solution if you need to go to him."

Wait . . . that last part is new and piques my interest. I know I said I didn't think I could watch him put himself through this, but I belong there with him. Whatever happens with Miller. I want—no, I *need* to be there for him.

"How?" I ask through a sniffle. The tears have finally stopped at the prospect that I can get to him.

"Mia has that book signing in Denver this week. She's flying out a few days early to catch this series. She'll be here tonight."

"I remember, but I am not sure how that helps."

"She worked in a coffee shop in college. Between the two of us, we can help Willa and Mikey cover."

"I can't ask her to do that, or you."

Poppy shakes her head. "You're not. We are volunteering and I know you would do the same. Let us help you. I mean, I'm honestly not sure how much help I'll be, but I can sweep and ring up customers."

I look at Willa, who's been working quietly beside us this whole time. She's standing with her hands on her hips, giving me a glare that honestly scares the shit out of me. "Why did you hire me?"

"Is that a serious question?" Wrong thing to say. Her eyes narrow even further. "Because I needed the help and you are grossly over-qualified, an excellent baker, and reliable."

"So, do you not trust me? Or are you a control freak?" she asks with her head cocked to the side. Damn her and her psychology degree. She is one-hundred percent using it on me right now.

"Um . . . No. I mean yes, I trust you. That felt like a trick question."

"If you want to go be with the man you love, don't let the shop stand in the way. We'll be fine. If Poppy and Mia want to hang out and help, that's okay. But I can handle it." She sighs, looking around the kitchen. "I've been meaning to talk to you about giving me more hours. I hardly have any classes over the summer, so it won't be a problem. Baking and making coffee isn't exactly rocket science. The other stuff, payroll, vendor orders, whatever—we can figure out how to have you do it from St. Louis."

I love Cruz and not just as my best friend. I am in love with him. Big, messy, in-love feelings and I sent him off to do something awful and hard, alone. There's a reason it hurt so much to watch him walk away. He was never supposed to do this alone. I should be by his side.

"I need to get to St. Louis," I say, looking at Poppy, not even sure where to start.

"Awe, you do love him. Let's get you there so you can tell him, because right now he probably needs to hear it."

I nod excitedly but don't say the words. It feels wrong to say them aloud to anyone but him. "I need to get to the airport. Can you take me?" I ask Poppy, gathering my things. I toss her the car keys. "You can drive my car."

"Slow your roll. Let's get you a bag packed and I'll see if I can find out from Hen where he's staying."

My roll comes to a screeching halt when I pull up the flights on my computer at Poppy's insistence. There are storms forecasted in St. Louis all day and everything is canceled or delayed by hours. All the later flights are full with people rebooking to try and get to their destinations.

"The next flight I can actually get on isn't until tomorrow afternoon. What am I going to do?"

"If you drove straight through. You would get there late tonight. But babe—"

I shake her off. I'm already on edge. Driving twelve hours would be awful. It would send me into a full-blown panic attack. "No, I don't want to do that. Not alone. I'll take the flight tomorrow and watch to see if anything else opens up sooner."

"I'll see what Hendrix can find out."

"Make sure he doesn't tell him I'm coming. If something goes wrong and my flight gets canceled or I can't get there . . . I already let him down once."

Poppy pulls me into a hug. "I doubt that. You know he loves you, too. He's loved you for years. Just travel safe and get to him in one piece. Mia and I will help as much as Willa will let us. You've got him and we've got you."

"Thank you. Both of you," I say, smiling over at Willa.

"Of course. I'm going to run so I can catch Hendrix before he leaves for practice," she says with one last squeeze before she heads back out the same way she came in.

I take a deep breath, looking around and mentally starting a to-do list. Willa and I put our heads together to come up with a plan for a week of coverage and pack up my laptop and charger. After I give her a quick rundown on how to do inventory, I head out to get things sorted out at home.

CHAPTER 41

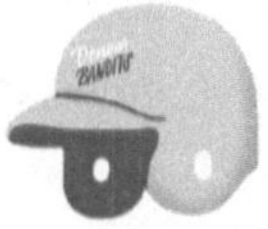

STORMY MOOD

PRESENT

When I left Rich's office four days ago, I tried to do what I promised. I owe it to Delilah to take care of myself. She was right in a lot of ways. This might be where I need to be, but this is my past. She's my future. Right now, the two are colliding and, even though I have to do this for my brother, I need to do it to ensure that my future with Delilah is everything I want it to be. Filled with hope and laughter, and separate from the darkness of my past.

I'll never forget my brother, and the grief will always be there, but I need this closure to build the life Delilah deserves. To be the man she deserves instead of the guy that's been chasing after his brother's ghost for the last three years.

As much as I've tried to rest, I'm antsy. Nothing about being in this city feels right. Everything is wrong without Delilah by my side. Instead of restful sleep, I tossed and turned when I tried to nap. Today it's even worse, but after a restless hour I gave up and decided to go for a walk. But when I stepped outside, the sky was a shade of greenish-gray that lets you know all hell is about to break loose.

I duck back into the hotel to escape the incoming weather. *Alone with my thoughts again. Fucking awesome.*

Swiping my card at my hotel room door, I settle on watching some baseball. If I can't play, at least I can watch some old games. I pull up the MLB app on my iPad and start flicking through the options.

My phone vibrates beside me. Foolishly, I still can't shake the hope that it's Delilah every time. We've never gone this long without texting. When I left, I knew that this would happen. That talking to me while I was away would be harder for her than giving me space. Every text and call would just reopen the wound for both of us. But fuck, I want to hear her voice.

When I pick up, it's Hen on the other end of the line. "Hey, man. How's it going?" I ask. Maybe he's talked to Delilah and can tell me how she's doing.

"I should be asking you that. How are things going in St. Louis? Did your P.I. have any updates for you?"

"Not really. He thinks this could be the break we needed, but he won't know anything concrete until after he meets with Miller's ex. He met with her to collect all the evidence but his team is going over everything with a fine tooth comb right now," I grit out. Just thinking about the fact that he's there and I'm stuck in this stupid hotel room alone makes me agitated.

"That's a step in the right direction? Does the hotel at least have a decent gym?"

"Um, no. I'm in a Hyatt by the Arch. I grabbed the first decent looking hotel I found near Rich's office downtown when I was on the plane. But I found a gym close by that I've been using here," I explain, glancing out the window. The rain is coming down hard, now pinging off the glass.

"How are the workouts going so far?" Hendrix asks just as lightning explodes across the sky.

"Calling them workouts doesn't feel right. Your grandma is more active than me right now. Fuck, Hen." I rake my hand through my hair, blowing out a breath. "I'm so bored stuck in this room, and I miss her so much it hurts."

"You could come home. No one would think any less of you." His voice is cautious, like he's afraid that it might not be the right thing to say.

"I can't. This isn't just about me or even Jarrett. Delilah deserves the best version of me and I need this closure to be that guy for her." The lamp next to me rattles as thunder cracks angrily outside, making everything vibrate. It mimics the turmoil I feel inside as I wait for word from Rich.

"What if this doesn't go the way you want, Cruz?" The question comes out uncharacteristically soft for Hendrix. I don't want anyone to handle me like I'm breakable, but I understand why he tempers it. It's a question that's been haunting me since I got on the plane alone. If this all goes to shit, will it still be worth it? Will I regret the decision I made, knowing it's hurting her?

"Then it's done. I stop looking for the answers. Finding out what happened that night wasn't the only promise I made to him. I'm not living up to the other promise to live my life to the fullest if I'm putting my future on hold. He wouldn't want that."

"You just walk away?" The question is colored with surprise.

"I just walk away. She's my future. Jarrett's gone—" My voice breaks and I clear my throat trying to keep my composure. "Delilah's not and I can't risk losing her. I told her in the beginning we could be friends if this didn't work out." I laugh maniacally, knowing now how stupid that was. This thing with Delilah is all or nothing. There's no way I could go back to just being her friend. It would tear me apart.

"That was really fucking dumb," Hendrix agrees as the lights in the hotel room flicker. The storm is really raging.

"No kidding. If it's up to me, it won't matter because I never plan on losing her." Saying it out loud only makes me want to call her more.

There's a beep indicating another call, just as I am about to say good-bye to Hendrix so I can call Delilah. I know I said I would give her space, but fuck it, I miss her. I pull the phone from my ear, torn between wanting it to be her and knowing it's probably Rich. It's the latter.

"That's Rich calling with an update. I gotta go. Later Hen. Thanks for checking in." My stomach flops with anxiety as I switch the call over.

"Tell me you have good news," I ask over the sound of the rain slapping against the building.

"Shit. Hold on." Rich goes quiet and the only noise coming through the speaker on my phone is distant thunder and the slap of rapid footfalls against wet pavement. "Sorry, this weather is nuts. The sky opened up on me and I had to make a run for it."

"Have you made any progress on her phone or the journals?" My fingers drum against my leg impatiently, the nerves causing the walls of the hotel to feel like they are closing in.

"Listen, Cruz, I don't want to get your hopes up, but I want you to be prepared for this to move fast. One of my guys is going to fly down to Miami to turn everything over to them as soon as he can get a plane out."

I swallow, suddenly at a loss for words. The space between my ears is filled with a buzzing sensation.

"Cruz, are you there?"

"Yeah," I say, letting my head fall back against the chair I dropped into while I was talking to Hendrix. "You're sure."

"Pretty sure. You might want to call your parents and prepare them. Once this goes to the police, there's no guarantee it stays out of the news."

That's a conversation that I've been putting off since the mystery calls from Miller's ex started coming in. They deserve to hear this from me. "Okay. I can do that today. Did you find anything new?"

"Victoria's a smart girl and not someone who's bad side I'd want to get on. She's been documenting everything and saving all this to bury him if things went south between them. Not that the asshole doesn't deserve it."

"Why the hell didn't she come forward sooner?" I ask, my voice taking on an angry edge. She sat on this for years. My family could have had closure right away instead of waiting all this time.

"She was in a hard spot. I'm not sure the extent of it, but he was emotionally abusive at a minimum," he says with a sigh.

Fuck, I hate Miller. He deserves all the pain that is coming his way. My blood boils with rage that he's been behind this the whole time. Living his life playing on the team that Jarrett should have been on. All this fucking time without paying for his role in my brother's death. "Do whatever you have to. I want him to pay." The words come out cold and detached.

I want to break something. If I were home, I would head straight to the cage and kill a few buckets of balls. Even if I could do that here, it's not allowed. All I can do is sit in this room and stew. I stand from the bed, pacing the small hotel room. The energy inside swirling like the wind outside.

"I'll do everything in my power to see he's held accountable for any role he had in Jarrett's death."

"Thanks Rich, keep me updated. I'm going to call my parents." I disconnect the call, cocking my arm like I might fire the phone against the wall. My teeth grind as I squeeze my eyes shut, fighting off the headache that's blooming behind my forehead.

"Fuck!" I yell to no one. I don't have the luxury of being able to throw a tantrum right now. Drawing in three deep measured breaths in I rein myself back in remembering why I am doing all this: Jarrett and Delilah.

There's practically a path worn down the middle of the room before I feel like I've got myself calm enough to call my parents.

CHAPTER 42

GIRLS TO THE RESCUE

PRESENT

Packing my bag takes me all of about fifteen minutes when I get home from *Buns & Roses*. But once that's done, the antsy feeling that's been consuming me all day returns. Like a madwoman, I try to stay busy to trick time in passing faster.

I've tried deep cleaning, which was pointless since I'd basically moved into Cruz's place to take care of him. When that failed, I sat down to read Mia's newest book. Despite it being one I would normally devour, it couldn't hold my attention. Finally, I hauled out my yoga mat and dumbbells to workout. It lasted all of ten minutes before I gave up. I was so jittery I was afraid I'd end up dropping a dumbbell on my foot.

My thumb hovers over the refresh button on my phone's browser. It's borderline obsessive how many times I've found myself in this exact situation today. *Click.* I bounce on the balls of my feet, watching the line crawl across the top of my screen. When the flights load, my stomach plummets. Nothing.

Maybe I should just drive to the airport and try to get a standby flight. I chew my bottom lip, grabbing my keys and suitcase to do just that. The startled gasp from the hallway almost makes me stumble over my carry on.

A surprised shriek echoes through the hall. I was not expecting to find Poppy standing on the other side of my door. And she's not alone. It never ceases to amaze me how Mia's a much prettier version of her older brother, and what I imagine Janet would have looked like at her age.

She's got the same almond-shaped eyes as he does, but hers are a striking blue-gray that you don't see very often. Her chestnut hair is a few shades darker than her brother's, hitting her collarbone in a wavy bob. She opens her arms as her full lips curl into a grin. All three of them, Janet, Hendrix, and Mia, have the ability to make you feel welcome with just a smile.

I step forward, accepting her hug. "What are you guys doing here?" I ask over Mia's shoulder.

"I figured you were going stir crazy over here, so we decided to come and keep you company, but it looks like you're leaving. Did you get an earlier flight?"

"Not exactly. I was losing my mind just sitting here. My plan was to wait at the airport for a standby flight." I step back into my apartment, holding the door so they can follow me.

"You could do that. Or we could all watch the game here tonight," Mia offers sweetly.

"No, you two should go. That's why you flew in early. I'd feel terrible if you missed it for me." That's mostly true. I don't want to be a burden, but friendly faces sound a lot better than pacing the airport alone.

"You can't talk us out of this. We can go to a game anytime. Now, what should we do for dinner?" Poppy asks, opening the drawer where I stash all my takeout menus. Fanning them out, she holds them up in front of Mia.

The raven haired beauty taps her chin for a moment, scanning the options before she plucks a sushi menu from the middle. "This will do."

We migrate to the living room, where we spread the menu out on the coffee table. Making the rash decision to order the sushi boat.

"I think we may have underestimated the amount of sushi that they could pack into a two foot long boat," Mia says forty-five minutes later, with wide eyes as we make room on the coffee table for the cute but very large raw fish vessel that Poppy is carrying in from the kitchen. The wooden monstrosity takes up most of the coffee table, leaving only the corners for our drinks.

"You know we can watch a movie instead." Poppy pauses her mission to load her plate full of rolls, looking at me with soft eyes from across the table.

I shake my head. "Oddly enough, watching helps." I tilt my head to the TV where the pregame show is on. "I feel closer to him. Even if he can't play, I know he's watching from his hotel room." I can picture him reclined against the headboard of some nondescript hotel room, his legs crossed at the ankles and one arm casually propped behind his head as he watches the game alone. Queue the churning feeling in my stomach from the guilt of letting him do this by himself.

"Stop looking at the TV like that." Mia's hand flies out, shoving at Poppy's shoulder who's biting down on her lower lip, heated eyes glued to the screen. Entranced as Hendrix goes through his stretches on the field, making his white pants pull tight across his butt.

"Can't help it, he's got a great ass and I love him." She pops a piece of sushi into her mouth, undeterred.

"Are you guys going to make me regret staying with Hendrix? If I hear even one mattress creak, I'm gone."

"It's not the mattresses you need to worry about with those two. Steer clear of the kitchen counter," I tell Mia.

Poppy's mouth gapes open like I just spilled her deepest secret, and Mia's hands fly up to cover her ears.

"That was uncalled for. To think I could have gone my whole life without knowing that information!" she shouts, looking absurd with her hands still clasped tightly around the sides of her head. "I'm a romance author. I need zero help imagining the scenarios those two have gotten into. Do you want to be responsible for permanently damaging my ability to write spicy, kitchen scenes?" The way she shudders next to me is almost comical enough to make me forget about all my worries.

"Oh, stop. I'll leave a container of Lysol wipes on the counter if it will give you peace of mind. Speaking of bookish things, tell us about your signing." Poppy's voice is raised, and she tugs on Mia's arm, trying to get her to uncover her ears.

She lets her hands drop to her lap. "You promise you're done assaulting my ears?" she asks, giving us both a pointed look.

I nod, pointing to my mouth, which is too full of sushi to respond.

"Scout's honor. Now spill," Poppy says, swallowing down her bite and raising her wine to her lips to wash it down.

"It's a big reader event. There's a huge group of romance authors in town. They host panels, parties, and of course there's a big signing. It's actually pretty cool. We get to interact with our readers and meet other authors." Mia's smile stretches wide across her face, showing off her straight white teeth.

"Oh wow. I didn't know that was a thing," I comment.

"You'll have a table next year. Voice actors are invited to this one as well." Mia nudges her shoulder.

Poppy's cheeks flame red. "Let me finish recording my first book first before you go signing me up."

"Stop," I chide. "You're going to be great. Not only do you have the talent, but you're one of the most determined people I know."

That just makes the red covering her cheeks creep down her neck. She ducks her head, popping a bite of sushi into her mouth with her chopsticks.

"What else are you going to do while you're here? Besides inevitably relocating to a hotel and the event?" I ask, excited to get to know Mia better.

She swirls the wine in her glass, watching it for a minute before responding. "I'm going to take a little road trip to Estes Park after the event wraps up. After this last book release, I'm feeling a little burned out. Maybe that fresh mountain air will give me that energy I need before I hole myself back up in my writing cave." She smiles like it's a light hearted joke, but it's not the full smile she had just a minute ago.

"You deserve a break. Stay a little longer and explore Colorado for a few weeks before you head back to North Carolina," Poppy suggests.

Mia shakes her head. "I can't. I have an obscene amount of meetings and a deadline with my publisher for the first draft of the next book."

"If you change your mind, I can help you plan out the road trip. Dean has a cabin near Snowmass that he doesn't use during the season. I'm sure you could disappear there for a while. Maybe a change of scenery would help," I offer softly, not wanting to overstep.

"It could be worse. I love what I do and it's not like I have writer's block or anything. Lately, I just feel like I am stuck on a hamster wheel."

"Think about it Mia. I'm sure Dean wouldn't mind." She pats Mia on the arm. "Oh, look Hen's on deck," Poppy says, pulling our attention back to the game.

The girls lounge on the couch with me for the rest of the game, sporadically picking at the sushi. If it were up to them, they'd have rolled out sleeping bags right there on the living room floor. When I catch Mia nodding off during post-game interviews, I shoo them out. They did enough already. I was an irrational mess, and they saved me from a lonely night at the airport by showing up when they did.

Still, their company was only enough to take the edge off temporarily. Later that night, I toss and turn, the same way I have for the last few nights. I feel more out of place in my own bed than I ever have. At one in the morning, I finally give in and wearily grab my keys and my suitcase, shuffling out the door into the darkness.

CHAPTER 43

CONFESSIONS

PRESENT

A distant dinging fractures the hazy images of Jarrett alone on the beach that night. When I roll towards the sound, I'm met with scratchy hotel sheets drenched in sweat. Slapping my hand down on the nightstand, I find my phone and struggle to silence the offensive noise. It takes several tries blinking to clear the grit from my vision before the time comes into focus—two-fifteen in the morning.

The glowing screen shows a notification for my security system. Suddenly, much more alert, I push up from the mattress and rest against the cool headboard. I tap the small square, opening the app.

The recording shows the door to the apartment pushing open. Her head's down, but I know without seeing her face that it's Delilah. My pulse races at the sight of her. She's there in my space where she belongs, and I don't even care why. For the first time since I left, some of the tightness in my chest loosens because she wouldn't be there if she still didn't want me.

She glances up at the camera, her shoulder slumped as she gives it a little wave before kicking her shoes off and stepping into the apartment beyond the reach of my camera. *She's back.* I want this all over. To find answers for my family and get back to my girl to start the rest of our lives together without this looming over us.

The nightmares are to be expected, with emotions running high. Rich turned all the evidence over to the police in Miami late yesterday. That should feel like a step in the right direction. Instead, I feel off-kilter. I've trusted him with this for the last three years, and now it's out of his hands.

This feels like our last chance to find out what really happened. I told Hen I'd walk away no matter what the outcome, but I'd be stupid to pretend that it won't be the hardest thing I've ever done if this all goes wrong.

When my eyes drift closed again, my phone is clutched in my hand. And this time, there are no dreams of my brother's broken body alone in the dark, wet sand.

The next morning I'm up at an ungodly hour. The storms stopped sometime overnight and I'm eager to free myself from the four walls of the hotel room. Pulling my hat down low on my head, I walk towards the greenway that runs along the Mississippi river. The pavement is still covered with puddles, but I'd walk through ankle deep water just to get out at this point.

When I get to the river, it feels like I can take a deep breath for the first time since I got here, and it has everything to do with the woman waiting for me back in Colorado. She was still there this morning. I know because the first thing I did when I woke up this morning was check the security cameras to see if she had left or stayed overnight.

I can't help but feel like she's there because she needs me the same way I need her. I walk for longer than I intended and by the time I turn around; I realize that it's been over an hour since I left the hotel. The clear skies and sunrise over the river has the path full of others with the same ideas as me. Nearly all of them are beaming and animated now that the storm clouds have moved out.

I'm almost back at the hotel when I stop at a coffee shop. It's going to be a long day. Rich and I are meeting so he can explain what to expect next, now that the police are taking over the case. But first I need to head to the gym for another mind-numbingly light workout.

I can't wait to be released to more intense workouts. Without Delilah or a physical outlet, I feel like I'm crawling out of my skin more often than not.

♥

The thirty minutes on a stationary bike did nothing to ease my tightly coiled muscles. As the day wears on I can feel my agitation down to my bones. Rich called me this morning, letting me know that something urgent came up and that he needed to push our meeting back to this evening. Despite his reassurance that it was a good thing, it only makes me more restless.

My phone vibrates with a message from Hendrix. He's been relentlessly checking in on me to make sure I am not going off the deep end.

HENDRIX:

Hey man. Practice sucks without you.
Everyone's mopey without their favorite captain here.

CRUZ:

I doubt that.

HENDRIX:

Don't underestimate how much you keep us all on the right path. We need you back. Any updates?

CRUZ:

No, my meeting with Rich got moved until later tonight. Something's going on, but he's been tight-lipped about it.

HENDRIX:

You trust him, right?

CRUZ:

I do. I know he's working hard to get answers.

HENDRIX:

Then let him do his thing. How's your head?

CRUZ:

It's been fine. Nothing alarming.

HENDRIX:

That's great news.

CRUZ:

Yeah. I'm ready to be back.

By late afternoon, I'm desperate to pass the time before meeting up with Rich. I go on another long walk after talking to Hen. It's the only way to make this nervous energy vibrating through me manageable.

The elevator doors ding, opening up on my floor. I'm looking down at my phone as I walk down the long hallway that leads to my room. Delilah left late morning and hasn't been back. I know because I've checked several times. She's probably at work, but I can't help the doubt that creeps in. Maybe she's not coming back this time.

I'm so lost in my phone that I almost trip over the pair of legs that are stretched across the worn maroon carpet. I glance around the hallway, checking to make sure I'm in the right spot. My voice comes out in a revenant whisper when I follow the legs up to their owner.

"Hermosa, what are you doing here?" She knocks the wind right out of me when she looks up at me from where she's camped out with her head resting on her carryon like she's been waiting a while.

"I couldn't do it anymore." Her hands twist in her lap as she stares up at me, her chin quivering.

The look on her face fucking guts me. After everything we've been through, she still doubts how I feel about her and whether I want her here. I'm going to remedy that, but first I need her in my arms.

Squatting down, I pluck her hands out of her lap, enclosing them in my larger ones and pulling her up to me in one swift movement. My arms wrap around her waist, catching her off guard and making a laugh huff out of her.

"Fuck, it's good to see you." My hands come up to her cheek, tilting her face up so she has to look at me. "This is where you belong."

Tears pool in her blue eyes, barely contained by her lashes. And I want nothing more than to take all her pain and sadness away. "I'm sorry I let you walk away when you needed me. I should have—"

"Shhh . . . It's okay. Come on, let's go inside," I say, pulling out my key card with one hand while I keep her anchored to me with the other. There's no way I'm letting her go again. I want to tell her that. Make her understand I want this forever, but I shove the words down. Soon, when this is all over and I can give her all of me.

Setting Delilah's suitcase off the side when the door clicks shut behind us, I guide her to the chair near the window. I lower us both into the seat, so she's pressed against me in my lap. "Are you the reason Hen's been so persistent about checking in on me?" I let my hands roam over her legs and hips. Still in shock that she came, and this is real.

"He was worried about you, but he was also on a mission to help me find you." She relaxes into my hold, covering my hands with hers and linking our fingers. "I didn't want to let you down again if I couldn't get here in time."

"Is that what you think? That you let me down?" I shift us, so that she's straddling me. "You've never once let me down. All these years you're the thing that's kept me going. When I lost my brother, I had a gaping hole in my soul. You helped mend me and make me whole again, Delilah."

"I should have been here with you. It was selfish to leave to deal with this on your own."

I trap her chin between my fingers, forcing her to look at me. "No. You've made me strong enough to handle this on my own."

"I was so scared, Cruz. Afraid that I was going to lose you to your grief, that you'd come back to me the shell of yourself that you were when we met. Then, with your injury, I was terrified that you were going to push yourself beyond what you could handle."

I run my nose along hers, whispering against her skin. "I understand, but I'm not just doing this for Jarrett. This was for us, too. You rebuilt my heart and soul, first by being my friend and now by being mine. You showed me I can still have the future I used to dream about." I take a deep breath before I continue drawing off the strength she gives me just by being here. "I will always miss my brother. Without him here, there will always be a part of me that is broken. But I don't want to live in the shadows of his death any more. No matter what happens when we leave St. Louis, we move forward. *Together*."

I pull back so I can see her face. The fear has faded from her gorgeous face and the lines that were etched on her brow moments ago have smoothed. They've been replaced with a gentle understanding. My lips tingle to tell her that she's the love of my life and that the only future that's worth all of this is one with her.

I can't do that, not yet. I need to finish what I started when I came to St. Louis, but that doesn't mean I can't show her. She leans in, bringing her forehead against mine.

"I want that. The future with you, all of it. You're not the only one that our friendship saved. When I felt worthless and shattered, you made sure to always give me what I needed. You lifted me up and helped me gain back my confidence. You gave me security. I didn't know I was missing by being there. Most of all, you made sure I knew I had value beyond being just a trophy on someone's arm. At every turn, you put me first, above everything else, without asking for anything in return."

Her words make my pulse race and my stomach flip. There's a sincerity in her voice and her eyes are filled with adoration. Delilah fucking loves me, her broken best friend. She just needs me to say the words first.

Her shaky breath fans across my face before she places a kiss on the corner of my mouth. "Are we okay, Cruz?" It's barely a whisper as she kisses the other side.

"We are more than okay and right now I'd really like to show how spectacular we can be."

"Yeah?"

"Fuck, yes. I need to be inside you like I need my next breath. Being here without you, knowing you were hurting. It was like I was missing all my most important pieces." I fight off a shudder as I remember the hollow feeling that overcame me the second the plane took off in Denver. It felt like I was leaving half of myself behind. The higher we climbed, the worse it got. "Not a single second passed that I didn't regret the way we left things."

"I'm here and I'm not going anywhere. It's me and you now." Her breath shudders as I dip my hands under her shirt, pulling her to me as I tug it up and over her head.

She's quick to do the same to me, running her hands over my chest and torso once she's freed me from my shirt.

"God, you look so perfect. I'm not sure it's possible, but I swear you got even more fucking beautiful."

She laughs when I lower my mouth and kiss the swell of her breast, my hands climbing up her ribs and cupping her through her bra. My lips blaze a path across her heated skin. Moving to the other side and giving it the same attention. "You just missed me. I'm a mess from the plane and running my hands over my hair while I was waiting for you."

"Not true, but I know a few ways to make you a mess." Without warning, I wrap my arms tightly around her waist and stand. Her ankles link around my back as I walk us across the room to the bed. "How do you want me first?"

"First?" Her chest is heaving when I lower her to the bed, dropping to my knees and making quick work of pulling her leggings and underwear down her hips. In a blink of an eye, I have her stripped to just her bra.

"Bra off," I say, pushing her knees apart. "I'm going to have you so many times tonight that you'll be begging me for a break."

She whimpers, her legs falling apart on their own. "Oh, god."

She's fucking soaked—swollen and wet. "It looks like you need it just as bad as I do." I tug her forward by the knees so her ass is hanging off the bed.

"I do. I'll always need you." She begs when I run my middle finger through her slickness. "Fill me up. Please, don't make me wait." Her hips push forward, trying to suck me in. I'm not going to make her wait. I need her just as badly. My cock strains against my pants, but it's not his turn. He's just going to have to wait because Delilah's right. I'll always put her first.

"I've got you. Now and forever. Hold those knees for me while I make you feel good." I murmur against her center, lapping at her clit softly as I ease my fingers inside her slowly. The pace I set is achingly slow. Working her up and pulling her back from the edge over and over again.

"No more. I can't take it. I need—" Her knees close around my head as she trembles under my touch.

"That's not how this is going to happen," I *tsk*, withdrawing my fingers to the tip and kissing her inner thigh lightly. "Who knows your body better than anyone else?" I ask, biting gently at her inner thigh.

She moans as I suck the spot to soothe it, leaving a pretty little red mark behind. "You . . . you do."

"That's right, and I always give you what you need, right?" I ask, sliding one finger back inside her.

"Yes. But . . ." She starts before losing herself as I add another finger, curling and rubbing as I kiss my way back up her leg to her clit. The second

I pull it between my lips with a sharp suck, she gasps, tensing underneath me.

"Oh shit, Cruz." She chants my name, like a song on repeat, as her walls clamp down on my fingers. I don't let up, continuing to lick and suck at her more softly now. I moan against her. Just as turned on by her pleasure, as if it were my own. "Too sensitive. I've never come that hard before." She pants, leaning up on her elbows as she scoots her body back, trying to put space between us.

Part of me wants to pull her back to me and show her that she can get there again and again on my tongue, but my dick might fall off if I don't get inside her right now. "If you're too sensitive, we can just cuddle." I offer with a devilish smile.

I'd stop, of course, in a heartbeat. Dickless or not, but I know that's not what she wants. I can see it when I look at her lust-filled eyes. The blue is barely a ring around her blown pupils.

She shakes her head slowly, wisps of blonde hair falling around her face. "Not a chance. Get up here and show me how much you missed me. Make me feel the way you need me." Vulnerability flashes across her face, and her chest flushes. Delilah blushing is my favorite, but not like this.

There should never be a moment of doubt that I want her. She's the only thing I want. If I have her, nothing else matters.

Pushing off the ground, I lean over the end of the bed so she's caged under me. Covering her hand with mine, I move down to cup my hard length, never looking away from her. "Feel this? It's just a fraction of the ways I need you."

Her dark lashes flutter against rosy cheekbones, and the most wanton sound passes between her lips. I almost fold in half from the sensation when she wraps her finger around me through my pants.

"You're my best friend, my future, fuck you're everything. All of it. Not just now, but for years. You've got to know that. Never doubt that without you, I'm not complete." I thrust into her hand. "This is just a bonus. I'll bury myself so deep inside you that you'll never forget what it feels like when we are together. But that won't be a problem right, because I'm your future too." It's not a question because I can't fathom a future where she doesn't feel the same.

"Yes," she says. Her voice cracks as she slips her hand inside the waistband of the joggers I'm wearing. "To all of it. Nothing else matters if I'm not yours. You were right. We were always inevitable."

"Good, then take my cock and get it nice wet with that pretty mouth of yours, so you can show me how well you can take my cock." She tugs my pants over my hips and I kick them off, letting them fall to the ground. My underwear follows just as quickly and then she drops to her knees in front of me, wrapping her lips around me and taking me all the way back.

It feels too good and it's not really what I'm after. "That's my girl. Now back on the bed. I want to feel you gripping me like it's the reason you were put on this earth."

Rising from the floor, she runs her tongue over her puffy bottom lip as she does what I asked, her eyes on me the whole time. She shudders when I run my cock over her still sensitive core, her saliva and arousal from earlier mixing.

"Fuck yes, you feel like heaven. Are you ready for me?" I ask, running my length up her slit again. Her heat surrounds me and it feels unbelievably good.

"Always." She moans when my head nudges her clit.

"That's it. Look at the way you take me so perfectly." Her head tilts down to where we are joined and I slowly ease inside her, making her mouth fall open. "You see that, Hermosa? I told you—fucking made for me."

I have to grit my teeth to keep it together. I'll never get over this feeling. Each time I'm inside her, I have to fight not to lose myself.

"Kiss me, Cruz." She's breathless, tugging me towards her by the back of my neck. "I need to feel all of you."

I savor every caress of my tongue against hers while I drive into her with the same unhurried tempo. This isn't a frenzied fuck because I missed her. It's much more. Even though I haven't said the words, I use my body to show her. Kissing her like it's the last time I'll ever get to. Letting my hands worship every inch of skin I can reach.

"Oh god. You feel so good. Don't ever stop." Her voice shakes as my cock drags out to the tip. The light coming in from the window catches a tear cresting the corner of her eye.

"Never," I promise, dropping my forehead to her shoulder as my own release builds, pulling tight at the base of my spine. My hand finds her clit between us, circling it until she's right there with me. She clings to me, holding tight where her hands are threading through my hair when we both tip over the edge together.

We lay like that tangled up in each other, quietly snuggling and talking in low voices about her trip here and me catching her up on everything with Miller.

After an hour and another leisurely round where she rides me with her legs wrapped around my waist, we move to the shower. I pass the time while we wait to hear from Rich by washing Delilah's hair.

I can't help myself when her eyes roll back and her muscles relax as I massage her scalp. It looks a little too much like the way she gets right before she comes. I drop to my knees to show her again how completely she owns my heart.

Delilah looks sated and adorable, wrapped up in a fluffy white towel as she lay diagonally across the bed after our shower. There's nothing I want more than to crawl in next to her and pretend the outside world doesn't exist, but I know we're on borrowed time.

As if I conjured him, my phone rings out from the nightstand. Delilah sits up on the bed, her face a mask of concern. Answering the call, I sink down next to her, letting her wrap me up in her arms as Rich gives me instructions on where to meet him.

CHAPTER 44

CONFESSIONS OF A DIFFERENT KIND

PRESENT

Cruz goes rigid under my touch. His voice is scratchy and broken. "The police station? I thought we were meeting at a restaurant."

I can't hear Rich's reply on the other end of the line, but the creases on Cruz's forehead smooth out. "If you say so. I have Delilah with me. We'll see you soon."

He hangs up the phone and I scramble to my feet, darting across the room to where my suitcase is. "What's going on?" I ask as I shove my legs into a clean pair of shorts.

"I don't really know. He didn't say much, just that this was a good thing and that he would walk me through everything that's happening when we get there." His face twists in confusion, and I pause with my arms through the sleeves of my shirt.

"What?" He can't hide this from me. I know him too well at this point.

Cruz shakes his head like he might blow off the question. "I'm not sure if it's a big deal, but it felt like it might be." He pauses to pull his own shirt over his head and I do the same, not wanting to hold us up. "He told me to pull around the back and suggested I throw on a hoodie and baseball cap, just in case. It was very cryptic."

"Oh, okay. Does he think there's going to be reporters there taking pictures, or is he just being paranoid?" I muse, thinking about the scenes we've encountered leaving the stadium or events together in the past.

"He's pretty even-tempered. I've never known him to blow things out of proportion." Cruz tosses me a hoodie from his suitcase. "Grab your sunglasses."

"Cruz. It's dark. I think that might be overkill," I start, but he levels me with a look that tells me this isn't a fight I'm going to win.

"There's no way in hell I'm going to let you be subjected to whatever it is that he's trying to protect me from. Sunglasses, please." His jaw is set, but the last word is a gentle plea, and I try to ignore the way his protective streak makes my knees go weak. Talk about an inopportune time for my lady bits to get all tingly from the way he wants to keep me safe.

"Yes, sir," I mumble under my breath as I grab them from the table. Cruz catches my wrist and pulls me against his chest.

"Don't think I didn't hear that." His arms band around me, holding me tight like I'm the only thing tethering him to the earth right now. "I'm going to make you repeat that again later under very different circumstances."

"Okay," I say around a swallow. "Right now, we need to get you answers."

"One second." His breathing is shallow as he fights to keep his emotions in check. "Just give me a second to hold you."

"Whatever you need," I tell him, returning the hug and resting my head against his pecs. I can feel the rhythm of his heart hammering under my ear, but the longer he holds me, the more it fades until it's nothing more than a mellow thumping.

"Okay, I'm ready," he finally says, but he keeps me right up against his chest for another minute before his chest falls with a ragged exhale.

The ride to the police station is short. Cruz does as Rich tells him and uses a back way into the lot and building. For good reason—there are reporters pulling in when we drive past the front entrance and loop around.

"What the hell is going on?" I ask no one, looking at Cruz, who looks just as dazed as I feel.

He parks in a dark spot hidden from the view of the street. "Wait there." Before I can protest, he's getting out of the car and running around to my side. When he opens the door, I slide out only for him to immediately tuck me under his arm, using his body to shield me from view should anyone come around.

The door opens as we approach and we are ushered inside by a gruff-looking guy with salt and pepper hair. I would guess he's in his late forties, but he's obviously taken good care of himself with enough muscle to rival Cruz, or any of the Bandits, for that matter.

"Rich, what the fuck?" There's no hostility in Cruz's voice. It is, however, full of trepidation.

"You must be Delilah. Sorry to meet you under these circumstances," Rich says, ignoring Cruz's question. I nod, too bewildered to do much more. "Come on, I have a room for us. Detective Flores will be there to help fill in the blanks from their side of the investigation."

Rich leads us through a maze of hallways before opening a door to a small conference room. "Grab a seat and I'll go get the detective."

Cruz drops into one of the worn chairs, clutching my hand in his lap between both his big ones as his heel taps nervously on the floor.

"Hey, look at me." His head turns to find me and I cradle his face with my other hand. "I'm here, okay? We've got this, whatever it is. You're not alone, not now. Never again."

He leans into my touch just as the door to the room opens and Rich steps in, followed by another man.

"This is Detective Mateo Flores. I've been working closely with him and my friend at the Miami precinct today."

"Nice to meet you both. We have a lot to talk about, so let's just jump right in," the detective says, dropping into a seat across from us.

"As you know, I turned everything over to the police in Miami yesterday," Rich explains it's not particularly helpful information and I can see Cruz's jaw tick with frustration.

"They reached out to me today to do what we call an agency assist. Typically, things don't move this fast, especially with multiple agencies involved. But Rich hit a gold mine," he explains as Rich opens the folder that he brought in with him.

"Miami is still waiting on a few pieces of evidence to come back from the lab, but they had enough between the phone and the bottle of GHB that we were able to request that St. Louis help with the arrest."

Cruz sits forward in his seat, gripping my hand tightly. I stroke the back of his hand gently with my thumb, trying to ease some of the anxiety I know is filling him right now.

"What does that mean? Was he arrested?" I ask without really meaning to.

"We had a few things working in our favor. He was in town, so Detective Flores was able to apprehend him quickly after Miami PD reached out," Rich adds, cracking open a bottle of water and offering it to me. When I nod, he slides it across the table.

"He was almost smug about the whole process and wouldn't shut up on the way to the station despite being read his rights," the detective adds.

"Miller's always been like that. Thinks he's smarter than everyone and that the rules don't apply to him." Cruz reaches across the table—Rich taking another bottle from himself. There's no love lost between him and Miller, but I've never heard his voice this cold.

It makes my arms prickle with goosebumps. The fear of his grief and anger consuming him was why I was so against him coming out here. He's promised to move on with our future when this is all over, and I need to trust that he will do that.

Like he can sense the way my nerves kick into high gear, he glances over at me, flipping our hands over and ghosting the pad of his thumb over my hand. Some of the angry drains from his face as he watches me.

"Sorry, Detective. My nerves are pretty shot here, so I'm sure Cruz is feeling the same. Can you spell it out for me?" Everything he said makes sense and points to them making progress. I don't need the details, I just need to know what this means for the man sitting next to me.

Detective Flores looks to Rich, who leans forward on his elbows. Looking Cruz in the eyes as he rolls his lips. The look he gives him sends chills up my spine and I scoot my chair close to Cruz, letting my head rest on his arm. I want to crawl in his lap and give him all the comfort I have to offer, but it's the best I can do given our setting.

"It's over. The short story is that he confessed to being at the beach with Jarrett that night. He slipped him the GHB. There was some sort of altercation after your brother accused Miller of giving him something. Ultimately, Miller says, Jarrett fell and hit his head. After he fell, Miller panicked and left him there. You're right, he's a selfish motherfucker. Miller was more concerned about his career than saving your brother's life."

There's a gasp, and it takes me a moment to realize it came from me, but my focus shifts to Cruz who curls around me, burying his face in my hair the best he can with the office chair separating us. Silent sobs rack his body, and it rips my heart in two. Seeing him like this, it's worse than I could have imagined, but I fight the pull to fall apart alongside him, letting my tears fall silently as I hold him.

Rich clears his throat, looking at me when he speaks. "We're going to give you some time. I'll be right outside when he's ready. I'm sure he'll have questions." I nod weakly, knowing he's right. "And Delilah . . . he's going to be okay."

"I know." My voice is raw as Rich slips through the door to give us privacy. When the door clicks shut, I do what I've been aching to do since

Cruz first tensed up and crawl into his lap, wrapping my arms around his neck.

"I've got you, Mi Amor," I whisper into his neck. "I've got you."

We stay like this for a while and I have no clue if it's been ten minutes or an hour. Cruz sniffles before lifting his head. "Thank you for being here. I thought I could do this without you, but I couldn't have."

"I'm never letting you do the hard stuff alone again. You hear me? It's you and me," I tell him, cradling his face in my hands.

He nods. "Let's get them back in here and then I want to get out of here."

I slide out of his lap and open the door, letting Rich know we are ready. He takes the same seat he vacated earlier.

"Detective Flores had some paperwork to take care of. I think I'll be able to answer all your immediate questions, but we can call him back in if we need him," Rich explains, looking between us.

"Did he say why he gave him the GHB?" Cruz's face is a mask. Like he's locked it all down to get through this conversation.

"Everyone knew Jarrett was about to get called up to play for the Commanders. Miller was afraid of him taking his spot. So he slipped the GHB into his drink. He wanted him to test positive for a banned substance." Rich pauses for a minute, giving us a second to process and ask questions before continuing. "Whether he thought it would save his ass or just wanted to fuck over your brother, I don't know. The alcohol and GHB combined likely made your brother disoriented. When he confronted him and they fought, it's probable that he lost his balance and hit his head. Miller called the taxi so someone would find him and bolted."

"My brother died so Miller could keep his spot on the team?" I try to cover it, but a sob breaks free when I hear the pain in Cruz's voice.

"I'm so sorry. Your brother didn't deserve what happened to him. Miller's going to go away for what he did, but I know that doesn't take away the loss of Jarrett."

Cruz stands from his chair, pulling me up with him. "Is there anything you need from me, or can we get out of here? I need to call my parents and then I just need some time. You'll keep me updated?"

"Of course. There's nothing you need to do." Rich shakes Cruz's hand before leading us out the door.

"Thanks Rich. I don't know how to repay you for finding out what happened to my brother. He's going to get justice because you believed me when I told you that his death wasn't an accident."

"I wish I would've gotten you closure sooner, but I'm glad you finally have it. The reporters are still out front, but the back is clear. The press release won't be until tomorrow afternoon."

CHAPTER 45

THAT HEA

PRESENT

The conversation with my parents is almost harder than when Rich gave me the news. Having to relay it all to them over the phone, and hearing them fracture as I explained it to them is gut-wrenching.

We talked about flying to Texas so that we could be there with them, but I was exhausted and didn't want to risk the news leaking before we could get there.

After everything, I just want to be home with Delilah. Not here, in the city that's taken so much from me already. I'm fighting heavy lids when Delilah comes out of the bathroom. It's late, well after midnight, and I'm crashing hard from the emotional toll and adrenaline.

She looks like a fucking angel as she crosses the room and slides into bed next to me. Her long blonde hair is braided to the side, and she's drowning in one of my shirts. The slumped set of her shoulders tells me she's just as worn out as I am, but she's never looked more beautiful.

When she slides into the bed next to me, I don't waste any time grabbing her waist and hauling her flush against my body. I've spent so long waiting. Waiting for answers, waiting for Delilah to be ready for something more with me. I can't wait anymore. I clamp my lips shut before the words can just spill out of me.

Delilah deserves more than a rush declaration of my feelings for her. And if I don't slow down and compose myself for a minute here, that's what she's going to get. My mind is screaming at me to tell her how I feel, but I don't want to leave any doubts that I mean every word, and it's not just the emotions of the day spilling over.

"Hey," she says, kissing my bare chest before she looks up at me with admiration. "How are you doing?"

I chuckle because it's a loaded question. My feelings are all over the place. I haven't processed Miller's involvement and the reason he did it. On the flip side, having answers, knowing that Jarrett didn't do this to himself, brings me a measure of relief like I can finally move forward. Nothing will bring him back, nothing will erase the hurt, but having Delilah by my side dulls the sharpness of the pain and anger.

I sit up, pulling her with me so we are both leaning against the stacked pillows.

"Having you here with me made everything easier. I'm not going to lie and tell you I'm okay, but I know I will be because we've got our whole lives ahead of us." I weave my fingers through hers, bringing it to my mouth to kiss her knuckles. I take a deep breath and let myself tell her exactly how I'm feeling. "Jarrett was my best friend and when I lost him, I never thought I would find anyone else that I would call my best friend, but then you walked into my life. Like you were sent from him to make sure I couldn't lock myself in the darkness you made each day a little brighter."

"That goes both ways, you know. After Brad, I tried to shut down, but you wouldn't let me." Delilah peers up at me, tilting her head closer to my chest. But I don't let her bury her face.

"That's because even then, I think I knew that someday you'd be mine. You weren't ready, so I waited and now I can finally be the man you deserve."

"Cruz, you've always been enough—" I place a finger on her lips, shaking her off. I want to get this out while I have the words and the composure to say them without fumbling over myself.

"You're part of my past. You've been there in the darkness and the light. You're my future, my world, my everything, Hermosa. Te amo, Mi Cielo." She gasps, tears clinging to her lashes. My thumb swipes them away.

"I love you, Cruz. I've loved you broken, whole, and everywhere in-between. You've been the man I deserved since day one. Your grief doesn't make me love you any less. If anything, it shows me how strong and loyal you are."

My heart is hammering against my chest at hearing her say the words. *Fuck, it feels fantastic to finally tell her how I feel.* My brother's smiling face pops into my head and I can't help but think he would give me hell for waiting so long.

Suddenly feeling energized knowing she feels the same way, sleep is the furthest thing from my mind. "Come home with me tomorrow. Don't go back to your place." The words tumble out before I can stop them. I didn't plan on asking her to move in, but I don't regret it. Not even when she pulls back, looking at me like I'm crazy.

"What do you mean? I'm already flying home with you," she says, looking adorable, like she doesn't want to make the wrong assumption.

"You are, and I suppose you can go to your apartment to get your things. I'll even come with and help you box them up. The All-Star Break starts soon, so even if I'm released to practice, I'll have free time to help you move."

"Move? You're asking me to move in?" Her nose wrinkles as she asks, and I bring my finger up to smooth the lines out.

"We've waited so long to love each other like this. I don't want to waste anymore time." If I thought she'd let me, I'd propose tomorrow. But we're going to need to ease into that.

"Waking up next to you every morning does sound pretty amazing. And I really enjoyed being there with you after you got hurt." Her hands loop around the back of my neck, pulling my lips down to meet hers.

"Think of all the fun we can have. Fun in the shower, fun in the kitchen, fun on the couch—" Her hand wraps around where I'm hard.

"I like fun." This time, her hand slips under my shorts, palming my length. "Maybe you should show me some of that fun now and make sure I know just how much you love me."

"I don't know. You still didn't answer my question. Move in with me. Don't make me wait any longer to start the rest of my life with you." I grip her ass and rock against her.

"Yes," she moans in response.

"Yes, you'll move in. Or yes, you like that?" I lower my head to her collarbone and nip the exposed skin there.

"Both. I'll move in with you as long as you don't stop." She sucks in a shuddering breath as I strip my shirt over her head.

"I'll never stop loving you, Hermosa." I roll on top of her, diving forward to capture her mouth in a hard kiss. I spend the next hour loving her before we are both exhausted.

The next morning, I wake up to Delilah curled around my body and I know this is exactly where I was meant to end up. Here with her, after everything that I've been through, she's my own, personal, slice of heaven.

THE END!!!

EPILOGUE

FOUR MONTHS LATER

When Cruz and I got back from St. Louis, the team rallied around us. Everyone insisted we postpone the trip to St. John until after the All-Star Break. There were several weeks where Cruz and I couldn't go anywhere without reporters hounding him for a statement.

As much as getting away would have been welcomed, he needed that time to work through his emotions. On top of that, there was no way he would have been able to enjoy himself while there was still so much happening with Jarrett's case.

Eventually, Miller was extradited to Miami and ended up pleading guilty and his lawyer convinced him that remorse might help him get a reduced sentence. With that behind us, we decided a postseason vacation was the perfect way for the guys to recover after being knocked out of the playoffs in the wild card round.

So here we are, over the Caribbean, on our way to a gorgeous villa— we even talked Xavier into coming along.

"I can't believe you changed into your bikini on the plane." I try to keep my smirk from turning into a full-blown chuckle as I survey Mia, whose swimsuit straps are peaking out from under her sundress. "Don't get me wrong, I fully support it, but I've never seen someone quite so eager to get to the beach that they change in an airplane bathroom."

"I need a drink in my hand, to read a book that's not my own, and sand between my toes. Besides, it's not like it's a commercial flight," she says, nodding to the bathroom on the private plane Dean secured.

"Hen, be a good brother and drop my luggage off at my room. Please," Mia begs with her hands clasped in front of her.

"Sure, right after I haul my girl off to our room I'll come back for your luggage," Hendrix says, giving Poppy a look that makes her blush.

"Nope. Not listening." Mia reaches into a bag and pulls out her Airpods, slipping them into her ears as she mumbles, "I think these are going to be my new best friend. What was I thinking, coming on vacation with two new couples? I need a break from romance, not to be immersed in honeymoon phase love."

"You've got us Mia," Dom says, waving a hand between himself, Xavier, and Dean.

A laugh sounds out from next to Mia. "Like she wants to spend her vacation putting up with your nonsense all week," Indie says, looking only at Dom. "No offense. You two are just guilty by association when your friend's the biggest man child on the team."

The corner of Dean's lip twitches up, but he doesn't jump to his friend's defense.

"Besides, Mia and I have lots of plans." Indie nudges Mia's elbow on the armrest. "Don't we Mia."

"Sure, if by plans you mean be a beach potato and see if I can grow roots. Then yes, we have plans."

"Exactly. The couples can do their coupley things, and you three can do whatever it is that you do." She waves her hand at the three guys. "Meanwhile, we will be perfecting the art of relaxing." A saccharine smile paints Indie's lips as she raises an eyebrow at Dom.

"Let me know if you need any help with that. I have a few ideas to help relax—"

"Dom!" Hendrix barks at him, leaning forward in his seat. "That better not be directed at my sister."

But it's not Dom who's looking at Mia. Dean quickly looks away, picking at an imaginary piece of lint on his shorts. Hendrix may not have noticed but his eyes were glued to where the strap of Mia's dress was sliding off her shoulder.

For the first time, Dom fumbles with his words. Not sure how to respond to that without getting into more trouble. And I'm not sure who he's more afraid of right now because both Indie and Hendrix are glaring at him with barely contained rage.

Mia jumps in, saving him from certain death. "Hen, knock it off. First, I'm capable of making my own decisions about who I spend time with and in what capacity. Second, while I'm sure you're a lovely companion, we are so far from compatible that you and I together is laughable."

"I'm a lovely companion. Thanks for noticing." Everyone turns to look at Dom, but he's oblivious, puffing his chest out with pride. It's Indie who speaks up, bursting his bubble.

"That's what you got out of that." Her head tilts back against the seat as she laughs, making Dom's lips pull down in a frown.

When the plane lands a short time later, we file into rental cars and head up the winding roads to the villa we will call home for the next week.

Arms wrap around me from behind as I stand on the back patio where there's a pool and stairs leading down towards the pristine beach. Mia and Indie dropped everything in the entryway and headed straight down there. Dom, Dean, and Xavier followed shortly after with a football and cooler in hand.

"Isn't it beautiful?" My hands cover Cruz's taking in the turquoise ocean and white, sandy beach.

"I've never seen anything more stunning." His lips hover over the shell of my ear, his voice is rough and husky.

"Are you trying to sweet talk me? You know it's completely unnecessary. I'm one hundred percent yours and head over heels in love with you already."

He chuckles against my neck, causing goosebumps to break out there. "I was just hoping you'd let me help you get into that bikini I saw on the top of your suitcase before we left."

"Help me get into it. Really, that's what you are going with?" Turning in his arm so I'm facing him, I walk my fingers up his chest and sink them into the hair at the nape of his neck. Cruz looks more relaxed right now than I think I've ever seen him. He's stayed true to his word and moved forward following his trip to St. Louis. He's even had several appointments with a therapist that Willa helped him find.

"Yes, I plan on being very helpful." I can feel him harden between us as his hands skim down my back to grip my ass and pull me against him.

"You do have really good hands." I suck in a breath when one of those hands sneaks under the waistband of the linen pants I'm wearing.

I'm not sure which one of us moves first but we both turn towards the villa and race to our bedroom.

BONUS EPILOGUE

FOUR MONTHS LATER

Delilah's been moping since the second we woke up this morning. She's not ready to leave St. John's, even though I promised we could come back again soon. There was plenty of downtime to relax between snorkeling, hiking, and shopping. After everything we've been through, she surprised me by extending the stay for a few more days after the crew left so she could give me the vacation I originally proposed when she was still too afraid to let me all the way in. As much as I'd love to squirrel her away here forever, real life is calling.

I'm confident that the plans I have waiting for her at home will cheer her up. It's been next to impossible to keep this secret from her, but I know it'll be worth it to see her face when she walks through the door of our apartment.

"Do we really have to go home?" she whines, her head falling to my shoulder as the Uber driver turns the corner to our street. The sun shining through the window catches on the dainty gold chain adorning her ankle, which is bobbing in the air, crossed over her knee. The one I picked out on the island with miniature charms on it. The tiny sun, moon, and star sway with the motion of the car. I reach out, running my fingers over it.

"We really do. I'm going to miss seeing you lounge around in bikinis all day. Think you could ease me back into the real world by walking around naked for the next few days?" I kiss the top of her head, smiling against her hair.

"Why do I think that would end up being counterproductive? We had to leave vacation to take care of responsibilities that would only end up with us never leaving the apartment."

"Yeah, I'm not seeing the problem with that," I tease as the car pulls up to the curb. After thanking the driver, I grab our bags out of the back and lead Delilah into the apartment. Excitement races through me as we get to the door. "Can you grab the door for me?"

I'm fully capable of setting everything down and going through first, but she needs to be the first inside for what I have planned.

Delilah slips the key into the door and turns the knob, looking over her shoulder as she pushes the door open. "Need any help?"

"Nope, I got it," I tell her with a smile as I look past her into the apartment where Janet is crouched down on one knee, holding on to the collars of Leia & Han. Both their tails eagerly wagging as they wait to be let loose.

As Delilah turns back towards the apartment, I nod at Janet, who releases her hold on them, letting them barrel towards us. Delilah drops to her knees, her mouth open in shock as she loves on them. "What did you do?"

"They still needed a home and we can give them one filled with love." I come to kneel next to her, patting Han on the head as he licks Delilah's face. "Thanks for your help pulling it off, Janet. I couldn't have done this without you."

"Of course. I'm happy to help facilitate a happy ending," she says with a wink and I choke on a laugh.

"Janet!" Delilah snorts, pushing up off the floor and crossing the room to hug her. "Naturally, it's part of your fairy godmother duties."

"Just make sure you give him the good stuff tonight, girly. These two are the cutest. He deserves it."

"I'm not sure I'm comfortable with this conversation." I push my hand through my hair, feeling out of place in this conversation. Hen would skin me alive for talking to his grandmother about our sex life.

"Don't be such a prude. You and Hen are cut from the same cloth, acting like I don't know what you get up to. I've lived a lot of years. There's nothing you've done that I haven't." Delilah bent over the bed in our Villa this week as I fucked her from behind while playing with a plug she packed to surprise me with, another first she let me have, fills my mind.

I'm not so sure Janet's right, but there's no way in hell I'm pointing that out. I clear my throat, trying to block the image out before I end up hard in front of my best friend's grandma.

Jesus, she's making me blush, but my girl just laughs like this is completely expected.

"Nope, boy. Don't give me that look or I'll start telling you stories and, by the way, your cheeks are flaming red right now, that's not something you're interested in."

"Let's skip story time. Thanks again Janet," I say, hoping to move on.

Janet gives Delilah one more hug before patting me on the shoulder and slipping out the door.

"That was very sneaky and very sweet." Delilah pushes up on her toes, kissing the corner of my lips as the dogs circle our feet.

"You know, now that we have these two, we should probably start looking for that house."

Delilah smiles up at me. "You think so?"

"Uh, huh. I do. I want it all with you, Hermosa. The dogs, the house, to make you my wife. See you pregnant with my baby."

"Let's practice that last one a little longer," she says softly, one arm looped around my waist while the other one scratches Leia's head.

"Just the last one?" I ask, tilting her chin up so I can see her face.

She nods, trapping that bottom lip between her teeth, knowing it's my fucking weakness. I may not be the first man to propose to her, but I'll be the first one to do it right and the first to call her "my wife." I kiss her deeply. I'm so damn in love with her. I still can't believe that I was lucky enough to find my best friend when I needed it most and now, she's my everything.

WHAT'S NEXT?

OTHER BOOKS BY LO EVERETT

MILE-HIGH HEARTS SERIES:

All on the Line - Poppy & Hendrix

All or Nothing - Delilah & Cruz

Calling it Safe - Coming Soon!

ACKNOWLEDGMENTS

With my first book it felt like the list of people to thank was endless. That list has only grown as the community around me continues to grow.

If you stuck around for book number two after reading *All on the Line,* you get the first shout out. Thank you for taking a chance on a new author—one that had no idea what she was doing when she sat down to start this journey. Those of you who are new to the Mile High Hearts Series welcome! The appreciation I feel for all my readers, new and old, is endless because without your support we wouldn't be here, together, right now. And there is no place else I'd rather be.

Thank you to my family who never fails to make me feel uncomfy by telling anyone who will listen that I write books—even their teachers. As much as I'd love to run and hide when that happens it's your pride in me that means the most.

To my friends—who may as well be family—Katie, Nykki, Anna, and Kendl, maybe someday you'll get to hear me talk about something other than books or kids sports. Thanks for continuing to put up with it, and for always being the first to tell me how amazing I am.

Tiffany and Amanda: for keeping me sane when I thought I might lose it at the end of this process. You made this big scary thing manageable and dare I say fun.

Abby, for your insight and kindness as I molded Cruz into a character I could be proud of. I am endlessly grateful for the time you spent reading and coaching me throughout the process.

Allison, for reading and loving Cruz and Delilah wholeheartedly. I'm lucky to count you as a friend, trusted confidant, and cheerleader.

Kat, Stephanie, Dawn, Andi, and Loriana your feedback from the beginning has helped shape this story into what it is today. I might be a little biased, but I think it kicks ass, and without your patience and dedication it wouldn't be the same.

Ali and Sara, for being my social media gurus when I can't figure the algorithms out or just don't have the time to be creative outside of writing. I love watching you guys take what I give you and turn into something amazing that I can share.

Caitlin, my editor, for never being afraid to tell it like it is. I'm not sure we'd be here today working together on this book, that I'm so very freaking proud of, if it wasn't for your willingness to have tough conversations. Even though it wasn't always comfortable you pushed me and it made for an even better book.